The HUNT

A NOVEL BY
Jan Neuharth

A PAPER CHASE FARMS PUBLISHING GROUP BOOK
MIDDLEBURG, VIRGINIA

PAPER
CHASE
FARMS
PUBLISHING
G R O U P

Published by
Paper Chase Farms Publishing Group
a division of Paper Chase Farms, Inc.
Post Office Box 448
Middleburg, Virginia 20118
www.paperchasefarms.com

This novel is a work of fiction. Names, characters, places, organizations,
business establishments, events and incidents are either products of the author's
imagination or are used fictitiously. Any resemblance to actual events, locales, or
persons, living or dead, is entirely coincidental.

ISBN 0-9729503-1-1 (Paperback)

PRINTED IN THE UNITED STATES OF AMERICA

First Paperback Edition 2004

Book design by Judy Walker

This book is dedicated with love to
Joseph, Dani, and A.J.

There are so many who have played an invaluable role in bringing this novel to fruition. Without them, this book might not exist, and, without a doubt, the journey would have been much less enjoyable.

My profound thanks and appreciation go to those who worked so hard to help publish this novel: Andrée Abecassis, for her kinder, gentler introduction to the world of publishing; Kaa Byington, for making editing fun; Jerry Gross, for his genius with plot and characterization, and for never settling for the simple solution; Janet Hitchen, for her extraordinary ability to capture life through a camera lens; Karen Stedman, for her keen eye, her professionalism, and her wit; Wendy Wainwright, for her prompt and meticulous proofing; and Judy Walker, for her brilliant design, her flexibility, her ability to create magic overnight, and for putting her heart and soul into her work.

My sincere heartfelt thanks go to my long-time friends, who enthusiastically devoted their time and candidly shared their thoughts: Carolyn Chambers, Fern Kucinski, Kate Palmquist, and Marly Perkins. This book is so much better because of you.

Last, but not least, I thank my family, all of whom were involved in this project from beginning to end: My beautiful mother, Loretta, for her gracious critiques, her gentle advice, and her undying faith in me; my father, Al, never one to mince words, for his "plain talk" feedback, his endless encouragement, his vision, and his love; my brother, Dan, a truly gifted writer, for his thoughtfulness, his tough editing, and his patient responses to my endless barrage of midnight e-mail questions; my children, for their love, their enthusiasm, and their understanding, especially when they found me at the computer working on the book, yet again; and, finally, my husband, Joseph, master of the hunt and of my heart, for his undoubting support, his love, his expertise, and his inspiration.

This novel was inspired by life in the Virginia hunt country. It is set in the idyllic small town of Middleburg, where I live, work, and play. Although some of the names of streets and places are real, this novel is entirely a work of fiction. The characters aren't based on real people. The Middleburg Foxhounds is a fictitious hunt. None of the conversations ever took place. Any resemblance to actual people, places, or events is truly coincidental.

If, after reading this book, you come away with a negative impression of the hunt-country crowd, please remember, this novel is a work of fiction. The folks in this community are some of the finest, most genuine people I know.

A glossary of foxhunting terms
can be found at the back of this book.

C H A P T E R

1

Zeb McGraw had been in the hayloft, crouched in the same spot, since before sunup, and he guessed it was about nine o'clock by now. He shifted his weight in a barely perceptible motion so he wouldn't be detected by the girl in the barn aisle below. The chilly, damp air penetrated his canvas hunting jacket, and he clutched his arms against his chest for warmth.

The girl below him hummed along with the radio in the barn. A female voice drifted over the airwaves, and the girl lifted the horse brush she was holding and sang into it as if it were a microphone.

"How do I show you, how much I want you? How can I know if, you want me too?" She twirled around, eyes closed, head flung back. "How do I tell you, how much I love you? How can I know if, you love me too?"

The music on the radio faded into a commercial and the girl lowered the brush and went back to grooming a big bay horse. She talked softly to the animal as she brushed him.

"So, Chancellor, my boy, you take good care of the boss out there today, all right? Give him a good run and take his mind off his work. All that complicated tax law stuff that seems to rule his life."

She stopped brushing and scratched the horse behind his ear, smiling as he cocked his head towards her and arched into her touch. "You make sure you bring Doug back safely to me. Okay, boy?"

Zeb viewed the girl thoughtfully. She wasn't the type he would have thought Doug Cummings would be interested in. He'd pictured Cummings with a rich, skinny broad, with painted nails, bleached hair, and lots of make-up. But this girl seemed to have the hots for Cummings. He wondered if Cummings felt the same way about her.

Zeb heard the sound of tires crunch on the gravel drive outside the barn. The engine died and a car door slammed, and Zeb saw the girl look over towards the barn door and smile.

"Hi, Babs," a man's voice said.

Zeb's pulse quickened. Was it Doug Cummings' voice? He couldn't be sure. He hadn't heard shit from Cummings for almost fourteen years. Zeb clenched his fists until his fingernails bit into his palms and drew his arms tighter against his chest.

He remembered the last time he'd seen Cummings. It was as clear as if it had happened yesterday. He was sitting in the front row of the courtroom on an uncomfortable wooden bench, just like a pew in church. His mama and his sister, Zelda, sat on either side of him. His kid brother, Zeke, was sitting right in front of him at a big brown table. Cummings sat at the table next to Zeke.

Zeb squeezed his eyes shut and relived the gut-wrenching moment when the judge had delivered Zeke's fateful sentence. He could still picture the panicked look on Zeke's face as Zeke turned to Cummings, pleading for Cummings to do something, anything, to keep him out of prison. But Cummings barely talked to Zeke. He just sat there in his fancy lawyer suit, acting like it was any other damned day in court.

Zeb drew a ragged breath and forced himself to focus on his mission. The only thing he could do for Zeke now was to even the score. Set things right. Zeb turned his attention back to the barn aisle below him.

He heard the sound of the man's footsteps on the brick aisle. The footsteps grew louder until the man stopped, just short of his field of vision. Then he heard the man's voice again.

"Well, Babs, I'm not sure I picked the best day for foxhunting. It looks like it's going to be a wet one."

"Yeah, it doesn't look too good, but I listened to Bob Riley's forecast and he said that the clouds would burn off and we'd have a nice day," the barn girl replied.

"I hope he's right, but I wouldn't place any bets on it," the man said.

Zeb saw the man reach his arm out and pat the horse on the neck. And then, finally, the man stepped into full view. It was Doug Cummings. Right below him. Almost close enough to reach down and touch.

Zeb felt a rush of energy and his pulse pounded in his ears. It would be so easy to kill Cummings. He could just drop down from the hayloft. But he fought back the urge. It wasn't time yet.

First, Cummings must suffer through hell on earth. Then he would die.

A fine mist of rain began to coat the windshield as Doug Cummings turned off the paved road and onto the gravel drive at Chadwick Hall. He frowned and cast a glance towards the November sky. Ominous gray clouds clung to the Blue Ridge Mountains in the distance, and a wispy fog was sliding down into the valley. The weatherman had been wrong again. It looked like they were going to have a wet go today.

The hunt meet was in the far back pasture, behind the manor house, and Doug followed the narrow drive as it snaked through a screen of cedar trees, wound behind the old stone barn, and curved up to the pasture gate. A dozen or so horse trailers were already in the field, and Doug drove slowly across the uneven ground, feeling his horse trailer sway with every bump.

He circled his rig around a green horse van and waved at a girl who was leading a gray pony down the ramp. He didn't recognize the girl or the pony, but the van belonged to one of the Hunt members. Doug finally found an open area and parked. He knew he'd be leaving the hunt early to head back to the office and didn't want to get boxed in by the other trailers.

Doug turned off the engine and felt the Range Rover rock back and forth as his horse stomped the trailer floor. "Hold on, Chancellor," Doug said, as he got out and walked back to open the hatch. The seventeen-hand bay horse whinnied as Doug opened the door, then lowered his head and poked it out the opening, his flared nostrils blowing clouds into the chilly air. Doug patted him on the neck. "Don't worry, boy. They're not going to leave without us."

Doug hung his tweed jacket in the tack room of the trailer and took his heavyweight frock coat off the rack. It wasn't as comfortable as his other scarlet coats, but it would protect him from the weather. He shrugged into the coat and put on his black velvet hunt cap, pausing to adjust it in front of the tack room mirror. As he reached up to smooth back the hair protruding from the rim of the hat, he noted a few more glints of silver at his temples.

Doug transferred his cell phone from his jacket to the breast pocket of his scarlet coat and picked up his gloves and hunt whip, which he set outside on the fender of the trailer.

Chancellor poked his head out of the open trailer hatch, and Doug patted him on the neck and picked a loose piece of hay out of his forelock. He had just taken the bridle off the hook inside the front of the trailer when he felt his cell phone vibrate. He fished his cell phone out of his breast pocket and flipped it open.

"Hello."

It was the senior associate on his tax team. "Doug. It's Mark. Sorry to bother you, but we have a major problem." Mark Hoffman's voice sounded as if he were in a tunnel, and Doug knew that he was on the speaker phone.

"What's up?" Doug asked, lightly shaking the bridle to untangle the reins.

"You are not going to believe this," Mark said in a tight, clipped tone. "Has Congress ever been ahead of schedule? I mean, in the entire fucking history of the United States government, has Congress *ever* been ahead of schedule?" The tunnel effect of the speaker phone amplified the nervousness in Mark's voice.

"Get to the point, Mark," Doug said.

"I just got a call from Congressman Weissman. They've moved up the House debate and they're ready to hear from you. Today. Like right now. As in, this morning."

Doug quickly hung the bridle back on the hook. "Did you stall him?"

"How am I going to stall him? He's a congressman, for Christ's sake. How the hell could I stall him? They want you there at nine-thirty."

There was a grim silence and Doug glanced at his watch. Damn. It was already eight forty-five, and he was a good hour and fifteen minutes away from Capitol Hill. That was without taking his horse home first.

"So, what did you tell him, Mark?" Doug asked.

"I told him the truth." Mark paused for a moment and cleared his throat. "I told Congressman Weissman that you were out chasing foxes in Virginia and that they'd just have to wait until you returned."

Mark's voice rose in pitch as he finished, and Doug heard boisterous laughter coming from whoever was in the room with Mark.

"I see. That's really funny," Doug said. "I think the long hours are getting to you if that's your idea of a joke."

"We all told Mark not to do it, Doug, but he wouldn't listen." Doug recognized the voice of the team's most junior associate, Judy Moran.

Doug smiled and picked the bridle up again. He rested the phone between his shoulder and cheek as he took Chancellor's halter off and slipped the bit in the horse's mouth. "I obviously didn't leave enough work to keep you busy. I'll try harder next time."

"Hey, Doug, are you sure you're foxhunting?" Mark asked. "We're hearing a lot of heavy breathing coming from your end of the phone."

"It's my horse." Doug slipped the last buckle into place on the bridle and took the phone back in his hand. "Now let's get serious for a minute here. Did you find the documents I left for you?"

"How could we not find them, Doug?" Judy asked. "You covered the whole conference table with them."

Doug chuckled. "Then you should have enough to do." He looked around the pasture and saw that most of the other riders were already mounted on their horses. "Is there a purpose to your call?" he asked.

"No," Mark replied. "We just wanted to let you know we have everything under control here."

"I can see that," Doug said. "Now get to work. I'll see you in a couple of hours."

"Okay, boss. Have fun. You deserve it," Mark said.

"Yeah, Doug," Judy said. "Seriously. We've got it all handled. Go relax."

Doug smiled and flipped the phone shut. Mark and his team of associates had been working almost night and day the past few weeks to prepare for the Tycoon Technologies hearing, and he was glad to see their camaraderie was still intact.

"Come on, Chancellor," he said, putting the reins over the horse's neck. He walked back and opened the rear doors of the trailer, released the butt bar, and tugged lightly on Chancellor's tail, signaling for him to back out. The horse obeyed, and Doug reached up and grabbed the reins as Chancellor stepped off the trailer. His horse's head was high and alert and he trembled slightly with anticipation. Doug removed the green wool cooler that covered Chancellor's back and folded it over the center divider in the trailer. Chancellor was already saddled, and Doug adjusted the white fleece saddle pad and checked the girth, then pulled his stirrups down, picked up his gloves and hunt whip, and climbed into the saddle. He tightened the girth, and then let Chancellor walk off on a loose rein.

The Smithers, who owned Chadwick Hall, were greeting riders at the front of the pasture where stirrup-cups were being served, and Doug guided Chancellor in that direction. He saw Pat Smithers standing in the center of the group holding a silver tray and he rode over to her.

"Good morning, Pat." Doug leaned down from his horse to give Pat Smithers a kiss on the cheek.

"Why, good morning, Doug. It's lovely to see you, as always," Pat replied. "Would you like a cookie?" she asked, holding the tray up towards him.

Doug declined the cookie but accepted a shot glass of sherry from Thomas, the Smithers' groom.

"Thank you, Thomas," Doug said, reaching down from his horse to take the glass from the silver tray the groom was holding. "I think we're going to need more than this today to keep us warm."

"Ah, well, it is a bit of a soft day," the groom replied, his southern drawl tinged with a trace of an Irish accent. "But never you mind. That's often some of the best foxhunting," he said, his wrinkled face crinkling into a smile.

Doug nodded and smiled back. "I hope that's true today," he said, placing his empty glass on the tray.

Doug looked around at the group of riders and saw Wendy Brooks, the hunt secretary, accompanied by a young blond woman.

"Good morning, Doug," Wendy said, riding up next to him. "I'd like you to meet a guest of the Smithers who'll be hunting with us today. This is Heather Prescott. She's from California."

"Hi. It's so nice to meet you," Heather said.

Doug nodded and tipped his hat. "Welcome to Virginia. Have you hunted before?"

"No, never. I'm so excited. This is like something out of a movie set," Heather replied. "And I just *adore* the outfit."

"I see you went all out," Doug said, gesturing towards Heather's clothing. Her attire was proper enough. Black melton coat, beige breeches, black dress boots, canary vest, white stock tie, and black velvet hunt cap. But Heather had obviously not purchased her riding clothes in Virginia. Her turnout was impeccable, but she had a Rodeo Drive kind of newness about her.

"Speaking of outfits, what's the deal with this?" Heather asked, reaching over and fingering the Robin's egg blue fabric and navy piping that covered Doug's collar.

Doug eyed Wendy, imploring her to rescue him, and pressed his leg against Chancellor's side, causing the horse to move away slightly.

Wendy intervened. "When gentlemen earn the privilege of wearing a scarlet coat, they display the colors of their Hunt on their collar," she explained to Heather. "It's referred to as 'earning your colors.'"

"Oh, really?" Heather replied, not looking at Wendy and sounding very uninterested. "I thought maybe you picked that beautiful blue color to match your eyes." She smiled at Doug and leaned over close to him again.

Doug pressed his leg against Chancellor's side again, but this time his horse didn't move. Chancellor was busy sniffing noses with the chestnut mare that Heather was on. Doug cleared his throat and gestured towards where most of the other riders were gathering. "It looks like the master is about to give a talk, so I'm going to head on over there." He nodded at Heather. "It was nice to meet you, Heather. I hope you enjoy hunting today."

Doug heard Heather's voice as he rode away. "I suppose it would just be wishful thinking to hope that he's single."

Doug smiled to himself and trotted over to where Richard Evan Clarke was addressing the field. "I'd like to thank the Smithers for hosting the Middleburg Foxhounds here today," the master said. "This is always a lovely fixture, and it is especially fitting today because it affords us plenty of woods to hunt in, where hopefully we can stay somewhat protected from this fine Irish weather."

There was a murmur of approval from the group and Jimmy Slater, an honorary whipper-in, leaned over to Doug and muttered under his breath. "What Richard really means to say is for once we won't all be bitching that we have to hunt in these damned woods."

Doug had filled in as a whipper-in on occasion and knew how much more difficult it could be to control the hounds through the woods. He smiled in response and looked around at the rest of the field. They had about thirty riders. A decent turnout for a Tuesday, especially with the lousy weather. "How many hounds is Smitty hunting today?" he asked Jimmy.

"He brought sixteen and a half couples. Including that new bitch hound the Oxford Valley Hunt gave us." Jimmy moved his horse closer to Doug and lowered his voice. "I saw you talking to Heather from California. What'd you think?"

"She seemed like a nice girl," Doug replied.

"She seemed like a *nice girl*? What, are you blind or something? She's a fox," Jimmy said.

Doug didn't say anything.

"Hey, Doug, come on. I heard that you and Nancy broke up," Jimmy said.

Doug raised an eyebrow. "News sure travels fast."

Jimmy shrugged. "It's Middleburg."

Doug smiled wryly and nodded.

"Actually, I heard it from Langley," Jimmy said.

Doug frowned and looked over at the other whipper-in, Langley Masterson. "Really? How did Langley hear about it?"

"I don't know. Maybe from Nancy."

Doug shook his head. "I don't think so. Nancy doesn't have much contact with Langley anymore."

"Well, then, I don't know how he heard about it," Jimmy said. "Anyway, what do you think about Heather from California?"

"She's all yours, Jimmy." Doug turned his attention back to what Richard Evan Clarke was saying.

"Harry Groves has agreed to lead the hilltoppers today, so the non-jumpers and anyone who wants to take it a little more slowly should stay behind and ride with Harry," the master said, gathering up his reins. He gave the field one last word of caution before heading out. "I'd like to remind everyone that the footing may turn slick today if this rain continues, so, as always, please be careful, and have a safe day of foxhunting. The Smithers have graciously provided a light tailgate hunt breakfast which will take place here immediately following the meet."

The huntsman, Winfield Smith, or Smitty as he was generally referred to, blew a short note on his horn to cast the hounds, and Richard Evan Clarke led the field down a trail into the woods. Doug trotted along enjoying the comforting sound of the horses snorting and blowing and the rustling of leaves beneath their hooves. The woods behind Chadwick Hall were dense and Richard kept to the trails. They rode under graceful sugar maples that were still ablaze in brilliant orange and yellow, towering dark red oaks, and the shimmering white bark of the sycamore trees. The dogwoods had already dropped most of their leaves, and Doug knew that most of the remaining color would be gone after the storm that was brewing.

They came around a bend and the master halted and held his hunt whip up, signaling for the rest of the field to follow suit. The far off notes of Smitty's hunt horn, encouraging his hounds to find a scent, drifted mournfully across the damp woods. But the hounds were silent. It was a blank covert. Richard checked for a few more minutes and then led the field on through the woods and let them jump a stone wall onto a gravel road, then across and up over a coop back into the woods again, where he picked up a canter.

Doug knew the territory well enough to know that the master was just killing time. Trying to give everyone their money's worth until the hounds got a scent. He wasn't just hanging in Smitty's pocket, following the huntsman, the way some other masters would. That wasn't Richard's hunting style. Richard Evan Clarke knew the territory like the back of his hand, and Doug was certain that if the hounds hit a scent Richard would give them a view of the fox.

They hadn't gone far when Doug heard Ruler, the lead hound, speak, then another hound spoke and confirmed, and then came the short staccato notes on Smitty's horn as he bid the hounds on. Soon the hounds were in full cry, and the master's canter increased to a gallop as he led the field on a run. Doug followed right behind Richard, and they emerged from the woods into a small pasture just in time to see a big red fox tear across the pasture with the hounds in full pursuit.

"Tallyho!" Richard called back to the field, tipping his hunt cap in the direction of the fox.

Doug could feel Chancellor's heart pounding as the thoroughbred lengthened his stride. Richard led them over a small coop back into the woods and then veered to the right as the trail split. Chancellor slipped on the turn as his hind hooves hit a patch of rock, but he recovered his balance and leapt right back into a gallop. The trail headed down a steep hill, and Doug checked Chancellor back to a trot, then let him jump the small ditch at the bottom of the trail and pick up a gallop again on the other side.

As he neared a clearing at the top of the trail, Doug saw a stone wall with a barbed wire fence on either side of it. Chancellor pulled on the reins, going for the jump, but Richard had stopped on the other side of the wall and appeared to be in some kind of trouble.

"Hold hard," Doug yelled over his shoulder, and he raised his right hand in the air as he pulled Chancellor to a halt in front of the fence. Chancellor tossed his head and spun around, ripping the reins out of Doug's hand.

"Cut it out," Doug said, grabbing the reins with both hands again and kicking Chancellor forward into the bridle. The horse grunted but stood still.

"What's the matter?" Doug asked, walking Chancellor towards Richard.

"Wire."

Doug could see the long strand of barbed wire tangled between the horse's legs.

"I'll get it," he said.

He jumped down off of Chancellor, took his wire cutters out of the case on his saddle, and handed his reins to the rider behind him. Then he climbed over the stone wall and slowly approached Richard's horse.

"Easy. It's okay," he said softly. He clipped the wire and pulled it out from beneath the horse, then ran his hands down the horse's legs. "I think he's okay, Richard. There are a few cuts, but they appear to be superficial."

"Thanks, Doug," Richard said. The master let his horse walk around and the animal appeared to be sound.

Doug hopped back over the stone wall and climbed up into the saddle, then turned Chancellor towards the jump and let him trot over it.

Richard waited until Doug had cleared the fence and then set off at a canter again. They could still hear the music of the hounds far off in the distance.

They galloped across the pasture and jumped a split rail fence onto Foxcroft Road, then cantered on down the road until they reached the crossing into Goose Creek, where they splashed across the water and climbed up the rocky bank on the other side. The master led the field through Stony Bank Farm where they caught up with the hounds. They ran for another twenty minutes, until the fox finally went to ground in a fence line near Hickory Vale Farm. The master gathered the field at a check on the back side of the pasture, and the huntsman called in the hounds.

"That old fox sure did you a favor going to ground when he did, Richard," Doug said, slightly out of breath, as he indicated the nearby property line of Hickory Vale.

"No kidding, Doug. The last thing I need is another run-in with Miss Lilibet," Richard replied. The new owners of Hickory Vale were from Texas, and when they had purchased the twelve-hundred acre farm the previous year they had graciously invited the Middleburg Foxhounds to hunt across their land. Foxhunting seemed like such a *civilized* sport, they had said. But when Miss Lilibet discovered that the Hunt did on occasion actually *kill* a fox, the hunting privileges were immediately revoked. Doug knew that Richard wouldn't take the field across Hickory Vale, but if the hounds were on a line, they wouldn't be so good at honoring Miss Lilibet's wishes.

"It's just a damned shame that Hickory Vale sits in the middle of our hunting territory," Richard said. "At least half of our fixtures lead to this territory one way or another."

"Well, we're still better off than most of the hunts around here," Doug replied. "At least our territory isn't getting carved up by subdivisions."

"Yes, and thank God for that," Richard said.

As they stood there, Doug looked out across the valley. The view was breathtaking, in spite of the thick, dark clouds that were sweeping across the landscape. The rolling hills seemed to go on forever, crisscrossing with stone walls and neat rows of fences, and dotted here and there with buildings. An occasional stream of smoke rose from a chimney to mix with the gloomy gray sky. The hounds gathered around Smitty, their tri-colored coats blended with the scenery, while the huntsman's scarlet coat cut a swatch of brightness in the dreary scene. There was a movement of scarlet through the trees, and Doug saw it was Langley Masterson, rounding up some stray hounds in the woods. Doug took a deep breath and let it out slowly. Time had a way of standing still at moments like this.

He looked at the horses around him. The high-strung ones refused to stand quietly, and danced, ready to go on. The veterans rested and caught their breath. Chancellor was alert, standing quietly, but not relaxed. Eager to be off again. Doug reached down and patted him on the neck. It looked like they were going to be there for a while. Smitty had cast the hounds to another covert, but so far they hadn't drawn a scent. The rain was still just a light mist, but the temperature was dropping and a chill was setting in. Doug watched as riders began to pass their flasks around, sharing the liquid warmth. He saw Jimmy Slater trot up to the group and offer his flask to Heather.

"Hi, Doug." Nancy Williams' soft voice broke into Doug's thoughts, and he turned around to see her behind him. Nancy had been hunting with the hilltopper group, and Doug saw that they had just joined the main field.

"Hello, Nancy."

Nancy brought her horse up next to his. "I'm sorry about the other night," she said, but Doug held his hand up to stop her.

"You don't have anything to be sorry about."

"Yes, I do," she said, blushing. "I know I was way out of line."

"Forget it," he said, shaking his head. "Your complaint was valid. My job does demand most of my time."

"No," Nancy replied. "I shouldn't have pushed you like that. I don't know what got into me. It must have been the wine or something. I'm sorry."

Nancy's horse was rooting at the reins, jerking her forward out of the saddle, and Doug reached over and grabbed the reins, forcing the horse to stand quietly.

"Doug." Nancy didn't say anything else, forcing him to make eye contact with her. "I'm okay with the way things were before," she said with what sounded like forced lightheartedness. "Really. I don't need more of a commitment from you."

Doug hesitated. This was not a conversation he wanted to have in the hunt field. "We can't go back to the way things were, Nancy," he said quietly, looking away. "You know that wouldn't work."

Her eyes filled with tears. "Why not? It was good between us. You know it was."

"Nancy, please," Doug said, looking towards the rest of the group. The two riders nearest to them quickly turned away. "Now's not the time or place for this conversation."

"Okay," she said, following his gaze. "Can we talk later?" She reached up with her gloved hand and brushed away a tear that was running down her cheek.

Doug sighed. There wasn't anything left to talk about. He couldn't give Nancy the time or commitment that she needed. But he'd talk if she wanted to. He owed her that. He nodded at her. "If you want to."

"After the hunt breakfast?" she asked.

"I don't know if I'll be at the hunt breakfast," Doug said. He didn't say that he had to get back to the office.

"Really? Why not?" Nancy asked.

Doug shrugged. "I may hack in early. But we'll talk. I'll call you."

"Promise?" she asked, smiling weakly as she brushed another tear away.

"I promise," he said, smiling back at her and releasing her horse's reins.

Doug turned his attention back to the rest of the group and feigned interest in the jokes that one of the members was telling.

"Hey, Doug. What's the difference between a dead fox on the road and a dead lawyer on the road?"

"I give up," Doug said, though he'd heard it a dozen times.

"There are skid marks in front of the fox."

Doug laughed politely and eased Chancellor away from the group. He glanced over at Nancy who was talking with Wendy Brooks. They were both looking at him. God, he hoped he hadn't raised Nancy's expectations by saying that he'd talk about their relationship.

Smitty's horn sounded from far off, calling the hounds in. "I guess Smitty's abandoned that covert," Richard called out. "Sounds like he's moving them down towards Hunter's Crossing."

Doug looked at his watch. Hunter's Crossing was heading away from the meet. That meant at least another hour of hunting. It was time to call it a day.

Doug rode over to Richard to pay his respects before leaving. "Thank you, Master," he said, tipping his hat. "I'm afraid I have to head in, but it was a good hour of sport. That was a nice view you gave us."

"Thank you, Doug. Are you taking anyone in with you?" Richard asked. "With this weather you might have some takers."

Doug shook his head. "I'm in a bit of a hurry to get to the office," he replied. "I'd rather hack in alone."

Richard nodded. "Fine. You'd better head off then, before anyone notices."

Doug mingled at the back of the field while the master set off towards Hunter's Crossing. He saw Nancy look at him, but then she followed along with the rest of the hilltopper group as they moved off. Doug waited behind until the last rider trotted off and then turned Chancellor in the opposite direction.

As he reached the tree line at the edge of the woods, Doug thought he heard someone call his name, and he pulled Chancellor to a halt. He turned in the saddle and looked back but didn't see anyone. He paused for a moment and listened but didn't hear it again. He shrugged and gathered his reins. He must have imagined it. Doug urged Chancellor back to a trot and headed into the woods.

CHAPTER
3

Doug trotted Chancellor along the trail through the dense woods, mindful of the footing. The misty rain had turned the blanket of autumn leaves beneath him sodden and slick. A crisp wind was picking up and Doug felt his horse shiver. He reached down and patted Chancellor on the neck, then ran his gloved hand along the horse's black mane, wiping off the water droplets that had gathered there. Chancellor responded by tossing his head and tugging on the reins.

"It's okay, boy, we're going home," Doug said, rubbing his horse's neck. He felt Chancellor's muscles quiver beneath his hand.

Doug turned off the main trail and headed down a steep passage that was a shortcut through the thick of the woods. In the summertime it would have been impassable, but now with some of the leaves off the trees, he could make his way through. He hadn't traveled more than a couple of hundred yards when he was startled by a faint scream, abruptly silenced, from somewhere behind him. Doug quickly pulled Chancellor to a halt and looked around, but the woods were quiet except for the rustling of the wind through the trees and the dull splatter of rain on the wet leaves.

He continued on cautiously at a walk but stopped short as the silence was broken once again, this time by a noisy thrashing in the brush. Doug turned his horse towards the commotion and Chancellor tensed. His ears pricked forward. His nostrils flared. The racket grew louder, closer, branches snapping and leaves crunching, and Chancellor spooked and bolted sideways as a riderless horse tore through the woods and thundered past them, its reins and stirrups flapping against its sides.

"Come on, boy," Doug said, clucking as he turned Chancellor towards the runaway. Chancellor leapt into a canter and took off after the fleeing horse. They were still in the heart of the woods, not on the trail, and the going was rough. A low branch slapped Doug across the cheek; he bent forward, almost burying his face in Chancellor's mane. He couldn't see anything ahead of him now and trusted Chancellor to choose the best path through the trees. Chancellor galloped on, winding sharply left and right as he avoided objects in his path. He stumbled once, and Doug heard the harsh scraping of steel horse shoes against stone as Chancellor scrambled through a rocky area.

Then the ground seemed to level off, and Doug felt Chancellor lengthen his stride. He was running straight now, no longer twisting through the trees. Doug cautiously raised his head and saw that they were on the trail, not far behind the runaway. As they grew closer, Doug recognized the horse and his pulse quickened. It was Sunday Stroll. Nancy's horse. He pulled Chancellor back to a trot.

"Whoa, Sunday," he murmured as they approached, and the horse pricked his ears and slowed his pace.

"Easy, it's okay," Doug said softly as he rode up alongside and grabbed Sunday's reins.

"Good boy," he said to Chancellor as he slipped the reins over Sunday's head, and Chancellor flicked his ears in response.

Then he sat back in the saddle and pulled on both sets of reins. "Whoa." Both horses halted. Doug let the horses stand and catch their breath for a brief moment and then turned back towards where he had heard the scream, leading Sunday along beside Chancellor.

Chancellor and Sunday trotted quietly, their heads bowed low against the rain. When Doug reached the spot where Sunday had first run past them in the woods he stopped and looked around.

"Nancy?" he called out.

No response. The throaty sound of the horses' heavy breathing filled the air.

He called louder. "*Nancy.*" He heard nothing but the faint echo of his voice, the horses' breathing, and the rain splattering on the soggy leaves. A forbidding chill crept through him. He shivered as he gathered up the reins and trotted on again.

As he approached a small clearing in the woods, both horses stopped abruptly, wheeled around, and tried to bolt back down the trail. Doug quickly pulled them up and turned them again towards the clearing. "Come on,

Chancellor," he said, clucking. Chancellor still balked, and he dug his spurs into Chancellor's sides and growled at him. "Get on up there." The thoroughbred cautiously moved forward with Sunday whinnying nervously beside him.

Doug urged the reluctant horses into the clearing but quickly pulled them to a halt when he saw what had spooked them. Nancy lay sprawled on the ground before him, not moving. Her body was twisted unnaturally, with her head bent back at an odd angle and her legs crumpled beneath her.

"Nancy, my God, are you all right?" he called out, as he jumped off of Chancellor and hurriedly tied both frightened animals to a tree.

Nancy didn't respond, and Doug crouched down beside her and shook her arm gently. "Nancy, it's Doug. Can you hear me?"

Still no response. She didn't appear to be breathing, and Doug tugged off his wet leather gloves and put his fingers on her neck, but he couldn't find a pulse. His heart pounded in his chest, and he silently repeated the CPR procedures in his mind. He carefully positioned Nancy's neck to check her airway, and his hands came away covered with blood. Then he saw the blood that crept around to the front of her white stock tie, still tied neatly around her neck.

Doug leaned down closer and gently lifted her head, just enough to see where the blood was coming from. It was hard to see much from his angle, but she had a head wound at the base of her skull, and it looked bad. He tore off his own stock tie and folded it into a makeshift bandage, then used it to apply pressure to the back of her head.

His hands were shaking, and he took a deep breath to calm himself as he rested Nancy's head back on the ground. He breathed into her mouth and performed a series of chest compressions. One, two, three. He counted slowly to fifteen. Then again. Two quick breaths followed by chest compressions. He repeated the procedure several times.

Doug stopped and checked for a pulse again. Still nothing.

Nancy's face was bloodstained where he had touched it, and Doug looked down and saw the blood on his hands and on the cuffs of his white shirt and the muddy mixture of blood and wet leaves that clung to his white breeches. An icy fear gripped him. His chest felt tight and cold.

He rose unsteadily to his feet, pulled out his cell phone and quickly pressed three numbers.

"Nine-one-one. What's your emergency?" a woman's voice asked.

"There's been an accident." His voice was shaky. "She's unconscious. Not breathing. She has a serious head injury. I need the rescue squad."

"What's your name, sir?" the woman asked.

"Doug Cummings," he replied.

"Where are you, sir?" she asked.

"In the woods. I'm in the woods. We were out riding," Doug said, pacing restlessly.

"You need to tell me where you are," the woman said.

Doug shook his head. "The rescue squad won't be able to get here," he said. "I'll bring her to them. At Chadwick Hall. That's off Snickersville Pike."

"Don't move the victim, sir. Just tell me where you are. The rescue squad will have her airlifted out if they need to."

Doug looked up at the towering trees around him. The woods were dense as far as he could see. They couldn't airlift Nancy out. There was no way a helicopter could get in. "I'm in the middle of the woods. They can't get a helicopter close enough. Send the rescue squad to Chadwick Hall," he repeated.

The woman's voice grew stern. "Sir, I repeat, do not move her."

"Stop telling me not to move her," Doug shouted. "She's not breathing. She needs help. Now. I won't just stand here and watch her die."

"You won't be helping her by moving her," the woman said. "You could make her injuries worse."

Doug cut her off. "Listen to me. I'm here and you're not. I'm in the middle of the goddamned woods. I know these woods. And I'm telling you they can't get an ambulance or a helicopter anywhere close to here. I'm moving her. Send the rescue squad to Chadwick Hall."

He flipped his cell phone shut and shoved it back into his pocket, then knelt down beside Nancy and carefully picked her up. Doug carried her over to Chancellor and draped her across the horse in front of the saddle. Then he untied both horses and let Sunday loose to find his own way.

Doug swung into the saddle and collected Nancy in his arms. He held the reins in his right hand and wrapped his left arm around Nancy, holding her close to his chest. He cradled the back of her head in his hand, holding the stock tie bandage firmly against her head wound.

An icy wind was blowing through the woods now, pelting the rain at them. Chancellor danced impatiently and spun around, almost unseating Doug. "Come on, boy," he murmured, kicking the horse into a trot. "Help me out here."

The ride back to Chadwick Hall was interminable, and by the time Doug rode into the pasture every muscle in his body seemed on fire in spite of the damp chill of the day. The rescue squad wasn't there yet, but he saw a small group of people who were setting up the hunt breakfast at the front of the pasture, and he called out to them for help. He pulled Chancellor to a halt and carefully dismounted, then let Chancellor go and set Nancy on the ground. The rain was hard and steady now. He grabbed a horse blanket from a nearby trailer to cover her with.

Still, no one came to help. "Come on, come on," he called out to the group again. "I need help over here."

Doug leaned over Nancy and felt for a pulse. But he still couldn't find one.

"I need help over here, damn it," Doug yelled again. Finally, a few people came running in his direction. He looked up at them. Thank God. Kathy Morris was among them. She was an EMT.

"What happened, Doug?" Kathy asked briskly, as she knelt down next to Nancy.

Doug moved aside slightly, giving Kathy more room. "I don't know, Kathy. I was hacking in and I found Nancy unconscious in the woods," Doug replied. "I already called nine-one-one. The rescue squad should be here by now." He glanced towards the entrance to the pasture. "I don't know what the hell is taking them so long."

Kathy checked Nancy's vital signs. "Was she breathing when you found her?" she asked.

Doug shook his head. He saw that Nancy's lips were purple. Her skin had a bluish cast. "She looks so cold," he said. His voice caught on the word "cold."

Kathy nodded. "How long ago did you find her?"

Doug pushed up the sleeve of his coat and looked at his watch, then realized that he had no idea what time it was when he had found Nancy. "I don't know. I tried to revive her and then I called nine-one-one. That probably took five or ten minutes. Possibly more. Then the hack over here seemed to take forever. I guess it took fifteen minutes. Maybe twenty."

Kathy loosened Nancy's stock tie and raised her eyebrows. She ran her fingers over some purplish marks on the front of Nancy's neck. "How'd she get these marks, Doug?" she asked.

Doug hesitated. He didn't know. "I don't know. I found her after she fell off." He thought for a few moments. "Maybe that's what caused her fall. Maybe she got tangled up in a branch or a vine and it knocked her off her horse." He shook his head. "I just don't know."

Kathy frowned but said nothing. She lifted Nancy's head and examined the wound, then gently rested her head back down. Doug watched anxiously as Kathy knelt there next to Nancy. Why wasn't she performing CPR?

"What are you doing? Why aren't you doing CPR?" Doug demanded.

Kathy looked at him and shook her head. "It's no use, Doug. Nancy's gone," she said quietly.

"No. She can't be," he heard himself say. But he knew it was true. And he realized he'd known it all along.

Then he heard the sirens of the rescue squad, and he saw Kathy stand and motion the others away. He remained alone, crouched by Nancy's still body. He reached out and gently moved a tendril of loose hair out of her face and pulled the blanket up around her. "I'm sorry," he whispered. He closed his eyes and bowed his head. "I'm so sorry," he repeated.

He felt a hand on his shoulder and he looked up. Kathy stood there looking down at him. "It's not your fault, Doug. It's a risk of the sport," she said. "We all know that. Nancy knew that. Come on. Leave her be now."

He shook his head but he stood up. The ambulance had reached the pasture and turned off its siren. Doug watched as it bounced towards them across the rugged land.

Kathy went forward and intercepted the rescue crew as they rushed out of the vehicle. Doug unbuttoned his coat, took off his hunt cap and ran his hand through his hair, wet from his sweat in spite of the chill. He saw one of the hunt members, Cassie Bryan, approaching, and he swallowed hard.

Cassie put her hand on his arm. "Doug, I wanted you to know that we caught Chancellor. My daughter's taking care of him. I just didn't want you to worry about him."

"Thanks, Cassie," Doug replied, avoiding eye contact and working hard to keep his voice steady. "What about Sunday?"

"We have him," Cassie said. "Smitty's going to take him back to the barn at the Hunt kennels."

Doug sighed and nodded. "Okay. Thanks. I'll be there in a minute." But Cassie didn't leave. Her eyes kept darting towards the left side of his face.

"You have some blood on your face," Cassie said.

Doug instinctively reached his hand up towards his cheek but then jerked it away in midair. His hand was smeared with blood too. He lowered his arm and looked down. A large dark red blotch spread across his canary vest and crept up the front of his white shirt. Doug's stomach flip-flopped. He had Nancy's blood all over him.

"Excuse me, Cassie," he whispered, and turned away. He drew a deep breath as he watched the rescue team move Nancy onto the stretcher and put her into the ambulance. They put a white blanket over her. He could see just the outline of her body and the sole of one black riding boot protruding from under the blanket. Then the rear doors of the vehicle clanged shut and Nancy was gone.

A young rescue worker picked his bag up off the ground and started towards the front of the ambulance, then stopped and looked at Doug. "You okay, sir? You need anything?"

Doug shook his head and lied. "No. I don't need anything. I'm okay."

The young man nodded sympathetically and looked past Doug towards the pasture gate.

Doug turned around and saw a sheriff's car pull up next to the ambulance. A stocky, middle-aged deputy got out and walked over towards them, his clear plastic raincoat flapping in the wind.

"Oh, no. It's that new guy. He thinks he's God's gift to law enforcement," the rescue worker said, shaking his head.

The deputy stared at Doug as he approached, his eyes traveling slowly from Doug's face down to his boots and back up again. "I'm Clyde Dickson," he said, chewing on something. "What's going on here?"

Doug stared back and didn't answer him.

"Carol Simpson's in charge. She's over there," the rescue worker said, pointing towards the other side of the ambulance. "I'll go get her."

The deputy ignored the young man and gestured towards Doug. "You've got blood all over you," he said, still staring. "What happened?"

Doug held the deputy's gaze without answering. He didn't like this guy's attitude. "There was a riding accident," he finally said.

The deputy turned his face to the side and spit out a wad of chewing tobacco. "Really? An accident you say? You look in pretty good shape to have lost so much blood."

"It's not mine," Doug replied.

"Excuse me?" the deputy said. "What's not yours?"

"The blood," Doug replied quietly. "It's not my blood."

Carol Simpson interrupted them. "Hello, Clyde. Hi, Doug." She reached over and put her arm around Doug. "You okay?" she asked.

Doug nodded.

"He's okay," the deputy said. "But he's wearing a lot of someone else's blood. And he doesn't seem to want to tell me what happened."

Carol squeezed Doug's arm. "There was a riding accident involving a woman who was a friend of Doug's," she told the deputy.

"Was a friend? You mean she's no longer a friend, or she died?" the deputy asked.

"She died," Carol said quietly.

"No shit? What happened?" the deputy asked, removing his plastic-covered sheriff's hat and smoothing back the thin strands of dark hair that crowned his balding head.

"We're not exactly sure," Carol replied. She dropped her arm from around Doug and looked at him. "Doug, Kathy said that Nancy was unconscious when you found her. Is that right?"

Doug nodded. "I wasn't able to revive her, so I called nine-one-one and brought her here."

"How'd you get her here?" the deputy asked, placing the hat back on his head.

"On my horse," Doug replied.

The deputy stared at him. "Why'd you move her?"

Doug stared back. "Why the interrogation?"

Carol interrupted. "Doug, I think Clyde's asking because it's generally not a good idea to move someone who's unconscious." She frowned at him.

"I must admit, I was surprised when I heard that you moved Nancy. I thought you knew better than to do something like that," she said.

"Well, it was my judgment call," Doug replied. "You couldn't have gotten the ambulance anywhere near her. You would have had to come in on foot. It would have taken too long."

Carol didn't speak, but her expression said that he had clearly done the wrong thing.

"Do you think that I made it worse by moving her?" Doug asked. "That you could have saved Nancy if I'd left her in the woods?"

Carol shook her head. "No, I'm not saying that," she replied. "I don't think anyone could have saved her."

The deputy studied Doug. "I still want to know where all the blood came from," he said.

Carol answered him. "Nancy had a nasty head injury. The back of her skull was crushed."

The deputy frowned and took a notepad and pen out of his shirt pocket. "What's your name?" he asked Doug.

Doug hesitated, debating whether or not to let the deputy go on grilling him. "Doug Cummings."

"Your full name."

"W. Douglas Cummings. The third," Doug said slowly.

"What does the 'W' stand for?"

"Nothing."

The deputy smirked and Doug saw him write "Attitude" in block letters across the top of his pad. "What's your address?"

Doug struggled to keep his cool. "Hunting Hollow Farm. Middleburg."

"I need a number where I can reach you, Mr. Cummings. I'm sure that there will be a follow-up investigation on this," the deputy said.

Doug stepped closer to the deputy and glanced down at the name above the man's badge. "Look, Deputy Dickson, what happened here today was a tragic accident. People fall off their horses all the time out foxhunting, and Nancy just fell wrong. Period. End of story. Don't try to make it into something else."

Doug saw a flicker in the deputy's eyes, but the man didn't back off. No one spoke for a moment.

"No matter how many questions you ask, nothing you can say or do will bring her back," Doug said quietly, stepping away.

Carol spoke up. "Doug's right, Clyde. Let's put an end to this."

The deputy glared at Carol but didn't argue with her.

Carol reached out and patted Doug's arm. "Go on," she said softly.

Doug gave her a slight nod and walked away.

The hunt was over and the pasture was busy with riders. As he headed towards his trailer, he heard a woman's shrill voice rise above the whinnying of the horses and slamming of vehicle doors. "Oh, my God, someone died?"

Doug glanced over in the direction of the woman's voice and saw Heather from California. She was crying. Jimmy Slater was standing next to her and put his arms around her. Doug quickened his pace and avoided eye contact with anyone as he walked to his horse trailer. He didn't feel like talking.

Someone had loaded Chancellor on the trailer for him, and Doug picked up his saddle and bridle and carried them to the tack room. As he reached up to put the saddle on the top rack, he heard a voice behind him.

"Doug, I just heard the awful news about Nancy. What happened?"

Doug turned around and saw Pat Smithers standing outside the trailer. He put the saddle away and stepped outside, closing the door behind him.

"I really don't know much more than you do, Pat. Nancy took a bad fall from her horse. I don't know how or why." He took a deep breath. "She was dead when I found her."

"Oh, no. Just like her father," Pat said, covering her mouth with her hand.

Doug nodded and they were both quiet for a moment.

"I was there, you know. When Buck Williams died," Pat said. "He was leading the field on a run, and I was just a couple of horses behind him when his horse stepped in a hole. He went down head first and never moved again. Just snapped his neck. Killed him instantly." Pat's voice cracked. "Oh, God," she said, and reached up to wipe her eyes.

Tears stung Doug's eyes, too, and he took a step towards the Range Rover. "I'm sorry, Pat," he said. "I just can't talk about this right now."

Clyde Dickson watched Doug Cummings drive his Range Rover and trailer out of the pasture. He saw Cummings glance his way, but Cummings didn't so much as give him a courtesy nod. Arrogant asshole. Clyde flipped him an imaginary finger.

"Cummings sure hightailed it out of here in a hurry," Clyde said to Carol.

"I imagine he just wanted to be alone," Carol replied. "You obviously couldn't know this, Clyde, but Doug and Nancy used to date. In fact, they just broke up. I guess that's hanging pretty heavy on Doug right now."

Clyde's pulse quickened and he raised an eyebrow. "Really? Any bad blood between them?"

"Oh, no, I don't think so," Carol said, pulling her raincoat closer around her. "I think they were still on friendly terms. At least I haven't heard anything to the contrary."

Clyde chewed on his tobacco and thought it over. He couldn't quite put his finger on it but something wasn't right. Finally, he shook his head. "I've got to tell you, there's something about all this that just doesn't set right with me."

"What do you mean?" Carol asked.

Clyde turned his head and spit the juice from his chewing tobacco, then looked at Carol and frowned. "The whole thing smells fishy to me. Cummings finds his ex-girlfriend in the woods. Dead. Covered with blood. And he picks her up, puts her on his horse, and brings her here. It doesn't seem right. A sophisticated guy like him, doing something dumb like that."

"Doug told you why he moved her," Carol replied. "He thought it was the only way he could help her."

"Yeah. I heard what he said. But I'm not sure I buy it."

"Why else would Doug move Nancy?" Carol asked.

"To cover something up. Maybe there was something in those woods he didn't want anyone to see."

Carol's mouth hung open. "Are you saying that you think there might have been foul play? That Doug might have been responsible for Nancy's death?"

"I'm saying that I don't buy his story, and I'm not going to just write this off as a riding accident," Clyde replied. "I'm going to request an autopsy."

"You can't be serious," Carol said, giving a little half-laugh.

Clyde didn't respond.

"You *are* serious. Oh, Clyde, I don't believe this," Carol said. "You're suspicious of *Doug*? Do you know who he is?"

"I don't give a fuck who he is. Pardon my French," Clyde snapped. "I know his type and it doesn't impress me. My daddy used to work for guys like him. They aren't all the model citizens they're made out to be. I know that better than most."

Carol pursed her lips. "I think you'd better be careful about jumping to conclusions, Clyde. There's no indication that this was anything other than a riding accident."

"I don't agree," he said. "What about her head injury? How'd she bash her skull in like that falling off a horse?"

"Any number of ways," Carol replied. "Nancy could have landed on a rock. Her horse could have kicked her in the head after she fell off. She could have hit her head on a branch. There's no telling."

"Her helmet would have protected her from that," Clyde replied.

"Not necessarily. There are all types of hard hats, and some are a whole lot safer than others. I really don't know what kind Nancy wore, but if she wore one without a chin strap to secure it, the fall could have knocked her hat off," Carol said.

Clyde wasn't deterred. "Okay. Then answer this. How come she and Cummings were both out there in the woods all alone? I may not know much about foxhunting, but I know enough about it to know that it isn't a solo sport."

Carol shrugged. "Doug said he was hacking in early, and I assume that Nancy was doing the same. That should be easy enough to find out."

He popped some more tobacco in his mouth. "Okay. Let's go talk to someone who knows," he said, gesturing towards the riders in the pasture.

"Come on, Clyde, there's no point in getting everyone all riled up. Why don't you let things settle for a couple of days? Request an autopsy if you want to. If anything suspicious turns up, then you can conduct an investigation. A couple of days won't make a difference."

Clyde considered her advice. "I suppose I could hold off on questioning anyone for a few days. But I won't wait to examine the site of the so-called accident. I want to get there before any evidence is disturbed."

"Well, I'm afraid you're out of luck there, Clyde," Carol said. "I believe Doug's the only one who can show you the spot where he found Nancy, and he just left."

Clyde looked down at his notepad and saw the blank space where he had failed to write Doug Cummings' phone number. He scowled. He was sure he could find it easy enough. But it pissed him off that Cummings had avoided giving it to him. "Tell me more about this guy," he said to Carol.

"Doug?" Carol asked.

"Yeah. Is he from around here, or is he a city boy?"

"Well, both actually. Doug's an attorney in Washington and he has an apartment there. The Watergate, I think. But he also has a farm out here. He grew up here. Doug's definitely a local," Carol said.

"An attorney?"

Carol nodded. "At a big Washington law firm that his father started. I'm telling you, Clyde, Doug's a rock-solid citizen. You're barking up the wrong tree with that one."

Clyde ignored her last statement. "He's single, I take it."

Carol nodded.

Clyde wrote "Womanizer?" on his notepad. "Does he have any family around here?"

Carol shook her head. "No. Doug was an only child and his parents passed away, oh, must be going on a dozen years by now. They both perished in that big hotel fire in Manila. A real tragedy. Douglas and Marie Cummings were well respected and loved in this community."

"Were they rich?" Clyde asked.

Carol shot him a look of annoyance. "Yes, I guess they were well-off. They owned a beautiful farm. Hunting Hollow. Of course, it belongs to Doug now."

"Rich," Clyde wrote. "Local." He tapped his pen lightly against the notepad as he thought about it. Then he circled the word "rich."

Clyde saw a woman wearing an outback coat and cowboy hat walking towards them.

"Excuse me, Carol," she said, nodding a greeting at Clyde, "I don't mean to interrupt, but there's something I feel you should know."

"Clyde, this is Kathy Morris," Carol said. "Kathy's an EMT, and she assisted Doug when he arrived here with Nancy."

Clyde nodded at her. "Hi, I'm Deputy Dickson."

"Pleased to meet you," Kathy said.

Kathy hesitated for a moment and her eyes darted towards the group of people standing around them. When she spoke she kept her voice low. "This may not mean anything, in fact, it probably doesn't, but I thought I should pass it on."

She stopped and Clyde nodded. He chewed on his tobacco, waiting for her to go on.

"It's about Nancy," Kathy said, pausing again.

"Yeah, go on. What is it?" Clyde asked.

"Nancy had some unusual marks on her neck," she said, looking down at the ground. The pointed toe of her cowboy boot tapped nervously against a tuft of rough pasture grass.

Now she had his full attention. Clyde's pulse quickened. "What kind of marks?" he asked.

Kathy spoke so quietly Clyde had to lean forward to hear her. "Purplish. Bruises. Almost like finger marks."

"You mean you think someone strangled her?" Clyde's voice was loud and he saw a middle-aged balding man in a red coat poke his head out of a nearby horse trailer to look at them.

Carol gasped and Kathy glanced at her. "I'm sorry. Maybe I shouldn't have said anything. It's probably nothing," Kathy mumbled, taking a step backwards.

Clyde looked at Carol, not bothering to conceal his smile. "I suppose I shouldn't say I told you so," he said, lowering his voice a bit.

Carol just glared at him, her lips pursed in a thin line.

"So, we've got an ex-girlfriend." He raised a finger. "Alone in the woods." Finger two. "Dead." Finger three. "With serious head trauma." Finger four. "And strangulation-type marks on her neck." Finger five.

He slowly wiggled his raised fingers. "I'd say that brings this inquiry to a new level, wouldn't you?"

Carol sighed. "I'm afraid to say I have to agree with you that an investigation is called for. But I'd still caution you to wait until the autopsy results are in first."

Clyde ignored her and addressed Kathy. "I'd like you to come back to my car and make a formal report."

Kathy nodded her consent and Clyde steered her towards his squad car, giving Carol a slow smile as he brushed past her.

When they had walked out of Carol's earshot, Kathy stopped and turned to Clyde.

"I may as well get it all out right now. There's something else that didn't set quite right with me," she said with a frown.

"What's that?" Clyde asked.

"It was something Doug said to Nancy, when he was kneeling by her side."

"Go on. Tell me."

"Doug told Nancy . . ." She hesitated for a moment. "Well, he said he was sorry."

Clyde raised an eyebrow. "Really? Sorry about what?"

Kathy shook her head. "I don't know. I guess that's what bothers me. At the time, it didn't really register. But then when I thought about it, along with the marks on Nancy's neck . . . well, like I said, it just didn't set right with me."

Clyde nodded. "It doesn't set right with me either. Come on. We need to get this all down on paper."

6

Doug felt his tension ease some as he reached the stone walls and four-board wooden fencing that surrounded Hunting Hollow. He drove along the black-fenced boundary until he came to the stone pillars that marked the farm's entrance. He turned off the paved road, drove through the open iron gates and onto the gravel drive that wound around stately oak, maple, and pine trees, towards his barn. Doug saw his farm manager, John, mending a fence board in the front pasture and three men in front of the house, fighting against the wind as they raked piles of wet leaves into bags.

As he neared the barn, his groom, Babs Tyler, came out to meet him and stood in the rain waiting for him to pull the rig to a stop in front of the barn. She walked purposefully to the back of the trailer, and by the time Doug had turned off the engine and climbed out of the Range Rover, she had already unloaded Chancellor. The tip of her nose was red and she sniffed, and then wiped her nose with the cuff of her sweater. She didn't have a raincoat on and water droplets clung to the fuzzy yarn on her gray sweater. She smelled like wet wool.

Babs wore no makeup and her face was leathery, making her look older than her twenty-five years. She carelessly poked a loose strand of hair into the rubber band that held back her ponytail.

"Hey, boss, what were you doing today, partying at the hunt breakfast and neglecting your horse? Look at him, all lathered up and shivering. You could have at least put a cooler on him."

Doug bit back an angry retort and took a deep breath before responding. She obviously had no idea what had happened at the hunt. "Babs, there was a bad accident out there today involving Nancy Williams. I rode for help and

Chancellor had a pretty hard workout. I didn't have the time afterwards to cool him out."

Babs snorted. "So, you were out there playing hero again. I know how much Nancy loves it when you do that. In fact, I almost wouldn't put it past her to stage something just to get your attention. Well, how bad was it? Is she okay?"

Doug shook his head. "She didn't make it, Babs."

Babs' mouth hung open. "Jesus, you mean she's dead? Oh, my God. Oh, Doug, I'm so sorry." Her eyes filled with tears and she looked more closely at him, then reached out and touched his cheek. "What about you, are you okay? You've got blood on your cheek." She looked down at the rest of him and her eyes widened. "It's all over you."

Doug backed away. "I'm fine. Please just take care of Chancellor. Give him a good rub-down and see that he gets a hot bran mash for dinner. I'll be back later to check on him."

Babs' face reddened and she turned abruptly and led Chancellor into the wash rack. Doug sighed. He hadn't meant to hurt her feelings, but the last thing he wanted to do was give Babs a play-by-play of what he'd just been through. He couldn't. Not right now.

Doug got his tack from the trailer and carried it into the barn. He hung his bridle and girth on the hook by the sink in the tack room and went around the corner to put his saddle on the cleaning rack. As Doug leaned down with his saddle, a loud bang sounded behind him. He turned and saw the outside door to the tack room blowing freely in the wind. He went to close the door, and for a fleeting instant thought he caught a glimpse of a figure near the far corner of the barn. Doug stepped out into the rain for a better look, but no one was out there. He dashed back inside and locked and dead-bolted the door.

Doug walked back out into the barn aisle. "Babs, you left the side door to the tack room unlocked. The wind just blew it open."

"No, I didn't," Babs replied. "I haven't used that door since Maureen delivered the blankets last week. And I locked it when she left. Just like I always do."

Doug didn't want to argue with her, even though he knew that Babs was the only one who would have had a reason to use that door. "Well, maybe John or someone else went through there. At any rate, I've locked it now and put my tack away. I'll see you later."

Doug turned to head out of the barn and Babs called out to him. "I almost forgot to tell you. Some guy was here looking for you early this morning, right after you left to go hunting."

Doug stopped and looked back at her. "Who was it?"

Babs shrugged. "He didn't say. He just said that he was a 'voice from your past' and he wanted to surprise you. He was dressed for deer hunting, but I don't think he was from around here. He sounded like a redneck. Like he was from West Virginia or someplace. He wanted to know how to get to where you were foxhunting today, but he didn't seem to know the area very well when I tried to give him directions. It was kind of weird. I didn't see a car or anything. He just seemed to appear out of nowhere."

Doug was surprised that someone would wander down to the barn like that. But he hadn't closed the front gates when he'd left to go foxhunting that morning. Anyone could have come onto the property. He remembered the figure he'd thought he'd just seen outside the barn. "If he shows up again, call me," he said. "And if I'm not around, have John deal with him."

CHAPTER

7

The telephone was ringing when Doug entered the house, but he ignored it and headed upstairs. He could hear Nellie answer the phone in the kitchen, telling whoever it was that he wasn't there. Nellie had helped raise him and had been his parents' housekeeper for years. She was getting older now and didn't really do much in the way of housekeeping anymore, but she had become like family to him.

Doug turned on the steam shower in the master bathroom and stripped off his clothes. His stomach turned as he saw the mass of blood that covered his clothing, and he quickly averted his eyes. The reality of Nancy's death was beginning to set in and exhaustion enveloped him. He stepped into the shower and stood there for a long time just letting the hot water beat down on him.

The shower warmed him, and he finally summoned up the energy to get out and dry off. He dressed in khakis and a flannel shirt and went down to his study. The light in the walnut-paneled room was dim, and the leather-bound law books that filled the floor-to-ceiling bookshelves seemed to close in on him. Doug walked around, switching on lamps.

He paused as he turned on the picture light for the portrait above the mantle. It was a painting of his father, dressed in hunt attire, his hunt whip held loosely across the chest of his scarlet coat. Doug ran his fingers along the bottom of the gilded frame, remembering the first time his father had taken him foxhunting. He closed his eyes and breathed deeply. He could picture it as if it were yesterday.

It was his ninth birthday, an unusually warm October morning, and fog lay in patches across the valley. The air had smelled dark and musty, and

Doug's tweed jacket itched his neck. He sweated a little as they waited for the stirrup-cup to be served, and when a man approached them with a silver tray, Doug's father explained to him that the shot glasses contained sherry for the adults and the Dixie cups held juice for the children. Doug gratefully took a small cup of apple juice from the tray and ate two of the cookies that were offered him. As they waited for the huntsman to cast the hounds, Doug's father predicted that the warm, wet conditions would make for good scenting, and he was right. The hounds hit a line right from the start and they ran for the first hour. His father had him on a lead line and kept him at the back of the field, controlling the pace so they barely even broke a canter, but Doug was intoxicated by the excitement of the chase and the camaraderie among the riders. He was finally part of it all, and he felt so much more grown-up than his newly acquired nine years.

The memory of his father brought on an overwhelming sense of loss, and Doug sighed and let his hand trail away from the painting.

He started a fire in the rugged stone hearth that dominated the eastern end of the room, then stretched out in front of it in his leather armchair. Doug put his legs up on the ottoman and reached for the phone to call his office.

"White, Baker and Cummings, how may I direct your call?"

"Hi, Jill, it's Doug. Can you get Marsha on the phone, please?"

"Certainly, Mr. Cummings. Let me transfer you."

He heard Marsha's pleasant voice come on the line. "Hello. Mr. Cummings' office."

"Marsha. It's me."

"Hi, Doug. Are you on your way in?" Marsha asked.

"No. That's why I'm calling. I'm not coming in."

"Is everything okay?" Doug could hear the concern in Marsha's voice.

He closed his eyes and took a deep breath. "No, Marsha, it's not. There was an accident in the hunt field today. Nancy's dead." His voice cracked.

"Oh, Doug, how terrible. What happened?" Marsha asked.

"She fell off. She was riding home alone, so we don't know exactly what happened." Doug didn't tell Marsha that he had been the one who found Nancy.

"That's awful," Marsha said. "I'm so sorry. What can I do to help?"

He sighed. "Cancel my appointment with Larry Greer at Tycoon Technologies. I'm due there in less than an hour."

"Consider it done. You also have an interview scheduled for this afternoon with Eric Schultz from *The Washington News*. Shall I cancel it as well?"

"What's that for?" Doug asked, frowning as he tried to remember.

"He's doing a story on the Bar Association awards. For the "People" section, I believe."

"Right. My public service award. Please cancel the interview. In fact, put if off indefinitely. I'd appreciate it if you'd also touch base with Mark Hoffman and explain the situation to him. Tell Mark to call me at the farm if he needs me for anything today. If I don't hear from him, I'll see him in the office first thing tomorrow morning."

"No problem. Anything else?" Marsha asked.

"Yes. I'd like you to send a messenger out with my mail and the file for the *Times* merger," Doug replied.

"Oh, Doug, are you sure? Why don't you just take some time off? Those things can wait."

Doug shook his head. "No. I need to have something to do."

"I understand," she said. "I'll call for a messenger right now. And if you need anything else, anything at all, I'm right here."

"Thanks," Doug said, hanging up the phone.

He got up and walked to the window. The rain was coming down in torrents and the wind pelted it against the thick glass panes. The view of the Blue Ridge Mountains, usually so breathtaking, was obscured by heavy dark clouds hanging on the horizon. There's not likely to be any hunting for a few days, he thought, looking at the flooded ground. That was probably for the best. He couldn't stomach going out there again any time soon.

Doug knew he should go and tell Nellie about what had happened, before she heard it from someone else, but instead, he flopped down on the couch in front of the warm fire and watched the flames dance across the logs.

He stayed that way for over an hour, until he heard the doorbell ring and Nellie came in with his mail. "Thanks, Nellie," he said, rising from the couch and taking the package from her. The large manila envelope was heavy and damp. His name on the front was illegible where the blue ink was splattered from the rain. He set it down on the coffee table.

"Nellie, can you sit down for a minute?" he said, gesturing towards the couch. "There's something I want to tell you."

Nellie sat down on the edge of the couch, her hands clasped together in her lap. "Oh, my, Doug. Something tells me this isn't going to be good news."

Doug gave her a small smile. "It isn't, Nellie." He reached out and put his hand over hers. "Nancy was killed in a riding accident today."

Nellie's pale blue eyes filled with tears and she gripped his hand in both of hers. "Oh, my Lord, that poor sweet lady," she whispered softly. "I hope she didn't suffer."

"No, I don't think she did," Doug said quietly. "I think that it happened very quickly."

They were both silent for a moment, then Nellie reached one hand out and patted Doug on the knee. "Are you okay?"

He started to nod, then shook his head. There was no use lying to Nellie.

"Let me make you some lunch," she said, rising from the couch. "You need to eat something."

"Thanks, Nellie, but I'm really not hungry." Doug regretted saying it as soon as he saw the disappointed look that crossed her face. He stood up. "On second thought, I am still a little chilled from the rain. Some hot soup sounds good."

Nellie nodded and started towards the door. "There now, that will make you feel better. You just stay here in front of the fire and keep warm, and I'll whip something up in a jiffy."

Doug sighed as he picked up the package of mail from Marsha and settled down behind his comfortable old cherry-wood desk. He tore open the packet and about halfway through the stack of mail, an envelope caught his eye. It was a flimsy white one, the cheap kind you could buy in any drugstore. His name was sprawled across the front in heavy black marker. Doug slit it open and found that it contained a death notice that had been torn out of a newspaper.

Reading it, Doug frowned, trying to remember why the name sounded familiar. Zeke McGraw. Then he remembered. It had been a long time ago.

He had been a first year tax associate at his father's firm, fresh out of Yale Law School, and Robert Dewitt, the head of the tax department and managing partner of the firm, had called him into his office.

"Doug, I'm sure you know that we pride ourselves here on the amount of hours our attorneys bill every year on *pro bono* work, helping out those who need an attorney but can't afford one," Dewitt had said.

Doug nodded, wondering what was in store for him.

"Well, I have a case here that I want you to work on. It's some criminal matter, no big deal. We got it through that new program we're participating in with the D.C. criminal courts. Shouldn't take up too much time, but it will look good to have some *pro bono* hours on your time sheet."

"A criminal case? Robert, you know I'm not a trial lawyer."

"I know that, Doug," Dewitt said, putting out his hand and motioning for Doug to sit down. "You don't have to be a litigator to handle this. I already told you, it's just a small criminal charge. Drugs or something. You'll plea bargain anyway. Very straightforward. You'll be fine. The litigation department is swamped right now with the Wellington trial, and since you just finished that research project for me, I volunteered you."

Doug glanced over the file. His client, Zeke McGraw, was a drug dealer from West Virginia who had a prior conviction for selling dope to kids in the local schoolyard. This time McGraw was in on a possession charge, arrested during a raid at a sleazy District nightclub. McGraw hadn't made bail and was being held in the D.C. jail, pending trial.

Doug met with his client in a small interrogation room at the jail and advised him that his best bet was to plea bargain for a reduced sentence. He had already met with the prosecutor and thought he could cut a deal where Zeke would be out in six months. All things considered, Doug thought that was pretty good. But Zeke McGraw would have nothing to do with it.

"I ain't going back to no prison. I done time before and I ain't ever going back. I want my day in court."

Doug couldn't believe what he was hearing. He didn't have enough experience to handle a criminal trial. He had to convince McGraw to accept the plea. "I really can't stress enough the risks of going to trial, Zeke. Giving this case to a jury would be like playing Russian roulette."

His client just scowled at him and Doug cleared his throat and continued. "You really have no defense, Zeke. The evidence against you is rock solid. They caught you red-handed. And the search was proper." He shook his head. "Frankly, I don't know what kind of a defense I'd even put on."

His client leaned over the table, his face less than a foot from Doug's. "You better come up with one, 'cause I ain't gonna cop no plea." He poked his finger at Doug. "You're gonna get me off."

A sour smell drifted from his client, and Doug leaned back in his chair and gathered his thoughts. "You're the client and, of course, ultimately it's your decision. I just want to make sure that you are well aware of the risks inherent in a trial. The outcome is wildly unpredictable. That's why I suggested the plea bargain."

Zeke McGraw snorted and settled back down in his chair. "I figure I got me a rich-boy lawyer like you, there ain't no way I can lose." He smiled, revealing a large gap where one top front tooth was missing. "You're gonna charm that jury into letting me off. They'll listen to you."

And so, Doug had no choice but to try the case. The trial lasted almost a full day and Doug suffered through the ordeal with Zeke's family breathing down his neck from the front row of the courtroom. His mother, with her pin-curl perm and flowered cotton dress, flanked on one side by Zeke's older brother, Zebulon, and on the other side by his sister, Zelda, who was visibly pregnant.

Right from the beginning of the trial, Zebulon whispered unsolicited words of advice to Doug in a voice loud enough to be heard by the jury. "Oh, man, that's a lie," Zebulon hissed when the DEA agent was testifying. "Zeke never did no drugs. The dude framed him." The judge admonished him twice, and Zebulon stopped only when the judge finally threatened to have him removed from the courtroom.

Doug tried his best to interject reasonable doubt into the prosecutor's case, but in the end the jury convicted Zeke on the drug charge, and the judge sentenced him to five years in prison.

"Motherfucker," Zeke swore at Doug. As the guard came to escort him from the courtroom, Zeke turned around towards his family. "What do I do, Zeb? I can't go back in. You know what happened last time. I ain't gonna survive." Zeke's voice was shrill and tight and his eyes darted wildly from Zebulon to his mother. Doug looked away and busied himself gathering papers from the table in front of him.

He heard Zebulon's twangy voice. "It's okay, bro. I'll figure something out. Don't you worry none. Zeb will take care of you."

The guard led Zeke through the door at the side of the courtroom and Zebulon turned on Doug. "You screwed up, asshole. What are you gonna do now?"

Had he screwed up? If someone more experienced had tried the case, what would have happened? Doug took a deep breath and looked at Zeke's family. Zeke's mother sat tight-lipped, her knuckles white where her hands gripped the pocketbook in her lap. Zelda scowled at him.

"Zeke knew that it was risky going to trial," Doug said. "He chose to gamble that he'd be better off with a jury than a plea bargain. Now he has to suffer the consequences and serve his sentence."

"That ain't good enough," Zebulon shot back. "You need to file an appeal or something."

Doug shook his head. "Don't get Zeke's hopes up. I don't see any grounds for an appeal. But I'll review the record and get back to you."

Doug reviewed the record, but didn't see a legitimate basis for an appeal. He even asked one of the litigators in his firm to take a look at it.

"Christ, Doug, why are you even wasting your time on this?" the lawyer asked after he had reviewed the file. "This case is a loser. McGraw should have copped a plea, but he insisted on a trial. Tell him he has to live with it."

Doug sighed. "I know. I just feel like I let him down."

The lawyer laughed. "That's just because it's your first trial. After a while, you get used to it."

So Doug drafted a letter to Zeke telling him there was no hope for an appeal and sent a copy to Zebulon. He never heard from or about Zeke McGraw again until now, some fourteen years later.

Doug frowned as he read the death notice. That was odd. It said Zeke had died in prison. But he should have been released years ago. Doug flipped the small clipping over, but there was no indication which newspaper it had come from. He wondered who had sent it and figured it was probably some attorney from his firm.

Doug crumpled up the clipping and threw it in the wastepaper basket.

C H A P T E R

8

The day of Nancy's funeral dawned gray and gloomy. Doug had spent the two days since Nancy's death in Washington, and he drove west out of the city on Interstate Sixty-six towards Middleburg, against the stream of headlights from the early morning commuters.

Doug had immersed himself in work since returning to the District, and his only contact with anyone in Middleburg had been when he'd called Nancy's mother. She had asked him to be a pallbearer, and he'd offered to deliver a eulogy, but she said no. She said she just wanted a short sermon from Father Andrews at the church, and she'd granted Wendy Brooks' request to recite a verse at the cemetery.

By the time Doug arrived in Middleburg the parking spots in front of the church were all taken, and he drove a block past the church into the center of town. He parked at the curb in front of the Red Fox Inn and fished in his pocket for a quarter for the parking meter.

A steady rain was falling, and Doug grabbed an umbrella from the seatback pocket as he climbed out of the car. He opened the umbrella as he hurried around the front of the Porsche and skirted a puddle on the red brick sidewalk as he fed the quarter into the meter. The meter whirred as it accepted the coin, and the digital-display showed that he was good for one hour. Doug frowned and reached in his pocket for more coins. He was certain the last time he'd used a meter in Middleburg, a quarter had bought him two hours.

Doug plugged another coin into the meter and headed towards the church. The streets of Middleburg were deserted, which wasn't unusual for a rainy, weekday morning. Activity would pick up around lunch time when the locals came to town to do their errands and collect their mail.

As Doug passed beneath the hand-painted signs that adorned the shops and businesses, he admired the way the community continued to maintain Middleburg's small-town charm. There were no fast-food restaurants, neon signs, or chain stores among the stone facades, and fox-carved wooden benches strategically placed around town invited people to sit a while and relax. Doug nodded a greeting at a woman changing the window display at the Piedmont Gourmet shop and crossed the street to the church.

The pews in the small red brick chapel were already crowded when Doug entered, and by the time the service commenced, the church was packed. Doug sat in the second row, behind Mrs. Williams and Nancy's brother.

Father Andrews walked to the pulpit. "We give Nancy back to you, oh God, who gave her to us. Yet, as you did not lose Nancy in giving, so do we not lose Nancy by her return."

Doug looked at Mrs. Williams. She sat rigidly, turned slightly sideways in the pew towards the pulpit, and as Father Andrews prayed, she reached up with one hand and dabbed at her eyes with a white handkerchief.

Doug swallowed a lump that swelled in his throat. Why did tragedy strike some families like this? First, Mrs. Williams' husband. Then her daughter. Both killed foxhunting. Should Nancy have given the sport up after her father's death? Would that have saved her? Or was her passing predetermined? If not foxhunting, would it have been a car accident, or some other mishap? Doug stared at Nancy's casket. If he'd been hunting with Nancy that day, if they hadn't broken up, could he have prevented her accident? Doug shook his head to clear his thoughts and forced his attention back to Father Andrews.

The priest's voice, solemn yet calming, boomed through the tiny chapel. "God lent his child Nancy to us for a while, for us to love and cherish while she lived. And though we now mourn her passing, we may take comfort in the knowledge that she has returned to God, our Heavenly Father."

When the funeral service was over, Doug joined Mrs. Williams and her son in the limousine for the short drive to the town's historic Sharon Cemetery. Doug blinked back tears as he helped place Nancy's casket in front of the new marble headstone, adjacent to Nancy's father in the family burial plot. He averted his eyes from the hole that had been dug in the red-clay soil and looked out at the sea of colorful umbrellas that dotted the graveyard. Across the cemetery, he could see the lonely obelisk that commemorated the unknown dead from the Civil War.

Father Andrews held his bible close to his purple-trimmed robe to protect it from the blowing rain. "Let us pray," he said.

After the priest led them all in prayer, Wendy Brooks stepped forward and placed a white rose on Nancy's casket. Her hands trembled as she unfolded a sheet of paper. She glanced briefly at the crowd. "I wrote this for Nancy," she said quietly. "I was inspired by a favorite poem of mine." Wendy began to read from the sheet of paper.

"Why do you mourn and grieve for me?
Fear not, my friends, my soul is free.
My spirit lives in all God's things,
The gentle music of the bird that sings.
The breeze in your face, the sun in the sky,
The glorious sound of the hounds in full cry.
The soft rain on autumn leaves,
The sought-out covert in fallen trees.
The ripple on the pond that you pass,
The crisp morning air, the frost on the grass.
The soothing echo of every hoofbeat,
As your horse delivers you home from the meet.
And when you hear the huntsman's horn,
I'll be galloping with you on one more run.
Please don't mourn and grieve for me,
Fear not, my friends, my soul is free."

Wendy folded the paper and reached up to dab at her eyes with her handkerchief. "It reminded me of what Nancy would say to us today, if she could," she said quietly, to no one in particular. She stepped back and handed the piece of paper to Mrs. Williams.

The graveyard was still for a moment, but for the gently falling rain and some muffled sobbing. Then the clear notes of "Gone Away" rang out from Smitty's horn. *"Da dada da da da dada da da da dada da daaaa."* Doug looked towards where the huntsman stood, formally dressed in scarlet, at the head of the casket, several yards behind Father Andrews. The playing of "Gone Away" caught Doug by surprise. It was an honor generally reserved for masters and hunting staff. He sought out Richard Evan Clarke and their eyes met. Richard gave him a small smile and Doug nodded his head in return. It was a nice tribute to Mrs. Williams and those whom she had lost.

Smitty walked over to the casket and placed the hunt horn on top of it, next to Wendy's white rose. "It was her papa's," he said, patting the horn gently. "She should have it now." Smitty's stout face turned red, and he made no attempt to wipe off the tears that streamed down his cheeks. He backed away from the casket, and Doug reached out and put his hand on Smitty's shoulder.

9

Zeb watched from the brick gardener's shed, just a few yards away from the gravesite. He stood by the weathered wooden door, which he had left open a crack. The door was old and warped, with a wide gap at the top, and rain blew into Zeb's face and coated his eyelashes with a mist. He blinked rapidly a couple of times but didn't reach up to wipe the water droplets away.

Zeb studied Doug Cummings, who stood at the gravesite next to an old woman dressed in a black coat. A fringe of white curls surrounded the old woman's black hat, and a black veil half covered her face. The old woman swayed on her feet and Cummings reached out and put his arm around her, then placed his other hand under her elbow. Cummings leaned down and spoke into the old woman's ear and she looked up at him and nodded.

A younger woman in a brown tweed jacket, long skirt, and boots stepped forward and placed a rose on the casket. Then she unfolded a piece of paper and began to read from it, but Zeb couldn't make out what she was saying. Cummings stood with his arm around the old woman and stared at the casket.

When the younger woman finished reading, Cummings reached up and wiped his hand across his cheek. Was he wiping away a tear? Or was it a raindrop? Zeb studied Cummings carefully and wondered what the dead woman had meant to him. Was Cummings suffering? Zeb shook his head. Nah. Cummings just stood there looking uncomfortable, like a normal guy at someone's funeral.

Zeb remembered how he'd felt at Zeke's funeral. Like a huge hand was inside his chest, squeezing his heart, trying to rip it out of him. He hadn't talked to anyone. Not even his mama. Or Zelda. He'd stood there alone by Zeke, promising Zeke he'd make it all okay. He'd make Cummings pay. No

43

matter what it took.

The crowd started to disperse and Zeb inched away from the door and quietly crouched in the back corner of the shed.

CHAPTER

10

The graveside service was over. Doug followed along with the others to the church parish house where a reception was held in the spacious gathering room. The corners of the large room were filled with flowers that had been transferred over from the chapel. Tables lined the center of the room, laden with pies, coffee cakes, and other sweets. Wet footprints splattered the varnished wood floor as people filed in from the cemetery.

As Doug helped himself to a cup of coffee, he spotted Carol Simpson across the room and walked over to her. He gave her a quick hug and spoke softly so only she could hear. "Thanks for intervening on my behalf with that deputy the other day."

Carol stiffened and her eyes darted quickly towards those who stood near them. "I don't know what you mean, Doug. I didn't intervene at all."

Doug frowned at her odd response. "Well, you definitely put a stop to his barrage of ridiculous questions. I just want you to know that I appreciated it."

Carol acted as if she hadn't heard him. "Excuse me, Doug. I think I'll help myself to something to eat." She turned towards the food table and left him standing alone.

Before he could react, Doug felt a hand on his arm and turned to see Heather from California standing next to him. She reached up and gave him a kiss on the cheek. "I'm Heather Prescott. We met at the hunt the other day, remember?"

Doug nodded, and Heather leaned closer, ran her hand up his arm to his shoulder, and lightly stroked his back.

"This all must be so hard on you. You look exhausted. Would you like to join me in getting something to eat?"

Doug backed away and looked at his watch. "No, I'm not hungry.

45

Besides, I didn't realize how late it was. I have to be getting back to Washington."

Heather linked her arm through his and tugged him towards the table. "Nonsense. Surely you can spare five more minutes."

Doug protested, but Heather held his arm tight, and he couldn't graciously extricate himself.

Langley Masterson was standing at the end of the food table by the plates, and he sidled over to Doug as they approached.

"Hello, Doug."

Doug nodded at him. "Langley."

Heather offered a plate to Doug, but he shook his head.

Langley stared curiously at Heather for a moment, before turning his attention back to Doug. "Well, Doug, it seems that we've both lost Nancy now, haven't we?" Langley asked.

"Yes, Langley, we have," Doug said quietly.

Langley nodded at him thoughtfully. "Yes, we have," he repeated slowly. "Except that you only lost her once. I've lost her twice."

Doug put his hand on Langley's shoulder. "Don't make it harder on yourself, Langley. Just try to remember the good times you and Nancy had."

Langley shook his head and shrugged Doug's hand off. "That's the whole problem, Doug. I've never been able to forget those good times."

Doug gave Langley a small smile, and then followed after Heather as she filled her plate.

"What was that all about?" Heather asked, as they reached the end of the food line and moved away from Langley.

Heather had a cup of coffee in one hand and her food plate in the other, and Doug reached out and held the coffee cup for her so she could eat. "Langley used to date Nancy, before I did."

"I gather that he wasn't the one who called it quits," Heather said.

"You're right about that. It was Nancy's decision."

"Did she dump him for you?" Heather asked.

Doug shook his head. "No, although I've always suspected that Langley thinks I played a role in their breakup. In reality, it was Langley's possessive behavior that killed their relationship."

"Possessive isn't always bad," Heather said, smiling.

"Well, Langley was overly possessive," Doug replied. "The final straw came one night when Nancy went out to dinner with friends, without telling

Langley where she was going. Langley searched the restaurants in Middleburg until he found her and caused a scene until Nancy finally left with him. That was it. Nancy stopped dating Langley after that."

Heather shook her head. "I can't imagine what Nancy saw in a middle-aged guy like him anyway. He's getting a pot belly and has lost half his hair. Is he rich or something?"

Doug raised an eyebrow. "You get right to the point, don't you, Heather?"

Heather just smiled.

"Yes. Langley comes from money," Doug said. "His family owns a three-thousand acre farm near Upperville, where Langley's father dabbles in race horses. Unlike Langley, his father is the epitome of a true southern gentle-man."

"And Langley? What does he do?" Heather asked.

Doug shrugged. "Foxhunts and spends his father's money."

Heather flashed him a smile. "Well, Nancy certainly made the right choice when she picked you over him."

Doug couldn't help smiling back. "Thanks." He handed the coffee cup back to Heather and looked at his watch. "I really have to leave now. It was nice to see you again, Heather. I hope you've enjoyed your stay in Virginia and that you have a safe trip back to California."

On his way out, Doug looked around for Mrs. Williams but saw that she was surrounded by people. He decided he'd call her later.

As he neared the door, Doug saw Kathy Morris immersed in conversa-tion with Wendy Brooks. Kathy's back was to him, and as he approached her, he heard her say something to Wendy about "foul play." Wendy said some-thing to Kathy, who spun around to face him.

"Doug, hi," Kathy said, blushing.

"Hi." He leaned down and gave Kathy a kiss on the cheek, and then did the same to Wendy.

Both women took sips from the coffee cups they were holding, but neither spoke. "I'm sorry, did I interrupt something?" Doug asked.

"Oh, no," Kathy said, too quickly. "We were just talking."

Doug studied them both. "I couldn't help but hear you use the words 'foul play,' Kathy. I hope you're not repeating Deputy Dickson's skepticism about Nancy's death."

Kathy smiled and seemed to relax. "Oh, so you know."

"Know what?"

Her brow creased into a frown and she blushed again. "About Deputy Dickson. That he's not sure Nancy's death was an accident."

Doug shook his head. "All I know is that he gave me a hard time. I thought he was just trying to throw his weight around. Is there more?"

"No. Not really," Kathy said, avoiding eye contact.

He was annoyed that Kathy would repeat what Dickson had said. "Well, I hope that speculation doesn't go any further. God forbid Mrs. Williams should hear that kind of talk."

Kathy nodded but didn't say anything, and Wendy just stared into her coffee cup.

"I'm heading back into Washington," he said, breaking the silence. Both women nodded. "I'll see you," he said, frowning, and opened the door.

Doug closed the door firmly behind him, and stood there, with his hand on the knob. The conversation with Kathy was unsettling. He couldn't believe she would repeat Dickson's nonsense. But she had. And he had the uneasy feeling that it went beyond idle gossip. He remembered how peculiar Carol Simpson had acted when he'd thanked her for running interference with Dickson. She'd almost seemed afraid to talk with him. He didn't know what was going on, but something wasn't right.

C H A P T E R

11

Clyde Dickson almost couldn't contain his smile as he sat across the desk from Sheriff Fred Boling at the Sheriff's Office in Leesburg. It was official now, just as he had suspected. Nancy Williams hadn't died from a riding accident. She hadn't been killed by falling on a rock or being kicked in the head by a damned horse. She had been murdered.

"It says it right here," the sheriff said, jabbing his finger at the piece of paper he held in his hand. "The cause of death was a combination of blunt force trauma to the head and strangulation." Sheriff Boling put the Coroner's Report down on his desk, removed his reading glasses, and rubbed his forehead.

"You know what this means, don't you, Clyde?"

Clyde nodded, but the sheriff continued before he could speak.

"It means that all hell is going to break loose. Things like this, cold-blooded murder, they just don't happen around here. As soon as word of this gets out, we're going to have reporters swarming all over this county. Why, I wouldn't even be surprised if this made the tabloids." He held his hands up in front of him and made quotation marks in the air with his fingers. *"Socialite Brutally Murdered on Foxhunt."* He snorted. "Like after the polo murder a few years back, there was this magazine headline, *'Hunt Country Blood Sport . . . Murder and Mystery in Middleburg'* or some shit like that. I guess I don't need to tell you what that did to the tourist business around here."

The sheriff shook his head. "Hell, I know that some folks in Middleburg would just as soon have the tourists stay away, but I've got the rest of the county to look after. If tourism drops off, Clyde, it'll hurt the whole damned county. The restaurants. The inns. The antique shops. The merchants. They'll all suffer."

Sheriff Boling leaned back in his chair and clasped his hands behind his head, a worried look on his face. "We need to do some damage control here, Clyde. Serious damage control."

"Yes, sir," Clyde said. He leaned down and spit tobacco juice into the empty Styrofoam coffee cup he was holding.

Sheriff Boling sat forward and studied Clyde for a minute. "You haven't been with the department very long, Clyde, but I like what I've seen from you. I think you're my kind of guy. And since I need someone I can really count on to head this murder investigation, I'm offering it to you."

Clyde smiled. All that sucking up he'd been doing was clearly paying off. "Why thank you, Sheriff. I'm right honored."

"Of course, there are some guys in the department who'll be pissed that I didn't hand this to them. But I'll explain that you're the logical choice. After all, you were the deputy on the scene. You won't need to waste any time being brought up to speed on this."

Clyde nodded.

"I don't know how much manpower I can give you on this, Clyde. You know we're short-staffed right now. But solving this murder is a top priority for me. You need anything, you come to me. I'll see that you get it."

Clyde's pulse raced. Perfect. He didn't want anyone else involved. He wanted to call all the shots on this one. Oh, yes. By the time this investigation was over, he'd make those rich equestrians sit up and take notice of Clyde Dickson.

Clyde leaned back in his chair and thought back to his first encounter with snooty horse people like Doug Cummings. He was fifteen years old and his daddy worked mucking stalls for William Clayton Barrington.

Clyde had accompanied his daddy to work one day, and was helping him tack up the horses for Mr. Barrington and his lady friend. It was a hot day, and the woman wore a thin white blouse, which revealed a lacy brassiere underneath. She had the most enormous breasts that Clyde had ever seen, and he swore that the woman was teasing him. She stood very close to him, feigning interest in just how he buckled the girth to the billet straps of the saddle. Her breast brushed very slowly against his arm. Clyde's palms grew so sweaty that the girth slipped from his hand.

The lady laughed, a low, rumbling laugh and leaned down to help him retrieve the dangling girth. Clyde was overcome by the flowery sweet smell of her perfume and the way her lacy white brassiere hugged her breasts. Her blouse, already unbuttoned three buttons, parted as she bent down for the girth. Clyde couldn't take his eyes off her chest. Although Clyde had never actually seen a woman's breasts before, except in a girlie magazine his best friend's father kept in his workshop, Clyde was certain that this lady had the largest, most perfect breasts he would ever see. He stood transfixed. The lady giggled softly and took the girth from his hand, and then Clyde looked up into the very angry face of William Clayton Barrington.

Clyde felt himself yanked up off the ground by the collar of his shirt. "You keep your eyes to yourself, young man, you hear me?" Barrington said.

Clyde felt the red burn of embarrassment creep up over his ears. "Yes, s-sir," he said, and stared at the brick pavers in the barn aisle.

Barrington released him and walked over to Clyde's daddy. "I don't want you bringing your boy back around here, you understand me, Dickson?"

Clyde's father had been "let go" a few weeks later, and his daddy had drifted from job to job after that, never very happy and never staying in any one place very long. He eventually found solace in a bottle, and drank himself to death just before Clyde's twenty-first birthday. At first, Clyde had blamed himself for his father's demise, but, over time, he had shifted the blame to William Clayton Barrington and those like him.

The memory triggered a burst of anger in Clyde and he nodded vigorously at the sheriff. He'd be more than happy to investigate these hunt-country snobs. Maybe he'd finally get the retribution he'd longed for. "Am I relieved of my other duties then? So I can devote my full attention to the investigation?" he asked.

The sheriff nodded. "Starting right now. Of course, I want you to keep me apprised every step of the way." He looked Clyde straight in the eye. "The outcome of this has serious implications for me, Clyde. I'm up for re-election next year, and this could be my ticket to a second term as sheriff. I won't forget anyone who helps me get there."

"I understand," Clyde said. "I'll do everything I can."

Sheriff Boling smiled and relaxed in his chair. "Now, you better get going, Clyde. You've got a murder to solve."

Clyde nodded and reached into his chest pocket for some more chewing tobacco. "I'll get right on it, Sheriff. But first, I have a suggestion. About damage control."

The sheriff nodded.

"Maybe we ought to go on the offensive with the media. Why not call a press conference?" Clyde suggested.

"A press conference? Weren't you listening to what I just told you?" the sheriff asked, an angry frown creasing his brow.

"Yes, I was, but, well, think about it for a minute. You just said yourself that reporters are going to be snooping around here, writing stories. Why not get them started on the right foot; tell them the story the way we want it told?"

"Which is?" the sheriff asked.

"Which is that we have no reason to suspect that there is a random murderer on the loose out here. That we believe Ms.Williams was killed by someone she knew, most likely someone she was foxhunting with that day," Clyde replied.

Sheriff Boling's mouth dropped open. "How'd you come up with that?"

Clyde shrugged. "It's the most obvious explanation. There's no evidence that anyone else was in the vicinity at the time of the murder."

The sheriff scowled at him. "There's no evidence of anything at all, Clyde, because we haven't conducted an investigation yet."

Clyde realized that he'd gone too far. "Yes, I know that," he responded quickly. "Of course, we need an investigation. A thorough investigation. But I did question Doug Cummings at the scene. And the rescue squad ladies too. There was no indication from them that anyone else was in the vicinity at the time of the murder. Other than the people out foxhunting. And the way Ms. Williams was killed indicates it was personal in nature. She wasn't raped. Or kidnapped. Or robbed. They didn't steal her horse." He gave a little laugh. "There's no motive. Except rage. Revenge. Hatred. The victim was strangled. That's a crime of passion." He raised his hands in a helpless gesture. "I just don't want the media scaring people away, Sheriff. Giving them the impression there's some serial killer running around out here. I'm thinking about damage control, that's all."

Sheriff Boling's scowl relaxed and he stared thoughtfully at Clyde. "You know, you may have something there, Clyde. I'm not willing to go as far as you just did, but you might be right about the press conference idea. Maybe we can use that to calm people's fears and let them know we're making this investigation our top priority."

Sheriff Boling scheduled the press conference for eleven o'clock, and

Clyde set up folding metal chairs in the lobby. But none of the half-dozen reporters who showed up for the briefing sat in the chairs. They made themselves at home, lounging around, perched on desks and counters, waiting for the sheriff to begin. Clyde was disappointed that none of the D.C. television stations had shown up. The reporters were mostly from the local community papers. The only big gun was one guy from *The Washington News.*

At five after eleven, Sheriff Boling walked out of his back office and greeted the reporters in the lobby. "Good morning, gentlemen." He smiled at the woman reporter from *Hunt Country.* "Good morning, Sharon." Clyde saw her smile back at the sheriff and he felt himself blush. No wonder she had laughed when he'd asked her to make a name tag for herself. She and the sheriff were obviously already on a first name basis.

"I have some disturbing news to deliver to you today," the sheriff said. He held up the Coroner's Report. "I have just this morning received word from the medical examiner that he believes Nancy Williams' death last week was not accidental, as we all had thought. In addition to the head trauma, which was consistent with an accidental death, he found evidence of strangulation." The sheriff placed the report on the desk next to him. "I'll have this available for you all to see, following the press conference."

Several reporters fired questions at the sheriff, and he held up his hands. "Let me finish, and then I'll be happy to answer your questions. You'll all get your turn."

The reporters settled down and Sheriff Boling continued. "Although we did conduct a routine investigation into Ms. Williams' death, there was no indication until this morning that a more thorough scrutiny was called for. But as soon as I received word from the medical examiner, a comprehensive investigation was launched. I can assure you we are giving this top priority."

The sheriff nodded at the reporters, indicating that he was ready for their questions. Several hands went up and he pointed to the reporter from *The Washington News.*

"Do you have any suspects?" Eric Schultz asked.

Sheriff Boling smiled at the reporter, looking much calmer than Clyde imagined he really felt. "Now, Eric, you know it's too early in our investigation for me to share that kind of information with you. We're going to talk to all the witnesses and collect all the evidence before we start jumping to conclusions here. But I can say that we've got some very strong leads that we'll be following up on."

"Can you give us any names that those leads point towards?" Schultz asked.

The sheriff just smiled at him. "How many different ways are you going to ask the same question, Eric?"

Eric Schultz smiled sheepishly and the other reporters laughed.

"Okay, then, will you tell us what witnesses you've interviewed so far?" Schultz asked, his pen poised over his notebook.

"Well, of course our main witness is Doug Cummings," Sheriff Boling replied. "I think most of you know that he is the one who found Nancy Williams in the woods."

"Is he a suspect?" Schultz asked, smiling.

Clyde held his breath, waiting for the sheriff's response.

Sheriff Boling laughed. "Well, Eric, I guess I'd better say that I'm not ruling out anyone as a suspect at this point. But I think Doug Cummings would more appropriately be called a witness." He looked around at the other reporters. "Next question."

"Do you have a motive?" Sharon Duncan asked.

The sheriff hesitated for a minute. "Not one that I can share at this time, Sharon. Just let me say that we have reason to believe that this killing was personal in nature. Not a random act. Anyone else?" He pointed towards another reporter, and Clyde half-listened as Sheriff Boling answered a few routine questions about the time and place of Nancy Williams' death.

Clyde studied Eric Schultz. That reporter was on the right track. Maybe they could work together. He chewed his tobacco and considered the possibilities.

"Thanks for coming. We'll be keeping you all informed as developments occur." Sheriff Boling concluded the press conference and retreated into his back office.

Clyde watched the reporters chat as they put on their coats. They seemed to be a pretty tight-knit group. A bunch of good old boys. And girl. Except for Eric Schultz. He was up at the desk, reading the Coroner's Report. The others drifted up there too, when they saw Schultz reading the report. Clyde watched as Schultz showed it to them, pointing at various things. They finished, and Schultz put the report back down on the desk, then headed towards the door with the rest of the group. Clyde held his breath. The others stopped by the coffee maker, where there was a half-empty box of Dunkin' Donuts.

"Hey, Deputy, can we have some of these?" one of the reporters called out to him.

Clyde nodded. "Sure. Help yourself."

Eric Schultz waved at them and walked out the door. Clyde threw on his jacket and followed him.

12

Clyde caught up to Eric Schultz just as he was getting in his car.

"I have some information that might be of interest to you," Clyde said, looking around to see if anyone was watching them. "Can we meet somewhere privately?"

Schultz stepped back out of his car. "Just say where and when."

Clyde's mind raced as he tried to come up with a place. "How about the parking garage behind the Tally Ho theatre? The top floor. In ten minutes."

He waited for Schultz's nod of agreement, then turned and walked back inside. The other reporters were still standing by the coffee maker, and he walked past them and knocked on Sheriff Boling's door.

"Come in."

Clyde went in and closed the door behind him. Sheriff Boling was sitting behind his desk. "I just wanted to tell you that I'm heading out now." He motioned towards the closed door to the front office. "I thought the press conference went well. You handled them like a pro."

The sheriff shook his head, but Clyde could tell that he was pleased by the compliment. "I regret saying that I thought the killing was personal in nature. I shouldn't have said that. I was trying so hard to convince them that we have everything under control, and all of a sudden I heard myself repeating what you had said earlier. I sure hope that's how this plays out."

"Don't worry, Sheriff. I think it will. I'm getting started on it right now." Clyde opened the door to the front office and was relieved to see that the reporters were gone. He waved at the sheriff and closed the door.

Clyde drove his patrol car the short distance to the municipal parking garage and followed the ramp to the top floor. He circled the crowded lot slowly until he spotted Eric Schultz sitting in his blue Honda, parked in the far corner. Clyde passed by without stopping and found a parking spot in the next row. He sat there for a moment, making sure no one else was on the floor, then got out and walked between the rows of cars. As he reached Schultz's car, he cast one last glance, but still didn't see anyone around. Clyde leaned down and opened the passenger door and climbed in, closing it quickly behind him.

Schultz smiled at him from the driver's seat, and Clyde thought the reporter's dark hair and beard made him look sinister in the dim light of the garage. "There seems to be a lot of cloak-and-dagger secrecy to this meeting, Deputy. I hope that means you've got something pretty spectacular to tell me," Schultz said.

Clyde's mouth was dry when he started to speak, and he had a hard time getting the words out. "First of all, I want to lay the ground rules." Clyde noticed that his hand was shaking and he gripped the armrest to quiet it, hoping that Schultz hadn't noticed. "This is all off the record. Just background stuff. You can't quote me on any of it."

Schultz let out a sigh. "Look, let's start at the beginning here. I don't even know your name. Or what this is about. Why don't you tell me what it is you think I should know, and we'll go from there. If it ends up leading to a story, and you don't want me to use your name, I won't."

Clyde nodded. "Okay. I'm Clyde Dickson. But I want my name kept out of it. You can't even tell anyone you know me. I'm just like that Watergate guy. What was his name?"

"Deep Throat."

"Yeah. That's it. I'm just like Deep Throat."

Schultz smiled and put his fingers in front of his mouth. "Okay. Why don't I call you Secretariat?"

Clyde's temper flared and he narrowed his eyes. "Are you making fun of me?"

"No, no. I think it's a good alias." Schultz dropped his hand from his mouth and his smile disappeared. "I'm all ears, Deputy Dickson. Tell me what information you have."

Clyde eyed the reporter, his nervousness gone. He was in control now. "There's more you should know about the Williams' murder. Off the record."

"Off the record," Schultz repeated.

"There is a suspect. Despite what Sheriff Boling said."

Eric Schultz sat up straighter in his seat. "Who?"

Clyde smiled and kept the reporter hanging for a moment. "Doug Cummings."

"Doug Cummings?"

"Yup."

"That's unbelievable," Schultz replied, shaking his head.

"Why's it unbelievable?"

Schultz paused. "Well, because he's Doug Cummings."

Clyde laughed. "Exactly. Because he had a rich daddy. And he's a lawyer. He's society."

Schultz nodded. "Yeah, basically. Why is he a suspect? He found her body."

"Found her? Maybe. But was she already dead?"

Schultz frowned. "Do you have evidence that she wasn't?"

"I'm not talking evidence right now," Clyde said. "I'm just talking suspicions."

Schultz nodded. "Go on."

"You know he was romantically involved with her?"

"Yes."

"Did you know he'd just broken up with her?"

"No."

Clyde smiled. "Well, he had."

Schultz shrugged his shoulders. "So?"

Clyde ignored him. "After he moved her from the murder scene and brought her back to Chadwick Hall, after she was dead, he sat there, bent over her lifeless body, and told her he was sorry."

"Sorry about what?"

"Good question. Sorry about what?" Clyde snorted. "Let me ask you something. If you found someone out in the woods. Dead. Bloody. Would you pick them up and move them?"

Schultz wrinkled his nose. "Probably not."

"Of course not. You'd go get help. Unless . . ." Clyde held up a finger. "Unless there was something in those woods that you didn't want anyone to see."

"Such as?"

"Such as evidence that might incriminate you."

Schultz didn't say anything.

"Cummings was covered with blood you know."

"Well, he picked her up and you said she was bloody."

Clyde nodded. "But he had it all over him. *All* over him."

Schultz frowned. "Why would he kill her?"

"Heat of passion. Rage. Happens all the time between ex-lovers. Even the rich aren't exempt from that."

"It's an interesting theory. But it's not evidence."

"I never said it was evidence," Clyde replied quickly. "But it raises suspicions. You asked if there was a suspect, and I'm telling you that there is. It's just not public information. Yet."

Schultz stared at him. "Why are you telling me this?"

"Because there will be a certain resistance to making this public. Because of Cummings' prominence. And I don't think that's right." He smiled at the reporter. "I believe in the public's right to know."

"If I decide to write about this, can I identify you as an unnamed source in the Sheriff's Office?"

"Oh, no. No. Absolutely not. They'd know right away who it was."

"Then I can't use it. *The News* has a strict policy. No unnamed sources. Unless we can establish their credibility somehow."

Clyde thought it over. "What if you heard the same information from another source? Could you use it then?"

"An unnamed source?" Schultz asked.

Clyde shrugged. "I don't know if she'd let you use her name or not."

"It would be my editor's call," Schultz replied.

Clyde took out his notepad and wrote down Kathy Morris' name. "This lady's an EMT. She was there. She's the one who heard Cummings lean over Nancy Williams' dead body and tell her he was sorry. She'll tell you about suspicions." He tore the page out of the pad and handed it to Schultz.

"If I have any questions, can I call you?" Schultz asked.

"Not at work," Clyde responded. He told Schultz his home phone number. "But if you get my wife, don't tell her who you are. Say you're selling insurance or something. Use a different name." Clyde put his hand on the door handle. "Remember. All of this was off the record. No hint of your source." He opened the door and got out of the car.

CHAPTER

13

"Damn it!" Sharon Duncan swore as she drove her car through the first floor of the parking garage. No parking spots. Again. She headed for the ramp to the second floor. Same deal there. She kept on going, all the way to the top.

"I remember when this garage wasn't even here," she muttered. Life around Leesburg used to be so simple. Before all the growth.

She wheeled around the corner and sped down the first row of cars, searching for a vacant spot. Her head was turned, looking over at the row to her left, when a movement in front of her caught her attention. She looked back and slammed on the brakes, just in time to avoid hitting a sheriff's deputy, who emerged on foot from between the row of parked cars to her right.

She lowered her window and stuck her head out. "Sorry, Deputy."

The deputy just glared at her and kept walking.

It's my lucky day, she thought. He must be in as big a hurry as I am. Sharon heard a car engine start up, and she looked around trying to locate it. There it was. Right where the deputy had come from. The Honda. She waited, tapping her fingers impatiently on the steering wheel, while the driver backed out of the parking spot.

The driver turned the Honda in her direction and as he got closer she saw that it was Eric Schultz. Her window was still down and she stuck her hand out and waved for him to stop.

"Hi, Eric." She waited for him to lower his window. "Say, that was some news about Nancy Williams, wasn't it? You could have knocked me over with a feather."

Eric just nodded and looked in his rear view mirror.

"What'd you think about the sheriff saying it was most likely she was killed by someone she knew?" Sharon asked.

He looked away. "I wouldn't put too much stock in that, Sharon. That's just speculation." Eric's eyes darted around the parking garage.

"What's wrong with you?" Sharon asked.

"Nothing."

Sharon followed Eric's gaze over towards the next row and saw a sheriff's car pull out and drive down the exit ramp.

"Oh, my God."

"What?" he asked.

"You were talking to that deputy, weren't you?"

He frowned at her but didn't answer.

"Oh, my God. You were. What did he say?"

"Come on, Sharon. I don't ask you about your sources. Don't ask me about mine."

"He's a *source*? This gets better and better."

"I've got to go," he said, easing off on the brake.

"Oh, no, you don't," she said, holding her hand out to stop him. "You owe me, Eric. I'm the one who got you started when you opened the bureau out here, remember? Introduced you to all the right people. Convinced them that you were okay, even though you were from Washington. You're not cutting me out of this one."

He hesitated for a moment, then shrugged. "We can't talk here."

"Then buy me lunch," Sharon responded. She'd just have to miss the deadline on the travel piece she was working on.

Eric motioned for her to come along, so she parked in his vacant spot and got in his car. "Where are you taking me?" she asked.

"Somewhere that doesn't have ears," he responded.

They decided on IHOP, and Sharon waited until the waitress had taken their order and filled their coffee cups before she lit into him again.

"Okay, Eric. Stop stalling. What did he tell you?"

Eric glanced at the couple in the booth next to them, then hunched over the table and spoke in a low voice. "Doug Cummings is a suspect in Nancy Williams' murder."

"What?" She screamed it, and the couple next to them gave her a dirty look. She covered her mouth with her hand. "Sorry."

She leaned over the table and whispered to Eric. "I don't believe it. They have evidence against him?"

Eric shook his head. "I'm not sure if they have evidence or not. I think it's just a suspicion right now. Several things that don't quite add up."

"Why didn't Sheriff Boling say that? He laughed at you when you asked if Doug Cummings was a suspect."

Eric nodded. "I know. I guess it wouldn't be politically correct to name Cummings. But Boling did say that he thought Nancy Williams was killed by someone she knew. And the only person that we're sure she knew who was out in those woods with her was Doug Cummings." He raised his hands in the air. "Two plus two."

"I don't believe it," Sharon said. "I just don't believe it. It sounds like pure speculation to me. You're not considering printing it, are you?"

He shrugged. "I haven't decided."

She frowned at him. "Eric."

"The most I'd say is that Doug Cummings has been named as a suspect. Period."

"Isn't that enough? You'd destroy him." Sharon sat back in the booth and folded her arms across her chest.

"It's a great story, Sharon. You've got to admit it; it's a really big story. And if he is a suspect, don't people have a right to know that?"

"Maybe. If the sheriff comes out and says it publicly."

"But that's the whole point," Eric responded. "That's part of the story. I have inside information that he's a suspect, but the sheriff is afraid to say it publicly. Just because of who Doug Cummings is." He pointed his finger at her. "Now that's not right. No other criminal suspect would get treatment like that. They'd be brought in for questioning. The sheriff would make sure we all knew about it."

Sharon shook her head, then reached up and brushed away a strand of blond curls that had fallen over her eyes. "I still don't think it's responsible journalism, Eric. I'm telling you, ever since the O.J. Simpson trial, all you big time reporters are acting more and more like you write for the tabloids. That line used to be so distinct. It's blurred now. What's news and what's sensationalism, Eric? I'm not sure you even know any more."

The waitress brought their lunch, but Sharon couldn't do more than pick at hers, and she didn't speak to Eric on the drive back. He pulled up behind her car and she immediately got out.

"Think it over carefully, Eric," she said before she slammed the door shut. "I hope you'll do the right thing."

Sharon sat on a stool at the counter in The Coach Stop restaurant in Middleburg sipping an iced tea and watching Doug Cummings. Her hunch had been correct. She knew that the Board of Governors of the Middleburg Foxhounds were meeting there for lunch and she had come hoping Doug Cummings would be present. He sat in a booth at the back of the restaurant with six other members of the board.

Sharon looked around the restaurant. It was packed to capacity with lunch patrons. Most were locals. But some looked like leaf-gazers. The Coach Stop was one of Sharon's favorite restaurants. Good food. Cozy atmosphere. The soda fountain counter gave the small restaurant a homey feel, while the local equestrian artwork that adorned the dark green walls lent it an air of elegance. Potted plants, placed discreetly at eye level, subtly divided the booths, making it the perfect place for meetings like the one Doug was having.

"Excuse me." The elderly man sitting at the counter next to Sharon interrupted her thoughts.

"Yes?"

"Are you from around here?"

"Yes."

"Oh, good. Maybe you can help us." The man gestured towards the woman sitting next to him. "Me and the wife, we're from Toledo, and we're out here on a day trip from the electrician's convention I'm attending in Washington, D.C. We were told that a lot of celebrities live out this way. Is there any kind of map that shows where they live? We have a rental car, and we'd like to drive by and see their houses."

Sharon smiled at the thought. "No. You won't find anything like that in

Middleburg. People out here are pretty private."

"Oh, I see," the man said. He turned and patted his wife on the arm. "I'm sorry, dear."

"It's okay, honey. Just out of curiosity, who are some of the celebrities that live out this way?" she asked Sharon.

"Well, there's Robert Duvall. He's the only real movie star celebrity who comes to mind," Sharon replied. "Elizabeth Taylor, when she was married to Senator John Warner, she lived out here. And Jackie Kennedy Onassis used to spend time here, before she passed away. Paul Mellon, Jack Kent Cooke, Pamela Harriman. They all lived here, but of course they're dead now."

"Robert Duvall. He's one of my favorite actors," the woman said. "Did you see him in *Lonesome Dove*?"

Sharon nodded. "I did. And if you're a fan of his you might want to drive on down the road a bit to The Plains. Robert Duvall used to own a restaurant there, called The Rail Stop. He no longer owns it, but it's a good restaurant. You might enjoy having a bite to eat there."

"The Rail Stop. I just love the names around here. What was the name of the cute little clothing store we saw earlier, honey?"

"The something filly," her husband replied.

"The Finicky Filly," Sharon offered.

"Yes, that's it," the woman said. "And the book store, called The Book Chase. And that restaurant that was down in the basement, The Hidden Horse. Someone told us that they used to hide horses down there during the Civil War, and that's how it got its name. Oh, and my very favorite. That quaint little coffee shop across the street called Cuppa Giddy Up. They make a right good cup of coffee there too."

Her husband paid the bill and they both climbed down off the stools. "Thank you so much for the information, young lady," the woman said. "It's been nice chatting with you."

Sharon smiled at her. "Nice meeting you. I hope you enjoy your day here." Sharon watched as the man helped his wife on with her coat and guided her out the front door of the restaurant. Sharon was getting used to people like them. Tourists. They flocked here from all over the world. To see the big horse farms. And do some antiquing. Maybe catch a glimpse of a celebrity. *People from away.* That's what the old-timers called them.

Sharon paid for her iced tea and waited patiently for Doug to finish his meeting. When she saw Doug's group start to get up from their table, she got down off her stool and walked up to the front, lingering by the door. She watched Doug walk through the narrow restaurant, stopping at several booths to say hello, and as he approached her, he smiled in recognition and nodded. She didn't know him well, but she'd run into him at many of the social events she covered for *Hunt Country*.

Just as Sharon started to speak to him, Kitty Baker, a local realtor, came up to Doug and grabbed his arm, whispering in his ear as she led him outside. Sharon hesitated briefly. She didn't want to intrude, but she feared she would miss her opportunity to speak with Doug, so she followed him out.

Doug's silver Porsche was parked at the curb and he stood by the open driver's door, still talking with Kitty Baker. "Mr. Cummings," Sharon called, waving to get his attention. "Could I talk with you for a couple of minutes?" She saw him glance down at his watch. "It won't take long; I promise. But it's really pretty important."

"Sure," Doug said.

Kitty Baker shot Sharon a look of annoyance. "Call me," she said to Doug, and went back into the Coach Stop.

Sharon blushed. She sensed she had interrupted more than a casual conversation. "I'm really sorry, but I think you'll want to hear this."

Doug smiled. "Don't worry about it. We were just chatting. What can I do for you?"

Sharon looked around. "Can we go somewhere more private? I don't want anyone else to hear this."

Doug looked at her curiously. "Sure. Come on, get in," he said, and motioned to the car door on her side, as he crawled behind the wheel.

Doug drove around the block and stopped the car next to a stone wall, under a clump of sugar maples. The cemetery where Nancy had been buried was behind them, surrounded by an ornate black iron fence and shaded by graceful oak and pine trees.

"I don't think anyone will bother us here," Doug said, clearing his throat and turning to face her. "So, what's on your mind?"

Sharon took a deep breath, not quite sure how to begin. "I was at the Sheriff's Office this morning for a press conference about Nancy Williams' death." She looked at him and hesitated, knowing she was about to drop a bombshell. "They've decided that it wasn't an accident. The autopsy revealed that Nancy was murdered."

Doug slumped back against the door. "Murdered?" he whispered, shaking his head. "That can't be." His eyes narrowed and he stared beyond her, out the window.

Sharon didn't say anything. She just sat there watching him. His handsome face was lined with worry. His penetrating blue eyes flickered back and forth beneath his black lashes, as if searching for an answer. After a few moments his gaze returned to her, as if he had just remembered that she was there.

"What did the autopsy show?" he asked quietly.

"There was evidence of strangulation, in addition to Nancy's head wound."

Doug squinted slightly and nodded, as if remembering something. "Nancy did have marks on her neck. But I can't believe that someone strangled her. *I was there.* It couldn't have been much more than five minutes from the time that I heard her scream to the time that I reached her. There was no one else there. I would have seen them."

Sharon didn't react. She just let him talk. Doug gripped the steering wheel, then pounded it with his fist, and his tone grew angry. "It just doesn't make any sense. Why would anyone want to kill Nancy? And how could they even know where she was going to be? You know there's no way to predict the exact route you'll take when you're foxhunting."

He rested his forehead in his hand and closed his eyes for a moment. Then he looked up at her again. "Do you think she could have surprised some deer hunters? That was on Helen Smith's land, and she's adamant about not allowing deer hunting on her property. Maybe Nancy rode up on some deer hunters and tried to tell them to leave. Half of those guys are drunk. If they were trespassing and got scared, there's no telling what they might do." He shook his head. "But I still think I would have seen them."

Sharon decided that it was time to tell him the rest. "Mr. Cummings, I think you should know that a deputy in the department named you as a suspect."

"Me?" Doug shouted. "Why in the world would anyone think I killed Nancy? I'm the one who tried to save her for Christ's sake." He shook his head, his lips set in an angry line. "Who was the deputy?"

"I don't know."

"I'll bet I know who it was," Doug said. "Did he say why I'm a suspect?"

Sharon shook her head. "I don't know. He didn't say it at the press conference. He said it later, to another reporter. Off the record. I just happened to hear about it."

"Who was the reporter?"

Sharon didn't answer. She wasn't sure she wanted to name Eric.

"Never mind," Doug said. "If you don't want to tell me who it was, I understand. I gather you've already gone out on a limb by telling me what you just did."

"Thanks for understanding," Sharon said quietly.

He straightened up in his seat and put the car in gear. "I know it took a lot of guts to tell me this, Sharon. You did the right thing. I won't forget it."

Sharon resisted an urge to hug him, or pat him on the arm. To offer some form of comfort. He was innocent. She was almost certain of it. And his life was about to be ripped apart.

Clyde decided to start his investigation by talking to Doug Cummings. He needed to have Cummings show him the murder scene. Even though he'd bet the rent that any useful evidence had already been removed.

When Clyde didn't find anyone home at the main house at Cummings' farm, he went on down the drive to the barn, where he found a young woman in the wash rack, clipping a horse.

"Is Mr. Cummings around?" Clyde asked, shouting to be heard above the buzz of the electric clippers.

"No, he's not," the woman replied, eyeing him skeptically.

"Any idea when he'll return?"

"Who knows? It's not my day to watch him," she said, shrugging.

Clyde instantly disliked her. Snotty bitch. She made a perfect match for Cummings. She had Cummings' same "fuck-you" attitude towards law enforcement. Well, she wasn't going to get rid of him that easily.

"Okay. Maybe you can answer some questions for me. I'm investigating the incident in the hunt field the other day," Clyde said, pulling out his notepad. "By the way, I'm Deputy Dickson. I assume you work for Mr. Cummings."

The girl nodded. "I'm Babs Tyler. And if you're here about Nancy Williams, I won't be much help. I wasn't there that day."

"That doesn't matter. Just tell me what Mr. Cummings told you about it, if anything," Clyde said, spitting into the vacant horse stall next to him.

Babs turned off the noisy clipper and stepped down off the stool she was standing on. "Doug didn't really tell me anything. Just that Nancy had an accident and that she was dead."

"Was he upset?" Clyde asked.

"Sure, what would you expect? He and Nancy were good friends." Babs shook her head. "I can't even imagine what I would do if I was trying to help someone and they died."

That got Clyde's attention. "Are you saying that she was still alive when he found her?"

Babs looked at him in surprise. "I guess so. I mean, that's what I assume happened. Doug said he tried to help her, but she died. Like I told you, he wouldn't really talk about it other than that. That's how I knew he was so upset." Babs sat down on a stack of hay bales that were lined up against the front of one stall. Clyde sensed that she was in no hurry to finish their conversation.

"What do you mean? Was it odd that he wouldn't talk to you about it?" Clyde asked, sitting down next to her.

"Actually, yes," Babs replied, fiddling with the clipper she still held in her hand. "Doug usually comes home from hunting and tells me stories about the hunt that day. He spends a lot of his time helping people out there, so I get to hear more about the mishaps than the hunting. You know, who fell off or who got lost, that kind of thing."

"So he usually comes home and talks about what happened that day, huh?" Clyde said.

Babs nodded. "Yeah. Sometimes he'll have a beer and chat with me while I put his horse away." She looked him over. "I guess you've probably never gone foxhunting, but it's quite an adrenaline rush out there. Sometimes it helps you wind down afterwards to relive the day." She snorted. "Although with most of the guys, the jumps get bigger and the chase gets faster every time they tell the story."

"But on that day, when Nancy Williams died, Mr. Cummings wouldn't talk to you about it. And that was unusual," Clyde repeated.

"Well, yes, at the time I thought it was strange. But, now that I think about it, who wants to talk about someone dying? I guess Doug just wanted to put that out of his mind." She looked quizzically at Clyde. "Doug's not in some kind of trouble, is he?"

Clyde smiled and didn't deny it. "I'm just trying to piece this whole thing together. Find out exactly what happened. Thanks for your time." He stood up and headed out of the barn, and then stopped. "Is there anyone else you can think of that I should talk to? Someone who would have been there that day and seen what was going on?"

"Well, the master, of course. That's Richard Evan Clarke. And probably the field secretary, Wendy Brooks. They always know who's there and what's happening," Babs replied.

Clyde wrote down their names. "All right. Thanks for your help. I may be back in touch."

"Do you want me to have Doug call you?" she asked.

Clyde thought it over. "No. I'll get in touch with him. In fact, I'd rather you not tell him I was here."

Babs frowned at him, then shrugged her shoulders and turned back towards the horse. "Sure. Whatever."

Doug glanced at the clock on the dashboard after he dropped Sharon off in front of the Coach Stop. Three-thirty. If he battled the traffic back into Washington, it would be almost five o'clock by the time he reached the office. It wasn't worth it. Anyway, he needed some quiet time to sort out what Sharon had just told him. It was all starting to make sense now. The way Carol Simpson had acted towards him after Nancy's funeral. And Kathy Morris and Wendy Brooks. And that damned deputy. They must have already known that the cause of Nancy's death was being questioned. That "foul play" was suspected.

Doug flipped open his cell phone and punched the speed dial button for his office.

"Hello. Mr. Cummings' office."

"Hi, Marsha. I got tied up out in Middleburg. Anything I need to know?"

"Oh, hi, Doug. Everything's pretty quiet here. Let me just check your messages. Oh, yes. Eric Schultz from *The Washington News* called again today. Twice. Remember, we canceled his appointment last week? He wants to do a story about your public service award."

"I thought we put him off indefinitely," Doug said.

"Well, I thought I had. I told him I'd call when you had an opening in your schedule. But he keeps persisting. I guess that's just the nature of the beast," Marsha replied.

"Put him off again."

"Okay. Other than that, I think things are under control here."

"Good. Then I'm going to stay out in Middleburg. There's no sense in battling traffic. Tell Mark and the gang that I'll give them a call in about half an hour. We'll work by phone. And, as of right now, I'm planning on going hunting tomorrow morning. If that changes, I'll let you know."

Doug flipped the cell phone shut and concentrated on negotiating the twisty turns on the narrow road. As he slowed to turn into his driveway, he saw a sheriff's car pulling away from his barn.

"What the hell's happened now?" he muttered, and stepped on the accelerator. As the sheriff's car drew near, he saw that it was Deputy Dickson behind the wheel. Doug slammed on the brakes and the Porsche fish-tailed to a stop on the gravel drive. He got out of his car and stood in the middle of the drive, hands on his hips, waiting for the deputy to do the same. But Dickson just sat in the sheriff's car, staring at him.

Doug walked over to Dickson's door, and motioned for the deputy to lower the window. Dickson slowly obliged.

"I don't know what you're doing here, Deputy, but I gather it has something to do with the disturbing news I just heard about Nancy Williams' death." He motioned for Dickson to get out of the car. "Why don't you get out of the car? I think we have some things to say to each other."

The deputy got out of the car with deliberate delay, and, after spitting onto the drive, he leaned against his car and folded his arms across his chest.

Doug chose his words carefully, keeping his temper in check. "I just heard about Nancy. That she didn't die from an accident. That they think she was murdered. I also heard through the grapevine that a certain deputy named me as a suspect in her murder." Doug stopped speaking and stared at the deputy. Dickson briefly met his gaze, then averted his eyes.

"That deputy wasn't you, was it, Dickson?"

Deputy Dickson didn't answer.

"Because if it was, you need to know that I don't tolerate dirty tactics like that."

Dickson cleared his throat. "Is that a threat, Mr. Cummings?"

"No. It's a fact. And it's also a fact that I didn't kill Nancy Williams. But apparently someone did." Doug drew a deep breath. "I want that person caught. So I'm willing to make a deal with you. You stop throwing my name around to the media as a suspect, and I'll help you as much as I can with your investigation." He paused. "Do you want my cooperation?"

Deputy Dickson smirked at him and spit out a glob of tobacco that landed next to Doug's foot. "Sure. I'd love your cooperation. That's what I was doing here. Looking for your cooperation."

Doug heard tires on the gravel and turned around to see his blacksmith, Kevin, driving towards them. He motioned the truck around them and waved as it passed, then turned back to Dickson. "So, where do you want to start?"

"The murder scene."

"Fine. Just be prepared. It's a long hike through the woods." Doug couldn't picture the hefty man riding a horse. "Unless you'd like to ride. That would be a lot easier."

"Naa. I haven't been on a horse since I used to ride bareback as a kid. I didn't have the benefit of riding lessons, and I've sure never ridden fancy horses like yours, Mr. Cummings."

Doug ignored the jab. "Okay. You walk, I'll ride. When do you want to go?"

"The sooner the better. How about tomorrow?"

"I'm hunting in the morning, but I could meet you after that," Doug replied. He narrowed his eyes at Dickson. "Have you talked to anyone else about me, besides the reporter?"

"I never said I talked to a reporter. But I did talk to your groom down there." Dickson pointed at the barn.

"Babs?" Doug thought she had more sense than that.

Dickson smiled. "Yeah. Interesting girl. Not very talkative at first, but then I couldn't shut her up."

Doug didn't bother to respond. He got into the Porsche and backed it up, then pulled up next to the sheriff's car and lowered the window. "Just to make sure you understand me, Dickson. If anything comes of the lies you leaked, if my name ends up in the media, you can rest assured that when this is all over, I *will* sue you." Dickson just scowled in response and Doug put the Porsche in gear and drove towards the barn.

When he walked into the barn, Doug saw Huntley in the crossties, with Babs standing next to him. Babs had put an aluminum twitch on Huntley's nose and was holding one of his ears. But despite her hold on him, Huntley still danced around and jerked his leg away from Kevin. Babs reached out and smacked the horse on the neck with the lead shank.

Doug frowned. "Hey, Babs, what's going on here?"

"Huntley's being a jerk today. If you want to take him hunting tomorrow, we need to get new shoes on him and Kevin doesn't have all day. I'm just trying to keep him quiet." Babs looked at Doug defiantly. "If you don't like the way I'm handling him, you can hold him."

Kevin made a strangled coughing sound and when Doug glanced at him he quickly looked away. Doug ignored her snide remark and kept his tone even as he replied.

"Babs, you know Huntley doesn't like to have his feet done. It doesn't do any good to get in a fight with him. All you need to do is use my good twitch, the one the Colonel gave me. You know those aluminum things are worthless."

Babs glared at him, one hand on her hip. "Like I don't know that? If I could find the Colonel's, I wouldn't be using this thing."

"What do you mean, *if* you could find it? You've lost it?" he demanded. Babs didn't answer, and Doug took a deep breath before continuing. "Babs, you know that twitch was a special gift to me from Colonel Wickens."

"Oh, come on, Doug. Stop making a federal case out of it. It'll turn up. The vet probably walked off with it when she was here worming last week. Just chill out. I'll find it," Babs said, turning away.

Doug stared at the back of her head and wondered what had set her off. It was Babs' nature to be gruff, but she'd been increasingly moody lately. Maybe she'd grown bored with her job and it was time for her to move on. He'd have a talk with her. But now was definitely not the time. He decided to leave before the confrontation escalated out of control and they both said something they would regret later.

"The hunt meet is at ten tomorrow at Stone Ridge. Please have Huntley ready for me to leave here at nine-fifteen." He rubbed Huntley on the head and nodded at Kevin as he walked out of the barn.

17

Zeb watched the barn girl sitting below him on a hay bale in the aisle. His stomach growled, and he thought about the packet of Hostess Twinkies he had in his jacket pocket. What the hell was she waiting for?

He heard the sound of a vehicle approaching on the gravel drive. Then the engine cut off, and a door slammed. Zeb listened to the footsteps in the aisle below and knew right away that it wasn't Cummings. The person was heavier and moved more slowly.

The barn girl rose from the hay bale as the person approached. "Thanks for taking your sweet time getting over here. Dr. Mitchell called over an hour ago to say you were on your way."

A tall, middle-aged man wearing riding pants and boots approached her. He was a large man, with thinning blond hair and a slight paunch. Looked kind of like the dude who played Frasier on TV.

The man scowled at her. "You're welcome, Babs."

"Sorry. Thanks for bringing it," she mumbled, reaching her hand out toward the man.

"Uh-uh. Not so fast," he said. He held what looked like a short branch in his right hand. It was about three inches in diameter and two feet long, with a loop of rope through one end.

As she reached for it, the man raised it above his head. "Let's do some bargaining first. What's it worth to you to get this back?"

The barn girl frowned at him. "Come on. I said thank you. Just give me Doug's twitch and leave so I can lock up here and go home."

The man ignored her. "How about body clipping Samson for me and braiding him for the Thanksgiving hunt?"

She stretched her arm for the branch, even though it was obvious she couldn't reach it. "I can't do that. I work exclusively for Doug. I don't free-lance on the side."

The man shrugged at her, still holding the branch out of her reach. "So make an exception."

"No." She jumped up towards the branch, trying to grab it from him. "Give it to me."

"Uh, uh, uh. Temper, temper." He laughed and waved the branch in the air, just above her grasp.

"Fine. Keep the damned twitch. I'm not wasting any more time on you. I'll tell Doug you have it and wouldn't give it back to me." She turned away from the man and stormed off down the aisle. "Now get out of here. I want to go home."

"Don't you turn your back on me, Babs."

The barn girl ignored him.

"I said, don't you turn your back on me." He started down the aisle after her.

"Fuck you," the barn girl said, turning to look back over her shoulder at him.

In one swift movement, the man leapt forward and swung the branch towards her, slamming it into her face just as she turned to look at him.

Zeb saw blood fly from her nose, and she sank briefly to one knee, then slumped to the floor. She sprawled on her back and lay there, groaning, with her hand covering her face.

"Don't ever talk to me that way, you bitch," the man said, standing over her.

The barn girl removed her hand from her face and glared at the man, then drew her right knee up to her chest, and kicked him in the balls.

The man dropped the branch and sank to his knees, both hands clutching his crotch.

"You fucking bitch," he hissed.

The barn girl scowled at him and put her hand to her nose, then drew it away and looked at her blood-covered fingers. "You've really gone off the deep end this time. And believe me, I'm going to make sure everyone in the Hunt knows about it."

The man snatched the branch off the floor, raised it high over his head, and waved it towards her in a threatening manner. "Don't you dare threaten me, Babs."

The barn girl snorted and grabbed at the branch. "I don't need to threat-en you. And don't fool yourself that you can intimidate me into keeping this quiet. Doug is going to go ballistic when he sees what you've done to me. Now give me the twitch and get out of here. You're such a pathetic loser."

The man jerked the branch back and then smashed it into her face again. The force of the blow pounded the barn girl's head into the brick aisle, and she moaned and then went silent. He raised the branch high and hit her again. And then again. His face was bright red and he narrowed his eyes as he swung at her.

"Don't you ever talk like that to me."

He lifted the branch high once more, and again, smashed it forcefully into her face. Her skull thudded hollowly against the bricks, but she didn't move a muscle.

"Don't ever talk that way to me ever again."

The man stared down at her, breathing heavily. The barn girl's face was an unrecognizable bloody mess and the man was splattered with blood. "Don't you ever talk that way to me again, you fucking bitch," he repeated hoarsely. Then the man rose and stumbled out of the barn.

Zeb sat silently, waiting to see if the man would come back. Five minutes passed. Then ten. The barn girl never moved. And then he heard the sound of footsteps in the barn aisle.

Zeb tensed in anticipation. Was it Cummings? Or had the man returned? He craned his neck to see farther down the aisle and waited impatiently. God, he hoped it was Cummings.

But then he caught sight of the top of a balding head and sank back in disappointment. It was the Frasier dude.

He watched the man kneel down next to the girl and put two fingers on her neck, as if looking for a pulse. After a few seconds he moved his fingers slightly. Waited. Then moved them again. Finally, the man removed his fin-gers, then stood, took a horse blanket off the front of a stall, and lay it down in the aisle next to the barn girl. Then he rolled her body over onto the blan-ket, so that she lay face down. The man wrapped the blanket around her, then picked up the bundle and carried it out of the barn.

He returned a few moments later, uncoiled the hose from the rack in the wash stall and began to spray down the aisle. From where Zeb sat in the hayloft above, the barn girl's blood blended with the red brick flooring, but pinkish bubbles formed in the stream of water from the man's hose. The man directed the stream of water towards the drain in the wash stall and kept spraying until the bubbles turned white.

Next, the man grabbed a towel from the shelf in the wash rack, wet it and wiped his hands and face with it, then used it to rub down the wooden wall in the aisle near where he had beaten the barn girl. He rinsed the towel out once, and then went back to cleaning the wall. Finally, he wadded the towel up, put it under his arm, and coiled the hose back on the rack.

The man turned the light off in the wash rack and stood for a long moment, looking around the barn. Then he walked to the tack room and went inside. When he came back out he was carrying a saddle and some other things in his arms. He paused to turn off the tack room light and close the door, and then Zeb heard his footsteps recede up the aisle. The lights went out and Zeb listened in the darkness to the sound of the doors at the end of the aisle slide shut.

Zeb remained still until he could no longer hear the crunching sound of tires on the gravel, and then he exhaled slowly. He reached into his pocket, took out the package of Twinkies, and tore into the cellophane wrap. As he stuffed one Twinkie into his mouth, he thought about how clumsy and undisciplined the killing of the barn girl had been. The man had no skill. No technique. No preparation. He'd beaten the barn girl as an impulse. Simply because he was mad at her.

Zeb popped the second Twinkie into his mouth and made himself a nest in the loose hay that covered the hayloft floor. He wanted to be around when Doug Cummings found out that the barn girl was gone. He wondered how long it would take the son of a bitch to figure out she was dead. And, when he did, would he even care?

Zeb was awakened some time later by the sound of quiet footsteps in the barn aisle just below him. He tensed, waiting to see if the person would approach the ladder that led to the hayloft. But the footsteps continued past the ladder, down the aisle, to the back side of the barn.

Zeb crept silently to the end of the hayloft and peered through the opening left by the partially closed hayloft door. It was dark out, but he could see enough to know that the barn girl's killer was back. The killer approached the horse trailer, opened the front hatch door, and tossed something inside. Then he closed the door firmly and walked back towards the barn. The killer moved cautiously, quietly, switching his head this way and that, looking all around him.

Zeb remained by the hayloft door at the back of the barn until he heard the barn doors at the front of the aisle slide quietly closed, and then he moved swiftly to the front hayloft door. He arrived just in time to see the killer get into the barn girl's car. The sound of the engine cut through the quiet and the car pulled slowly away from the barn and up the drive, with the headlights turned off.

Zeb looked around the drive and parking area, but there were no other vehicles in sight. The killer must have come on foot, so he could drive away in the barn girl's car. That explained why he hadn't heard him arrive. But that didn't excuse the fact that he had allowed the killer to get so close while he had slept. He'd been sloppy. But he wouldn't let it happen again.

Zeb looked at the sky. It must be two, three o'clock. Logic told him that no one would arrive at the barn before daybreak, but he still wouldn't risk drifting off to sleep again. He moved back to the center of the hayloft and settled down at his post next to the opening in the hayloft floor.

CHAPTER

18

Doug spent the night at the farm and rose Friday morning at six-thirty, prepared some toast and fruit for breakfast, and sat down at the kitchen table with *The Washington News* spread out in front of him. He scanned the "A" section first, then "Sports," then "Business." Doug finished eating and pushed away his plate, then picked up his coffee cup, leaned back in his chair, and turned to the "Local" section.

He paused with his cup halfway to his mouth when he saw the photograph on the front page. It was a color picture of Nancy and him, on horse-back, standing side-by-side at a hunt meet. The leaves were in full color, and the picture must have been shot during cubhunting because they were wearing their tweeds. Each held a stirrup-cup and they were both smiling at the camera. The caption beneath the photograph read, *"Murder victim Nancy Williams and ex-boyfriend Doug Cummings, riding to hounds during happier times."* The bold headline was off to the right. *"Murder in Middleburg, Foxhunting Death Not An Accident."* Doug put down his coffee cup and read the article.

"The posh hunt-country community of Middleburg, Virginia was shocked to learn yesterday that the official cause of death of local resident Nancy Williams was classified as murder. Ms. Williams' death was previously believed to be the result of a riding accident." Doug skimmed the article until he got to the third paragraph. *"Sheriff Fred Boling declined to name any suspects at this time, saying only that they have reason to believe that the murderer was someone Williams knew. Boling said that the key to their investigation is Doug Cummings, a Middleburg resident and partner in the Washington law firm of White, Baker and Cummings. Cummings, who recently*

broke off a personal relationship with Ms. Williams, says he was horseback riding in the woods when he stumbled upon Ms. Williams' body. Authorities say Cummings reportedly moved Williams to another location and then sought help. Sheriff Boling labeled Cummings a witness, but sources close to the investigation say that they will be looking to Doug Cummings for answers to several troubling questions. Cummings was contacted by The Washington News, but declined the request for an interview."

Doug looked at the by-line. Eric Schultz. Damn. That's why the reporter had called yesterday. The phone rang and Doug walked over and picked up the cordless phone on the counter.

"Hello."

"Doug. It's Marsha. I'm sorry to call you so early, but have you seen *The Washington News* this morning?"

He sat back down at the table. "Yes. I just finished reading it."

"Oh, Doug, I'm so sorry. It makes you look like you have something to hide, and it's my fault. I just assumed that Eric Schultz was calling yesterday about the interview for the "People" section, and I never even spoke with him. I just left him a message on his voice mail that you were not interested in an interview at this time. And I'm afraid I was kind of rude. I really tried to discourage him from calling back." Her voice was shaky and she sounded congested, as if she might have been crying.

"Look, Marsha, you just did what I asked you to do. You had no way of knowing that Schultz was calling about an interview for a different story, but I should have. I knew that a reporter might be writing a story naming me as a suspect in Nancy's murder. I just didn't make the connection that it might be Schultz. But it's water under the bridge now. Besides, I don't know that it would have made a difference in the article, even if I had spoken with Schultz yesterday."

"So, what are you going to do?"

Doug sighed. "I'm not sure there's anything I can do. I just hate that the firm's name got dragged into this. I'll get together with Robert Dewitt about it as soon as I get in."

"I'm sure you are going to be flooded with phone calls," Marsha said. "What time should I expect you?"

Doug knew that it wouldn't look right if he didn't show up at the hunt that morning. Besides, he had to meet Dickson later to show him the murder scene. He decided that he should stick with his plans to go foxhunting, and then go to the office later.

"I'll be in after lunch," he said. "And when people call, make sure you tell them I'm out foxhunting. I don't want anyone to think I'm avoiding them."

Doug went upstairs to dress. He would shower and shave before hunting so he could get to the office more quickly afterwards. As he rubbed on some after-shave, Doug couldn't help recalling Lady Hawthorne's sharp words to him, almost twenty years earlier. He had been foxhunting in Ireland and had greeted the master, Lady Hawthorne, at the hunt meet with a tip of his hat and a kiss on her hand. She was a crusty old woman and a stickler for tradition, and although she'd been charming at dinner the prior evening, she lashed out at Doug that morning.

"You Americans!" she had chewed him out. "Don't any of you have any bloody sense? How do you think my hounds are ever going to find a scent with that damned perfume you're wearing? We might as well all go home right now, it's going to be a frightful day."

Doug smiled at the recollection, in spite of his mood, and looked out the bedroom window towards the barn. Usually Babs would have pulled the trailer around in front of the barn by now, ready for him to load his horse. But the drive stood empty. Doug frowned. It wasn't like Babs to be running late. He finished tying his stock tie and hurried down to the barn.

As soon as Doug rounded the corner of the drive and approached the barn, he knew something was wrong. Babs' car wasn't there, and the stable doors were drawn tightly closed. Doug slid the barn doors open and turned on the stall lights. Chancellor's deep whinny greeted him from down the aisle, and Huntley banged his hoof against the stall door. Doug peered into Huntley's stall. Not a speck of hay. The horses obviously had not been fed.

"Damn you, Babs. I didn't need this today," he muttered. He glanced at his watch. If he hurried, he might still be able to make the hunt meet.

He tossed each horse a flake of hay from the bale that Babs had set out in the aisle, and fed grain to all the horses except Huntley. Huntley would have to wait for breakfast until after foxhunting.

Doug retrieved the tack room key from the hook on top of the door frame, but the door handle turned easily in his hand even before he inserted the key. He shook his head in exasperation. Babs had left the door unlocked. Again.

Doug flung the door open and flipped the light switch. His saddle and hunting bridle were on the saddle rack, with a clean saddle pad folded neatly on top. At least Babs had managed to clean his tack.

Doug hastily saddled Huntley and led the horse out to where the Range Rover and trailer were parked, behind the barn. He opened the ramp, tossed the lead shank over Huntley's neck and clucked to him to go on the trailer. The horse started up the ramp, then snorted loudly and backed up.

"Come on, Huntley. Get on in there." Doug smacked him on the rump and clucked again, but Huntley just turned sideways on the ramp and planted his feet firmly.

Doug checked the hay net in the trailer and found it full of alfalfa hay. He grabbed a handful and tried to lure Huntley inside, but Huntley just stretched out his neck for the hay, and kept his feet where they were on the ramp.

"What's the matter with you today, Huntley?" Doug asked. "Are you being stubborn because you missed your breakfast?"

He got a bucket of grain, shook it in front of the horse's nose, let him have a mouthful, and placed the bucket in the trailer. Then he put the lead shank over Huntley's nose, jerked it a few times, and walked up the ramp, clucking in encouragement. Huntley started to follow Doug, then stopped abruptly and flew backwards, pulling the lead shank out of Doug's hand.

"Damn it." Doug kicked at a clump of loose hay on the ground and grabbed Huntley's lead shank. He had more important things to do than spend all morning trying to load his horse on the trailer. Doug put Huntley back in his stall, fed him, and, after making sure all the horses had water, put his tack away in the tack room. As he reached for the switch to turn off the lights on his way out, the empty saddle rack where Babs usually kept her saddle caught his eye. Doug looked down and saw that Babs' grooming box was gone as well.

Had she walked out on him? He had a hard time believing that she would do such a thing, but her absence was looking more and more suspicious. Doug locked the tack room and as he turned to head out of the barn, he noticed the empty blanket rack on the front of Chancellor's stall. That was where Babs had displayed the wool cooler Chancellor had won for Best Turned Out at the Virginia Field Hunter Championships. Doug had presented the cooler to Babs as a gift, and she was more proud of it than any of the ribbons or trophies in the tack room. But the blanket was no longer there. She must have taken it with her.

Doug groaned. That confirmed it. Babs wasn't just late for work. She had taken her belongings and quit. He turned out the barn lights and headed back up to the house, dreading the thought of having to find a replacement for Babs, on top of everything else he was dealing with.

Nellie was in the kitchen cooking when he walked in. "Oh, Doug, I'm so glad you came back. I was worried about you, going off foxhunting in this cold without a proper breakfast. I was so mad at myself. I overslept this morning. I was hoping to get up before you and have breakfast all fixed, but by the time I woke up you were already gone. Oh well, never mind that now; come and sit down. I've made you your favorite blueberry pancakes. I thought I was going to have to eat them all by myself. This should warm you up and help put some meat back on your bones. You are getting way too thin, Doug. I worry about you."

Doug sat down at the table. He didn't argue with her, but he had to suppress a smile when Nellie put a heaping plate of blueberry pancakes in front of him. He hadn't liked blueberry pancakes since he was a child, but Nellie loved to cook them for him.

Nellie poured Doug a steaming cup of coffee and some fresh-squeezed orange juice and sat down at the table with him. "Doug, honey, you can tell me it's none of my business if you want to, but I read the newspaper this morning and I'm frightened for you. It made it sound like you're in some kind of trouble." She patted his hand and held it in her soft grasp. "Even though I'm just an old woman and can't do much, I can set those people straight. I'll tell them that you could never do anything like murdering some-body." Nellie shook her head, pursing her lips. "Why, that's just crazy to even think about. I helped raise you from a baby, and I dare say I know you better than anyone else on the face of this earth, now that your dear mother and father are departed, and I will just tell them that they must be crazy to even be thinking such a thing." Nellie's voice broke and she dabbed at her eyes with her apron.

"Nellie, it's all right," Doug said, putting his arms around her and hugging her gently. "It's not as bad as you think. No one really thinks that I murdered Nancy. Some deputy just thought he could get away with throwing my name out, to take attention away from the fact that he doesn't have any real leads on Nancy's murderer. Unfortunately, the *News* ran it. The worst thing that's going to happen to me is that people will be talking about me for a while. But that will all die down soon enough."

As he held Nellie, Doug was aware of how frail she had become. He clasped both of her worn hands in his. "I actually have a problem much more serious than what you read about in the newspaper," he said. Nellie frowned at him, and he quickly continued. "It seems that Babs has quit, leaving me with a barn full of horses and no one to take care of them. If I didn't have to deal with the ramifications of this *News* article and prepare for the Tycoon Technologies hearing, I would just take a few days off and do the barn myself, until I hired someone. Right now, though, I can't afford to do that." Doug looked at Nellie. "I really don't know what to do."

Nellie's frown relaxed. "Now, Doug, you just stop worrying about that right now. I've seen more grooms come and go from that barn than you can shake a stick at, and it always works out for the best. First thing, I'm going to call John and have him come over and take care of the barn right now. He's done it before in a pinch and he'll do just fine. Then I'll set about finding you a replacement for Babs. Don't you even think any more about it. Those horses will be taken care of, if I have to go down there and do it myself." Nellie stood up and headed for the phone.

Doug smiled at her. "Nellie, I don't want you down in the barn, but if you wouldn't mind overseeing everything, it would be a great help." He left while Nellie was on the phone and went to his study. He had over an hour until he had to go meet Dickson. Doug picked up the phone to call Robert Dewitt.

Clyde drove through the pasture gate into the field where the hunt meet was being held, and hesitated, not quite sure where to go. He looked around the pasture, astonished by the chaotic atmosphere. There seemed to be no rhyme or reason to how the horse trailers and vehicles were parked in the big field.

Clyde shook his head as he watched the people riding around on their horses, chatting with each other, laughing, eating and drinking what was offered to them on silver trays. The idle rich. With nothing better to do on a Friday morning than to ride around on their horses, chasing some poor pitiful fox.

He had come to the meet hoping to talk to the master, Richard Evan Clarke, and the field secretary, Wendy Brooks, as Babs Tyler had suggested. But now he wasn't sure where to find them. He searched the group, looking for a familiar face. Doug Cummings had said he would be there, but Clyde didn't see him. He drove slowly through the pasture until he finally saw a man in a red coat getting on his horse. Clyde parked next to him and got out of his car.

"Excuse me, are you Mr. Clarke?" Clyde asked.

The man looked at Clyde in surprise and, not even bothering to speak, pointed towards a big white horse van parked a few trailers away. Clyde's cheeks burned as he walked off towards the van. They were all alike, these horse people. They seemed to have some unwritten code about who and what was important, and he obviously wasn't on their list.

Clyde saw a tall, white-haired man in a red coat getting up on his horse. "Mr. Clarke, I have some questions I need to ask you," Clyde said.

The man looked down at Clyde from his horse. "Why, Deputy, I don't believe we've met. I am Richard Evan Clarke and you are . . . ?"

"I'm Deputy Clyde Dickson," he said, awkwardly shaking the master's hand.

"There, now, that's better. I always feel much more comfortable talking with people I know. What is it I can do for you, Mr. Dickson?" Richard Evan Clarke asked, ignoring Clyde's title.

"I need to ask you a few questions about the day Nancy Williams died."

"No, Mr. Dickson. I think this is hardly an appropriate time or place for that." The master's horse swung his hind end in Clyde's direction and Clyde jumped backwards and glared at the master. He had the impression that Clarke could have controlled his horse if he wanted to, but he just smiled at Clyde and let the animal dance around.

"Of course, I'm eager to cooperate with any investigation of Ms. Williams' death," Richard Evan Clarke said. "If you think I can be helpful in any way, just call my secretary and set up an appointment. I'd be happy to talk with you at a more suitable time. And by the way, Mr. Dickson, my friend Doug Cummings told me about your little talk yesterday, and I can assure you, you're barking up the wrong tree with that one." Before Clyde could respond, the master tipped his hat and rode off.

Clyde watched as the other riders gathered behind the master and trotted off towards the woods. He shook his head, still shocked by the treatment he'd just received. He turned to head back to his car when he saw a woman, not dressed in riding clothes, getting into a Jeep Cherokee. What the hell, Clyde thought, I'm already here, I might as well ask her if she was around the day Nancy Williams was murdered.

He walked over to her. "Excuse me, do you usually come to these hunts?"

She looked at him and smiled. Finally, a friendly face. "Why, yes, I do," she replied. "I'm Wendy Brooks, the field secretary of the Hunt. I'm not hunting today because I had a little accident and am grounded for a few weeks." She pointed down and Clyde saw that she had a cast on her foot.

"Wendy Brooks. I was looking for you. Can you spare a few minutes?"

"Why, sure, I guess so," she replied.

"It's about Nancy Williams," Clyde said. "I don't know if you've heard this already, but the autopsy showed that Ms. Williams' death was no accident."

"Yes, I know."

"Were you there the day she died?"

Wendy nodded. "Yes, I was."

"Tell me what you remember about that day. Anything at all."

"Well, I remember that the weather was bad. It was very cold. And rainy."

"Did you see Nancy that day?" Clyde asked.

"Yes. Of course. We hunted together all morning until she decided to hack in early."

"Why'd she do that?" Clyde asked.

Wendy glanced around the pasture, and then back at Clyde. "She wanted to ride back with Doug Cummings," she said quietly.

Clyde smiled. Bingo.

"They rode back together?" Clyde asked. He couldn't believe Cummings had lied about something so easy to verify.

"Yes. Doug said good-bye first, and then when Nancy found out that he was going in, she followed right after him."

"Did you actually see them together?" Clyde asked.

Wendy pursed her lips and stared off across the pasture, as if trying to remember. "Yes," she finally said, nodding. "Yes, I did. Just as Doug was going into the woods, I called out to him and I saw him stop and wait for Nancy to catch up. Then I went on and joined the rest of the field."

"Ms. Brooks, would you be willing to come down to the Sheriff's Office and give me an official statement, repeating what you've just told me?" Clyde asked.

"Well, sure, if you want me to. I'd like to help in any way I can. Nancy was a dear friend of mine."

Clyde nodded. There was a brief silence and then Clyde asked, "Ms. Brooks, do you think that Doug Cummings might have murdered Nancy Williams?"

Wendy hesitated. "Deputy Dickson, you must understand that Doug Cummings has a lot of friends around here, and he has been very good to this Hunt. I wouldn't want to be quoted as saying anything bad about him."

Clyde nodded, hardly daring to breathe.

"It's just that on that day, when Nancy was killed, Doug was acting kind of strange. Just like, well, in a bad mood or something. Usually he's real friendly and very helpful to everyone, but on that day he was different. I think it was the first time I ever saw Doug leave early without asking if anyone wanted to go back with him. I remember thinking that was peculiar." Wendy sighed and looked at Clyde. "Like I said before, Nancy and I were close friends and she used to confide in me. I know that she was still in love with Doug and was trying to get their relationship going again. Nancy told me that she had tried to talk with Doug about it during the hunt that day, but he put her off. That's why she followed him, so they could talk." Tears filled her eyes and she shook her head. "I've felt so guilty, but these thoughts have been running through my mind ever since I read the *News* this morning. I know that Nancy was with Doug that day. And as much as it pains me to say it, I think he must have killed her. There's just no other explanation."

Clyde reached out and put his hand on her shoulder. "I know how hard this must be for you, Ms. Brooks, but you have been very helpful with all that you've told me. I really appreciate it. Rather than drag this out and make you relive this all again another day, why don't I go to my office with you right now and get your statement, so you can have it over and done with. I'll even drive you, and then bring you right back here."

Wendy protested lightly, but then agreed, and got into the sheriff's car with him.

"I thought I'd see Doug Cummings out here today," Clyde commented, as he started the car,

"Well, actually, so did I," Wendy replied. "Doug was supposed to lead the hilltopper group this morning, but he never showed up. Richard had to find someone else to take it over."

Dickson smiled. He assumed that *The Washington News* article was responsible for Cummings' absence that morning.

C H A P T E R

20

Clyde managed to record Wendy Brooks' statement, drop her back off at her car, and arrive at the meeting with Doug Cummings, just on time. They had agreed to rendezvous in the field at Chadwick Hall, where the hunt meet had been held on the day that Nancy Williams died. When Clyde drove into the pasture, he saw that Cummings was already there. He was immaculately dressed in gray wool suit pants, navy barn coat, light blue shirt with a yellow tie, and black paddock boots. A slick city lawyer, dressed for a day in the country.

Clyde felt a surge of resentment as he looked at Cummings leaning against his shiny black Range Rover. It was the fancy model. A 4.6 HSE. Clyde sat in a vehicle like it at the auto show they'd recently held at the Convention Center, and he knew that the price tag exceeded his own annual salary. Even the color of the vehicle screamed money. He tried to remember the fancy name they'd given it. Oh, yeah. *Java Black*. It figured that Cummings would drive a vehicle like that.

"I hope those shoes are made for walking, Deputy," Cummings said, as Dickson got out of his car. "I'm sure your schedule is as busy as mine, so let's get going." Cummings headed towards the woods.

"I thought you were going to be riding," Clyde said.

"I changed my mind," Cummings replied, keeping his eyes fixed on the trail ahead of him.

Clyde followed along in silence for a few moments. "I went out to the hunt meet today to talk to a few folks. I thought I'd see you there."

Cummings shot him a look and it seemed to Clyde as if he picked up the pace. "I changed my mind about that too."

They hiked in silence for a few more moments, and then Clyde spoke up again. "You read *The Washington News* this morning?"

Cummings turned to face Clyde and stopped so suddenly that Clyde almost bumped into him. Cummings' hands were on his hips and he looked pissed. "Look, Deputy, I'm only here today because I'm interested in finding Nancy's killer. And because I gave you my word that I would help you. But I don't want to be your friend, and I sure don't want to make small talk. As for the article in the *News*, you can rest assured that I'll deal with that in due course."

Cummings towered over him, too close for comfort, and although he hated himself for doing it, Clyde backed up a step. Cummings continued to stare him down for a few moments, then turned back up the trail.

Clyde choked back a response. He was afraid that if he pissed Cummings off any more, he wouldn't show him the murder scene. But he fumed as he followed along, staring at Cummings' backside. I'm going to nail you, you arrogant S.O.B. You can't intimidate me into backing off.

They hiked for a good thirty minutes and by the time they stopped, Clyde was gasping for air. I sure as shit hope he knows where he's going, Clyde thought. His sides were starting to cramp from the fast pace, but he was damned if he was going to give Cummings the satisfaction of asking him to slow down.

"This is it. I found her right about here," Cummings said, and motioned to an area in the center of a clearing that was about twenty feet wide.

Clyde carefully walked around the clearing, then knelt down and examined the ground where Cummings claimed Williams had lain. He could see remnants of hoof prints and what looked like a few foot prints, but any evidence of a struggle or whatever else might have been there appeared to have been covered up by the newly fallen leaves or washed away by the rain. Clyde half-heartedly groped through the blanket of leaves, not really expecting to find anything, and grunted in surprise when his hand brushed against something soft and spongy.

He carefully brushed the leaves away, and his pulse quickened when he saw a crumpled pair of golden-brown leather gloves. Although the gloves were twisted and the fingers balled-up, Clyde estimated them to be rather large. Most likely those of a man rather than a woman.

Clyde heard the rustling of leaves as Cummings approached. "Those are my riding gloves," he said, kneeling down next to Clyde.

"Fancy that," Clyde replied. "Want to tell me what they're doing here?"

Cummings frowned. "I remember taking them off when I was trying to help Nancy. I couldn't feel her pulse with them on. I guess I left them here."

"Well, you won't be wearing them again any time soon. They're evidence now," Clyde said. He pulled a plastic evidence bag from his jacket pocket and, using a twig that lay nearby, carefully scooped the gloves into the bag and sealed it.

Clyde continued searching through the leaves, but to no avail, and finally stood up and brushed the dirt off his knees. He circled the perimeter of the clearing, stopping to search beneath trees and brush that might conceal anything.

"Which way did she come from, when she rode into the clearing?" Clyde asked.

Cummings scowled at him. "I don't know. I wasn't here. But if she took the same trail I did when she left the hunt, she would have come from there." He pointed towards a narrow trail that fed into the clearing on the opposite side from where they had entered.

Clyde walked over and examined the area. The approaching trail curved sharply just before it intersected with the clearing, making it impossible for someone coming from that direction to see into the clearing before they entered it. A perfect secluded spot for an assault.

Clyde popped some tobacco into his mouth and tried to reconstruct the scenario. "Are there other clearings like this along these trails?"

Cummings shrugged. "Sure."

"Why would Ms. Williams stop in this clearing then, instead of one of those?"

"Who knows? I guess that depends on why she stopped or whether she had a choice. We'll probably never know that," Cummings said.

Clyde snorted and smiled at Cummings. "Oh, yes, we will. As long as I'm handling this investigation, we'll find out."

Clyde's mind raced as he stared down the empty trail, trying to envision how it might have happened. The trail was pretty narrow for them to have ridden side-by-side. Chances were, Cummings was probably in front, with Williams following him. If he was already mad, if he was looking for a way to silence her, he could easily have entered the clearing ahead of her and then turned around and been waiting for her when she entered. He could have surprised her and grabbed her off her horse, no problem. Or, maybe, he didn't plan it.

Perhaps they rode into the clearing together. The clearing was a good place to stop and talk. Maybe they stopped to talk and she got him angry. Either way, Cummings' temper probably just got the better of him and he lost it. Maybe he knocked her around first and that's how she hit her head. Maybe he strangled her after he saw how bad it was, to cover up what he had done. As he thought about her head injury, Clyde recalled his discussion with Carol Simpson about Williams' riding helmet.

"Did Ms. Williams wear a helmet when she rode?" he asked Cummings.

"Sure."

"Was she wearing it when you found her?" Clyde asked.

Cummings hesitated for a moment. "No, she wasn't."

"That surprise you?"

Cummings shook his head. "No. I don't recall that it even registered at the time. Nancy's hard hat didn't have a chin strap. It could have come off easily in a fall."

"Then it should still be around here someplace," Clyde said.

"Yes."

Clyde resumed his search among the trees at the edge of the clearing, and Cummings did the same. A few minutes later, Clyde heard Cummings call him.

"Deputy. Over here. I think I found it."

Clyde walked over towards where Cummings' voice came from and saw him crouched down behind the trunk of an enormous oak tree.

"There it is," Cummings said, pointing at a black velvet riding helmet that lay upside down in a pile of leaves.

"Any way of proving it's hers?" Clyde asked.

Doug nodded. "Look inside. Nancy was always losing things at the barn where she boarded, and she told me she was going to put her name on everything."

Clyde reached out with his pen and turned the hat over. Nancy's name was printed boldly in marker on the label inside.

"Too bad it's been out in the weather so long. I doubt you'll get any evidence off of it," Cummings said.

"Oh, I wouldn't bet on that," Clyde replied, smiling at him. "It's incredible what forensics can do these days." He put the hat in an evidence bag, then stood up and looked back at the clearing. "How do you think it ended up behind this tree?"

Cummings just shrugged and shook his head.

"Looks to me like someone threw it here to get it out of the way," Clyde said. "I'm surprised you found it so quickly. Almost like you knew where to go."

Clyde could see Cummings' cheek muscles tighten as he clenched his jaw. "Okay, Dickson, that's enough. I don't want to be accused of cutting short your investigation, but I won't stand here and listen to your foolish accusations any more. Finish up, so we can head back. Unless, of course, you think you can find your way back alone. If you do, I'll leave now."

Clyde realized that he'd crossed the line and he backed off. "I've about finished for now," he replied. "But I'm going to seal off this area and come back and look more thoroughly later." Clyde cordoned off the area with yellow police tape, wondering all the while whether he would ever be able to find the place again. He doubted whether Cummings would willingly lead him back there a second time.

CHAPTER

21

When they arrived back at the cars, Doug climbed into the Range Rover and sped off, ignoring the bucking of the vehicle as it bounced over the rough terrain. As he drove, he reached into his breast pocket, took out his cell phone, and tossed it on the seat next to him. He'd call Marsha when he was on the road.

He noticed a hunt whip lying there when he put the phone down, but at first it didn't register with him. He kept on driving for a moment, then looked back at the seat again and slammed on the brakes.

Doug slowly reached over and picked the hunt whip up, holding it so he could read the initials engraved on the silver band at the base of the horn handle. He traced the initials slowly with his fingers, then leaned his head back against the seat. "B.W." Buck Williams. It had belonged to Nancy's father, and Nancy had carried it with her in the hunt field. He hadn't thought about it until now, but he was certain Nancy must have had it with her the day she died. What was it doing in his car?

He saw Clyde Dickson drive up next to him, and started to open his window and flag the deputy down, but then thought better of it. He couldn't explain how the whip had gotten into his car, and he knew Dickson would figure out a way to turn it against him.

The deputy stopped his car next to Doug's, but Doug just waved at him and motioned for him to go on.

As Doug watched the receding taillights of the sheriff's car, his mind raced with possibilities. He was certain that Nancy's whip hadn't been in his car when he'd driven to Chadwick Hall that morning, so someone had to have put it there while he was in the woods with Dickson.

Doug's thoughts were interrupted by the ringing of his cell phone.

"Hello."

"Hi, Doug. It's Marsha. Are you on your way in?"

"Yes."

"Good. Because Robert Dewitt and the members of the executive committee would like to meet with you as soon as you arrive."

"Oh, Christ."

"No, Doug. I think it's okay. Steffie told me they want to give you a vote of confidence."

Steffie was Dewitt's secretary. He hoped she knew what she was talking about. Doug looked at his watch. It was almost noon.

"Tell them I can meet with them at one o'clock."

Doug flipped the phone shut and looked again at the hunt whip. What the hell should he do with it? The obvious answer was to give it to Mrs. Williams. He put the whip on the floor under the passenger seat and headed towards his office.

22

Steffie had been right. The executive committee did give him a vote of confidence. They were gathered in the main conference room and Robert Dewitt led the meeting.

"Doug, we just want you to know that we're behind you one hundred percent. I'm sure that you'll want to deal with *The Washington News* in due course, and our litigation department is at your disposal. In the meantime, we will present a united front and trust that this will all blow over soon."

Doug breathed a sigh of relief. "Thanks, Robert." He nodded at the others. "Your support means a great deal to me. I don't take it for granted."

Doug worked with the Tycoon Technologies team all afternoon, but left the office around five-thirty to head back to the country. He had accepted an invitation to a dinner party at Sallie Rogers' home in Middleburg that evening, and he felt that it wouldn't look right if he backed out. Especially after missing the hunt that morning.

When Doug got back to the farm, he decided to make a quick stop at the barn to see how the horses were. John Montgomery, his farm manager, was there and had everything under control, just as Nellie had said he would.

"Hi, John. Thanks for pitching in and helping out here. I know you'd rather be out there on the mower. I really appreciate you helping out with the horses," Doug said, shaking his hand.

"Sure thing, Mr. Cummings. I was happy to help out. I'll do it for as long as you need me to, you know I will, but I had an idea about that, if you don't mind my saying something."

"No, of course not, John. What do you have in mind?"

John took off his work hat and crumpled it in his hands as he spoke.

"Well, I don't know if you remember my oldest boy, Billy. He's finished up with school and he's looking for work. I was thinking maybe since you was needing someone to help out in the barn, well, maybe you might consider Billy." He looked at Doug, almost as if expecting him to be angry, and then continued. "That boy, he has good horse experience. He used to work at the track galloping every morning. I think he'd do a right fine job for you."

John paused again and took a deep breath. "There is one thing that you need to know though. A while back, last summer, Billy started hanging with the wrong crowd. One day they was all riding around together and they got busted. Billy didn't have no drugs on him, but he was in the car with the rest of them so he got charged too. They let him off with a fine and probation, but now he's got a criminal record and he's having a hard time finding a job. He wants to work real bad, Mr. Cummings, and I know he'd do a fine job for you, I'd make sure of that. But if you don't want him around here, I understand that, I really do. I just thought I'd ask."

"John, if you say Billy is a good worker, I'm sure he is and I'm more than happy to give him a chance," Doug said. "I'd like to talk to him first, though."

"Why, yes sir, Mr. Cummings, he's right over there in my car. I thought that in case you might consider hiring him, I should bring him along." He turned around and motioned to Billy to come over.

Doug smiled at the boy and shook his hand. "Good to see you, Billy. Your father says you might be interested in working for me here in the barn."

"Yes, sir, I would. I'd work real hard for you too." Billy's voice shook.

"Good. Then let's give it a try. I've got to run now, but I'll get together with you this weekend and we can go over the details. It's really pretty simple. Huntley and Chancellor are the only horses that require full care. The babies and broodmares just need to be fed and looked after." Doug smiled at the boy. "I'm glad you're here, Billy. If you're half as good a worker as your father, I've made the right decision."

As Doug was about to leave, he remembered the horse trailer. When he had gone to meet Clyde Dickson, he had just unhitched the Range Rover and left the trailer as it was. "Billy, I left the trailer open behind the barn, could you please close it up?"

"I already done did that, Mr. Cummings," John replied. "Funny thing though, I found this dirty towel in the front of the trailer. It smelled real funny, kind of like that deer scent the hunters use to attract the bucks. I don't know, maybe someone was hunting and wiped their hands on it or something, but I didn't think it should be in the trailer so I threw it away."

That's odd, Doug thought. He hadn't noticed a towel in the trailer that morning, but then, he had been pretty distracted. He wondered if the odor from that could have been responsible for Huntley's bizarre behavior. Doug shrugged. "That's fine, John. I don't know why that would have been there." Right now, a dirty rag in his trailer was the least of his worries. He left John and Billy and headed up to the house to get ready for Sallie Rogers' dinner party.

Henry, Sallie Rogers' butler, answered the door, took Doug's coat and showed him to the library, where the other guests had already gathered. A warming fire crackled in the huge stone fireplace, and classical music softened the sound of voices and laughter. As Doug entered the room, the conversation stopped. All eyes seemed to focus on him.

"My, my, if it isn't the man of the hour. Doug, my darling, it's so good to see you." Sallie Rogers' rich voice boomed from across the room. "Come here and let me see what that beating you took in the *News* today has done to you."

Doug smiled at her and crossed the room. "Hi, Sallie," he said, leaning down and kissing her on the cheek.

Sallie patted the area next to her on the couch. "Here, I saved a spot for you. Please forgive my poor manners in not rising to greet you, Doug, but my arthritis is acting up again. Now, sit down and tell me all about it."

Doug accepted a glass of Dom Perignon from Henry, and sat down on the couch next to her. "Sallie, please at least let me have a sip of my champagne first," he said, smiling.

"Of course, how thoughtless of me. You just relax a bit. You must have had a horrendous day." Sallie patted his knee. "Now, let me think, do you know everyone here?"

Doug looked around the room at the eight other guests. As always, Sallie had it evenly matched. Boy, girl, boy, girl, boy, girl. Doug nodded a greeting at the familiar faces, until his eyes rested on a woman sitting in a wing chair in the far corner. He smiled. "Hi. I'm Doug Cummings. And I hope you don't read *The Washington News*."

The woman returned his smile coolly. "Nice to meet you, Mr. Cummings. I'm Anne Sullivan."

"Forgive me, both of you. Where are my manners tonight? Doug, Anne has become a dear friend of mine. She's been helping me try to settle some of Stephen's real estate deals. She's a damned good lawyer, if you ever need one." Sallie flinched. "I'm sorry, Doug, I didn't mean to imply anything by that last remark. Someone change the subject, quickly, before I get myself into more trouble."

Everyone laughed and Gretchen Moore, one of the guests, started telling a story about how terrible her horse had been when she had ridden him in a George Morris clinic the previous week. "I kid you not. You all know Class Attack. She's about as perfect as they get. But when Classy heard George's voice boom over that sound system, she short-circuited. I don't know what set her off. Maybe she knows George doesn't like spotted horses."

Doug turned to Sallie and quietly asked how she was doing. When Stephen Rogers had passed away the year before, Doug had been Sallie's estate tax advisor and helped probate her husband's estate.

"I'm fine, Doug. But what about you?" Sallie's pale blue eyes fixed intently on him, demanding an honest answer.

Doug returned Sallie's gaze. "It's been a rough day, Sallie, but I'm all right." He tried to lighten up the conversation. "Come on, now, I didn't come here to sit around and mope all night. Let's get on with your party."

Sallie's look told Doug she wanted to talk more about it, but she nodded at him and turned her attention back to the rest of the guests. "Did any of you hear about what happened to Pam Richards when she was over in England at that polo clinic last week?"

Doug excused himself and went over to the fireplace, occupying himself by adding some logs to the already blazing fire. Meagan Clarke, Richard Evan Clarke's niece, followed him and sat on the ottoman by the hearth. She leaned in close to Doug and lingered over a peck on his cheek. "Hey, Doug, I just had a great idea. Are you busy this weekend?"

"Why do you ask?"

"Well, I got a phone call from my brother right before I came over here. It seems that he had a room reserved at The Inn at Little Washington for the weekend, but now he has to work and can't go. Rather than lose his deposit, he asked if I wanted to use it. Of course, I said yes. How could I refuse?" Meagan smiled coyly at Doug. "I had planned to take a good book and go down there for the weekend, but I'd much rather forget the book and take you. What do you say? I thought maybe you could use a change of pace right about now. No strings attached. Just a little 'R and R.'" She reached out and rubbed his shoulders.

He smiled politely at her. "Thanks for the invitation, Meagan, but, unfortunately, I've got some commitments this weekend that I can't get out of."

Meagan stuck out her lower lip. "Well, I guess I'll just have to take that old book after all. Maybe some other time, huh?"

Henry came in and announced that dinner was served, and Doug went over and offered his arm to Sallie. Sallie was only sixty-two, but she had debilitating arthritis in one hip and needed assistance to get around.

Doug was seated to Sallie's right at dinner, with Anne Sullivan across from him. He studied Anne as she talked with Sallie. She was probably in her mid-thirties, tall and trim, athletic looking. Her blond hair was pulled back in a bun and her hazel eyes dominated the features of her chiseled face. Anne laughed at something Sallie said. Her smile was infectious, revealing two rows of perfectly straight white teeth, her mouth framed on both sides by soft dimples. Doug found her intriguing.

There was a lull in the conversation and Doug broke in. "So, you're a real estate lawyer. Do you have an office out here?"

"Actually, I'm a criminal lawyer. I was just helping Sallie out on a few real estate matters. And, yes, I do have an office out here. In Aldie."

Sallie turned to Doug. "Doug, darling, don't tell me you've never heard of Anne. Why she's almost a local celebrity. Remember the Allen Claghorne trial? He was that nice farmer who was accused of murdering his wife and her lover while they were making love in the hayloft of the barn. Anne represented Allen and proved that the wife's lover's ex-lover was really the murderer. Oh, well, never mind. It was big news out here, but I'm sure it didn't make much of a splash in Washington. I keep forgetting that you only come out here to play with your horses and don't really get involved with the local gossip. Anyway, Anne's a brilliant criminal attorney."

Doug smiled. "Well, I apologize for my ignorance. How long have you lived here?"

"I moved here from Vermont a couple of years ago."

"Quite a change from Vermont. Do you like it here?"

"Yes, I do, but I still miss Vermont sometimes," she replied, looking down at her dinner.

"What brought you down here?"

Anne hesitated briefly before answering him. "I moved here to be with a friend."

Doug glanced quickly at her finger. No ring. Of course that didn't mean anything. "Do you ride? I don't recall ever seeing you out hunting."

"I used to hunt and show some, but I sold my horse when I moved down here, and I've only ridden sporadically since then. I'm afraid I'm pretty rusty," she said, smiling slightly.

"That's no excuse. It's like riding a bicycle. You never forget," Doug said. "And there's no shortage of horses in Middleburg. You should come hunting with us some time. We have a hilltopper group, so you could take it nice and slow. I have a very quiet Irish hunter that you would love."

Their conversation was interrupted by Tom Smythe. "Hey, Doug," he called from down the table. "Where were you today? I ended up having to lead the hilltopper group." He shook his head. "I don't know how you stand it. What a bunch of wimps. It was either too fast, or too steep, or too windy, or too muddy, or too something. You owe me one, man." Tom grimaced. "I always used to envy you out there alone with all those women, but you must either be a saint or a masochist to put up with them."

Doug grinned at him. "They're not so bad, Tom. We usually have a good time out there. They were probably just testing you."

"Yeah, right. So, where were you anyway?"

Doug hesitated. "My horse wouldn't load."

"Who, Chancellor?" Tom asked.

Doug shook his head. "No, actually, believe it or not, it was Huntley."

"Aw, come on, man. I don't believe it. Mr. Dependable?" Tom had tried on numerous occasions to buy Huntley from Doug for one of his students. "Want to sell him?" Tom asked, pretending to pull out his wallet.

Doug just smiled and shook his head. His thoughts returned to what John had told him about finding a dirty towel in the trailer. The more he thought about it, he was sure that was why Huntley had acted up that morning. What he didn't know, was how the towel got there. He hoped it hadn't been left by deer hunters as John had speculated. They had no business anywhere on his property.

Doug thought fleetingly of the deer hunter that Babs had told him about. He tried to recall what day that man had shown up. Then he remembered. It was the day that Nancy had died.

Doug's thoughts were broken by Gretchen Moore, who was seated to his right. "Doug, Tom was asking you why Babs wasn't able to get Huntley on the trailer this morning. She can usually get the horses to mind her just by looking at them," Gretchen said, laughing. "I remember once when my mare wouldn't stand still for me to get on at the meet, and Babs came over to help. She was so curt, I don't know who was more intimidated, my horse or me. It worked though. She had me up on that horse before either one of us had time to think about it."

Doug kept his tone light. "Babs doesn't work for me anymore, so if any of you know any good grooms, send them my way. I'd hate to spend the rest of the hunt season trying to get my horses on the trailer."

"What happened, Doug? Babs was with you for so long. Did she leave you without any notice? Or did you fire her? Tell me the scoop." Gretchen fired questions at him.

Doug hated gossip and didn't want to be responsible for hurting Babs' chances to get a job elsewhere. Babs was a good groom and he'd give her a decent reference. "Let's just say we had a parting of the ways," he replied.

"Oh, come on, Doug. You have to tell me more than that. Give me the dirt. I can't believe she would leave before you had a replacement, if you two parted on good terms." Gretchen's words were slurred and she seemed well into her wine.

"Babs didn't leave me high and dry, Gretchen. I do have someone else to take care of the horses, at least on a trial basis. He just wasn't around this morning when I needed him."

Malcolm Douglas' husky voice interrupted from the other end of the table. "I keep telling you, Doug, you need to get yourself a good colored boy to work for you. I'm telling you, they know their place. You won't get any back talk from them. Those young girls you employ think they're God's gift to the horse world." Malcolm laughed and raised his wine glass.

Doug didn't try to hide his look of distaste. "You know my farm manager, John, is black, Malcolm. And he's as good a worker as they come. But I don't choose my employees by the color of their skin." He gave Malcolm an icy smile. "That goes for my friends too, Malcolm."

"Oh, lighten up, Doug, and don't give me that Martin Luther King bull-shit," Malcolm grumbled.

Doug bit back a response and turned his attention to Tom Smythe. "So, tell me, Tom, other than the whiners in the hilltopper group, how was the hunting? Did you have a good day?"

"We had a kill," Tom replied. "But it was an old mangy fox and it didn't give us much sport."

The conversation turned to foxhunting for a while. Doug half-listened as Tom told a story about a run they had. He felt Sallie's hand on his knee under the table and he looked at her.

"Thank you," she mouthed.

He nodded, and as he turned back to the conversation, he noticed Anne Sullivan looking at him. But when he met her gaze, she quickly glanced away.

After a few moments, Sallie suggested they all retire to the living room for dessert and coffee. Doug lingered behind and kept his distance from Malcolm. As he was heading into the living room, Doug heard Anne Sullivan ask Henry where a phone was so she could make a phone call.

"Here, Henry, I'll show Ms. Sullivan to the phone. You go ahead and serve dessert. Just make sure Gretchen Moore gets a strong cup of coffee before she drives home."

Henry nodded, chuckling. "Yes sir, Mr. Cummings. I'll be sure to do that."

Doug turned to Anne. "Follow me, I'll show you to the back bedroom, where you'll have some privacy."

He showed Anne the telephone on the nightstand in the guest bedroom and then left her to make her call. But when he reached the hallway, he stopped. He had no interest in joining the rest of the group in the living room. He'd much rather talk with Anne. So he stood in the hallway and waited for Anne to finish her call.

When Anne came out and saw him still standing there, a look of surprise and slight irritation crossed her face.

"Everything all right?" Doug asked.

"Yes, fine, thank you." She frowned at him. "You didn't have to wait here for me. I think I could have found my way."

"It's my pleasure. I've had about as much dinner party small talk as I can stand." He leaned against the wall and smiled at her. "So, Annie Sullivan, I've made it my mission to get you back up on a horse. What do I need to do to get you to go riding with me?"

She studied him for a moment and then the corners of her mouth lifted into smile, but her eyes were cold. "It's Anne, not Annie, and I don't think there's anything you can do, Doug. Please excuse me."

Before he could respond, she brushed past him and walked down the hall. Doug stared after Anne's retreating figure and felt his cheeks burn with embarrassment. What had he done to deserve that reaction?

Doug sighed and closed his eyes, leaning his head back against the wall. What a day.

He stayed by himself in the hall for several moments, then reluctantly joined the others in the living room. Sallie caught his eye and motioned to the empty chair next to her. Thankfully, Anne Sullivan was seated across the room.

Doug poured himself a cup of decaf from the coffee service on the sideboard and sat down next to Sallie. Malcolm Douglas was bragging to the others about a rare collection of hunting journals he'd purchased in England to donate to the Sporting Library. Doug tuned him out.

He felt a hand on his arm and he looked over at Sallie.

"Are you all right?" she asked softly, leaning close to him.

He nodded. "Sure."

Sallie studied him. "No, you're not. What's bothering you?" She nodded in the direction of Malcolm Douglas. "Is it what Malcolm said earlier?"

"No. It's just a combination of everything I guess." He paused. "I just got the cold shoulder from your friend Anne Sullivan."

"Ah." Sallie smiled. "I must admit to playing matchmaker when I invited Anne tonight. I thought you two might hit it off." She glanced over at Anne for a moment. "I guess the timing was wrong. Anne has been through some trying times lately. In her personal life. She's probably not ready for a relationship just yet." She smiled at him. "At least not with a man as worldly as you."

Doug frowned at her.

"Don't be offended, Doug. I meant that as a compliment," Sallie said.

He sighed and set his coffee cup on the table next to him. "I'm not offended, Sallie, but do you mind if I say good night? I'm really beat and I have an early day tomorrow."

"Of course not, Doug. I know it's been a long day for you. Thank you so much for coming." Sallie offered her cheek to him for a kiss.

Doug kissed Sallie and stood up, avoiding eye contact with Anne Sullivan as he said good-bye to the group.

24

Anne watched from across the room as Doug said his good-byes. He seemed to purposefully avoid looking in her direction, which was just as well.

There was no doubt, she had overreacted to his offer to take her riding. And she knew that she should apologize to him. After all, he was Sallie's friend. But she definitely didn't want to encourage him to ask her out again. She had no room in her life for a man like Doug Cummings. These days, she was drawn more to "steady and faithful," than to "tall, dark, and handsome."

She studied Doug as he shook hands with Tom, and kissed Meagan on the cheek. What was underneath that cool, confident exterior, she wondered? Was he really so nonchalant about *The Washington News* article? Or was that just a front?

Doug took his coat from Henry, said one more good-bye to Sallie, and then left the room. He never even glanced in her direction. Anne's cheeks burned and she quickly looked away. Fine. It was better that way. At least she didn't have to worry about him calling her for a date.

Gretchen Moore's voice broke into her thoughts. "Anne, *hello*, are you listening?"

Anne shook her head. "No, I'm sorry. I didn't hear you."

Gretchen rolled her eyes. "I was asking you what you thought about the story in *The Washington News* this morning? Do you think that Doug is really a suspect?"

Anne frowned. "I really have no way of knowing that, Gretchen. It certainly doesn't sound like they have any evidence linking him to Nancy Williams' murder. But I'd say it's pretty obvious that someone in the Sheriff's

Office isn't exactly a fan of Doug's."

"But what if he is a suspect?" Gretchen asked. "Whose side do you think people will take? Doug's or Nancy's? Remember how divided the community was over the Polo murder?"

"Oh, Gretchen, we all know Doug didn't murder Nancy," Sallie said. "No one who knows Doug would believe such a thing. Besides, I'm confident that the proper authorities will track down whoever is responsible for this awful crime. I just hope they don't take too long."

"Oh, they'll find him eventually. But the bastard will probably hire himself some fancy criminal lawyer who'll come up with an excuse to get him off," Malcolm said, winking at Anne. "Better be prepared for a phone call, Anne."

Gretchen leaned towards Anne. "You wouldn't really represent him, would you?" she asked, wide-eyed.

Anne hesitated. "I can't answer that question without knowing all the circumstances."

Gretchen gasped. "Oh, my God. You would. I don't believe it."

"Someone has to represent him. Or her," Anne said quietly. "Everyone's entitled to a defense."

"Even a murderer?" Gretchen asked.

"Accused murderer," Anne responded automatically.

"Oh, come on, don't give us that 'innocent until proven guilty' crap," Malcolm said, snorting. "You don't really believe that."

"Yes, I do," Anne replied evenly.

Malcolm grunted and studied her while he took a long puff of his cigar. "You know what really intrigues me? I'd like to know what makes a pretty lady like you want to spend your life trying to put vermin back out on the streets."

Anne took a deep breath before responding. "Not everyone who gets charged with a crime is 'vermin' as you call them, Malcolm. A lot of innocent people get arrested. And many people commit crimes due to extenuating circumstances. Those people can make something out of their lives, if they're given a second chance. That's why I chose this profession."

Malcolm blew out a white cloud of smoke. "Okay. I can buy that. But what about the other ninety-nine percent? The guilty ones. Why do you defend them?"

Anne sighed. "They're all innocent as far as I'm concerned, Malcolm.

Until proven otherwise."

No one spoke for a moment, and then Malcolm laughed. "I think you and Doug ought to get together, Anne. Since you're both such high-minded civil libertarians."

Anne just smiled coolly in reply.

Sallie intervened. "Malcolm, darling, you can be a real pain in the neck at times. Please stop teasing Anne. We all know she's a great attorney, and we're very proud to have her in this community. But should you ever need a criminal lawyer, Malcolm, she may not take your call."

Everyone laughed, and Sallie motioned for Henry to pass the dessert tray around.

Clyde was listening idly to the scanner as he sipped his coffee and delayed dressing for church, hoping to find a reason to excuse himself from the Sunday ritual. The report of a dead body caught his interest, and he turned up the volume.

The crackling voice of the dispatcher called out the location. "Poor House Hollow Road, in the woods behind Hunting Hollow Farm."

Clyde drew a sharp intake of breath. "Goddamn it." Hunting Hollow Farm was Doug Cummings' place. Clyde threw on his coat and ran out the door, not even bothering to tell his wife that he was leaving. He radioed from his car for more detailed directions and gave instructions that the deputies on the scene not touch the body until he arrived.

Clyde parked by the other squad cars on the road and climbed down through the woods in the direction of the voices of the other deputies. As he grew close, a putrid stench almost overpowered him and he could tell by the others' expressions that the corpse looked bad. The body was clearly that of a female, but her face was bloody; her features battered beyond recognition. Bits of leaves and earth clung to her mangled flesh.

Clyde took out his handkerchief and covered his mouth and nose. There was something about the body that was familiar to him, but what? He forced himself to stare at the body. What the hell was it?

She wore a beige wool turtleneck and blue jeans. Nothing special about that. He looked at her feet. Paddock boots, so she was probably a horse person. Nothing special about that. And then he saw it.

"Holy shit," he muttered. The worn brown paddock boots with the hole in one toe were the same ones he had been staring at on Babs Tyler three days before. He remembered them vividly, because he'd thought at the time that Doug Cummings should pay his groom more, so that she could at least afford decent shoes.

Clyde shook his head. "You're a sick son of a bitch, Cummings," he said under his breath. "You were pissed that she talked to me, so you killed her." Clyde forced himself to calm down and think everything through. He had to be very cautious, play it strictly by the book. He didn't want to risk making any mistakes that might jeopardize the case against Cummings.

"Okay, boys," he said. "Let's get the medical examiner in here. I don't want anyone touching the body or the scene before he has a look at her."

The other deputies didn't seem to understand his urgency. They were slow to respond. "Come on, come on," he barked. "I don't have all day here. This a crime scene. Let's get it marked off. One of you get on up to your car and radio for the M.E. to get his ass over here pronto. I don't give a damn if you have to pull him out of church."

Clyde watched as one of the deputies strung the yellow crime scene tape around the trees and the other traipsed through the woods back towards his car. As he waited, he reached into his pocket and popped a wad of chewing tobacco into his mouth.

After a few moments, the deputy returned from his car. "Did you get Brady?" Clyde asked.

"They're going to page him."

Clyde scowled. No telling how long that might take. "Who found her?" he asked, nodding his head towards the body.

"A local farmer. He was out looking for a missing cow and stumbled across her body."

"Where is he?" Clyde asked.

The deputy pointed behind him. "He lives up Poor House Hollow Road, about a half mile. He went home and called us, and after he showed us where to find her we let him go back home again. He was pretty shook up."

"Did he touch her?"

"He said he turned her over with his boot, to see if she was alive. Then, when he saw her face, he hightailed it out of here."

"He see anything else? Anyone around?"

The deputy shook his head. "Nah. I don't think he'll be any help. Like I said, he was just out here this morning looking for his cow. From the looks of her, I'd say she's been here a couple of days."

Clyde nodded. "All right. Let's search the area. See what we can come up with."

It took almost an hour for Scott Brady, the medical examiner, to arrive. He took one look at the body and immediately turned on Clyde. "Where do you get off calling me out of church, Deputy? Another few hours wouldn't have made a difference here. You should have known that. Too much time has passed for me to be able to pinpoint the time of death."

Clyde stood up to him. "Maybe so, but I know the sheriff will want to give this top priority. This is the second woman we've found murdered in the woods, and that's going to have everyone in an uproar."

Brady nodded. "Well, I'd say you're right about that." He knelt down next to the body and opened his bag, and Clyde watched impatiently as Brady collected samples and examined the body.

"What do you think?" Clyde asked. "Was this girl murdered by the same guy as the Williams woman?"

Brady frowned at him. "You know I can't answer a question like that, especially before I've conducted my autopsy."

"Okay. But you see the similarities, right?"

"Well, both victims appear to have been beaten in the head, however, this beating was considerably more vicious than the other one. And the previous victim was strangled. I don't see any evidence of that here." He rubbed his chin thoughtfully. "Both victims were found in the woods, but not in the same vicinity. Both were female, but the other woman probably had a good ten years on this girl. Neither showed any signs of sexual assault, although I haven't finished my full examination of this girl yet." Brady shook his head. "I reckon you're right to be thinking along those lines, Deputy, but I sure wouldn't go so far at this point as to say we have a serial killer on our hands."

But you don't know that they both had the misfortune of knowing Doug Cummings, Clyde thought. "Will you be able to tell if the same murder weapon was used on both of them?" he asked the medical examiner.

"I don't know, but I'll do my best to look for any similarities," Brady replied.

Clyde asked Brady to make this autopsy a top priority and to get the results to him as soon as he was finished. Brady left and Clyde looked around the site again, trying to determine how Babs Tyler got there. There was no sign of a struggle and no blood other than where her head had rested on the ground. He figured that she was murdered elsewhere, then dumped out here.

He thoroughly searched the area again, but didn't find anything new.

Damn. Clyde grabbed the tree branch next to him and rested his head on his arm. It was just like with Nancy Williams. How the hell was he supposed to find any evidence in the damned woods?

26

Clyde sat in his car for a while, pondering what to do next. He should give the sheriff a call and fill him in on what had happened. And he should call home and tell his wife why he had disappeared in such a hurry. He should start his investigation. Find out where Babs lived. Whether she had a roommate. Who saw her last, and when. But he had another priority.

Clyde started his car and drove up the road until he reached the entrance to Hunting Hollow. He started to turn in, then saw that the iron gates were closed tight. Clyde put his car in park, got out and swung the heavy gates back, then drove his car through, leaving the gates hanging wide open.

Clyde drove down the long driveway to the main house and parked by the front door. He got out and rang the bell, and after a few minutes it was answered by an elderly woman.

The woman gave him an icy look, and wiped her hands on her apron. "May I help you?"

"I'm here to see Mr. Cummings."

"Let me see if he's available." She started to close the door in Clyde's face, but he stuck his foot in the way.

"I'll wait for him inside," Clyde said, pushing the door back open and stepping into the house.

Clyde watched until she vanished out of sight at the end of the hallway. While he waited for Cummings, he looked around the entry hall. Jesus Christ. There were at least a half-dozen oil paintings on the walls. Of horses. And hounds. There was a large bronze horse on a half-round wooden table. The table looked old and fragile. Probably an antique. Clyde looked down at the Oriental carpet that covered the hardwood floor. Shit. He wondered how much money was tied up there.

William Clayton Barrington had lived in a fancy house like this. But he'd paid his help so poorly that Clyde's father had struggled to put proper food on the table for his family. Clyde pictured the hole in Babs Tyler's paddock boot. Cummings was obviously a tightwad with his help too.

Clyde heard footsteps and saw Cummings walk down the hall towards him, a newspaper in his hand.

Cummings didn't give him a chance to speak first. "I don't know why you're here, Deputy, but I don't like you showing up unannounced. I told you I'd cooperate with you, but I'd prefer to do it over the telephone."

Clyde held his hand up. "Now just wait a minute, Cummings. Give me a chance to tell you why I'm here. I came by to tell you that we found her."

"Found *who*?" Cummings asked.

"Babs Tyler."

"Really? Well, that's nice. I didn't know that you were looking for her," Cummings responded.

Whew. What a cool character. Cummings hadn't even flinched. "Yeah, well, we weren't really looking for her because we didn't know that she was missing. Why is it you didn't report that, Cummings?" Clyde asked

Cummings glared at him. "Where are you going with this?"

"I'm just trying to figure out why you didn't call and file a missing persons report when your groom disappeared, Cummings. The only explanation that I can think of is that you already knew where she was," Clyde said, shaking his head.

Cummings cocked his head and smiled. "And where was that?"

Clyde exaggerated a false look of shock. "Why, Mr. Cummings, lying dead in the woods, of course."

Cummings sank back against the wall, a very convincing expression of disbelief on his face. "Babs is dead?" he asked.

Clyde snorted and shook his head. "Yeah, Cummings. Beaten to a bloody pulp and left to decay like a stinking piece of meat. But then, you already knew that, didn't you?"

Cummings took a step towards Clyde and narrowed his eyes, anger now replacing the look of disbelief. "Are you accusing *me* of her murder?"

Clyde smirked. "You'll make it a lot easier on yourself if you'll come in voluntarily. We sure do have a lot to talk about."

"Do you have a warrant?" Cummings demanded.

Clyde stared at Cummings and chewed on his tobacco for a moment, then shook his head slowly. "No. But I can get one."

Cummings grabbed the door handle and pulled open the door. "Stop playing games with me and get off my property, Dickson, or you'll regret the consequences." His voice was low, but threatening.

Clyde knew he'd pushed Cummings as far as he could, so he stepped outside. "Okay, Cummings. But you're just making this harder . . ."

Before he could complete his sentence, Cummings slammed the door in his face.

Doug leaned against the closed door and took a deep breath. Babs was dead. He should have known that Babs wouldn't have walked out on him. Why hadn't he tried to find her? Or called the police? If he had, they might have found her in time.

Doug pounded his fist against the door. What the hell was happening? First Nancy. Now Babs. And this crazy deputy seemed determined to pin it all on him. He had no doubt that Dickson would be back with a warrant, if he could find a judge to issue one.

Doug went to his study and sat down at his desk. He needed a lawyer. He leaned forward, his elbows resting on the desk, his fingers laced together, debating whom to call. No one in his firm practiced criminal law, but he figured that was the best place to get a good referral.

He reached for the phone to call one of his litigation partners, but stopped. Doug stared thoughtfully at the receiver for a moment, and then slowly put it back in the cradle. He wasn't sure that he wanted to drag his firm into it at this point. If Dickson couldn't get a warrant, it might amount to nothing, and there was no use getting the partnership up in arms.

Doug got up and walked to the window. The more he thought about it, he wasn't sure he wanted a Washington attorney anyway. It was probably smarter to retain a local attorney. Someone who knew the ropes. And knew the judges.

Doug considered the local criminal attorneys he knew. There was Jock Weatherly. And Cameron Sutherland. He had hunted with both of them and he knew they were part of the good old boy network. But neither one impressed him as being exceptionally bright.

Then he remembered Anne Sullivan. Sallie Rogers had said that Sullivan was the best criminal lawyer around, and he trusted Sallie's judgment.

Doug hesitated, remembering Anne Sullivan's attitude towards him at Sallie Roger's dinner party. But he didn't care how she treated him, as long as she was the best lawyer around.

He found her listed in the phone book, with both an office and home number, and when he didn't get an answer at the office, he dialed her house. A woman answered after the second ring. Doug decided not to identify himself. "Hi, may I speak with Anne Sullivan please."

"This is Anne."

Doug took a deep breath. "Anne, this is Doug Cummings. We met at Sallie Rogers' dinner party the other evening." Before he could go on, she cut him off.

"Mr. Cummings, I thought I made myself clear the other evening. I am not interested in going riding with you. Please don't call here again."

"Wait. Don't hang up. That's not why I'm calling. This is business. It's important. Anne?"

"Yes, I'm still here," she said quietly.

"I need a lawyer. A criminal lawyer actually. That's why I'm calling."

"All right. Call my office in the morning. I know I have a busy schedule this week, but I'll tell them to try to work you in."

"I'm afraid it can't wait until tomorrow," Doug said. "I'm in trouble, Anne. Maybe big trouble. A deputy just left here, threatening to come back with an arrest warrant. I need some legal advice and I need it now."

Her voice softened. "Tell me what happened."

"I'd rather not talk about it over the phone. Could we meet somewhere?" Doug wanted to get away from his house, in case Dickson showed up with a warrant.

"I can't leave home right now. I don't have a baby sitter." She hesitated. "I guess you could come over to my house if you want to."

Doug let out a sigh. "Thanks, Anne. I really appreciate it."

He wrote down the directions to her house and told her he was on his way. Doug took time to look for Nellie before he left and found her ironing in the kitchen. She glanced up as he walked in.

"What was that all about, Doug? That deputy was so rude. Is he the one who's been causing all the trouble?" she asked.

Doug nodded. "I need to talk to you," he said. He took Nellie by the hand

and led her to a chair at the kitchen table. He sat down in the chair next to her.

Nellie grasped her white apron between her hands and twisted it nervously. "Oh, no, Doug. Is this more bad news?"

He nodded and reached out for her hands. "Babs is dead," he said quietly.

One of Nellie's hands flew to her chest and she made the sign of the cross. "Oh, my dear Lord. What happened?" she whispered, as tears ran down between the soft wrinkles on her face.

"Apparently she was murdered."

Nellie gasped. "Who would do such a thing?"

"He accused me." Doug stood up. "I'm on my way to talk with a lawyer now."

"My goodness, Doug, can I do anything to help?"

Doug attempted a smile. "Just continue to believe in me."

28

Doug drove into Anne's driveway fifteen minutes later. The gravel drive cut through a thick shelter of evergreen trees and sloped down to an old Virginia-style farm house. An immense porch ran the length of the white wooden structure. Glossy black rockers flanked the front door on both sides, and as Doug mounted the stairs, they rocked vacantly in the wind.

Doug rang the bell and within a few moments Anne opened the door, with a little girl by her side. Anne smiled politely. "Come on in."

Anne took his coat and Doug rubbed his hands together to warm them. "Brrr. It's getting cold out there. I wouldn't be surprised if we got some snow tonight."

"Yippee," the little girl cried. "I love snow. Then we won't have any school tomorrow and we can build a snowman."

Anne smiled down at her. "Let's not get too excited yet." She introduced the girl to Doug. "This is Samantha. Samantha, can you please say hello to Mr. Cummings."

The girl looked shyly at him and stuck out her hand. Doug crouched down and shook her hand, smiling at her. "Hi, Samantha. It's very nice to meet you. How old are you?"

Samantha held up four fingers. "I'm going to be five in February."

"You're almost five? That's pretty grown up," Doug said, letting go of her hand and standing up. "I want to thank you for letting your mommy spend some time working with me today. I hope it doesn't interfere too much with your play time."

"Aunt Anne's not my mommy. My mommy and daddy are in heaven." Tears welled up in Samantha's big brown eyes; she reached out and grabbed

Anne's hand and buried her face against Anne's stomach.

Doug didn't know how to respond. He looked at Anne. "I'm sorry."

Anne hugged the child. "It's okay, sweetie. It makes me feel sad too. Let's go and see if we can't find something in the kitchen that might make us feel better." She turned to Doug. "Have a seat in the den," she said, motioning towards the room on her left. "I'll be right back."

Doug went into the den, feeling foolish. It seemed like he was always putting his foot in his mouth around Anne Sullivan. He leafed restlessly through a *Chronicle of the Horse* magazine while he waited for Anne to return.

"I'm really sorry," he said when Anne came in. "I shouldn't have assumed Samantha was your daughter. If you need to spend some time with her, I can wait here. Or, I can come back later."

Anne shook her head. "Don't apologize. Your assumption was a natural one. Samantha's all right. She's playing happily now. Thanks for your concern. Why don't you have a seat and tell me about your situation." Anne motioned for Doug to sit on the couch, and she got a legal pad from her desk and sat down in the chair across from him.

Doug sat perched on the edge of the couch. "Where do you want me to begin?"

"Why don't you just tell me everything, from the beginning. I'd rather know too much than too little. Take your time."

Doug told her the sequence of events as well as he could remember them, starting with his discovery of Nancy in the woods and Dickson's apparent bias against him. Anne listened quietly and took occasional notes, until he told her about Babs.

"Isn't that the groom that you were discussing at dinner the other night?" she asked.

Doug nodded. "Yes."

Anne raised her eyebrows. "At that time, did you have any reason to believe that she might have met with foul play?"

"Of course not. If I had, I would have called the sheriff. I just thought she had walked out on me."

"Was that the type of behavior that you would expect from her?" she asked.

Doug thought about it. "Actually, no. Babs worked for me for five years and the best trait she had going for her was her reliability."

"Didn't you think it was odd that she would walk out on you?" she asked, frowning.

Doug felt a rush of anger start in his chest and rise to his temples. Anne didn't believe him. He stood up. "Look, Anne, I came here because I wanted to retain you as my attorney, not get the third degree."

Anne put her hand up. "Hold on, Doug, don't get your feelings hurt by my questions. I am on your side, but those who aren't will ask the same things, and I want to hear the answers before they do." She motioned to the couch. "Please sit back down and continue. If it makes you more comfortable, I'll hold off on my questions until after you've finished."

Doug sat down on the couch. He sighed and ran his hand through his hair, avoiding Anne's gaze. "I guess this is getting to me more than I thought. I'm not dealing very well with this deputy breathing down my neck." He met her eyes. "To be honest, I've been asking myself the same questions. I should have made an attempt to find Babs. I should have known that something was wrong."

He shook his head and thought about it for a moment. "There's just something about it that still doesn't make any sense to me. Babs' saddle and grooming box disappeared when she did. That's the reason I thought that she had walked out on me." He raised his shoulders questioningly. "But if Babs didn't quit, if she didn't show up for work because she'd been murdered, why were her things gone?"

Anne shrugged. "Maybe she did take her things and walk out on you, and was murdered after that. It helps your case if you have a convincing reason why you didn't report her missing."

Doug nodded. "Well, at the time I thought that I did. We had a disagreement the night before, and I was irritated with her to the point that I really didn't much care if she did quit. When she didn't show up and her things were gone, I just assumed that she had walked out in a huff."

"What was your disagreement about?"

"Nothing major. The way she was handling one of my horses," Doug said. Then he remembered the twitch. "And she had lost, or misplaced, something of mine. It didn't have any great monetary value, but it was given to me as a gift and had sentimental value. I didn't like her casual attitude about it."

"Was anyone else there, when the two of you had this disagreement?" Anne asked.

"My blacksmith was. Why?"

"I just don't want to be surprised if some witness turns up with a version of your encounter with Babs that might give you a motive in her murder," Anne said. "Was the disagreement heated or violent in any way?"

"No. Babs was just being confrontational. That's how Babs was."

Anne wrote something down. "Let's talk alibi for a moment. I know you found Nancy Williams, but prior to that, can anyone place the two of you together that day?"

Doug thought about it. "We hunted together that day, but that was about it. We were never alone, if that's what you mean. I'm not sure, but I think I was the first one to hack in. I know that Nancy was still with the rest of the field when I left."

"Did anyone see you leave?"

"I paid my respects to the master, so I know he saw me. I slipped out kind of quietly after that."

"Why?" Anne asked.

Doug shrugged. "I was cold and wet and wanted to get to the office as quickly as possible. When other people come along, I have to adjust my pace to theirs."

"What about Nancy? To the best of your knowledge, was she alone when she left the field?"

"I assume she was, but I don't know for sure."

"Okay," Anne said. "Let's move on to Babs. What time of day was it when you had your disagreement?"

"Late afternoon."

"Did you see her again after that?" Anne asked.

"No." Doug shook his head.

"Did you go back to the barn?"

"No. I went up to my house and stayed in all night."

"Was anyone there with you?"

"Just my housekeeper."

"Tell me about her," Anne said.

"Well, she's been with my family since I was a child," Doug began. "Nellie must be pushing seventy by now. She has a suite in my house, and she cooks some and oversees the place."

"Did she cook you dinner that evening?"

Doug thought about it. "I don't really remember. She could have."

"Do you recall the last time you saw her that evening, or the last time she would have seen you?"

"No. But I'm sure it was not any later than dinner time. Nellie usually retires by eight or nine o'clock."

"Do you recall speaking to anyone on the phone that evening?"

"God, Anne, I don't know. That night had no significance to me at the time. There was no reason for me to remember anything about it."

"That's all right. I'm just asking. If you don't remember, that's fine. What about the next morning when Babs didn't show up for work? Do you remember what you were doing then?"

Doug nodded. "Oh, yes. I remember that morning well. I got up and read *The Washington News*, saw the article about me, and then spent some time on the phone with my secretary."

"Good. Can you remember the timing?" Anne asked, writing something on her legal pad.

"I think Marsha called shortly before eight o'clock and we probably talked for thirty or forty-five minutes." He paused, calculating. "Then I showered and dressed and went to the barn. I probably got there shortly after nine."

"Was anyone else at the barn?"

"No."

Anne put her pen down. "When did you next see or speak to anyone?"

"I don't know, it was probably ten or so. I spent a good forty-five minutes to an hour in the barn. Then I went back to the house and Nellie was up."

"Is it safe to say that, from the time you got off the phone with your secretary," Anne paused and looked at her notes, "say around eight-thirty, until the time you saw Nellie, around ten o'clock or so, no one can vouch for your whereabouts?"

"Yeah, that's safe to say. Not much help, is it?"

"Look, Doug, from what you've told me, I don't believe that any judge will issue an arrest warrant for you. There's no hard evidence and weak circumstantial at best. The only real connection you have to these murders is that you knew both women; you were in the woods alone in the vicinity of Nancy Williams when she was murdered, and Babs Tyler was found dead in the woods near your property. That's not probable cause. I am concerned, though, that this deputy seems to have it in for you. These things seem to have a snowball effect, and it sounds like this guy is trying really hard to build a case against you. At some point, weak evidence, if you have enough of it, can gather strength. That's why I was hoping to establish an alibi, so we could put this whole thing to rest."

"So, where do we go from here?" Doug asked.

"I'd like to pay Deputy Dickson a visit tomorrow and hear what he has to say. Hopefully, I can get him to show me anything he has on you. I'll know a lot more then."

Doug was overwhelmed by a sense of helplessness. He was a lawyer, a partner for God's sake, and yet he couldn't think of a damned thing to do to help his own defense. Criminal law was so foreign to him. His mouth was dry, and when he spoke his words sounded thick and inadequate. "What should I do?" he asked.

"Be as normal as possible. Go to work, go hunting. Do whatever you otherwise would do. It's a waiting game at this point." Anne handed him her card. "This has my beeper number on it, as well as my office and home. I can always be reached at one of those numbers. If Deputy Dickson shows up, have someone find me immediately."

They both stood up and Anne put out her hand. "Let's get together in a day or so at my office. I'd like to go over everything again in greater detail, after I've had a chance to see where Dickson is coming from."

As they reached the front door, Doug turned to Anne. "Thanks for taking the time to meet with me. I hope I didn't upset Samantha too much."

"No need to thank me, Doug." Her reply was polite, though not exactly friendly. "I'll be in touch."

CHAPTER
29

Zeb watched Doug Cummings from the shelter of a clump of trees in front of Hunting Hollow. It was almost midnight and Zeb had been there since Cummings had returned home late that afternoon. The night was clear and the air was frigid, but Zeb barely noticed as he watched Cummings through the window.

Cummings was in his study, sitting at his desk, across the room from a crackling fire. He had been writing on some papers for over an hour. He finally stopped and tossed his pen on the desk. Cummings leaned back in his chair and rubbed his eyes.

Zeb raised his Winchester and viewed Cummings through the scope. Cummings massaged both temples with his hands and ran his fingers through his hair. Then he settled back down, with both hands clasped behind his head. Eyes still closed.

Zeb set the sight of his rifle on Cummings' temple. Killing Cummings would be a piece of cake. Hell, he could drop a deer at three-hundred yards. Only person he knew who could shoot better than him was his sister Zelda. Shit, she outgunned Zeke and him every time.

Zeb lowered the rifle, ever so slightly, and zeroed in on Cummings' chest. His finger stroked the trigger. Lightly. Itching to pull it.

Pow. Pow. Pow. Zeb closed his eyes. In his mind he pulled the trigger and shot Cummings. Twice in the chest. Then in the head. He could picture it so clearly. The fleeting look of disbelief on Cummings' face. The way Cummings' body recoiled as each shot tore into him. The dark stain of blood that spread across Cummings' chest.

Zeb lowered his rifle and watched as Cummings rose from his chair, stirred the fire, turned out the lights, and left the room.

None of the curtains in the house were drawn and Zeb could see Cummings plainly through the front windows as he climbed the stairs. Zeb had already sneaked inside twice when Cummings was away and he knew the layout of Cummings' entire house. The old biddy Cummings had for a house-keeper must be blind as a bat and deaf as a doornail, because she'd never even known he was there.

Zeb watched Cummings cross the upstairs hall and enter his bedroom. He waited as Cummings disappeared from sight, then reappeared, and walked back towards the bed dressed only in boxer shorts. The lights went off and Zeb stared at the darkened window for a few moments. He pictured Cummings lying in an enormous king-sized bed that was larger than Zeke's entire prison cell had been.

Then a figure appeared at the darkened bedroom window and Zeb squinted, trying to see better. His eyes focused and he saw it was Cummings. Cummings stood there for several moments, his hands on the window frame, just staring out at the black, frosty night.

Zeb's hand tightened on his rifle and his finger stroked the trigger again. Not yet. Not quite yet.

Doug left the farm well before dawn Monday morning, a good hour before his *Washington News* was delivered. He picked the paper up at the newsstand in the lobby of his office building when he arrived, shortly before seven-thirty.

Doug waited until he was at his desk with the door to his office closed, before he opened the paper. There it was, page one of the "People" section, Eric Schultz's byline. *"Hunt Country Murder Spree, Possible Result of Love Triangle Gone Awry?* Related Story, Page 1A." There was a photograph of him at some social affair, dressed in hunt attire, drink in hand, talking with several women.

"The quiet streets and bricked sidewalks of bucolic Middleburg are awash in sorrow again this morning, the wealthy residents in shock over the death of yet another member of the horsey set. Many residents expressed horror and dismay at the allegations that one of their own, W. Douglas Cummings III, millionaire socialite and confirmed playboy, may be responsible for the recent tragic hunt-country deaths of Cummings' ex-lover Nancy Williams and his horse groom Babs Tyler. Friends say that Cummings' whirlwind fairy-tale romance with Williams was ill-fated from the start, just another in a long string of [Cummings'] relationships destined to go nowhere. 'What's most surprising,' said one acquaintance of Cummings, 'is that Doug would do anything to risk losing Babs Tyler. You know, out here, a good groom is second only to God.'

"Many in the tweedy, moneyed, foxhunting set voiced concern for their own safety. 'I haven't owned any shotgun shells for years, but I do now,' one long-time resident said. But another local scoffed at the idea. 'You know, I've

lived here for over fifty years and have never locked my door. I'm certainly not about to start now. Why, I don't even think I could find the key anymore.'

"As the search for answers in these two shocking deaths continues, the eternal chase for the fox goes on, undisturbed, across the rolling Virginia countryside. The locals say that Williams and Tyler would have wanted it that way."

Doug had just finished reading the article when someone knocked on his door, and he quickly shoved the paper in his briefcase and closed the lid.

"Come in."

Robert Dewitt walked in, a rolled up *Washington News* in his hand. He nodded at Doug and strode over to the desk, looking grim, as he slapped the paper against his palm.

"Mind if I sit?" Dewitt waved at one of the chairs across the desk from Doug.

"No, of course not, Robert, sit down." Doug stood and waited until Dewitt was seated. "Want a cup of coffee?"

"No, thanks." Dewitt squirmed uncomfortably in the chair. "I don't know quite how to begin, Doug." He avoided Doug's eyes. "It's really none of my business how you got yourself into this mess, or how you are going to get yourself out of it, but it is my concern when it starts to affect the firm, and it has. Our clients simply will not tolerate having your name, our name, splashed across the front pages of *The Washington News* day after day. I've already had a dozen calls this morning, and it's not even eight o'clock yet. So far, I've been able to calm everyone down, but I can't continue that indefinitely."

"What are you suggesting, Robert?" Doug worked to keep his voice even.

Dewitt stared at the pen he was fidgeting with. "Doug, I'm afraid I have to ask you to lie low for a while, until this all blows over."

"I don't know what you mean by that, Robert. *Lie low.*" Doug's heart thumped in his chest.

Dewitt's face reddened. "We need to be able to disassociate ourselves from you, Doug."

"Disassociate?" Doug almost managed to keep the anger out of his voice. "What happened to the vote of confidence that you gave me on Friday?"

Dewitt held the newspaper up. "That was before this." He made eye contact. "Look, Doug, if it were anyone else, I'd ask them to leave the firm, but I won't do that to you. I owe your father that. I just need to put some distance between us. I need to be able to tell our clients that you are on a leave of absence, pending the resolution of this matter."

"Has the partnership voted on this?" Doug demanded.

"No, I don't think that's necessary," Dewitt responded. "As managing partner, I have the authority to handle things at this point. Please don't force me to take formal action, Doug. You might not like the outcome."

"What about my clients? What about the Tycoon Technologies hearing?"

"I've already spoken with Larry Greer. He wants Mark Hoffman to handle the hearing."

Doug's stomach tightened into a knot. "Mark? He's never testified before Congress, Robert. He's a good lawyer, but I think that's over his head. There's too much at stake for Tycoon Technologies."

"Well, it's their decision and that's what they want. You can coach Mark. From behind the scenes."

Doug stared grimly at Robert. "Did you bother to plead my case with Greer?"

Dewitt shook his head. "No, Doug, I didn't. I think they're right." He stood up. "Look, Doug, why don't you just do us both a favor and take some time off? Don't fight me on this. If you look at this from my point of view, from the firm's point of view, I know you'll agree that this is the right thing to do. Hopefully, this situation will be short-lived and we can all put it behind us."

Doug's instinct was to fight Dewitt's decision, but he knew that Robert was right. "Fine, Robert. I'll do it your way. I don't anticipate this going on much longer anyway. I've retained an attorney and I expect things to be resolved very quickly. In the meantime, I'll work with Mark on Tycoon Technologies and my other clients."

"That's fine. You can work by phone or he can come over to your place." Dewitt opened the door. "Good luck, Doug. Keep me informed." Dewitt rushed out, closing the door behind him.

Doug felt a tightening in his chest, and he reached up and loosened his tie, forcing himself to take several deep breaths. He hadn't thought that this mess could get any worse, but it had. Doug quickly emptied his desk drawers of anything confidential, selected the client files he wanted to take along, then buzzed Marsha to come in.

"Marsha, I'm going to be working at home for a while, so I need to have copies of these files." Doug motioned to the stack of legal folders on his desk. "I'll wait if you can copy them now please."

"Of course. Is there anything else you'll be needing?" she asked.

"Not that I can think of right now. Thanks, Marsha."

"Very good, sir, give me a few minutes and I'll be back with these."

Doug paced his office while he waited for Marsha to return. He paused at the window and looked down at the city from his penthouse perch. The sun was brilliant now, shooting beams of golden warmth through the clear, crisp morning air. Doug watched as commuters jammed Pennsylvania Avenue, horns blaring, everyone in a hurry to get to work. Everyone except for him.

Marsha returned with the copied files packed neatly in a cardboard file box. "I put your client telephone list in here too, Doug, and some of your administrative firm files. I thought you might be needing them."

Doug smiled at her. Good old Marsha. Loyal to the bitter end. "Thanks, Marsha. I'll be calling in every day, and of course you have all my numbers in case you need to reach me for anything." He picked up his briefcase and the box and headed for the door.

"Doug."

He turned around. "Yes?"

"I just want you to know that I think what the firm is doing to you is wrong. If you ever need me for anything, I'm just at the other end of that phone." Marsha's voice cracked. "Of all people, you don't deserve this." Tears filled her eyes and she stopped.

Doug nodded his appreciation at her, not trusting his voice. He managed to make it to the elevator without seeing anyone and punched the call button impatiently. The elevator was slow to arrive, but he had it to himself on the ride down.

Doug saw heads turning as he walked through the lobby, and he quickened his pace. He knew the stares must be because of the *News* piece. People obviously had no idea that he had just been asked to "disassociate" himself from his firm. But he felt conspicuous carrying the box of files nonetheless.

The parking attendant brought Doug's car around and helped put the box in the trunk. "Looks like you've got quite some work here, Mr. Cummings. That's sure to keep you busy."

Doug handed him a tip and mumbled an agreement.

He drove to the Watergate and was greeted by the daytime doorman, George, in his usual judicious manner. No hint of a reaction to the *News* article. George was well trained to be discreet.

His apartment was naggingly quiet, and the air was flat from having been closed up for the past few days. Doug switched on some lights, turned on CNN, and flopped down on the couch.

He stared mindlessly at the news for a while then started channel surfing, looking for a distraction. After an hour or more, he turned off the television and threw down the remote control. He decided to head out to the country and see what, if anything, Anne Sullivan had been able to do on his behalf.

Anne Sullivan knew something was up as soon as she walked into her office that afternoon. Her secretary, Cyndi, was standing in the front hallway and her young associate, Leslie McCashin, rushed breathlessly out of the conference room and closed the door behind her.

Leslie grabbed Anne's arm and pulled her aside. "What a hunk!" she whispered. "I had no idea when I came to work here that you had clients like him."

Anne turned towards her office and motioned for Leslie to follow. She waited until Leslie was inside and then shut the door firmly behind them. "I don't know what or whom you are talking about, Leslie, but your behavior is entirely inappropriate. You're a lawyer, not some lovesick teenager, and if you want to continue working for me, you'll learn how to lend some dignity to this profession. Do I make myself clear?"

Leslie blushed and nodded.

"Fine. Now tell me what this is all about."

"Doug Cummings is here, waiting for you. We told him we weren't sure when you would be back, but he insisted on waiting, so I had Cyndi set him up in the conference room," Leslie replied.

"Okay, let me return a few calls and then I'll see him. Tell Mr. Cummings I'll be with him shortly. And, Leslie, please try to remember that Mr. Cummings is a client of this firm, not some 'hunk' that you're trying to pick up in Georgetown, or wherever it is you go these days."

Anne had to suppress a smile as Leslie left the room. One of the reasons she enjoyed having Leslie in the office was her youthful energy and enthusiasm. Her lifestyle was so foreign to Anne that she often found herself laughing at

Leslie's tales of her somewhat promiscuous personal life. But this was different. Anne did not find Leslie's interest in Doug Cummings at all amusing.

Doug was seated at the conference table when Anne walked in. The knot in his tie was loosened and pulled slightly to the side, and the top button of his white starched shirt was unbuttoned. His navy blue suit jacket hung on the back of his chair. His shirt sleeves were rolled up to just below his elbows.

He rose when Anne entered and she shook his hand, then sat down next to him. "Doug, I'm surprised to see you. I don't really have anything new to tell you. I haven't been able to hook up with Deputy Dickson yet. Has something else happened?"

His smile was cold. "Yes, as a matter of fact it has. It seems that I've been relieved of my duties at my law firm, at least for the time being, so I thought I'd come out here and see if you'd made any progress." He motioned towards the door behind Anne. "I'm sorry I didn't call first. I'm afraid I've been a burden to your staff, whom I must say have been more than accommodating."

Anne turned to see Cyndi standing in the doorway.

"Excuse me, I was just wondering if I could get you any more coffee, or a soft drink perhaps?" Cyndi said.

Anne looked at Doug, who shook his head no. "We're fine, Cyndi, and please close the door behind you."

Anne turned back to Doug. "I apologize for their behavior. You are not the typical client we see around here, and I'm afraid they don't quite know how to handle it."

"Please, don't apologize. Believe me, they've been the highlight of my day." Doug rose and started to pace the room. "I don't mean to disrupt your office or your day, Anne, but I really need some action here. If I don't put this thing to rest soon, my career is over. That is, if it isn't already. Isn't there anything you can do to speed this up?"

Anne hadn't focused on Doug's case yet. Her morning had been spent at a bond hearing for another client. Actually, she hadn't considered him a priority at all since no charges had been filed yet.

"Tell me what happened. What do you mean, you've been relieved of your duties at your firm?" Anne asked.

He sat back down and leaned forward. His elbows rested on the table and his hands were raised, palms together. Anne noticed that his fingers were long and powerful, his nails neatly groomed.

"Did you see the piece in the *News* this morning?" he asked.

Anne nodded.

Doug smiled grimly. "Well, so did our key clients. And they weren't happy about it. So the powers that be in the firm want to be able to tell the clients that I'm on a leave of absence until this is resolved. They're hedging their bets, ready to cut me loose if things get worse, or to welcome me back with open arms if I come out of this smelling like a rose. But I have a gut feeling that if there's any more negative publicity, they'll want me out of the firm. Completely."

"I'm sorry, Doug, I guess I didn't realize the urgency of your situation. I will try to track down Deputy Dickson this afternoon." Anne looked at her calendar. "How about if we get together first thing tomorrow? I can spend all day on your case if need be."

"Is there anything I can do in the meantime?"

Anne studied him for a moment. He was scared. Understandably so, since it appeared that his career was on the line. "You have to pull yourself together, Doug. I know how hard this must be for you, especially now with what happened at your law firm today. But appearances are extremely important in a case like this. You need to lead as normal a life as possible."

Doug shook his head. "That's easy to say, but my work is my life. That is what I do."

"Well, you also ride and go foxhunting, I know that. And you have friends out here. Get together with them. Take advantage of this time to do some of the things you don't otherwise have time to. You'll be buried under your work again sooner than you might think."

Doug opened his mouth as if to argue with her, but then closed it again. He nodded. "Okay. I had planned to go hunting tomorrow, so how about if I come here right after that, say late morning?"

"Perfect. I'll try to have some answers by then. We can figure out where to go from there," she said, rising from her chair.

Anne opened the conference room door and was walking Doug to the front when Cyndi interrupted them.

"I'm sorry to interrupt, Anne, but Bud Malone is on the phone insisting that he talk to you right now. He says it will be quick."

Anne apologized to Doug and picked up the phone at Cyndi's desk. While she was on the phone, Anne saw Leslie come out of the library and walk over to Doug.

"Um, hmm," Anne said to Bud, as she strained to hear what Leslie was saying to Doug.

"I understand that you have a fabulous barn at your farm that Peter Burns built," Leslie said.

"Yes, I do, but how do you know that?" Doug asked.

"I just hired Peter to build a barn at my place, and he said he would try to arrange a time when I could see yours to get some ideas. Of course, I won't be building anything nearly as grand as what you have, but he still thought it might be helpful for me to take a look at what he did for you. He probably wants to show off a little." Leslie flashed a smile at Doug.

"Well, you made a good choice. Peter did a great job for me. And you're welcome to come over any time to take a look."

"Gee, thanks." Leslie looked at her watch. "You're not going over there now by any chance, are you? I'm finished up here, unless Anne has something else for me to do."

Doug nodded. "I'm headed over there right now." He glanced out the window. "Actually, the weather's so nice today; it would be a great day for a hack. You're welcome to come along if you like."

"I'd love to," Leslie said, ignoring the glare Anne gave her. "I just need to make sure Anne doesn't need me for anything."

"Bud, can I call you right back?" Anne asked. "Great." She hung up the phone.

"Anne, I've taken your advice and decided to go out for a ride, and Leslie here has graciously agreed to come along and keep me company. That is, unless you need her here for something," Doug said, smiling at Leslie.

Anne felt the color rise in her cheeks. "How kind of you to invite her, Doug. Leslie, why don't you come into my office; we'll see how the afternoon schedule looks."

Anne ushered Leslie into her office and all but slammed the door behind her. "Just what do you think you are up to?" she demanded.

"What do you mean?" Leslie asked.

"You know very well what I mean, Leslie. I already spoke to you once today about your behavior towards Doug Cummings, I shouldn't have to repeat myself." Anne's voice shook with anger.

"Wait a minute, Anne, that's not fair," Leslie replied. "You were talking about my demeanor in the office, not what I do on my own time."

"Have you forgotten that he's a client?"

"He's your client, not mine. I don't see anything wrong there," Leslie responded.

Anne tried to remain calm. "You may be right that it's technically not an ethical violation, but I don't like it. It doesn't look right. Besides that, Leslie, he's a client here for a reason. He's likely to be charged with murder."

Leslie's eyes widened. "Are you saying that you think he's guilty?"

"Come on, Leslie, you know I would never say that about any client. But it's another reason that I think it would be a mistake for you to go out with him."

"I'm not going out with him. We're just going riding." Leslie stared defiantly at Anne. "Are you going to tell me that I can't go?"

"No, I'm not, but I strongly advise against it."

"Will it affect my future here?"

Anne hesitated. "No," she said finally.

"Okay, then, I'm going." Leslie stood up and went to the door. "I'm sorry if you're upset, Anne, but I do have a right to a life away from here and right now I can't think of anything I'd rather do than spend the rest of the day with Doug Cummings. He's gorgeous and charming, and I can assure you he's no murderer. I'll be perfectly safe." She left Anne's office door open when she walked out.

"Is everything okay?" Anne heard Doug ask.

"Sure, it's fine. Let's go." Leslie replied.

Anne watched out her office window as they walked to their cars. Leslie laughed at something and grabbed Doug's arm, and he smiled back at her. Anne felt a surge of jealousy and backed away from the window.

"Cyndi?" she called out. "Could you please call the Sheriff's Office and get Deputy Dickson on the phone for me?"

Clyde was still angry as he sat at his desk that afternoon waiting for Anne Sullivan to arrive. The only one who seemed to have the guts to go after Cummings was the *News* reporter, Eric Schultz. Everyone else seemed scared to confront him. Especially the sheriff. The sheriff had ordered him to back off of Doug Cummings, at least publicly, and refused to let him go after an arrest warrant. In fact, Sheriff Boling had reamed him out.

"Goddamn it, Clyde. I told you how high the political stakes are for me on this. What the hell do you think you're doing, going after Doug Cummings? He's Middleburg's golden boy for Christ's sake."

"So what? Does that mean that he should be above the law?" Clyde asked.

"It means you better be damned certain before you start throwing his name around."

"I didn't throw it around. I just came to you with it and suggested that we get a warrant."

"You didn't throw it around? You leaked it to the media."

"No, sir, I didn't," Clyde lied. "I did not give Doug Cummings' name to the media."

The sheriff glared at him. "Oh, yeah? Then how come it keeps showing up in *The Washington News*?"

Clyde took a deep breath. "That's what I'm trying to tell you, Sheriff. I'm not the only one who thinks Doug Cummings might be responsible for these murders. I have a statement from the hunt secretary saying so. And I'm sure there are others. But everyone's afraid of saying so publicly because of who Cummings is. I know it seems like a political risk, but think of the rewards when you turn out to be right."

"*If* I turn out to be right," the sheriff replied. He looked at Clyde thoughtfully for a moment. "You come back to me with more evidence, and maybe I'll reconsider. But for now, keep his name out of it."

"Are you telling me to redirect my investigation?"

"I'm telling you that the heat is on for you to solve these murders. I won't tell you who to go after or not to go after. Just keep Cummings' name out of it. For now."

Clyde threw a pencil down on his desk and looked at his watch. Where the hell was she? The sheriff was due back in an hour and he didn't want Boling to see him talking with Anne Sullivan.

Then he noticed a pretty blond lady come in the office and saw the deputy out front point in his direction. It must be Anne Sullivan. As he watched her approach, Clyde wondered what kind of woman could spend her life representing killers like Doug Cummings.

Clyde didn't bother to rise when Anne introduced herself. He indicated the chair next to his desk and reached in his pocket for his tobacco.

Anne Sullivan seated herself and put her briefcase on his desk. "I know you're a busy man, Deputy, so I'll be brief. I'm here today because you have been harassing my client, Doug Cummings, and issuing false and misleading statements to the media."

"I haven't issued any statements to the media," he said.

"Yes, you have, Deputy. And please don't interrupt me. I wasn't finished. You issued false and misleading statements to the media and threatened to arrest him. As I know you are aware, Mr. Cummings pledged his full cooperation to you in helping to find Nancy Williams' killer and, of course, the same holds true as to Babs Tyler. Instead of working with him, however, you have chosen to wage a media war against him. You and I both know that you don't have sufficient evidence against my client to get a warrant, or you would have arrested him by now."

Clyde straightened up in his chair and glared at her. God, he hated women lawyers. If you stood up to them, they accused you of discrimination. If you didn't, the guys said you were pussy-whipped. "Oh, I have evidence all right, plenty of it. I'll arrest Cummings; it's just a matter of time," he replied.

"Really?" she said, with an annoying smile. "The way I figure it, your only evidence as to Nancy Williams is that Doug Cummings was alone when he found her in the woods, and he happened to have recently terminated a personal relationship with her."

"Alone when he found her? Alone when he killed her you mean. No one's going to believe that cockamamie story of his that he moved Williams to try to get help reviving her." Clyde shook his head. "You don't move someone with a neck injury. Everyone knows that. Cummings moved Nancy Williams to cover up the fact that he had murdered her. Plain and simple."

"Nice theory," Anne replied. "But it's pure speculation. Maybe you can enlighten me and explain how that adds up to probable cause for murder."

"Well, now, that might not, if that was all I had. But I've got more." Clyde leaned forward and spit into his wastebasket then settled back into his chair. "Try this on for size. I have a sworn statement from the hunt secretary, Wendy Brooks, that Cummings was in a bad mood during the hunt on the day that Williams was murdered and that Williams and Cummings left the hunt together that day to ride back through those woods. So they could talk about their relationship." He smiled. "And there was an EMT on the scene, Kathy Morris, who will testify that she heard Cummings tell Williams' corpse that he was sorry." He paused for effect. "I also interviewed Babs Tyler, and she told me that Cummings said that Nancy Williams was still alive when he found her in the woods." Clyde made an exaggerated effort at shaking his head. "Too bad for Babs Tyler that she told me that, though. That's what got her murdered."

"Why do you say that?"

"Why, I saw it with my own two eyes. When I told Cummings that Tyler had talked to me about Nancy Williams' death, he about blew his top. It was no coincidence that she turned up missing the next day. It also doesn't look too good for your boy that he didn't show up like he was supposed to at the hunt that morning, the day that Tyler disappeared."

Clyde couldn't keep himself from hammering her with more damaging news. Scott Brady, the medical examiner, had called him shortly before Anne Sullivan had arrived, and informed him that he thought it was likely both Babs Tyler and Nancy Williams were beaten by the same type of object. Brady couldn't say for certain that the same weapon was used on both victims, but he felt there was no doubt that their beating wounds were substantially similar in nature.

"Oh, one more thing, Miss Sullivan. It seems that the same murder weapon was used on both of these victims. I'd say that makes Doug

Cummings' connection to these two women rather significant, wouldn't you? It's also a well known fact that Babs Tyler and Nancy Williams didn't get along very well. In fact, I have one witness who says that she saw the two of them in a cat fight at the hunt meet one day, and it was over Doug Cummings." Clyde winked at her. "I guess maybe the love triangle just got out of hand."

Anne Sullivan shrugged her shoulders. "All of that is very interesting, but what about some real evidence that connects my client to these two murders. Do you have any of that?" she asked.

Clyde's face turned red. What a bitch. "Look, lady, that's about as real as you can get."

She flashed him a smile. "No, not really. I mean hard evidence. Something that a judge or jury might pay attention to. Like prints, fiber, hair, stuff like that."

"Oh, I'll give you plenty of evidence. I'm just waiting on the results from forensics," Clyde responded.

Anne smirked, and stood up. "Thanks for your time, Deputy Dickson. I found your theories fascinating."

CHAPTER
33

If Doug had not already been mounted on his horse when he saw the photographers arrive at the hunt meet, he would have loaded Chancellor back on the trailer and left. Now, there was no way for him to get out of there without being seen. He saw Richard Evan Clarke across the paddock and rode over to him, staying out of the way of the cameras.

"Richard, I seem to be a walking magnet for the media these days, and they're out here in full force this morning," Doug said, pointing the photographers out to the master. "The last thing I want is for you or the Hunt to suffer from my negative publicity. What do you want me to do?"

Richard looked long and hard at Doug before answering him. "Doug, my friend, let's get one thing straight. I am and always will be proud to have you as a member of this Hunt, and I will stand by you no matter how rocky the road ahead. I appreciate your concern, but you need not trouble yourself with how this might affect the Hunt. Believe me, we'll come through it just fine. Now, having said that, I think we should cast the hounds a tad early today and head for the Bellevue Woods." He climbed up on his horse and motioned to the huntsman to get under way.

Smitty blew his horn and cast the hounds, and the master and Doug followed close behind. The early departure took most of the riders by surprise and Richard waited briefly at the entrance to the Bellevue Woods for the rest of the field to catch up. Doug smiled as he saw the photographers run back to their vehicles. They'd have little chance of following the hunt by car in this territory.

Although the Bellevue Woods was usually not the best hunting territory around, that morning was an exception. The hounds hit a line right away and

Richard led the field after them through the winding trails in the woods. The terrain was steep and Doug was glad that he was riding Chancellor. Huntley would have had a hard time keeping up.

As Doug hunted up front with Richard, he admired the master's ability to follow the hounds by sound alone. The hounds were far off to their left, out of sight, but their music filtered across the woods to the field. Richard had the field properly positioned, even though it wasn't good viewing territory.

They galloped on for ten minutes or so and when they rounded a bend, Doug could see bright sunlight ahead. They had reached the edge of the woods, and Doug followed right behind Richard as they galloped into a large open pasture. Doug recognized the territory. They were at Homestead Farm.

Richard halted his horse and held his hand up, signaling for the field to follow suit. "Hold hard." Riders quietly passed the word along to those behind them. The cry of the hounds was still faintly audible, far off in the woods. Doug watched Richard as he listened and scanned the tree line up ahead. No one spoke.

Then Richard took off his hunt cap and pointed just as a large red fox burst out of the woods and ran across the pasture in front of them, followed a few moments later by the hounds. "Tallyho!" someone called out, and the field was off and running again.

As Doug started off after the master, he noticed that one of the riders was having trouble with her horse and had dismounted. He pulled Chancellor up and rode over to help her.

"Is everything okay?" Doug asked.

The woman looked at him and got back up on her horse. "Yes, it's fine, thanks. He just has a loose shoe." She started off back towards the rest of the field, her horse clearly lame at the trot.

Doug trotted up to her. "Wait. He looks pretty sore. Let me see if I can pull the shoe."

"No, I said he's fine. Please, just leave me be." Her voice was shrill and she quickened her horse's pace.

"No, he's not. He's lame. Why won't you let me . . . ?" Doug stopped in mid-sentence. He understood. The woman didn't want to be alone with him. He pulled his horse up and let her catch up with the others on her own. He didn't blame her for her reaction. Anyone who had read the papers recently had good reason to be afraid of him. Doug waited until the woman had reached the field before he cantered up to join them.

The fox went to ground in a thicket twenty minutes later and the field checked while Smitty called in the hounds. They were at the edge of Foxfield Farm, which bordered Hunting Hollow on the back side, and Doug decided to hack home, rather than go back to the trailers where the photographers were probably waiting. He paid his respects to Richard and set off through the woods towards his farm.

The air was crisp but the sun warmed him, and Doug was in no hurry. He slowed to a walk and gave Chancellor a loose rein. The hunt had been good therapy. He was glad he had gone. He drew in a deep breath of clean autumn air and let it out slowly. He felt relaxed for the first time in days and smiled as he thought of the famous quote of Winston Churchill. "There's something about the outside of a horse that is good for the inside of a man." Amen.

When Doug rode up to his barn and dismounted, he saw Billy walking Junior, one of Doug's yearlings. The young horse was lathered with sweat and breathing hard.

"What's going on, Billy? Is something wrong with Junior?"

"I'm sorry, Mr. Cummings, it's my fault. I had him tied on in his stall while I was grooming him, then I went out to get a curry comb. The next thing I knew, Junior came racing out of the stall and ran right past me out of the barn. It took me almost twenty minutes to catch him, that's why he's so hot. He didn't do nothing to hurt himself though, I checked him all over."

Doug handed Chancellor to Billy and checked over the colt himself, agreeing that he looked fine. "I should have warned you about him, Billy. Junior is an escape artist, and, as I recall, chewing on lead ropes and halters has always been a favorite pastime of his. He's just one of those clever thoroughbreds who's too smart for his own good and is always getting himself into trouble."

Billy hooked Chancellor up to the crossties in the wash rack then took Junior from Doug. "Like I said, Mr. Cummings, I'm real sorry. It won't happen again."

Doug smiled at the boy. "It's forgotten, Billy, and, please, call me Doug. I've been trying to get your father to do that for years." He grabbed a bottle of Evian and sat on a hay bale, watching as Billy gave Chancellor a rubdown.

"So, how are things going for you, Billy? Did the note I left you adequately explain the routine around here?" Doug asked.

Billy looked down at the ground and mumbled, "Yeah, I guess so. I ain't really had time to read all of it."

"Okay, why don't we go over it when you finish up with Chancellor, and you can let me know if you have questions about anything."

The boy nodded halfheartedly, not looking at Doug.

"Is something wrong, Billy?"

Billy frowned and nodded. "Yeah, Mr. Cummings, it is. I guess I should have told you right off, but I don't read and write so good. I'm sorry. I was waiting for my father to come and help me read your note."

Billy's answer caught Doug by surprise. He knew the statistics about rising illiteracy rates, but it was still shocking to him that a student could go through school and still not know how to read. Doug thought it over. "Billy, I think I have a solution for you. Nellie is the best English teacher I know. I still remember her drilling me about my grammar when I was in school. I know she'd be happy to teach you, and it would help her too, by giving her something to do. I think she's been pretty lonely lately." He paused, studying the boy. "Billy, you are a hard worker and you have a great future ahead of you, but there are a lot of doors that will never open if you aren't able to read and write. You can learn; I know you can. Please let Nellie help you."

Billy looked at him. "Do you really think so?"

"I know so, Billy. I'll be happy to ask Nellie if you like, but I think it would mean more to her coming from you."

"No, that's okay. I can ask her." Billy put a wool cooler on Chancellor. "Thanks, Mr. Cummings," he said, as he walked the horse out of the barn.

"Doug," Doug said, smiling at him.

"Doug," Billy repeated, smiling back.

Doug looked at his watch and decided he'd better get on his way to Anne Sullivan's office.

He followed Billy outside. "Billy, I've got to get to a meeting. Have you driven a truck and trailer before?"

"Oh, sure, lots of times. A horse van too."

"Great. After you finish with Chancellor, could you get your father to drive you to the hunt meet and bring the Range Rover and trailer back here?"

"Sure," Billy replied.

"The keys are in the ignition and it's parked at Willow Grove Farm, in the pasture on the right, just after the main drive. Do you know where that is?" Doug asked.

"Yes, sir, I'll find it no problem; don't you worry."

"Thanks. I don't know yet if I'll be hunting again this week, but if I do,

I'll take Huntley. I'll let you know for sure tomorrow."

Doug got into his Porsche and waved to Billy as he headed up the drive. He had kept the front gates closed and locked, and as he slowed down to open them, he saw a television crew waiting on the other side. He spotted the PNN logo emblazoned on their camera. *Premier News Network.*

Doug hesitated. If he'd been in the Range Rover, he would have turned around and used the farm road to get out the back way, but that wasn't an option in the Porsche. The terrain was far too rough. He turned off the car and got out, pocketing the keys. He unlocked the gates and tried to swing them open, but was blocked by the van, parked on the other side. The crew consisted of two women, one carrying a microphone, and a man dressed in jeans and a canvas jacket, who looked at him through the lens of a television camera.

One of the women stuck a microphone in Doug's face and the cameraman hovered off to the side. "Mr. Cummings, what can you tell us about the deaths of Nancy Williams and Babs Tyler?" the woman asked.

Doug opened the gates enough to squeeze through and put up a hand to shield himself from the camera. "You are trespassing on private property; I'm asking you to turn off that camera and get off my property."

Their only reaction was to back up slightly, shifting with Doug as he moved forward. The woman shoved the microphone back in Doug's face, the camera still rolling. "Mr. Cummings, how do you respond to the recent allegations that you are the one responsible for the murders of Nancy Williams and Babs Tyler?"

Doug reached out and shoved the camera so the lens pointed towards the ground. "I said, please turn off the camera and leave my property."

The woman reporter continued to hold the microphone in front of his face. "Mr. Cummings, is it true that you and Babs Tyler had a disagreement the night before she disappeared?"

Doug was a half foot taller than the cameraman, and he grabbed the camera from the man and held it high over his head, out of the cameraman's reach. "You obviously didn't understand me when I asked nicely, so I'll have to communicate in a way that you can relate to."

The man backed away, his hands in the air, shrieking at Doug, "Don't break it, man, just calm down, I'll turn it off. Just don't break the fucking camera."

Doug waved the camera slightly, threatening to throw it if anyone came near, and climbed into the PNN van. The keys were in the ignition, as he had suspected they would be, and Doug started the van and backed up onto the road, sending the gravel flying. The PNN crew ran after him and pounded on the van door. But they jumped back as the van lurched forward and stood screaming obscenities as Doug drove out of sight down the country road.

Doug pulled over about a half-mile up the road, intending to leave the van there. He looked at his watch. If he walked back for his car, he'd be even later than he already was for his meeting with Anne Sullivan. He put the van in gear again. He'd drive it to Anne's office, and then have it returned to the crew.

The mood was tense in Anne's office. Leslie had been in a foul mood all morning. Anne was worried that it had something to do with her riding date with Doug Cummings the previous day. She knocked on Leslie's office door.

"Come in."

Leslie was sitting at her desk. "Leslie, I don't mean to pry, but do you mind my asking what's bothering you?" Anne asked.

Leslie scowled at her. "Nothing. I just got up on the wrong side of bed, that's all."

"Alone?"

Leslie just looked at her.

"Look, Leslie, I don't want to rehash what we talked about yesterday, but I think I have a right to know if your foul temper has anything to do with Doug Cummings. He's due here for a meeting. I don't want to be caught in the middle if something unpleasant happened between the two of you."

"Don't worry, Anne. It was just the opposite. That's the problem. Nothing happened. Nothing at all."

Anne let out a sigh. "Good. I think that's for the best, Leslie, for everyone."

"That's easy for you to say," Leslie responded, a pouty frown on her face. "I was so sure he was interested in me. We had a fabulous afternoon, and he took me to the Black Coffee Bistro for dinner. We had a bottle of wine and sat and talked for hours. Then he offered to drive me home, since I was a little tipsy, and you know what happened? I got a peck on the cheek. Period. I felt like I was on a date with my brother. He was a perfect gentleman, said how much he had enjoyed it and that we should do it again some time, but I know he'll never call me."

They were interrupted by Cyndi, calling out from the front office. "Anne, come and look at this."

They rushed up front and joined Cyndi at the window, just in time to see Doug Cummings get out of the driver's side of a *Premier News Network* van, parked in front of Anne's office.

Doug waved when he saw them at the window and hurried up to the front door. "Good morning, ladies; sorry I'm late. May I use your phone?"

Without waiting for a reply, he picked up the phone on Cyndi's desk and quickly pressed the numbers. "Billy, I'm glad I caught you before you left to get the trailer. There's been a slight change of plans. My car is sitting at the top of the driveway; you can find keys for it in the tack room. I need you to bring it to me, if you could. I'm at Anne Sullivan's law office in Aldie. Right on Route Fifty, near the Little River Inn. I have a vehicle here that I need you to drive to Middleburg. John can meet you there. Oh, and one more thing. If you see some reporters waiting by the gate, offer to call them a cab."

He hung up and turned to Anne. "I really am sorry I'm late. I ran into a little bit of a roadblock."

Anne shook her head. "Something tells me I don't want to hear this, Doug."

"Why?" He held his hands up innocently. "I didn't do anything wrong. A television crew was blocking my drive and I couldn't get out, so I borrowed their van to drive over here."

"Oh, great. Please don't tell me they got the whole thing on film."

He grinned. "Well, they did, but when I turned the camera off for them I somehow managed to erase the tape."

"You know you're probably going to get slapped with a suit over this. I don't see PNN letting this slide," Anne said.

Doug shrugged. "That's what I have you for."

Anne hated that cocky attitude. "No, Doug, it's not. You retained me as your criminal attorney, not your baby sitter. And you're not making my job any easier by creating negative publicity for yourself." She took a deep breath. "The judge and jury are not the only ones whom you'll be tried by, Doug. You'd better not forget about the court of public opinion. If you want to save your reputation and get on with your life once this is all over, you'd better start caring about what image you portray to the media."

Doug scowled. "Fine. I apologize. The next time I find the media trespassing on my property, I'll be nice and civil and invite them in for tea. Will that make you happy?"

"What would make me happy . . ." Anne stopped and bit back her retort. "Forget it. Never mind. Let's drop that subject. What's done is done. Why don't we go into the conference room. I'll fill you in on my meeting with Deputy Dickson."

Doug followed her without a word.

They sat down and Anne briefly summarized her meeting with Clyde Dickson the previous day. "I was basically pleased with what I found out. Number one, he doesn't have enough for an arrest warrant, at least not now. But that's not to say he's not still working on it. His theory, as you read in the *News*, is that you, Nancy, and Babs were involved in some sort of love triangle and, when things got out of hand, you murdered them. As far as I know, that theory is based on one witness' statement that Nancy and Babs didn't get along very well and had been seen having a fight over you."

She looked through her notes. "He made a couple of factual allegations that don't fit with your version of what happened, so let's go through those first. Apparently, he has a statement from Wendy Brooks, the hunt secretary, that you were angry with Nancy Williams at the hunt on the day that she was murdered. Do you recall anything like that?"

"No. Definitely not. I wasn't angry with anyone. I do recall being cold and wet, and anxious to get back to the office. I suppose I wasn't in the best mood, but it wasn't directed at anyone in particular, most certainly not Nancy," Doug replied.

"Wendy Brooks apparently also said that you and Nancy left the hunt field at the same time that day. Is that true?"

Doug stared at her. "Are you serious?"

Anne nodded. "Yes. Dickson claims that's in her statement."

He frowned. "Anne, that's absolutely not true. I left alone. I didn't see anyone from the time I left the field until I found Nancy lying in the clearing. Why would Wendy say that?"

"I don't know, Doug, but it's a problem for us. Let's talk it through. Were the two of you riding together at all that day?"

Doug shook his head. "No. Nancy was riding with the hilltoppers. I went first flight. We spoke briefly at a check, right before I left. But that was it."

"If she had followed after you when you left, would you have noticed?" Anne asked.

"That depends on how far away she was." He frowned. "It's always bothered me, though, the fact that she was hacking home alone. That's something that Nancy normally would not do. Maybe she did follow after me. As I recall, I was going at a pretty good pace that day. Nancy probably wouldn't have been going fast enough to catch up with me."

"Okay, let's leave that until I can get a look at Wendy Brooks' statement to see just exactly how she described it." Anne consulted her notes. "Dickson also says he has a statement from someone named Kathy Morris who claims that she heard you tell Nancy you were sorry. Back at the hunt meet. After you knew that Nancy was dead."

Doug shook his head, a puzzled look on his face. "I really have no idea what she's talking about, Anne."

"Do you remember this Kathy Morris being there?" Anne asked.

"Sure. She's an EMT. She was at Chadwick Hall when I arrived there with Nancy. She examined Nancy and tried to help, but it was too late."

"But you don't recall saying anything along those lines to Nancy?" Anne asked again.

Doug shook his head again. "No, I honestly don't. I guess that I could have. I *was* sorry. Sorry that she was dead. Sorry that I hadn't been able to save her. Sorry that our relationship hadn't worked out."

"Do you remember if Kathy made any comment to you about Nancy's death?" Anne asked.

"Yes. She said that it wasn't my fault and that I had done all that I could to help Nancy. I appreciated her saying it, because at the time I was uncertain whether I had been right to move Nancy."

Anne nodded. "Dickson mentioned that. His theory is that everyone knows not to move someone with a head or neck injury and that you moved Nancy to hide the fact that you murdered her."

"He's got an explanation for everything, doesn't he?"

"Yes, he does." Anne checked her notes again. "He also claims Babs told him that you said Nancy was still alive when you found her."

Doug stared at her. "That's simply not true. I never said that. I may have said that I tried to save her, but I never said that she was alive when I found her."

"Speaking of Babs, let's move on to her. Dickson says that on the night before Babs disappeared, he saw you get extremely angry at Babs for having spoken with him about Nancy Williams' death. He thinks that was your motive to murder her. He also pointed out that you were supposed to be at the hunt on the morning that Babs disappeared, but that you never showed up. His theory, of course, is that you were either busy committing the murder or hiding the body."

Doug scowled. "That's bullshit. I wasn't angry at Babs; I was just surprised to learn that she had talked to Dickson. As far as the hunt the next day, the reason I wasn't there was that my horse wouldn't load on the trailer. I already went over that with you."

"Calm down, Doug. I'm not questioning what you already told me, I'm simply telling you what Dickson's theory is. May I continue?"

Doug shrugged, not bothering to answer.

"The only other bit of new information I was able to get from Dickson is that Nancy and Babs were allegedly beaten with the same object. That eliminates the possibility that they were both random, unrelated murders, and bolsters Dickson's theory that the murderer is someone who had a close connection with both of the women, i.e., you. Of course, that's just his theory and, as far as I know, he has no murder weapon and no other physical evidence linking the murders to you." Anne glanced at her notes one more time, then put her legal pad down.

Doug stared at her. "Do you mean to tell me that Nancy and Babs were actually murdered by the same person?"

"If the same murder weapon was in fact used on both of them, I'd say there is little doubt," Anne responded.

"My God, Anne, that means there really is some lunatic out there who killed both those women. If he has already killed twice, it's likely he will again."

Anne didn't understand Doug's reaction. Was he trying to tell her something? She measured her words carefully. "You sound surprised by that, Doug. Haven't you known all along that they were killed by someone?"

"Sure, of course. But I never really believed that the two deaths were connected."

"Why not?"

"I don't know," he said. "I just thought that was a bogus theory. That Dickson was searching for some way to connect them both to me and not focusing on trying to find out what really happened."

"What did you think had really happened?"

Doug paused briefly. "I guess I thought maybe some deer hunters killed

Nancy. As for Babs, I really don't know. I don't know anything about her lifestyle or who she hung out with, but I guess I thought maybe she went home with someone she shouldn't have and got into trouble."

"What do you think now?" Anne asked.

He shook his head. "I just can't see a connection. Nancy and Babs really didn't have much contact with any of the same people, except me of course. But someone better come up with something soon, before this guy strikes again."

"We don't know that it was a man, Doug. Women can kill too. But at any rate, it's Dickson's job to find the killer. My role is to make sure that the evidence doesn't implicate you."

Doug glared at her. "Oh, that's right, I forgot. Nancy and Babs didn't mean anything to you. You criminal lawyers aren't concerned about truth or justice. Your job is just to create reasonable doubt."

Anne's face flushed with anger, but before she could respond, the door burst open and Samantha came running in. "Aunt Anne, look at what I made in school today." Samantha climbed up onto Anne's lap and proudly displayed a construction paper turkey.

Anne told the little girl how beautiful the turkey was then turned to Samantha's nanny, Ingrid, and quietly explained that they had interrupted a meeting and asked her to take Samantha out.

"No, I don't want to leave," Samantha whined. "You said we could have lunch together today. Ingrid and I brought a picnic from the bakery to have with you."

"Okay, sweetie, we can do that later. You just go and play for a little while. I'll come and have a picnic with you when I finish my meeting with Mr. Cummings," Anne said, trying to hand the struggling girl to Ingrid.

"Come on, Samantha. You and I can go downstairs and make a picnic in the basement, and your Aunt Anne can come down when she is finished," Ingrid said kindly, reaching her arms out.

Samantha pulled away from the nanny and clung to Anne. "No. I'm hungry now. I want to have the picnic here while you have your meeting."

Anne turned to Doug in apology, as she stood to carry Samantha from the room. "Excuse me, I'll be right back."

"Wait, Anne," Doug said. "I think it's time for a break anyway. Why don't you eat lunch with Samantha? That's fine with me."

Samantha turned to Doug, smiling. "You can eat with us too. We brought lots of food."

He smiled at her in return. "That's very nice of you, Samantha, but I think your Aunt Anne would probably like to spend some time alone with you. Maybe we can have a picnic some other day."

"Uh-uh. Aunt Anne doesn't care if you eat with us, and it will be more like a real picnic if we have more people. Please say yes. We have cookies and everything."

Doug looked over the girl's head at Anne and raised an eyebrow.

"Samantha, it's fine with me if Mr. Cummings joins us for lunch one day, but I don't think he has time in his schedule today. He's very busy and we have a meeting we need to finish."

Samantha looked imploringly at Doug. "It won't take that long. We can eat real fast, and then I can help you with the meeting if you want me to."

Doug laughed. "Now that's an offer that's hard to refuse."

"Goodie," Samantha said, jumping down from Anne's arms. She reached for the white paper bags and began setting out all the food. Samantha jabbered happily with Doug throughout lunch, and Anne was happy not to have to make conversation.

Anne finished eating first and excused herself to make a few phone calls. When she returned, she found Samantha sitting on top of the conference table in front of Doug, laughing at whatever Doug was telling her. Ingrid sat in the chair next to him, smiling.

Anne walked over to the table. "Hey, guys, what are you doing?" she asked.

"We're pretending we're sitting in front of the camp fire, and Doug is telling us scary stories. Come on and listen, Aunt Anne," Samantha pleaded.

"I can't right now, Samantha. Mr. Cummings and I need to get back to work." Anne looked disapprovingly at Doug. "Besides, I don't think it's a very good idea for you to listen to scary stories. You might have a bad dream."

"Oh, no, Aunt Anne. They're not that scary. Just one more? Please?"

"No, Samantha. We gave in to you and had the picnic. No more begging. Enough is enough. I have to get back to work."

"Oh, okay." Samantha reluctantly climbed down from the table into Doug's lap. "Thank you for the fun picnic and stories, Doug. I really like you. I hope we can play again." She reached up and gave him a tight hug around his neck.

Doug tousled Samantha's hair affectionately. "I hope so too, Samantha."

Samantha kissed Anne good-bye then grabbed Ingrid's hand and skipped out of the room.

Doug rose and held Anne's chair out for her while she sat down. "She's quite a little girl. She must bring you a lot of joy."

Anne nodded. "Samantha is very special. She has been with me a relatively short time, but I can't imagine my life without her. I often worry about the scars that the death of her parents has left on her, but I think she is adjusting quite well so far."

"She seems to be very well adjusted, not to mention perceptive," Doug said with a slight grin.

"Why do you say that?" Anne asked.

"Because she figured out that I'm a good guy and that it's okay to like me, which is more than I can say about the other member of her family."

Anne felt herself blush. "Can we get back to work?"

"Why? Why does that make you uncomfortable? You know it's true." Doug leaned on the edge of the table, close to her. "I know that in the kind of law you practice, you don't care whether or not your client is a good guy or a bad guy. In fact, I assume you'd rather not know. But I also know that it's human nature to put in a little extra effort, go the extra mile, for the clients that you like. And, quite frankly, it really bothers me that you don't like me."

Anne avoided his gaze. "That's not true that I don't like you, Doug, and I can assure you that I will represent you to the fullest extent of my ability. I'm sorry that you think otherwise."

"Oh, come on, Anne. This isn't about your ability as a lawyer to represent me. If I had doubts about that, I'd change attorneys in a heartbeat. I'm talking about your personal attitude towards me, which from the day I met you at Sallie Rogers' dinner party, has ranged from frosty to hostile." Doug sat down and pushed his chair back, resting the toe of one riding boot casually on the edge of the conference table.

It was obvious to Anne that Doug wasn't going to drop the subject, but she didn't know how to respond. She looked down at the table, avoiding his gaze, and an embarrassing moment passed where the only sound was the clicking of her pen top, on and off.

"Well?" Doug said.

"Well, what?" Anne replied.

"I'd like to know if I've done something to offend you."

"Look, you're right," she finally replied. "I have been unfriendly, maybe even rude at times, and I apologize for that. It's hard for me to explain why. I really don't have any animosity towards you personally, Doug. I guess that your type just seems to bring out the worst in me sometimes."

"My type? What is that?" Doug asked.

"Doug, please. Let's get back to work."

"I want to know."

Anne sighed. "Fine. Do you really want me to spell it out?"

Doug nodded.

"Come on, Doug. It's not as if you don't know. You cultivate the image. A carefree playboy. No, correction, a rich, carefree playboy. No responsibilities. No ties. Able to talk your way or buy your way out of any situation." Anne tried to keep her tone even, but she knew her disdain shone through.

Doug sat up in his chair. "Well, I appreciate your brutal honesty, Anne, but you couldn't be more wrong. If that's my reputation, it's undeserved. If it's just your perception, I'd suggest you make an effort to get to know people a little better before you jump to conclusions like that. You never know what you might be missing."

Doug stood up and put his hunt coat on. "I hope you don't mind if we call it a day. I'm exhausted and I think we've already covered everything we need to." He nodded curtly at Anne and walked to the door. "Keep up the good work, Counselor. You know where to find me if you need me."

Anne stared after him. Oh, God. Had she really just talked that way to a client?

She quickly rose and rushed to the hallway just in time to see Doug walk out the front door. She hesitated for a moment, debating whether to follow him outside and apologize.

Leslie's voice broke into her thoughts. "My, Doug sure stormed out of here in a hurry. Is everything all right?"

Leslie stood by Cyndi's desk, right next to the conference room. She had a strange smile on her face and Anne wondered if she had heard their exchange.

Anne felt her cheeks burn. "Yes, Leslie, everything's fine." She turned back into the conference room, closed the door, and sat down in the chair Doug had occupied. There was a smudge of dirt on the conference table where his boot had rested and she reached out and gently wiped it off.

Who did she think she was fooling? She knew what her attitude towards Doug was really about. There was no use denying it. She was attracted to him and had been since the first night she'd met him. Not that anything would ever come of it. He was her client. She would never cross that line. But she was falling for him nonetheless.

She sighed and leaned her head against the back of the chair. Even if Doug weren't her client, she had no room in her life for a man like him. Especially now that she had custody of Samantha. Samantha needed stability. A father figure. And that was something Doug Cummings definitely was not.

CHAPTER

35

Sharon Duncan was sitting at her desk in the news room when Doug Cummings called.

"I'd like to talk to you about a story that I think you might be interested in," Doug said. "Could we meet somewhere?"

"S-sure. Right now?"

"Whenever you can get away. The sooner the better."

"Okay," Sharon said, trying to keep the excitement out of her voice. "I can get away now, if you like. You name the place."

"How about if we meet in the bar at the Landsdowne Resort in thirty minutes?"

"Fine," Sharon replied. "I'll see you there."

Doug was seated at a table in the far corner when Sharon arrived. He rose and pulled out the chair across from him, waiting for Sharon to be seated before settling back down.

"Would you like something to drink?" he asked.

Sharon looked across the table and saw a bottle of Perrier in front of Doug. "Just a Coke please," she replied.

Doug signaled the waitress and placed the order.

"Pepsi okay?" the waitress asked.

Sharon nodded. "That's fine."

Doug waited until the waitress was beyond earshot then leaned forward in his chair.

"What I'm about to tell you is off the record. I don't want to be quoted or identified as your source. Is that agreeable?" He spoke quietly.

Sharon swallowed hard. "Agreed," she replied.

"Okay." Doug picked up a pack of hotel matches off the table and fingered them, flipping the cover open and shut. "Stop me if you've already heard this. I'm not sure how much Dickson has leaked at this point."

Sharon nodded.

"The medical examiner has determined that the same murder weapon was used on Nancy Williams and Babs Tyler. That means that they were both killed by the same person." He paused, looking Sharon squarely in the eye. "That person was not me."

Sharon started to protest that she had never suspected him of the murders, but Doug held his hand up and stopped her.

"I wasn't implying that you did, Sharon. That's not the issue. Please, let me continue." He smiled at her and she nodded again, her hands clasped tightly on the table in front of her.

"Dickson and the news media are obviously focusing on the angle that I am the murderer and that Nancy and Babs died as the result of some kind of personal relationship that they had with me. And, as long as that is what people are hearing or reading, they won't have any concern for their own safety," Doug said, setting the matches down.

"Okay," Sharon said. "Go on."

"I think someone should write a story that will make people—women—aware of what's going on. Someone needs to warn them in a way that will make them listen, make them take precautions for their own safety." He looked closely at her, as if trying to read her reaction. "You know that won't be an easy sell, Sharon. We're talking about Middleburg for Christ's sake. People go riding alone. And they go to their barns alone at all hours of the day and night. They feel safe here. Most of them don't even lock their doors."

Sharon shook her head slightly. "Mr. Cummings, it sounds like you are asking me to sensationalize this. To write a story just to get everyone all riled up about these murders."

"I just want you to present the facts in a way that will make people realize what's happening here," Doug replied. "And, by doing so, maybe you'll help save someone from being this guy's next victim."

The waitress appeared with Sharon's drink and Doug leaned back in his chair. Sharon didn't know how to respond. She realized that what Doug Cummings was asking her to do could just be a clever ploy intended to turn the attention away from him. But she didn't think so. Her instincts told her that he was innocent. He was right about one thing, though. The locals hadn't been warned that there might be a serial killer in the area. And as far as she knew, the fact that the same murder weapon was used on both women had not yet been released. She could break that story and at the same time warn people to be more careful. There certainly wasn't any harm in that.

"Okay," Sharon said. "I don't know if it'll help, but I'll write the story."

"Thank you," Doug said, letting out a sigh.

Sharon studied him for a moment. "Mr. Cummings, can I ask you a personal question?"

"What's that?" Doug asked.

"Why are you asking me to do this?"

"Because two women I cared about have been brutally murdered, and no one is doing anything to find out who did it or to stop it from happening again." He shook his head. "I don't want to pick up the paper or turn on the news tomorrow morning and learn that another woman has been killed by this guy."

Doug left and Sharon stayed at the table, outlining her story. She had never broken a big news story before, and she prayed that the daily press didn't learn about the weapon evidence and publish it before her piece ran. The latest issue of *Hunt Country* had just hit the streets. It would be a week before the next paper came out.

Doug sped down the winding road towards the Morven Park Mansion, where the Masters of Foxhounds Association was holding a rally. The last thing he felt like doing was going to the Beacon of Support bonfire, but he had promised Richard Evan Clarke that he would show up.

Doug tried to remember the number of bonfires that had burned on hillsides throughout the land at the last rally. Thousands in the United States. Even more in Great Britain. He couldn't recall exactly.

Richard said that tonight's rally was an independent event, confined only to Morven Park. It was the Masters of Foxhounds' quick response to an announcement that day that an anti-hunting bill had been re-introduced in Parliament.

The parking lot at the entrance to the Morven Park Mansion was already full, so Doug parked on the grass along the side of the driveway. From the looks of the number of cars, there was a strong attendance for the rally.

Doug walked up the drive, and as he rounded the bend to the mansion, he saw a large group of people gathered on the front lawn. Well over a hundred, he estimated. He searched for Richard, but he had a hard time picking out faces in the fading light.

"Hello . . . good to see you . . . great show of support here tonight . . ." He murmured greetings and shook a few hands as he walked through the crowd. Finally, he spotted the master standing under the light on the front porch of the mansion, holding a microphone.

Knock, knock, knock. Richard tapped the microphone. "May I have your attention, please." The buzz of conversation stopped and people turned towards the porch.

"First of all, I'd like to thank each and every one of you for coming here tonight. I am very pleased to see such a tremendous showing of support for the sport of foxhunting. It will be recognized and appreciated by our compatriots in Great Britain. I know it's cold out tonight, so we won't drag this out too long. We'll wait just a few more minutes for full darkness and then we'll light the bonfire.

"As I'm sure most of you are aware, a beacon is the historic symbol of alarm in England. For centuries, the British people communicated word of enemy invasions by lighting beacons from hilltop to hilltop, until the news reached its destination. With our beacon here tonight, we send out our word of alarm, because the fight in England is our fight as well.

"We must join forces in spreading the word to all animal enthusiasts of this threat to our liberty, our freedom, and our country lifestyle. We, who live in and love this countryside, we are the caregivers to animals and the natural habitat. And yet, animal rights organizations have made it their political agenda to try to dictate animal welfare issues that they do not truly under-stand. While animal rights activists may have a right to believe as they wish, they have no right to force those beliefs upon us. They have no right to destroy our traditions. They have no right to change our lifestyle. We see through their sham of political correctness. We recognize their strategy of divide and conquer. And we will defeat it."

There was a roar of applause and cheers of support, and Richard held up his hand to silence them. "Now, let's send out our message of alarm with the lighting of our beacon. For those of you who didn't bring a flashlight, we have extras up here." He gestured towards a long table that was set up on the porch. "We also have some coffee and hot cider." Richard put the microphone away and walked down the porch steps.

Doug went over to him. "Nice speech, Richard." He motioned towards the crowd. "You have a good turnout."

"Doug, thank you for coming," Richard shook his hand. "Yes, we have quite a crowd here."

Doug lowered his voice. "Any animal rights activists show up?"

Richard shook his head. "No, thank God. I don't think they got wind of it in time."

"Mr. Clarke, we're ready for you to light the bonfire," a voice called from below.

Richard clasped Doug on the back. "Grab yourself a cup of coffee and a flashlight. I'll see you down there."

Doug nodded. He didn't want coffee, but he took a flashlight from the table and walked with the crowd down the hill to the bonfire.

"Let's all turn our flashlights on and aim them towards the sky," Richard called out.

Beams of light shone out across the darkening landscape, and the bonfire started to crackle as Richard held a torch to it. The smell of the fire drifted across the night air. Doug inhaled deeply. It was a comforting mixture, the cold fresh air and the scent of burning wood, the crackling fire and the slowly moving beams from the flashlights. Peaceful.

"Now, please join me in the singing of John Peel." Richard began to sing the old English foxhunting ballad, and other voices joined in. Doug quietly sang along.

As they sang the last verse, Doug eased away from the group. He didn't feel like sticking around and socializing. Maybe he was just being paranoid, but it seemed as if no one was too keen on talking with him. Other than Richard, no one there had done much more than offer him a polite greeting.

He slipped away into the darkness and headed towards the Porsche. As he started down the drive, he realized that he still had the flashlight in his hand. Oh, well, he'd return it to Richard at the hunt on Saturday.

Doug opened the driver's door and tossed the flashlight on the passenger seat, then winced when he heard what sounded like breaking glass. What had he left on the seat? He climbed into the car and looked over at the seat. The flashlight lay on top of a photograph in a brown wooden frame. The glass on the front of the frame had shattered.

Doug moved the flashlight and gingerly picked up the frame. It was a photograph of Babs holding the blue ribbon that Chancellor had won for Best Turned Out at the Virginia Field Hunter Championships. Doug slowly placed the picture back down on the passenger seat. The last time he'd seen the photograph, it had been hanging on the wall in his tack room. It had disappeared the same day that Babs did.

Doug heard voices through the dark and saw the beams of several flashlights approaching. He quickly reached out and closed the driver's door, and the interior light in the car went out.

As he sat in the dark, he gripped the steering wheel with both hands. Who had put the picture in his car? And where did they find it? Then he remembered how Nancy's hunt whip had appeared in much the same way, on the seat of his Range Rover. A chill crept over him. Someone was playing games with him. Was it the murderer?

Anne arrived at the hunt breakfast at Richard Evan Clarke's farm just as the riders were returning from the hunt. She had intended to show up early so that she would have time to chat with Richard and then leave before the party really got under way, but she'd been delayed by a phone call from a client.

Anne accepted a cup of hot cider from the waitress at the front door. "Do you know where I might find Mr. Clarke?" she asked the waitress.

The girl shook her head. "Sorry."

Anne looked around but didn't see any familiar faces, so she retreated to a warm spot in the library in front of the fireplace.

More than half of the people in the room were dressed in hunt attire, and most of the riders' boots and breeches were mud splattered. Anne watched one man, whose backside was coated with muck, animatedly entertain the others with a detailed description of his spectacular fall.

"And I heard you missed the kill," another rider said to him.

He groaned. "Thanks for reminding me." He turned to a teenaged girl in the group. "How was it, Tara? Your first kill."

Anne noticed the girl had a smudge on each cheek and she shuddered. The girl had been blooded. The age-old tradition of wiping blood from the dead fox on the faces of those riders who had witnessed their first kill.

The girl wrinkled her nose, and as Anne listened for her reply, she was grabbed in a bear hug from behind. She whirled around and smiled when she saw that it was Richard Evan Clarke. She reached up and gave him a peck on the cheek. Richard had been the godfather to her best friend Nicole, Samantha's mother, and Anne and he had grown very close following Nicole's death.

"Anne, my dear, I'm so glad you came. It's been far too long. You look fabulous. How's my pet Samantha?"

"She's doing great, Richard; thanks for asking. How about you? Still enjoying a good day of hunting, I see." Anne held on to his arm.

"Anne, I couldn't even conceive of my life without it," Richard replied. "I'll never give up foxhunting, you know, no matter how ancient I get. When my time is up, I plan to die while hacking back to the trailer after a good run."

Anne laughed. "If I know you, Richard, you'll probably get your way, though not any time soon I hope."

He smiled at her. "You really are a sight for sore eyes. I wish I could see more of you. Are you ever going to join us in the hunt field?"

She shook her head. "Not in the foreseeable future. My case load has been pretty heavy lately, and I try to spend whatever spare time I have with Samantha."

"Yes, I've heard about some of your cases. I was very pleased to learn that you are representing Doug Cummings. He's a close friend of mine, and I fear that he's in some hot water. I'm glad to know that he is in your very capable hands. How's it going?"

"Well, the case they are trying to build is purely circumstantial, but it has the potential to be a convincing one. Unfortunately, Doug's lifestyle seems to lend itself to the type of speculation they are engaging in."

Richard nodded. "Yes, I can see that. Doug's really not the sort he's made out to be, you know, but with women throwing themselves at him the way they do, people just assume that he's a real ladies man. And, of course, the fact that he's approaching forty and still a bachelor enhances that reputation. It's really too bad. Doug's a decent and honorable man from a good family, and I hate to see his name get muddied by this. Although I have faith that you'll see he is exonerated from any criminal charges, I fear that the damage to his reputation might be devastating."

They were interrupted by Doug, who came around the corner and clasped the master on the back. "Thanks for a great day of sport, Richard. You gave us an incredible view of the kill. That was some of the best hunting we've had all year."

Richard put an arm around his shoulders. "Doug, speak of the devil. We were just exalting your virtues."

Doug glanced at Anne. "I'm sure that was a very one-sided conversation."

Richard raised an eyebrow questioningly. "I think that must be my exit cue," he said, giving Anne a kiss. "Enjoy yourselves, and, please, eat up. As usual, Margaret has ordered enough to feed an army."

Anne waited until Richard was out of earshot, and then turned to Doug. "Doug, I owe you an apology. I was way out of line with what I said to you the other day. I hope that you'll forgive me. I want to continue to represent you, and I really will do my very best for you. If you no longer feel comfortable with me, however, I understand."

Doug groaned. "What the hell is that supposed to mean, Anne? 'I still think you're a jerk, but it was very bad manners of me to say so?'"

Anne's face flushed with anger, but she bit back a retort. "I'm trying to apologize, Doug. You could at least have the graciousness to accept it. I don't think you're a jerk, and it was wrong of me to stereotype you the way I did."

Doug's expression softened. "Okay, all right, I accept your apology." He flashed her a smile. "I promise that I will make every effort to live up to the newly found faith you have in me, Counselor."

Anne shook her head and couldn't help smiling back. "You're impossible, Doug. I'll bet your mother didn't stand a chance with you."

He laughed, but then his smile faded. "Well, at least she isn't around to suffer the humiliation this would have caused her." He stared at the fire for a moment, then shook his head and turned to her. "I want to see Richard's new stallion. I'm thinking of breeding one of my mares to him in the spring. Care to have a look?"

"Oh, Doug, thanks, but I really need to be going," Anne said, gesturing towards the door.

"Come on, the party's just starting. Allow yourself to have some fun for a change. No one's going to hold it against you, I promise." He smiled at her again.

Anne hesitated and Doug guided her gently by the elbow. "Good decision. Come on."

A small group was gathered at the stable, watching as Richard's groom paraded the stallion, Impressive Gent, around the barnyard. His neck was arched and steam clouded from his nose as he snorted. His feet seemed to barely touch the ground as he trotted before them.

Doug whistled softly. "Richard wasn't kidding about this one. Where did you find him, Michael?"

The groom beamed at Doug. "You won't believe me, Mr. Cummings, but I found him around here, almost right in our own back yard, at the livestock auction. I've dreamed of finding a horse like this one all my life, but I knew for sure no horse person in their right mind would ever willingly part with a horse like this. So, I've been going to the auctions, looking for a diamond in the rough."

Michael shook his head. "You wouldn't believe what bad shape he was in when he came on the auction block. All skin and bones and the meanest son of a bitch you'd ever care to see. But I saw something in his eyes, something that told me he was special, and I bought him. I knew Mr. Clarke would have fired me on the spot if I brought Impressive home looking like that, so I took him to a friend's barn. I kept him there a good six months, working with him and fattening him up, then I brought him here for the boss to take a look at him. The rest is history."

Doug started chatting with Michael about the breeding schedule, and Anne suddenly became aware of another conversation next to her.

"Well, from what I hear, he was the last person alone with either of the two ladies before they were murdered, God rest their souls." The speaker lowered her voice to a whisper. "You do know, of course, that the three of them had a thing going. Pretty kinky too, or so I'm told."

Anne cast a glance at them. The woman speaking was older, probably in her sixties, her two female companions somewhat younger.

"I shudder just to think of all the times I let him help me when I was out foxhunting. Why, I even hacked in alone with him a time or two. Of course, at the time I had absolutely no idea the danger I was in," the older woman said, clucking her tongue.

Doug walked back over to join Anne, and the conversation next to her stopped.

"Are you ready for some lunch?" he asked.

"Sure." Anne was silent as they made their way back to the house, and Doug stopped halfway.

"Did I do something wrong down there?" he asked.

"No, of course not." She avoided his eyes.

He just stood there with his hands on his hips. "Tell me."

"Oh, it was those ladies down there. They were gossiping about you. It bothered me. That's all."

"That's nothing new, Anne. I guess I've almost gotten used to it. Every place I go, it seems as if heads turn and conversations cease. I can't let it get to me."

"No, you shouldn't. I just was taken aback by it, that's all. Sorry I mentioned it."

He smiled at her. "It's okay. It feels good to have someone on my side, even if it is my lawyer."

They walked across the terrace and through the French doors directly into the dining room. Anne looked around. Richard had really outdone himself. A bronze of a huntsman and several hounds stood in the center of the table, surrounded by flowers that were intertwined at the base with the hounds and the horse's legs. The blossoms climbed up curly willow branches above the rider and into the crystal chandelier above. A blazing fire crackled in the huge stone fireplace, and rich sounds of classical piano music floated in from the other room.

Doug handed Anne some silverware and a plate, and they both went around the table filling their plates with a little bit of everything. Venison stew, pheasant, poached salmon, asparagus, wild rice, and field greens.

"Let's find a place to sit; then I'll get us something to drink," Doug said.

They found a grouping in the living room with two empty chairs, and Anne sat down and balanced her plate on her lap.

Doug put his plate on the needlepoint seat cushion of the chair next to her. "What can I get you to drink?"

"A Perrier would be great, thank you."

A well-dressed, pretty woman sitting next to Anne leaned close and gestured towards Doug. "Who's he?" she whispered.

Anne looked at her. "Doug Cummings."

"Is he yours?" She had a British accent, and 'yours' had at least two syllables.

Anne laughed. "No, not really."

"Well, I'm frightfully sorry for you, then." She smiled at Anne. "Hi, I'm Priscilla Haughton."

"Hello. I'm Anne Sullivan."

Doug came back with their drinks and handed Anne her Perrier.

"Thank you."

He picked up his plate and sat down next to her. Priscilla leaned forward, as if to speak to him, but a man sitting on the other side of Doug started talking to him about Richard's stallion.

Priscilla looked at Anne and rolled her eyes. "Men and their horses."

Anne smiled. "Do you ride?"

"Not for years now. Ever since Mummy married husband number four, who was allergic to horses. He made her sell the whole lot of them. I'll tell you what though, if they had hunt breakfasts like this in England, I might take it up again."

"What are the hunt breakfasts like in England?"

"We don't really have them. I mean, sometimes a chap will invite everyone round to his house after the hunt, but it's nothing like this. You're lucky if he sets out a bottle of whisky and some Scottish eggs."

A waiter came by and collected their plates and Doug turned to Anne. "Would you like some dessert?"

"No, thanks." She glanced at her watch. "I really need to head home."

Doug stood up. "I'll walk you to the door."

"Nice meeting you," Anne said to Priscilla.

"My pleasure."

Doug walked her to the door and waited for the valet to bring her car around.

"Thanks for a nice afternoon, Doug. I'm glad you talked me into staying. Will you give my regards to Richard?"

"Sure. I'm going to be heading out soon myself. One of my associates dropped off some work for me to review. I'd like to get it done before the hunt ball tonight."

"Oh, is that tonight?" Anne asked absently.

"It is. You mean you're not attending? I can't imagine how you could pass it up. You must have something more exciting planned, like curling up in front of the fire with a good book."

Anne smiled. "If you don't think it's enjoyable, why are you going?"

Doug shrugged. "I'm on the Board of Governors of the Hunt, so I should at least put in an appearance. And there's nothing wrong with the hunt ball. I actually used to enjoy going. It's just that going out socially these days is a bit of a strain. I'm never quite sure who it's safe to talk to. That's one reason it was so nice having your company today. At least I knew you weren't going to flip out if you were left alone with me."

"Well, surely your date tonight will be good company."

Doug shook his head. "I don't have one."

"Why not?" She regretted her question as soon as it was out.

Another shrug. "It's too much hassle. Besides, I can't afford to get involved with anyone right now."

The valet brought Anne's car and Doug walked her around to the driver's side. She settled in and was just about to close the door when Doug put his hand out and stopped her.

"Anne, wait. I just had an idea. Why don't you come to the hunt ball with me tonight?"

Anne stared at him in disbelief. "You're kidding, right?"

"No, I'm dead serious. Come on, it'll be fun."

"Doug, I can't go to the hunt ball with you."

"Why not?"

"I just can't. It wouldn't look right. I'm your lawyer. I can't date a client."

"It wouldn't be a date. You could come along to protect me. At the rate I'm going, you never know when I might need my attorney present."

Anne couldn't suppress a smile.

"Come on, please say yes. We both deserve a relaxing evening out." He held up both of his hands. "I'll be on my best behavior, I promise."

"I don't know if Ingrid can baby-sit," she heard herself say weakly.

Doug grinned. "If she can't, bring Samantha along. I'll pick you up at seven." He closed her door and was back inside the house before she could protest.

38

Doug frowned as he walked into his bedroom and saw his scarlet tails lying in a crumpled heap on the floor. He had hung the formal wear up on the door of the armoire before leaving for the hunt that morning. Doug picked the coat up and removed the plastic wrap. It looked fine. He was just about to hang it up again when Nellie rushed into the room carrying his white tuxedo shirt.

"Oh, dear, I can see I'm just in time. You were probably wondering where this was." She shook her head. "I swear that old dry cleaner gets worse every time we use it. I guess they can get by with it because they're the only game in town."

Doug smiled at her. "What damage did they do this time, Nellie?"

"Why, they pressed your collar tabs unevenly, just like they did last time. And I specifically told them to take extra care with it." She showed the collar to him. "I worked on this for over thirty minutes just to get the line out where they pressed it wrong. I don't know why you refuse to let me wash and iron all your shirts for you. If it's not the collar they bungle, it's the buttons."

"Fine, Nellie, if you want to do my shirts yourself, that's okay with me. Let's just stop using the cleaner out here. I'll take the dry cleaning back to Washington with me. The cleaner the Watergate uses does a decent job." He took the freshly ironed shirt from her and held it up. "Thanks for fixing the shirt, it looks great."

Doug hung the shirt up with his scarlet coat. Nellie must have inadvertently knocked the coat down earlier when she had taken his shirt.

"Hey, Nellie, I don't mean to kick you out, but I'd better get in the shower or I'm going to be late."

"You'd think no one ever took the time to teach you proper grammar, Doug. 'Hey?' What was it I used to tell you when you were a boy? 'Hay is for horses, young man. That's no way to address someone you respect.' Don't you remember me telling you that?" She shook her head. "Now you're a famous lawyer and you're still talking that way." Nellie walked out and closed the door behind her, still grumbling.

Doug smiled after her. Nellie would probably always treat him like the little boy that she helped raise.

He showered, shaved, dressed, then stopped to check his appearance in the bedroom mirror before leaving. As he reached his arms up to straighten his white bow tie, Doug noticed that one of the three gold Middleburg Foxhounds' buttons on the right sleeve of his scarlet tails was missing.

Damn it. The dry cleaner really was a disaster. Doug looked at his watch. He'd be late if he had Nellie sew on another button, so he decided to cut the third button off his left sleeve. That way, at least both sleeves would match.

Doug tried cutting the button off without removing the coat, but it was awkward. First, he nicked a small piece of cloth with the manicure scissors. Then, when he finally succeeded in snipping the button off, it flew across the room. Muttering, he picked the remnants of thread off the sleeve, then turned off the lights and went downstairs.

"Wish me luck, Nellie," he said.

"Why, what for, Doug?"

"I have the pleasure of the company of a very interesting lady tonight."

"Oh, Doug, I'm so glad. You enjoy yourself."

"I have every intention of doing just that." Doug turned back to her as he reached the door. "Nellie, when I came home today the back door was unlocked again. I hate to harp on it, but you've really got to be more careful about locking up, especially with what's been happening around here lately."

"I'm sorry, Doug. I don't remember using that door today, but I'll be more careful from now on." She walked with him to the door. "Oh, Doug, I almost forgot. Someone from your law firm called here earlier and asked for your cell phone number. He said it was important that he get in touch with you. I gave him the number. I hope that was all right."

"Who was it?"

"I'm not sure he told me his name. But he did say he was from your law firm."

Doug nodded. "Of course that's all right, Nellie. My cell phone number is listed in the firm directory, but maybe whoever it was called from home and didn't have the directory with him."

CHAPTER

39

Doug arrived at Anne's house a few minutes before seven. Samantha answered the door, dressed in a princess costume.

"Hi, Doug. That's a really cool coat. You look so-o-o handsome. I'm going to pretend that I'm going to a ball tonight too, and my prince is going to look just like you." She grabbed the ends of his long scarlet coattails and danced behind him.

Doug laughed. "Samantha, look at you. You are the prettiest princess I've ever seen."

"Wait until you see Aunt Anne. She's going to be the most beautifullest lady at the ball."

Doug could hear Anne come down the hall, going over instructions with Ingrid. "Samantha can select a TV dinner, but she has to eat the dinner before the dessert. Don't let her tell you otherwise. Since it's not a school night, she can stay up until eight-thirty and then read one bedtime story before going to sleep."

Doug caught his breath when he saw her. Anne wore a long black velvet gown that hugged her body, with a slit up the front that revealed her long slender legs as she walked. The strapless neckline was bare and her hair, normally held back in a bun, was loose and brushed her shoulders. She looked magnificent. Whoa, boy, he warned himself. She's your lawyer, and she's off limits.

He gave Anne a kiss on the cheek. "You were right, Samantha. Your Aunt Anne is going to be the most beautiful woman at the ball."

Anne blushed. "I hope this isn't inappropriate. It's all I had."

"You look fabulous."

"Thank you. And you look quite elegant in your scarlet."

"Thanks. Ready to go?" Doug helped Anne into her long black mink coat and handed Ingrid a slip of paper. "I've made reservations at The Ashby Inn for dinner. I've written the number down for Ingrid."

Anne turned to the nanny. "I also have my pager with me. Beep me if you need me for any reason. I shouldn't be out too late."

Ingrid smiled at her. "Please don't worry. You go and have fun. Samantha and I will be just fine."

Doug knelt to give Samantha a hug. "Goodnight, princess."

"Nite-nite, Doug. Hey, you smell good. My prince is going to smell like that too."

"God, she melts your heart, doesn't she?" Doug said as they walked to the car.

Anne smiled at him. "Every day."

It was a short drive to The Ashby Inn. Doug pulled up in front and walked Anne up the stairs to the front door. "I'll go park around back and see you inside. I've requested a table by the fire in the pub."

By the time Doug parked and entered the restaurant, Anne was already seated at the table, looking at the menu.

"See anything that looks good?" he asked as he sat down.

She nodded. "Everything."

The waiter removed a bottle of Taittinger Comtes de Champagne from the ice bucket next to their table and held it out for Doug to see. Doug looked at Anne. "I took the liberty of ordering champagne, but if you'd prefer something else just say so."

"No, champagne sounds lovely, thank you."

Doug waited while the waiter poured the champagne and then held his glass up in a toast to Anne. "Here's to my lawyer," he smiled, "who also happens to be a beautiful and engaging dinner companion. Thank you for joining me."

Anne set her glass down. Her smile disappeared.

"What's the matter?" he asked.

She shook her head. "You said this wasn't a date."

That was hardly the reaction he expected. "It isn't a date. But does that mean I'm not allowed to pay you a compliment?"

She shook her head and gave a small smile. "I'm sorry. I'm not very good at this." She raised her glass. "Cheers."

Doug touched his glass to hers, then set it down on the table. This should be an interesting evening, he mused. He opened his menu. "Have you decided what you'd like?"

"I think I'll have the Dover Sole."

"Sounds good. I'll have the same." He signaled to the waiter and placed their order. Then he picked up his glass and leaned back in his chair, wondering what subject was safe to talk about. "Tell me what brought you down to Virginia and about how Samantha came into your life," he said.

Anne hesitated for a moment. "It's actually a tragic story. Samantha's mother, Nicole, was my closest friend. We met as roommates in college. A few years before Samantha was born, Nicole was injured in a car accident and had to have a blood transfusion. As it turns out, the blood was infected and Nicole contracted HIV. She didn't find out that she was infected until she was pregnant with Samantha, and by that time she had already transmitted the virus to her husband, Roger. Samantha, fortunately, was not infected. Around the time Samantha turned two Nicole and Roger both started to suffer from the illness, and they realized they had to make plans for Samantha's future. They asked me if I would consider taking custody of Samantha and I agreed. I moved down here about two years ago to help take care of them and be with Samantha. Nicole passed away last year, then Roger about six months ago."

He reached over and touched her hands, which were nervously twirling the stem of her champagne glass. "I'm sorry, Anne. I had no idea."

She shook her head. "It's okay. It's Samantha I worry about. It was very tough on her watching them slowly fade away, and to lose both her parents at such a young age has threatened her sense of security in her world."

"What about Samantha, are you going to adopt her?"

Anne withdrew her hands and sat back. "That's a decision I'm still struggling with. I love Samantha. From my perspective, I would love nothing more than to adopt her and legally become her mother. But I have a nagging doubt whether that would be the best thing for Samantha."

"Why? She obviously loves you very much."

"Yes, she does. But if I had to pick the ideal family for Samantha, she would have a mother and a father, maybe a brother or sister. I know that's what Nicole and Roger would have wanted, if they had a choice."

"Don't sell yourself short, Anne. You have so much to offer that little girl. There are a lot of kids out there with single parents. You can't honestly think she would be better off with total strangers."

"I just don't know, Doug. That's why I haven't finalized anything yet."

"Have you asked Samantha what she wants?"

"She says she wants me," Anne said quietly.

"Well then, isn't that your answer?"

Anne didn't respond.

Doug shook his head. "I'm sorry. I don't mean to tell you what to do. It's got to be a very tough decision. I admire you for giving it such thought." He sighed. "Well, I sure managed to put a damper on the evening, didn't I?"

Anne smiled at him. "No, you didn't. It actually did me good to talk about it. Thank you for listening." She held up her glass. "How about some more champagne?"

Doug lifted the bottle out of the ice bucket and reached over to fill her glass. "Since I'm playing chauffeur tonight, I'm going to have to count on you to do justice to this bottle."

She laughed softly. "You're not trying to get me drunk, are you?"

Doug just smiled. He knew that no matter how he responded, he was doomed.

The hunt ball was well under way by the time they arrived at the Middleburg Community Center, and the dance floor was already packed with people. Anne waited at the door while Doug checked her coat. She looked around the big room. The decorating committee had done a great job.

Italian white lights twinkled along streamers hung from the high ceiling. Lush evergreens wrapped with gold and silver taffeta bows adorned the walls and doorways. The round tables were covered with dark green cloths, over-laid with gold, and ivy topiary trees with gold and silver balls served as centerpieces. The historic mustard-colored building had been transformed.

Doug returned and took Anne by the arm. "Let's find Richard's table." He spoke close to her ear to be heard above the music.

She nodded and he steered her to the front corner of the room. Places had been reserved for them at Richard's table. There were some drinks on the table, and an evening bag hung off the back of one chair, but no one was there.

"They must all be dancing," Doug said. He held a chair out for her and once she was seated, he put a hand on her shoulder and leaned down next to her. "Can I get you something from the bar?"

Anne's head was reeling a bit from the champagne. "You go ahead, I'm fine."

"I'll be right back."

Her skin tingled where his hand had rested on her bare shoulder, and she reached up and touched it as she watched him make his way through the crowded room to the bar. There was a line, and Doug caught her eyes across the room. "Sorry," he mouthed.

She smiled at him. "It's okay."

As she watched Doug, Anne saw a young woman approach him. She was tall and thin, with long, dark hair that flowed almost to the waist of her silver-sequined, backless gown. She kissed him on the cheek and slipped her arm through his. She said something and laughed, and Doug smiled back at her. Then she moved closer to him and said something into his ear. Doug put his arm on her back as he listened to what she was saying.

Anne watched as the crowd in front of Doug inched forward and he slowly made his way to the bar. All the while, he and the young woman continued to talk, seemingly engrossed in their conversation. Doug never looked back over towards where she was sitting, and Anne felt her face burn with embarrassment. They'd been there five minutes and Doug had already abandoned her. She should have known better than to come there with him. She straightened up in her chair and turned away.

Anne felt self-conscious, sitting there all alone, and reached for the water glass that sat on the table in front of her. The outside of the glass was wet with condensation, and as she sipped from the glass she felt water drip onto her lap. She unfolded a white linen napkin from the table and dabbed at her gown, then folded the napkin neatly and placed it back on the table. Hesitantly, she looked over towards the bar again. Doug was third in line now, with the young woman still attached to his arm. They were chatting away, and Doug seemed in no hurry to get to the head of the line.

Anne's embarrassment flared into anger and she pushed back her chair and rose from the table. She wasn't going to just sit there all night, waiting for Doug to return. She searched the crowd for someone she knew, and spotted Leslie McCashin standing at the edge of the dance floor. She made her way across the room to Leslie.

Doug appeared at her side about fifteen minutes later. "Here you are. I've been looking all over for you," he said, casually slipping his arm around her shoulders.

Anne shrugged his arm off, but didn't think she could manage a civil reply, so she ignored him and continued talking with Leslie. "I love your necklace, Leslie." She reached out and fingered the diamond solitaire on the simple gold chain. "Is that the one you bought at the estate sale?"

Doug waited while Leslie told Anne about the necklace, and then intervened again. "The band's pretty good, Anne. Feel like dancing?"

Anne spun to face him, making no attempt to cover her anger. "Look,

Doug, don't feel that you have to spend your evening with me just because we came together. I'm perfectly fine on my own. I'm sure that there are a whole slew of women just dying to dance with you. Why don't you go and ask one of them?"

"What's wrong, Anne?" Doug asked, reaching out and putting his hand on her back.

His touch on her back was tender, which made Anne even angrier. She turned back to Leslie. "Leslie, Doug was wondering if you'd care to dance."

Doug cleared his throat. "Excuse us for a minute, Leslie," he said, gently gripping Anne's arm and pulling her aside. "Anne, what the hell is going on? Why are you so upset?"

"I'm not upset, Doug." She shook his hand off. "I'm having a great time." Her voice cracked and she looked away just as Richard Evan Clarke approached them.

"Hello, you two," the master said jovially. "You've finally arrived. I was beginning to wonder if you had decided to skip the ball altogether. I'm glad you're here. Now, remember, Doug, you can't monopolize her all evening. I want to have at least one dance with her."

Anne grabbed Richard's arm. "I would love to dance with you, Richard. How about now?"

Richard smiled at Doug. "Your loss, old boy. I promise I'll return her later."

As Anne danced with Richard, she saw Doug lead Leslie onto the dance floor. He looked over in her direction, and she quickly looked away. She knew that she was behaving childishly, but she couldn't help herself. She wasn't about to spend the evening competing for Doug's attention. Anne danced with Richard for two numbers, and then the band took a break.

Richard held his arm out to her and led her off the dance floor. "Would you like to go to the table?"

Anne saw Doug head in that direction and she shook her head. "I see someone I want to talk to, Richard. I'll be there in a few minutes." She turned towards the other side of the room. Now what? She decided to get a glass of wine, and as she waited at the bar she felt a hand on her arm.

"Anne, isn't it?"

Anne turned and saw the British woman she'd been talking to at the hunt breakfast.

"Yes. Priscilla, good to see you."

Priscilla fanned herself with her hand. "I'm just dying for something cool to drink. My date's a bit of a bore, so I've been hiding from him on the dance floor."

Anne smiled. "Who's your date?"

Priscilla waved her hand towards a group of men who stood nearby. "He's the one in the scarlet tails who looks a bit like a stuffed turkey."

Anne laughed.

"I'm serious. See him over there? He's busting out all his buttons. Why, that coat probably hasn't fit him for at least twenty years. Not that I imagine he ever looked dapper in it to begin with. He's too bloody short and round."

It was their turn at the bar and they each ordered a glass of white wine. Then they stood off to the side of the bar.

"Look there," Priscilla said, pointing towards Richard's table. "There's that handsome chap you were with this afternoon. He looks quite dashing in his scarlet. Are you with him again tonight?"

Anne started to nod, then shook her head. "Sort of."

Priscilla laughed. "What does that mean? Lover's spat?"

"No, it's not like that," Anne said quickly. "We're just friends."

"Well, too bad for you. Maybe I'll steal him for a dance later."

Anne smiled politely. "Sure."

The crowd around the bar was thinning out as people began to take their seats. "I think they're about to serve dessert. We'd better get back to our tables," Priscilla said, with a little wave.

Anne felt conspicuous standing there alone, so she made her way to Richard's table. Doug was seated when she got there, with an empty chair next to him. Anne saw another empty chair across the table, next to a man dressed in scarlet, and she sat down there. Leslie was seated on the other side of the man and she leaned over and introduced him to Anne.

"Anne, this is Langley Masterson. He's an honorary whipper-in with the Hunt and has been entertaining me with all kinds of fascinating hunting stories."

Anne nodded at him. "Hello. It's nice to meet you."

Langley smiled back. "The pleasure is mine. Are you here all alone?"

Anne hesitated. "I came with Doug Cummings."

Langley laughed. "Oh, I see. You're the flavor of the week."

Anne's cheeks burned and she managed to smile politely before she turned away from him. She sipped her wine and avoided looking at Doug at first, but after a few minutes she glanced in his direction and caught him staring at her. He tilted his head slightly and raised an eyebrow, giving her a small smile. A charming, 'are you still mad at me' kind of look. Anne's pulse quickened. She blushed and glanced away.

Maybe she'd been too hard on Doug. He really couldn't help it if women kept throwing themselves at him. Maybe he'd had no choice with that woman at the bar. Perhaps he was simply being friendly. After all, he had come looking for her afterwards. She looked towards Doug again and found him still watching her. This time she didn't look away. He raised his shoulders and mouthed, "Friends again?" And Anne couldn't help smiling at him.

Doug smiled back, as he rose from his chair and started around the table towards her. Anne moved her chair back slightly, preparing to turn and greet him, but she was interrupted by the man seated to her right, who asked her to dance. Caught off guard, she heard herself say "yes."

The man guided Anne to the dance floor and immediately held her close. He began swaying to the music, then his hands began to roam. First, down her back and over her buttocks. Then they brushed against her breasts. Anne tried to pull back, but his grip held her tight.

"You're so beautiful," he whispered in her ear. His words were slurred, and she figured he was drunk. Anne pushed against his chest and to her surprise he released his grip. Then she saw Doug standing next to them.

"Okay, Neal, you've had your turn. Anne's my date tonight. I'm cutting in."

Doug put his hand on her back and guided her to the far side of the dance floor. "Are you all right?"

She nodded. "Thank you."

The music finished and Doug turned to take her back to the table, but she stopped him. "Doug, wait."

He turned back and looked at her. His expression was guarded.

"Dance with me."

Without a word, Doug drew her to him. The music was slow and Doug held Anne lightly as they danced. The song ended and blended into another one, and they kept dancing.

Anne reached up and whispered in Doug's ear, "I'm sorry."

Doug held her tighter and she rested her head on his shoulder.

She felt the soft wool of Doug's coat against her cheek, and smelled the pleasing mixture of his after-shave and the clean starch of his shirt. She inhaled deeply and felt a faint lightheadedness.

She gently fingered the sleeve of his coat where she held his arm and felt his muscle beneath it. And then she was suddenly acutely aware of the broad, comforting strength of his chest. His sturdy shoulders. And the powerful way he guided her so effortlessly around the dance floor. Everything about Doug was so male. His scent. His touch. The deep rumbling in his chest as he hummed along with the song.

The warmth of Doug's hand on her back radiated through her velvet gown and she moved closer. Oh, God. What was she doing? She closed her eyes and buried her face against his chest. It's just a dance, she told herself. Just a dance.

"I long to hold you, again in my arms," the female vocalist sang. Doug rested his cheek against her hair and drew her hand up to his chest. Anne kept her eyes closed, willing the song not to end. *"I long to touch you . . ."*

Doug's hand stroked her back, gently pressing her closer, and she molded her body to his, eyes still closed, savoring the moment.

"I long to hold you, forever in my arms."

The song ended and the band picked up a jazz number. Doug slowly pulled away. "Come on, it's hot in here. Let's go get some air." He grabbed Anne's hand and led her outside through the back door.

A blast of cold air greeted them. Doug took his scarlet coat off and put it around Anne's shoulders, then took her by the hand again. "Follow me."

He led her across the small parking lot and up a gentle slope to a wooded picnic area. Doug stopped and leaned against one of the picnic tables. He slipped his hands around Anne's waist and pulled her close to him.

Anne's arms went around his neck. "What are we doing?" she whispered.

Doug leaned down and kissed her mouth lightly. His hands slid through her hair and held her face close to his, tracing her lips with his fingertips. Her skin was smooth, and he closed his eyes and inhaled the musky scent of her perfume.

Anne's arms tightened around him and drew his mouth back to hers. Her fingers were ice cold against the nape of his neck, and Doug reached up, without breaking from the kiss, and laced his fingers through hers. "You're freezing," he whispered, drawing her hands against his chest.

He felt her mouth curve into a smile against his. "It's okay," she murmured.

Doug kissed her softly again then leaned his head back, just enough to see Anne's face. A nearby streetlight shone on her through the bare trees, and shadows flickered across her as the branches swayed in the stiff breeze. Anne's cheeks were flushed and her breath made little puffs in the frigid air.

Her fingers gripped his lightly, tugging him closer, and she smiled quizzically at him. "What?" she said.

"Let's go home," he said quietly.

"Home?"

"To my place." He released her hands and nuzzled her neck, gently, letting his hands roam around to her back and down to her hips, pulling her closer to him. His lips brushed against her forehead. "Where we can take our time, and I can kiss you without worrying that you're going to freeze to death."

A frown creased Anne's brow, and she stiffened and shook her head. "God, Doug, what are we doing? I can't go home with you. We shouldn't even be out here. You're my client. This isn't right."

He held a finger to her lips. "Shhh, it's okay."

She struggled out of his arms and backed away. "No, it isn't. I can't get involved with a client. It's unethical."

"I'm more than your client, Anne. Besides, it's too late. We're already involved." He reached out for her hand and pulled her back towards him.

She took a step forward, but maintained a distance between them. "I mean it, Doug. You're my client. And I won't be added to your long string of one-night stands."

Doug sighed and placed his hands on her shoulders. "It's not a one-night stand, Anne. I'm not like that."

"Yes, you are."

He leaned forward and cupped her face in his hands. "No, I'm not," he said quietly, gently stroking her cheeks.

"Stop it. Don't touch me. I can't think when you do that." Anne pushed his hands away. "Please."

"You're serious," Doug said, letting go of her.

She nodded. "Yes, I am. I'm sorry. I don't know what I was thinking. I just got carried away."

"You got *carried away*?"

She pursed her lips. "Come on, Doug, let's go back inside. It's not doing either of us any good to stand out here and argue. I won't have an affair with a client, not under any circumstances." She smoothed her hair back and straightened her gown.

"An affair?" he repeated. "Is that what we're doing? Having an affair? I felt like we were just getting to know each other. Maybe even starting to like each other."

Anne just stared at him, her lips set in a firm line.

Doug shook his head in disbelief. "I don't get it. Who are you?"

"What kind of a question is that?" she asked.

"Who are you? Who's the real Anne Sullivan? You're soft and warm one minute. Concerned. Passionate. And then, the next minute, you're throwing daggers at me. You switch. Just like that." He snapped his fingers.

Anne flinched and he thought he saw a hint of tears in her eyes. She took his coat off and held it out to him, but he made no move to accept it and she laid it on the picnic table. "Come on, Doug, please. Let's go back inside."

He shook his head. "No, you go. I'll be in after a while." Doug walked her to the top of the path and watched as she made her way across the parking lot and down to the back door of the Community Center. He waited until the door fell closed behind her, then returned to the picnic table.

As he picked up his coat, he caught a whiff of Anne's perfume. Damn it. What kind of game was Anne playing with him? He slammed his fist down hard on the picnic table and something sharp gouged into his hand, but he ignored it. He flung his coat over one shoulder and pushed through the hedgerow into the athletic field, swearing as a branch snapped back and stung his cheek.

42

Anne ran into Leslie as soon as she entered the ballroom.

"You look pale, Anne, are you all right?" Leslie asked.

"I'm fine," Anne lied. "Just a little chilled. It's getting cold out there."

"What were you doing out there, anyway?"

"I went out for some fresh air."

Leslie raised an eyebrow. "Alone?"

Anne snapped at her. "No, Leslie, I wasn't alone. Doug was with me. And, yes, to answer your next question, he's still out there."

Leslie backed off, looking hurt. "Sorry. I was just curious. I didn't mean anything by it."

Anne nodded at her. "Of course. Forget it. Excuse me, Leslie, I need to go to the ladies room."

As Anne headed up the stairs, she stole a look behind her, just in time to see Leslie head outside through the back door.

Anne repaired her lipstick and brushed her hair, then went back downstairs. The crowd was beginning to thin a little. She looked around the room for Doug. She didn't see him anywhere, so she sat down at a nearby table, grateful to rest her feet, which were swollen and aching from her evening shoes.

Twenty minutes later Doug had still not returned and Anne wondered whether he had gone home and left her there. She decided to claim her coat and then try to find another way home. But when she came back from the cloak room, she saw Doug talking with Richard Evan Clarke.

As Anne approached them, she could see Doug using a white handkerchief to dab at a deep scratch on his right cheek. When she got closer, she saw that his hand holding the handkerchief was also cut.

"What happened, Doug?" Anne asked.

Doug glanced in her direction, but avoided eye contact. "I got in a fight with a tree, and the tree won." His tone was forcibly lighthearted.

She looked at his injuries more closely. "You should really get those cleaned out. They could get infected."

"Thanks for your concern, Counselor, I'll be fine. Are you about ready to call it a night?" Doug still didn't make eye contact with her.

Richard interrupted. "Please, stay for just a few more minutes, if you could. I'm going to give some brief remarks, and I'd like to introduce the board members."

"Are you sure you want to introduce me looking like this?" Doug asked, dabbing again at his cheek.

Richard chuckled. "Certainly. It just looks like you had a rough go of it out hunting today."

Doug looked at Anne, who nodded. "Okay, Richard, but I'm going to hold you to your promise to be brief," Doug said.

As Doug and Anne stood together in uncomfortable silence, waiting for Richard to take the stage, a woman with a professional-looking camera hanging from her neck approached them. She raised the camera as if ready to take a shot of them, but Doug looked at her and shook his head. The woman raised an eyebrow questioningly, and pointed to his cheek. Doug just smiled and shook his head again, and she lowered the camera and strolled off.

"Who was that?" Anne asked.

"Sharon Duncan. She's a reporter for *Hunt Country*."

Anne turned her attention to Richard, who had just taken the microphone up on the stage. Richard gave a brief welcome and thanked all the volunteers who had helped with the evening's festivities. He was beginning the introductions when he lowered his hand holding the microphone and looked towards the back of the room. Anne turned her attention in the direction of Richard's gaze, but she couldn't see anything. She just heard raised voices. Then the president of the Hunt rushed up and spoke to Richard. Richard, looking shocked, raised the microphone again.

"Ladies and gentlemen, it seems there has been some kind of an accident outside. I ask you all to remain in here until you hear otherwise, so that we don't get in the way of the authorities. As soon as I know more about what is going on, I'll be back to you."

Approaching sirens pierced the air, and flashing beams streamed in through the skylight windows, like strobe lights, overpowering the delicate white lights above.

Richard put the microphone down and quickly made his way to Doug and Anne. He motioned for them both to follow him into the kitchen.

Richard's face was ashen. "I'm not going to mince words. I'm afraid we have a desperate situation on our hands."

Richard paused for an instant, then locked eyes with Anne and continued. "Leslie McCashin was just found murdered out in the parking lot. The local police are on their way and the sheriff has been called." He glanced at Doug. "I think it would be best if you're not here when the authorities arrive, Doug, especially looking like you do right now."

"Richard, what the hell . . ." Doug said, but Richard put his hand up and stopped him.

"There's no time for talk now, Doug. You need to get away from here and confer with your lawyer." Richard turned to Anne. "You know I'm right, Anne. Get him out of here. You can use the caterer's door." Richard turned away and left them there.

Anne backed away from Doug. The image of Leslie heading out into the parking lot in search of Doug flashed through her mind, and she stared at the scratches on Doug's face and hand. What had caused them? Had they come from a struggle with Leslie?

A cold knot of fear gripped her stomach. What a fool she had been. She knew what Doug was accused of, yet she'd been blind to the fact that he might be guilty. Even now, even though the facts were staring her squarely in the face, it was hard for her to believe that Doug was actually a murderer. Somehow, he still managed to look so damned innocent, standing there in his elegant evening wear, a look of disbelief convincingly plastered on his handsome face.

Anne struggled to push her feelings aside and reach some level of objectivity. Doug was her client, and she needed to think like his lawyer. Richard was right. She should get Doug out of there.

She held out her hand. "Give me the car keys. I'll get the car and pick you up around the corner by the library." When Doug didn't respond, she snatched the keys from his coat pocket and pushed him towards the door. "Go on. I'll be right there."

Zeb watched the blue flashing lights from his perch in the lifeguard stand next to the swimming pool at the Middleburg Community Center. He was starting to shake from being out in the cold so long, and he blew into his hands to warm them. All the while, he never took his eyes off the cops in the parking lot. He knew he'd have to leave before the cops started searching the area, but for now they were still gathered around the dead woman.

Zeb had watched it all happen. He'd seen the barn girl's killer beat and kill the woman. Rape her too. Right out there in the parking lot. But the killer was gone now. He went back into the Community Center and was probably still inside, acting as if nothing had happened.

The sound of approaching sirens caught his attention, and Zeb craned his neck to look up the driveway. A sheriff's car pulled into the drive and parked, and a deputy got out and joined the crowd around the dead woman.

As Zeb watched the cops, he wondered if they'd pin this murder on Cummings too. It looked more and more like Cummings might be arrested for the barn girl's murder. And the murder of the foxhunting lady. And even though sending Cummings to prison hadn't been part of his original plan, he wasn't entirely against the idea. He wouldn't mind having Cummings rot in some stinking prison cell. Let Cummings live how Zeke had lived. Let him know how Zeke had felt.

Zeb stiffened as the side door to the Community Center opened and Cummings came out. Cummings stood for a moment, looked around, and then set off at a jog through the garden.

"Go on, Cummings. Run if you want," Zeb whispered. "I'll hunt you down."

Zeb unfolded his stiff frame from the lifeguard chair and climbed down the ladder. He was ready to make contact with Cummings.

CHAPTER
44

As Doug stood in a thicket of trees behind the library, waiting for Anne, he felt his cell phone vibrate. He reached into his pocket.

"Hello."

Silence.

"Hello? Anne?"

No response. He was about to flip the phone shut, when he heard a low chuckle.

"Who's there?"

The chuckle grew louder. "How's it feel to be you right now, Mr. Hot Shot Lawyer? Eh?" The man's voice had a twangy West Virginia-type accent.

"Who is this?" Doug demanded.

He was greeted by raucous laughter, and Doug held the phone away from his ear until the laughter died down.

Doug was tempted to hang up, but he had a sick feeling in his stomach that maybe this had something to do with the murders. "Do I know you?" Doug asked.

"Oh, yeah. Only you probably don't remember me, 'cause you're such a hot shot lawyer and it ain't worth your time remembering someone like me." The laughter was gone, and the man's voice was chilling.

Doug tried to keep him on the phone. "Help me out then."

"*Help you out?*" His voice was surly. "Okay. You fucked up my kid brother's case and sent him to the slammer. And now you're going to rot in some stinking prison cell, just like he did. And when all those freaking faggots fuck your ass, you're gonna be beggin' to die, and then you'll know how Zeke felt."

Click. It sounded like he hung up.

"Hello?"

No response.

"Damn." Doug flipped the phone shut.

"Doug?" He heard Anne's voice call out softly, as she walked between the high hedges at the top of the path.

Doug stepped out in front of her.

Anne jumped back. "God, Doug, you scared me. What are you doing hiding up here?"

His mind was still on the cell phone call and he stared at her for a moment, then held his phone out. "I was on the phone."

"You were on the phone? Don't tell me you spoke with someone about what happened tonight?"

"We have to talk," he said quietly.

"You're right about that. But not here. Come on, let's go." She handed Doug the keys and walked back towards the car.

Doug followed her and started the car. "Where to?"

Anne hesitated for a moment. "I guess my house." She looked towards the Community Center where red and blue flashing lights sliced through the night sky. "But don't drive through town. Go the back way, down St. Louis Road, to Snickersville Pike."

Clyde stamped his feet and blew on his hands, trying to fight off the cold, as he waited for the medical examiner to finish inspecting Leslie McCashin's body. He poured himself another cup of coffee from his thermos. It was going to be a long night.

The remaining party guests were being detained inside the Community Center. Clyde was certain that there was a witness in there with some piece of helpful information, and he wasn't going to let anyone out until he had their name and had conducted a brief interview with each one. The snooty master of the Hunt, Richard Evan Clarke, was putting pressure on him to let them go, but he didn't care.

Clyde saw Scott Brady packing up his case, and walked over to him. "What have we got?"

Brady shook his head. "He's getting a lot more violent. Looks like he kept on at her even after she was dead. I suspect that many of her injuries were caused by postmortem trauma."

Clyde almost couldn't contain his excitement. "So our guy did it?"

The Medical Examiner nodded. "I'm pretty certain. Same MO with one exception."

"What's that?"

"This woman was sexually assaulted. Looks like she was raped."

Clyde's upper lip curled in distaste. "Sick son of a bitch. He as much as left his fingerprint. You've got to get me some DNA evidence Brady. ASAP."

Brady nodded. "I'll do my best."

Clyde watched as the body bag was zipped closed, then turned to the other deputies. "Okay, guys, comb the area. If our guy left anything behind, you sure as hell had better find it."

He climbed into his car, trying to get warm, and watched as the deputies methodically made their search. Their flashlights bobbed around, in the trees and between the cars, little spot lights, hunting for clues.

About ten minutes into the search, one of the deputies came running over to his car. "Deputy, come over here. I think we found something."

Clyde followed the deputy to where the Middleburg Police Chief stood, pointing his flashlight at an area next to the outline of where the victim's body had been. There, glinting in the beam of light, was a small gold button. Clyde knelt down to get a closer look.

"This has something written on it. Can you read what it says?" he asked the deputy.

The young deputy next to him peered closely at the button. "Looks like the letters 'MF.'"

Clyde's stomach turned. That didn't help his case against Doug Cummings any.

The Middleburg Police Chief snorted. "Well, that really narrows it down, doesn't it?"

Clyde looked up at him. "What do you mean?"

"There were probably at least a dozen guys here tonight wearing a coat with buttons like that," the police chief responded.

"Why? I don't get it," Clyde said.

"Come on. Think about it. 'MF.' Middleburg Foxhounds."

Clyde drew in his breath. "Who would wear those buttons? Every member of the Hunt?"

"Naa. Only those guys who wear the red coats," the police chief said.

Clyde's hopes soared. Doug Cummings wore a red coat. "Okay, bag it," he said, barely able to contain his excitement. "And be damned sure not to touch it."

He watched as one of the deputies gingerly picked the button up with a pair of tweezers and dropped it in the evidence bag. The deputy whistled. "Would you look at this? This must be our lucky day. There's still some red thread attached to it. That's going to make proving the match a piece of cake."

Clyde's adrenaline was pumping. He was hyped to make the arrest. Now he just had to convince the sheriff. He left the other deputies to finish searching the area, and headed inside the Community Center to start his interrogations.

Anne hesitated inside her front door, trying to decide where she and Doug should go to talk. She finally decided on the kitchen. Anne turned on the overhead light and motioned towards the rectangular Country French pine table in the center of the room.

"Have a seat. I'm going to put some coffee on," she said, reaching for some fresh roasted beans to grind.

While she waited for the pot to brew, Anne kept her distance from Doug. She set the mugs out and got cream and sugar. Anything to avoid having to make small talk with him.

But Doug hardly seemed to notice her. He sat quietly at the table and seemed to be lost in his thoughts.

Anne poured cups for them both and then joined Doug at the table. She sat across from him, perched on the edge of her chair.

"Okay, Doug. What do you want to tell me?"

Doug looked at her and rose from his chair. He started to pace, then stopped next to Anne and ran his hand through his hair.

"Anne, I know you are going to think I'm crazy when you hear what I have to say, but just hear me out. I have a theory about what's been happening here."

Anne leaned even farther forward in her chair. She wished he weren't standing so close to her. Almost as if reading her thoughts, Doug started to walk again. He had his hands in his pockets and was looking down at the floor.

Then he stopped and turned around, looking her squarely in the eye. "I think someone is killing these women as some kind of retaliation against me, possibly trying to frame me for their murders."

Anne looked up at him in astonishment and almost choked on her coffee. "I know it sounds ludicrous . . ."

She interrupted him. "Ludicrous? You're right about that."

"Just hear me out," Doug said, and he sat down across from her. "Fourteen years ago, when I first started practicing, I had a *pro bono* case, a criminal case, for a client by the name of Zeke McGraw. The trial didn't go well and he was found guilty and sentenced to prison."

"Oh, I see. And now you're going to tell me that he killed Nancy, and Babs, and now Leslie, and that he's trying to frame you for those murders." She knew it was unprofessional, but she didn't even try to keep the contempt out of her voice.

"No. Zeke didn't do it. He's dead. I think his older brother, God, I can't even remember his name right now, I just remember it started with a 'Z,' I think he's behind it."

Anne stood up. "Look, Doug, I'm sorry, but I just can't sit here and listen to this."

Doug slammed his fist on the table so hard it made her jump. "Damn it, Anne, can't you just listen to what I have to say before you pass judgment on me? You're my lawyer for Christ's sake."

He was right. She sat back down and gave him a curt nod. "Go on."

Doug took a deep breath. "When I was waiting for you by the library, I got a call on my cell phone."

Anne forced herself to listen as Doug relayed the phone conversation to her.

"He called you on your cell phone?" she asked, when he had finished.

Doug nodded.

"How do you think he got the number?"

He frowned and was silent for a moment. Then he nodded. "Of course. That's it. When I was leaving tonight, Nellie told me that a man had called the house today and asked for my cell phone number. It must have been him."

Anne stared at him. "Go on."

"Well, I've been sitting here thinking about several other incidents that have happened recently. Like the day Nancy was murdered. Some strange guy showed up at my farm looking for me and told Babs he was a 'voice from my past.' I think now it must have been McGraw's brother. Babs gave him directions to where we were hunting, so he would have known where to find me and could have killed Nancy. Then, later that day, I received a newspaper clipping, a death notice about Zeke McGraw. It was sent anonymously."

"Do you still have it?" Anne asked.

Doug shook his head. "No. I threw it away."

"Then, the day Babs disappeared, when I couldn't load Huntley on the trailer, my farm manager found an old rag in my trailer that smelled like deer scent. I think that's why Huntley wouldn't go on the trailer."

"So?" Anne said.

"So, I don't know how the rag got there. Maybe this McGraw brother put it there to frame me, so I couldn't get to the hunt and wouldn't have an alibi for Babs' murder."

"Oh, come on, Doug, that's a little far-fetched. Who would even think of doing something like that?"

"McGraw would. He's from the backwoods of West Virginia. I'll bet you anything he's a deer hunter. He'd know that other animals would react to the deer scent. And there's more. A week or so after Nancy died, someone put her hunt whip in my car. And then the same thing happened after Babs died. A picture of her, that used to hang in my tack room, appeared in my car."

"Are you saying someone put them there to frame you?" Anne asked.

Doug frowned. "I don't know. Either to frame me or just to torment me. The point is, it's the perfect setup. And that's what I think Zeke's brother is doing. Setting me up to go to prison for these murders. All three of these murders have happened to women I know, when I've been alone, without an alibi. Like tonight, with Leslie. I was outside alone and all he had to do was find a victim and bingo, I'm the obvious suspect. I think he's been following me and he just waits for an opportunity. Tonight, it was Leslie. There's no telling who it might be tomorrow."

Anne rubbed the back of her neck. "Doug, I don't know what to say. You've caught me off guard here. But in spite of all that you've told me, you don't have anything concrete that exonerates you. A stranger visits your barn. A newspaper clipping you no longer have. A call on your cell phone." She shook her head.

Doug nodded. "Of course. He's made sure of that. But now that we know about it, there has to be a way to expose him."

She didn't respond.

"Anne?"

She glanced at him, but avoided making eye contact.

He scoffed. "You think I killed them. Don't you?"

Anne met his gaze. "Tell me how you got those cuts tonight, Doug."

He looked away. "I ran into a branch when I went for a walk."

"And that cut your face and your hand?"

"No, Anne." His voice was quiet. "I was so angry and frustrated after you left me and went back inside, that I hit the picnic table. That's how I cut my hand."

Anne blushed and looked away and Doug reached over and touched her chin, forcing her to look at him again. "I did not see Leslie out there, Anne. And if I had, I wouldn't have murdered her."

Anne stood up and walked to the window. Doug seemed so sincere about his innocence that it was hard not to believe him. But she was attracted to him, and she no longer trusted her judgment.

When Anne finally spoke, she chose her words carefully. "Just so we understand each other, Doug, please remember that it's not my job to rely on what I personally believe, but rather to figure out what I think a jury will believe. I will investigate the whereabouts of this McGraw brother tomorrow. In the meantime, I must warn you that I believe they may show up with a warrant for your arrest at any time. You have to mentally prepare yourself for that. And I don't know whether I can get you out on bail or not. I'll try, but you must know that I see a judge ruling against us on that."

Doug stood up. "Is that it then? I just go home and wait?"

Anne nodded. "That's all you can do right now." She walked him to the door. "Call me if the cops show up. No matter when it is."

Doug hesitated, his hand on the knob. "Anne, about tonight, what happened between us . . ."

She interrupted him. "Tonight never happened, Doug."

He stared into her eyes. "Is that how you want it to be?"

She nodded.

"Okay," he said quietly, closing the door as he went out.

By the time Doug arrived home it was nearly one a.m., and he turned off the downstairs' lights and wearily climbed the stairs to his bedroom. He hung up his scarlet coat and loosened his tie, but then realized he was so hyped from the evening's events that it would be useless to even attempt sleep, so he went back down to the library and poured himself a cognac.

Doug sank down on the overstuffed leather couch and sipped his drink. He felt the warmth of the liquor flow through him, and he kicked off his shoes and leaned back, closing his eyes.

He dozed off after a while, and was awakened later by the distant sound of pounding, muffled, yet most certainly coming from somewhere within the house. He sat up. Something was wrong. He tried to focus on what it was, and then he snapped awake, and remembered what had happened.

The banging continued and angry voices mixed with the thuds. Flashing blue lights intruded from outside. Doug was alert now, and the full reality of what was happening hit him like a blast of icy air. He looked at his watch. Two-fifteen. It had to be the police.

Doug got up and put his shoes back on, then slowly went to the front door and turned on the outside light.

"Who is it?"

"Deputy Dickson. Open up."

Doug unlocked the door and opened it, but didn't step back to allow entry. "Isn't it a little late for house calls, Deputy?"

Dickson shoved a warrant in Doug's face and pushed past him. "I have a search warrant, Cummings, get out of my way."

Doug didn't bother to argue and stepped back as three other deputies rushed in behind Dickson.

"Okay, fellas, you know what you're looking for. Tear the place apart until you find it." Dickson closed the door behind them and leaned against it. His hand rested on the gun in his holster.

Doug watched as the three deputies split up. One went upstairs and the other two headed in opposite directions on the main floor.

Dickson smirked at Doug. "Pretty nasty scrape you've got on your face there, Cummings. Did Ms. McCashin scratch you before or after you raped her?"

Doug inhaled sharply. "Oh, God. Leslie was *raped*?"

Dickson snorted. "Don't waste your theatrics on me, Cummings. I know what you're all about."

"Doug?" They both turned towards the back hall as Nellie walked towards them, dressed in a flannel nightgown and quilted bathrobe, her long gray hair loose from its braid. "My goodness, Doug, what's going on here?" Nellie asked.

Doug walked over and put an arm around her. "I'm not quite sure myself, Nellie. The deputy is apparently looking for something that couldn't wait until morning. Why don't you go back to bed? I'll tell you all about it tomorrow."

Nellie put a trembling hand on Doug's arm. "No, I'll wait up with you. I couldn't sleep with them roaming around anyway."

One of the deputies came down the stairs, carrying Doug's scarlet evening coat, and Doug and Nellie waited while the deputy huddled with Dickson.

Doug watched as the deputy showed a small evidence bag to Dickson. Dickson handed the coat back to the deputy and strode over to Doug.

"Doug Cummings, you are under arrest for the murder of Leslie McCashin. You have the right to remain silent, anything you say can and will be used against you in a court of law."

Doug gently pushed Nellie behind him, then walked past Dickson towards the phone.

Dickson drew his gun and yelled at Doug, "Freeze right there, Cummings, or I'll shoot."

Doug stopped, raised his hands and slowly turned around. "I'm not going anywhere, Dickson. I'm just exercising my Constitutional right to call my lawyer."

The two other deputies had come running at the sound of Dickson's command, and the three of them stood by, waiting for direction from the deputy. "Cuff him," Dickson ordered.

"Hey, wait a minute," Doug shouted angrily at the young deputy who was standing over him. "You're not touching me until I've had a chance to call my attorney."

The deputy looked uncertainly at Dickson. "I said cuff him. He can make his call from the jail," Dickson snarled.

As the deputies half-dragged Doug out of the house, he remembered that Nellie was standing there. "Everything's going to be okay, Nellie. Phone Anne Sullivan . . ."

Before he could finish his sentence, the deputies shoved Doug into the back seat of the patrol car and slammed the door.

48

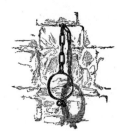

When Anne arrived at the jail in Leesburg, Doug had already been booked and taken to a cell. The lobby was deserted except for a middle-aged deputy sitting behind the front desk, with a Stephen King paperback book resting on his belly. Anne identified herself and asked to see Doug.

"Why, that's not possible, Miss, ah, Sullivan," the deputy said, with a thick southern drawl. "He's been taken to his cell for the night. No one's going to question him before morning, so he really doesn't need to see a lawyer right now. I'd suggest you come back tomorrow, during regular hours."

Anne read the man's name on his badge. "Deputy Thomas, I must not have made myself clear. I'm Doug Cummings' lawyer and I want to see my client. Now. You can either do as I ask and let us both get on with our jobs, or you can force me to call Judge Hitchin and wake him up at this ungodly hour. And believe me, Deputy Thomas, I'll be sure to mention your name."

The man's beefy face grew flushed. "Well, ah, I guess you could see him for a couple of minutes. You go on to the interview room. I'll bring him there."

Anne nodded at the deputy. "Thank you, Deputy Thomas. I can see you and I are going to get along just fine." She walked down the hallway to the attorney/inmate interview room before he had time to change his mind.

Doug was handcuffed when the deputy led him into the room. "You want me to take his handcuffs off, ma'am?"

Anne nodded at the deputy as she studied Doug. She'd had similar meetings with many clients, but the sight of Doug, dressed in orange prison garb with "Inmate" emblazoned across his chest, turned her stomach.

They both sat down on opposite sides of the table and Anne waited to speak until after the door closed behind the deputy. "Are you all right?"

Doug nodded.

"As you know, the magistrate denied bail, so I'll request that a bond hearing be set for first thing Monday morning. I'm afraid that you're stuck in here at least until then. Now, tell me what happened."

Doug shook his head. "I still don't really know what it was all about. Dickson and three other deputies showed up with a search warrant. They went through the house. One of them found my scarlet tails, the coat I wore last night, and showed it to Dickson. Then he arrested me."

"Could you tell what it was about the coat that interested him?" Anne asked.

"It seemed like they were looking at the sleeves, but it was pretty hard to tell," Doug replied. "He also had something in an evidence bag, but I couldn't see what it was."

"Was that all that happened?"

Doug nodded.

Anne sighed. "Okay. I'll find out what the charges are based on when I meet with Timothy Shaw, the prosecutor, on Monday morning. In the meantime, we need to focus on your situation here." She looked critically at him. "You need to get that cut on your face cleaned up."

Doug scoffed. "Really, Anne, I appreciate your maternal instincts, but a little cut on my face is the least of my worries right now."

"Forget my maternal instincts, Doug. I save those for Samantha. I simply don't want to appear before Judge Hitchin at a bond hearing Monday morning with a client who looks like he just got in a bar brawl, or worse yet, looks like he was injured while committing the murder that he's charged with."

"God, Anne, that reminds me, Dickson referred to this cut when he was at my house. He asked if Leslie scratched me before or after I raped her." Doug shook his head. "I can't believe I forgot to tell you that before."

Anne stared at him. "Leslie was raped?" she repeated.

Doug nodded and leaned forward in his chair. "I'm sorry I blurted it out like that."

Anne closed her eyes for an instant. Who did this, Doug? Was it you?

"Anne?" Doug reached out and touched her hand.

Anne pulled her hand away and sat back in her chair, avoiding making eye contact with him.

Doug clasped his hands together and took a deep breath. "Look, Anne, I know this is going to sound very coldhearted, but I've got to ask."

She studied him for a moment. "Go on."

"Doesn't the fact that Leslie was raped make it better for me? For my defense?"

Anne frowned. "In what way?"

"Because now there's a way I can prove that I didn't do it. Just run a DNA test and have me eliminated as a suspect."

Anne weighed the possibilities. "I want to think this over, Doug. At this point, I'm not inclined to run out and agree to DNA testing."

"Why not?"

"Well, because DNA test results can be interpreted in different ways. Look at what happened in the O.J. Simpson trial. I just don't want to rush into anything that could backfire on us."

He scowled at her. "That sounds to me like the kind of advice you'd give a client that you thought might be guilty. I'm telling you, Anne, I did not rape and murder Leslie and if there's a test out there that can prove my innocence, I'm going to take it."

"Remember, Doug, we don't need to prove that you are innocent. We just need to interject reasonable doubt into the prosecution's case. Sometimes, a defendant can hurt his own case by trying to prove his innocence and then failing to do so convincingly. I don't want to fall into that trap."

"Well, I'm not *some defendant*, and I will not settle for an acquittal based on 'reasonable doubt.' I have a life to live once this is all behind me, Anne, and I won't spend it having people, yourself included, wonder whether or not I really committed those murders. It's all or nothing for me. If you can't play by those rules, I'll find someone who will."

Anne sighed and looked at her watch. It was almost five a.m. "I can play by those rules, Doug. I just feel that it is my duty to point out the drawbacks to that approach. Besides, even if we can prove that you didn't rape Leslie, you'll still face the murder charge. Timothy Shaw is a very smart prosecutor, and I'd be surprised if he didn't turn the DNA evidence around and use it against you."

"How the hell could he do that?"

"Simple. Maybe the rapist and the murderer are not the same person. In fact, maybe Leslie wasn't raped at all. Maybe she had consensual sex with someone, maybe it even got a little rough. Maybe you found out about it afterwards and became so insanely jealous and outraged that you murdered her."

"That's insane, Anne. Who would believe a theory like that? What's he going to say, that Leslie was having sex with someone at the hunt ball, out in the parking lot?" Doug stopped and blushed.

Anne gave him a small smile. "It's really not so far-fetched when you think about it, is it?"

Doug sighed and rubbed his hand over his eyes. "Christ, Anne. Isn't there any way out of this?"

"I think that we have a really good chance, Doug. The last thing I want is for you to get discouraged." She stood up. "Right now, we both need to try and get some sleep. I'll be back later today with a change of clothes for you to wear to court on Monday. I'm sure you already know this, but I'll say it anyway. Don't speak to anyone about your case. Not a guard, not another inmate, no one. Certainly not Dickson or anyone else who might try to interrogate you. They have a right to question you, but only if I'm present. Any questions?"

Doug shook his head. "No."

Anne knocked on the door and Deputy Thomas opened it.

"Deputy Thomas, there's one other thing I need you to do for me," Anne said. "Mr. Cummings needs to have some immediate medical attention given to the cuts on his face and hand. I know I can trust you to handle that for me."

"Ah, Miss Sullivan, how do you expect me to, uh, do that at this time of night?" he drawled.

"That's up to you, Deputy. As I'm sure you can see, these are very nasty wounds, and I know that the last thing you want to have happen is for my client's injuries to become infected due to lack of care on your part. Use whatever resources you feel are necessary, Deputy Thomas." Anne smiled at him. "I'll leave you to look after Mr. Cummings. I can let myself out. Thanks again for being so cooperative."

Anne put her hand on Doug's shoulder as she walked by. "Try to get some rest, Doug. I'll see you later."

Anne saw Doug again briefly that day when she returned to drop off his court clothes.

Doug looked pale and exhausted, but someone had done a pretty good job cleaning up the cut on his face. Anne figured that after he had a shave, he'd look presentable enough for the bond hearing the next day.

"I dropped some clothes off for the hearing tomorrow. They'll do for now, but we'll need to do some shopping before a jury sees you."

"Why, what's the matter with my clothes?" Doug asked.

Anne smiled. "Nothing if you're in Washington or New York. But we're in rural Virginia, Doug. Armani suits and Hermès ties don't play very well out here. You know as well as anyone that this is a blue blazer and khakis kind of town. By the way, I had the pleasure of meeting Nellie. She helped me select your clothes. She said to tell you she's doing fine and that when you get home, she is going to cook you the biggest plate of blueberry pancakes you ever saw."

Doug smiled. "How is she really doing?" he asked.

"She's okay. Nellie may be getting up there in years, but I think she's a pretty tough cookie. She also has undying faith in you, Doug, and absolute confidence that you'll prevail in all this." Anne changed the subject. "Let's talk briefly about the bond hearing tomorrow. We won't be getting into any of the substantive issues of the case, just character issues, whether you're a flight risk, things like that. I'll need a background bio, so I can show the judge what an upstanding citizen you are. Who can provide me with that?"

"Call my secretary, Marsha." Doug gave her Marsha's home phone number.

"Fine. Now your job tomorrow is to stay calm, no matter what the prosecution may say about you. I don't want the judge getting the impression that you're hot headed."

Doug took a deep breath and sat back in his chair. His fingers drummed nervously on the table. "What are my chances for bail?"

"I honestly don't know, Doug. Bail is not usually granted in murder cases, but then you're not the typical defendant. Your good character is definitely on our side, and I intend to focus on that as much as I can. Judge Hitchin is a fair judge. He won't be afraid to do what he thinks is right."

There was a rap on the door. "Time's up, Counselor."

"Okay, just give us another minute," Anne replied.

Anne looked back at Doug. "Any questions?"

"What can I do to help between now and tomorrow?"

"Honestly, the best thing you can do is to try and get some rest. I know that probably seems like a ridiculous request, but I need you to be as relaxed as possible tomorrow. I want the judge to see you as concerned, but not distraught. The perfect picture of someone falsely accused."

"I am falsely accused, Anne. And by the end of this, I hope even you are going to believe that," he said quietly.

50

The bond hearing was set for ten o'clock Monday morning. Anne arrived at the courthouse at nine-thirty, hoping to catch a word beforehand with Timothy Shaw. The media were everywhere and she hurried into the attorneys' lounge before they spotted her.

Anne found Shaw waiting in the lounge.

"Good morning, Anne," Shaw greeted her pleasantly. "I was glad to see that you're defense counsel on this case. It's always nice to work with opposing counsel that you respect and trust."

Anne smiled at him. "You can stop with the flattery, Timothy. What do you want?"

"I want some samples from Cummings, so I can run DNA tests. If you cooperate now, I'll give you a good plea." Timothy Shaw wasn't one to play games. Anne knew that he was offering a deal most defense counsel would jump at.

"You skipped a step, Timothy. What amount of bail can we agree on?" Anne asked, knowing full well what his response would be.

Shaw laughed heartily. "I see. That's how you want to play it. There will be no bail, Anne. Your guy's not going to be seeing sunshine for a very long time."

"Fine. We'll let Judge Hitchin decide that." Anne started to walk away, then she stopped and turned back around. "Oh, Timothy, I'm just curious, how well do you know Clyde Dickson, the deputy who arrested my client?"

Shaw shrugged. "This is the first time I've worked with him. Why?"

Anne leaned closer to him and spoke in a hushed tone. "Well, let me give you a word of caution. Just between you and me. That guy's a loose cannon and for some unknown reason, he's got it in for my client. I know you play things by the book, and I wouldn't want the shoddy way in which he has conducted this investigation to reflect poorly on you. He's bad news, Timothy. Just be careful." Anne picked up her briefcase and started towards the courtroom.

"Anne, wait a second." Shaw caught up with her. "Give me an example."

Anne laughed. "What, and help you see all the pitfalls in your case? Oh, no, Timothy, I'll wait to point those out for the jury." She paused, shaking her head. "I must admit, though, I was shocked to hear that you would proceed with a case like this. I would have expected more from you."

"I don't know what you mean, Anne. Doug Cummings raped and murdered Leslie McCashin and murdered those other two women too. Only with Leslie McCashin, I have the evidence to prove it."

Anne flashed him a look of disbelief. "Oh, come on, Timothy, you don't have any evidence. It's all just Dickson's speculation."

"Not true. I have real evidence," he countered.

Anne just smiled at him.

"Fine, I'll share it with you. I don't care. I have a button that was found next to the victim's body at the crime scene. I also have another button, identical in appearance, that was found at your client's home, hidden in a plant, and I have the scissors that your client used to cut it off his coat. Luckily for me, they all had enough fiber evidence for forensics to be able to confirm that both buttons came from Cummings' coat. I should have the results in a couple of days." Shaw stepped back, his hands on his hips, and looked smugly at Anne.

Anne's pulse quickened in excitement. A button from Doug's scarlet tails? She could blow all kinds of holes through that theory. Hell, Anne thought, I can even introduce testimony that I was wearing Doug's coat outside at the hunt ball that night. I walked across that parking lot wearing Doug's coat. She knew that it would cause all kinds of problems if she had to testify to that, but at least it was a defense Doug could use as a last resort.

She glared at Shaw. "A button? You don't even have the forensics' results yet and you're charging Doug Cummings with these heinous crimes just because Dickson brought you a button?" Anne shook her head. "Just heed my warning, Timothy. I'd hate to see your promising career halted by this case." She glanced at her watch. "See you in court."

Anne made a mad dash to the courtroom, issuing several "no comments" to the throng of reporters, and had just finished organizing her papers on the counsel table when the bailiff brought Doug in. He looked perfect. Just the demeanor she wanted. The cut on his cheek was barely visible from a distance, and Anne had to admit that the Armani look gave him an air of confidence. Hardly the picture of a serial killer.

She stood up to greet him and waited while they took off his handcuffs. "You look great," she said. "I take back everything I said about your clothes."

Doug smiled. "Thanks. You don't look bad yourself."

The door to the judge's chamber opened and the court clerk called out, "All rise. The Court is now in session, The Honorable Judge John Hitchin presiding. God save the Commonwealth and this Honorable Court. You may be seated."

The clerk called their case. "The matter of the Commonwealth vs. W. Douglas Cummings, the Third, will now be heard."

The judge glanced at the papers before him on the bench, and then looked out at the courtroom, his wire-framed glasses resting on the tip of his nose. "Before we start this proceeding, I have a word to say to the spectators and the media in this courtroom. I am a firm believer in open court proceedings and the presence of the media in the courtroom. I will not, however, tolerate any disruption of the legal process that is our purpose here today. Therefore, you all stand forewarned that if any disturbance occurs in this courtroom, I will close these proceedings immediately. That means no beepers going off, no cell phones ringing, no one going in and out of this courtroom once we have started this hearing. If anyone cannot stay for the duration, he or she should take leave now."

Judge Hitchin waited, giving anyone so inclined a chance to leave, but no one moved. The courtroom was silent.

"Fine, then, let's proceed." The judge looked at Timothy Shaw, his glasses still perched low on his nose. "We have before this Court today the issue of bail in this case. Do you agree with the defense that bail is appropriate, Counselor?"

Shaw stood up. "Absolutely not, Your Honor. The defendant stands accused of the most violent of crimes, rape and murder, and would pose a threat to society if he were to be released on bail. In addition, Your Honor, the defendant has the inclination and the financial means to flee this jurisdiction should he be given such an opportunity."

Judge Hitchin looked at Anne. "How do you respond to that, Counsel?"

Anne stood up and gestured towards the lectern that stood between the two counsel tables. "May I speak from the podium, Your Honor?"

Judge Hitchin nodded. "Thank you, Counselor. Mr. Shaw always seems to think that's too long a trip for him to make." The judge looked pointedly at Timothy Shaw, who turned crimson under his gaze. There was a light titter from the audience, then silence as the judge glared in their direction. He looked back at Anne. "You may proceed, Ms. Sullivan."

Anne took a deep breath before beginning. "Your Honor, the man seated at the defense table today is not your ordinary defendant, nor is this case a typical case." She gestured towards Doug, making brief eye contact with him. "Mr. Cummings is a member in good standing of the bar of the Commonwealth, as well as the District of Columbia, and has been for almost fifteen years. He volunteers his time to serve on the boards of a dozen charitable and educational institutions, including the University of Virginia and Yale University. His family is native Virginia. Mr. Cummings grew up in this community."

Shaw jumped to his feet. "Your Honor, the next thing Ms. Sullivan is going to tell us is that the defendant was a Boy Scout. None of this has any relevance to the crimes the defendant stands accused of."

"I'm simply trying to establish Mr. Cummings' character, Your Honor, which is clearly relevant to the issue of bail."

Judge Hitchin motioned for Shaw to sit down. "You may continue, Ms. Sullivan, but please spare us the part about the Boy Scouts."

Anne smiled. "Yes, Your Honor. Mr. Cummings is very active in this community and serves on several local boards, including the Board of Governor's of the Middleburg Foxhounds, the Board of Trustees of the Middleburg Community Council, and the Board of Directors of Middleburg Merchant's Bank. In other words, Your Honor, Mr. Cummings is a pillar of this community. Mr. Cummings has a stake in having his name cleared in this community and in having his good reputation restored. He's not going to flee this jurisdiction. This is his home. This was his family's home. All that matters most to him is here." She gestured towards the window and the spectacular view of the Blue Ridge Mountains beyond. "Doug Cummings is an innocent man, falsely accused. He's got every reason to stay and fight, and nothing, Your Honor, nothing at all to gain by flight."

The judge looked at Timothy Shaw. "Mr. Shaw."

Shaw stood up, looking uncertain whether he should go to the podium, but Anne still occupied it. "Your Honor, the defendant isn't at all anxious to clear his good name. We've received absolutely no cooperation from the defense in the investigation of this matter."

"That's not true, Your Honor," Anne said quickly. "Just prior to the start of this hearing, Mr. Shaw and I were discussing Mr. Cummings' desire to voluntarily submit samples for DNA testing, so that he may put this matter to rest. Mr. Cummings is insistent that DNA tests be run, Your Honor. As soon as possible."

"I beg the Court's pardon, Your Honor, but defense counsel never agreed to such a test," Shaw responded.

"Only because our conversation was interrupted, Your Honor. As I stated before, Mr. Cummings is insistent on such tests being run," Anne replied.

"Fine, then," the judge said. "The two of you get together and get it scheduled. Do you have anything else to say before I rule, Ms. Sullivan?"

"Yes, I do, Your Honor." Anne took a brief moment and looked over at Doug, then back to the bench. "When I stood up here today, I told you that bail was proper for two reasons. One, Mr. Cummings is not an ordinary defendant, which I have just shown. He's honorable, he's reputable, and he's determined to clear his name. In addition, Mr. Cummings poses no flight risk. But the second reason that bail should be granted in this case is perhaps an even more compelling one. This case, Your Honor, makes a mockery of this Court. It's a harassment suit, if a charge this serious can be characterized that way. It's based on speculation and innuendo."

Shaw was on his feet again. "This isn't an evidentiary hearing, Your Honor. Defense counsel is going way beyond the scope of these proceedings."

Judge Hitchin frowned at Anne. "Counsel, my patience is wearing thin here. Mr. Shaw is right. I think you're straying beyond our purpose here today. Wrap it up please."

"With all due respect, Your Honor, I disagree. My client's freedom is at stake here today, and I believe that this Court may, no, must, look at the strength of the charges against Mr. Cummings in order to determine whether or not he poses a risk to others, and whether it is appropriate to infringe on his liberties, to lock him up, while the Commonwealth drags him through a long, drawn-out trial process."

The judge didn't interrupt, so Anne quickly continued. "Your Honor, the charges against Mr. Cummings were filed because of one, only one, shred of physical evidence. A tiny button. And the Commonwealth has no evidence that this button even has any connection to Mr. Cummings. It just looks similar to a button he owns. And, by the way, Your Honor, it also looks similar to buttons that countless other men were wearing on their coats in the vicinity of the murder on the night in question. A Middleburg Foxhounds' button, found at the Middleburg Foxhounds' Hunt Ball." Anne shook her head. "But the Commonwealth didn't charge any of those other men, Your Honor. No, they decided instead to rush out, in the middle of the night, before they could run any tests, and charge Mr. Cummings with the crime. And, now, Mr. Shaw would like to throw away the key."

Judge Hitchin frowned at Shaw. "How do you respond to that, Counselor?"

Timothy Shaw walked to the podium and Anne, showing him a hint of a smile, sat back down next to Doug.

"Your Honor, Ms. Sullivan is correct only in that we don't have any test results back yet to confirm the connection that this evidence has to Mr. Cummings. However, when this case is viewed in its entirety, the connection is quite clear."

"Mr. Shaw, this case will be viewed in its entirety in due course, and you'll have your chance to argue your case against the defendant. But it seems to me that at this point in time, you've made some pretty strong assumptions, perhaps, and I say perhaps, without the proper foundation to back them up. I trust that by the time this case goes to trial, you'll have that foundation, or you'll not come into my courtroom. But for our purposes here today, this doubt as to the strength of the charges against the defendant, along with the evidence as to his good character, makes me inclined to release Mr. Cummings on bail pending the trial of this matter. Do you have anything else to say, Counselor?"

"Just that I believe that you should take Mr. Cummings enormous wealth into account, Your Honor, in determining whether there is any amount of bail that could assure his return for trial," Shaw replied.

Judge Hitchin took off his glasses and leaned forward. "Counsel, I find it hard to believe that there is not some amount of money that even a man of Mr. Cummings' alleged vast wealth would be unwilling to forfeit, but quite frankly, even if there were not, I don't see how I can possibly take that argument into account, since you have failed to provide any such evidence before the Court today."

Anne smiled. The judge was right. It was Shaw's burden to produce evidence of Doug's net worth.

Shaw blushed. "Your Honor, I assumed that you wouldn't consider bail in a case such as this."

"Well, Counselor, you assumed wrong."

The judge straightened up in his chair and addressed the courtroom. "Having heard all the arguments presented here today, it is my determination that this case is an appropriate one for the defendant to be released on bail and that amount is hereby set at one hundred thousand dollars. I am also imposing a requirement that the defendant surrender his passport, and that he not travel more than one hundred miles outside of this jurisdiction." He banged his gavel on the bench and rose from his chair.

Pandemonium broke loose in the courtroom, and some members of the media struggled to approach Doug. The bailiff led Doug and Anne through the front of the courtroom to an upstairs conference room, where they would remain until the arrangements to post the bond were completed.

Anne waited until they were alone and then turned to Doug. He smiled and reached out his hand and touched her awkwardly on her elbow. "Nice job, Counselor," he said. "Thank you."

Anne tried to contain her enthusiasm, and she cautioned Doug that the bail could be revoked at any time, based on the discovery of further evidence. But even she had a hard time being pessimistic. "Let's not forget, though, that we're still facing a murder trial, Doug. This victory today, although it may seem sweet right now, is a far cry from an acquittal at trial."

Doug's smile faded. "Believe me, Anne, I haven't forgotten that for one moment. But right now, just to know that I am free to go home, that I don't have to spend tonight sleeping on that cold, hard bunk, surrounded by bars, that means more to me than you could ever imagine."

She nodded. "Okay. Let's get the wheels rolling to get you out of here."

Doug leaned back comfortably against the rich leather seat of Anne's Jaguar and watched Anne as she drove. They were out of the vicinity of the courthouse, and he heaved a sigh of relief. "Fill me in on this whole business about the button from my coat. What was that all about?"

"A Middleburg Foxhounds' button was apparently discovered at the murder scene. And when the police searched your house, they allegedly found a pair of scissors and a button, identical in appearance to the one found at the murder scene, hidden in a plant," Anne replied. "Their theory, of course, is that when you returned home Saturday night, you realized that you had lost a button sometime during the evening. Fearing that perhaps you had lost the button during your struggle with Leslie, you removed a second button from the other sleeve of your coat, thinking that it would be less obvious to anyone investigating that the first button was missing."

Doug stared at her. "That's right. They're right. That's exactly what I did."

Anne glanced quickly in Doug's direction. "What?"

"They're right that I cut the button off. They just have the wrong motive." Doug straightened up in his seat and looked around. "Can you pull off this road somewhere? We need to talk about this."

They were just passing Oatlands Plantation, a property of the National Trust for Historic Preservation. Anne turned off the highway at the entrance to the estate and pulled into the public parking lot by the mansion, turning off the engine.

"Talk," she said.

Doug turned sideways in his seat, facing her. "When I got dressed to pick you up for dinner, before the hunt ball, I realized that one of the three buttons on the right sleeve of my coat was missing. I knew that I would be late if I asked Nellie to sew another one on, so I decided to cut one off the left sleeve, so that at least both sleeves would match. I had a hard time getting the other button off, and when it came loose, it popped across the room. I guess that's how it ended up in a plant. I didn't bother to look for it, I just put the scissors down and left to go and pick you up."

"Let me see if I understand this. Are you saying that you did lose a button off your coat, but that it was lost before the hunt ball, and that the fiber test results will show that the button found at the murder scene did not come from your coat?"

Doug narrowed his eyes. "Perhaps, but I was thinking of another scenario. When I arrived home to get dressed that evening, my coat was lying in a heap on the floor, rather than hanging on the armoire where I had left it that morning. I just assumed that Nellie had inadvertently knocked it off when she had come in earlier to see if my shirt needed pressing. Now, I'm not so sure that's what happened."

Anne frowned. "Go on."

"What if McGraw's brother came into my house and took the button from my coat, then planted it at the murder scene, to frame me?"

Anne just stared at him.

"Well?" Doug asked, when she didn't respond.

"Doug, I just don't see a jury ever buying that theory."

"Do you have another explanation as to how a button that I was not wearing on the night in question ended up at the murder scene?"

Anne didn't answer.

Doug shook his head. "No, I didn't think so."

Anne sighed. "Okay, let's assume McGraw did do this. How easily could he have gotten into your house?"

"As a general rule, I keep the place locked, but on that day, I think he could have walked right in. When I arrived home, the back door was unlocked. It has also happened on several other occasions recently. I think that Nellie is getting forgetful about locking the door."

"Do you have an alarm?" she asked.

"Yes, but I very rarely turn it on."

"I think that you'd better start using it."

Doug nodded. "So, where do we go from here?"

"I'm going to get busy finding out about Zeke McGraw's brother," Anne said, starting the car. "Where can I find you later, if I need to get in touch with you?"

Doug thought about it briefly. "I think I'll go to my law firm."

Anne pulled the car back onto the highway and headed towards Middleburg. "All right. I'll call you there if I need you; otherwise, let's touch base at the end of the day and I'll fill you in on what, if anything, I've learned."

They drove in silence for a while. Doug was dreading the thought of spending the evening at home all alone. He looked at Anne. "I have an idea. Why don't you and Samantha come to my house for dinner tonight? Nellie would love to cook for someone other than just me, and I know that she and Samantha would get along great. Then we can go over what you learn today."

Anne glanced over at him. "Sure. If we can make it an early night."

"Of course. Why don't you come over around five? That way you and I can chat for a few minutes and we can still eat by six."

They were approaching the entrance to Hunting Hollow and Anne slowed the car to a stop. The gates were closed and the driveway was swarming with reporters. She looked at Doug. "Is there any other way into your farm?"

He shook his head. "Not in this car. There's an old service road through the woods, but you'd never make it without four-wheel drive. Why don't you drop me off here? I'll jump the fence and go across the pasture."

"I don't like that idea," Anne said. "If they see you, they'll be all over you. We don't want the image of you sneaking into your farm to show up on tonight's news. You had a victory today. That's what we want them to focus on. I really think we should go through the gates, and use this opportunity to issue a statement."

She smiled pleadingly at him. "I know the reporters really bother you, but believe me, it's far better to have the media on your side than against you."

"I didn't think they were on anyone's side."

Anne nodded. "Right. Objective reporting and all that. Let's just say that sometimes the unbiased reporting of the facts seems more fair and objective than at other times. In my experience, the governing factor is often what rapport, if any, the reporter has with the subject." She put her hand on his arm. "Please humor me and put up with it. I'll be right there with you."

He smiled. "How can I refuse, when you put it like that?"

52

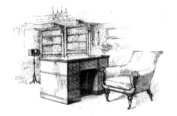

The lobby at White, Baker and Cummings was empty when Doug arrived.

"Hi, Jill," Doug greeted the receptionist. "How are things?" He peered into his mail slot, checking for messages.

"Good afternoon, Mr. Cummings," Jill replied, glancing nervously around the lobby. "Can I help you with something?"

"Relax, Jill, I work here, remember? There's no need to treat me like a visitor. I still remember the way to my office."

As Doug walked towards the hallway that led to his office, he saw Jill pick up the phone.

Doug opened the outer door to the suite where his office was located, and stopped when he saw Marsha working at a desk adjacent to another partner's office.

"Marsha, what did they do, loan you out to Findley, since I haven't been around to keep you busy?" he asked her.

Marsha glanced quickly around, then got up and pulled Doug by his arm into the copy room, closing the door behind them. "Doug, I've left messages everywhere for you. I tried to warn you."

He frowned. "What are you talking about, Marsha?"

She shook her head. "When I arrived for work this morning, they were emptying out your office and told me that I'd be working for Mr. Findley from now on."

Doug threw open the door and stormed back out into the suite, heading for his office.

"Doug." Robert Dewitt's voice boomed from behind him. "I need to talk to you."

Doug turned around and glared at Dewitt, then continued on into his office. Marsha was right. The room was empty. Literally. Even the furniture was gone.

Dewitt followed Doug into the office and closed the door behind them.

Doug wheeled around to face Dewitt, one hand on his hip, the other gesturing around the barren room. "What the hell is going on here, Robert?"

"Calm down, Doug. I'll be happy to discuss this with you if we can keep it civilized. If not, you'll be escorted out." Dewitt leaned against the wall, his arms folded across his chest.

Doug took a deep breath and fought hard to control his temper. "Something tells me this isn't going to be much of a discussion, Robert, but go ahead."

"All right. I'll cut to the bottom line. You are no longer a member of this firm. I'm certain that I don't have to tell you why. We've sent your furniture and other personal items to storage, awaiting your instructions as to what you'd like done with them." Dewitt inched closer to the door as he spoke.

Doug just stared at Dewitt and shook his head. "I'm no longer a member of this firm?" he repeated. "You can't do that, Robert. You can't unilaterally kick me out of the firm. Read the By-laws."

"Not only can I, Doug, but I have. You read the By-laws. There's a morals clause in there that gives me the absolute power to take this action." Dewitt responded.

Doug walked to the window and leaned his palms against the glass, trying to contain his anger. He took several deep breaths, then turned back to face Dewitt. "Look, Robert, I understand you feeling that you had to take certain actions to protect the firm from my negative publicity. I really do. But I think we can work together on this. I would be agreeable to taking a complete leave of absence from the firm, pending the resolution of the criminal charges against me. Wouldn't that satisfy the critics?"

Dewitt put his hand on the door knob. "There will be no negotiating, Doug. The decision has been made and the action taken." He opened the door and motioned for Doug to exit. "We have nothing else to talk about. I would like you to leave now. If not, I'll call security."

Doug banged his fist against the wall behind him. He strode over to the door and stopped in front of Dewitt. "I'm just curious about one thing, Robert. Did it matter to you at all that my name is on that door?" Doug gestured towards the front of the firm.

"Why, that's not your name, Doug. That's your father's name. I'm surprised that you could have forgotten that." Dewitt turned and walked away.

Although Doug had worked out at the gym and finished with a long hot shower, he was still seething at what Dewitt had done. As he paced his study, waiting for Anne and Samantha to arrive, he poured himself a scotch on the rocks and took a long drink. He closed his eyes and sighed as he felt the cold liquid burn his throat.

All his instincts screamed at him to mount an immediate battle against the firm, but logic told him that would be suicide. He knew he had to wait until he no longer had a murder charge hanging over his head. Doug looked at the portrait of his father hanging above the fireplace, and hoped to God that there was no looking back from beyond. The doorbell rang and Doug put down his drink and went to answer it, struggling to shake off his mood.

"Hi, Doug." Samantha rushed inside and tugged off her coat, which was splattered with raindrops. "It's starting to rain outside and maybe if it gets cold enough it will turn to snow and then we can build a snowman. Will you help me? Will you?"

Doug laughed. "Wait a minute, slow down. Don't I even get a hug?"

He bent down and Samantha threw her arms around his neck. "Look what I brought for us to play with," she said, opening the backpack she had brought and showing him her collection of toy horses. "Aunt Anne says that you like horses, so I brought some of my Breyer horses and some of my Pony Tails. Which ones do you want to play with?"

Doug ruffled her hair affectionately. "Tell you what, let's take these into the kitchen where Nellie is fixing dinner, and we can set them up in there. There's a fire in the fireplace and they'll be nice and warm."

"Okay, but they can't play too close to the fire because they might get burned and besides that, horses are afraid of fire you know," Samantha said, working diligently trying to zip up the backpack.

Doug straightened up to greet Anne. She gave him a light embrace and touched her cheek to his. "I found out some interesting things today. Let's get Samantha settled and I'll fill you in."

Nellie and Samantha hit it off immediately and Doug led Anne back to the study. "Have a seat," Doug said, indicating the couch. "Can I get you something to drink?"

"I'd love a glass of white wine."

"Chardonnay okay?"

Anne nodded.

Doug poured her wine and freshened his scotch, then sat down beside her on the couch. "Here's to hoping that your day was better than mine," he said, raising his glass to her.

Anne returned his toast, and took a sip, then put her glass down on the coffee table. "Why, what happened? When I left you, your day was going pretty well."

Doug shrugged and stared at the fire. "Never mind, forget I said that." He looked over at her. "You said you have some interesting news. What is it?"

"Doug, something is obviously bothering you. Wouldn't you feel better if you talked about it?" Anne asked.

Doug closed his eyes briefly. Part of him wanted to tell her what Dewitt had done, but he couldn't bring himself to speak about it. He shook his head. "Maybe later. You tell me what you found out."

"Okay. I spent the afternoon on the phone with the prison where Zeke McGraw was incarcerated and was able to speak with several of the guards who had worked around him. It seems that it was common knowledge around the prison that McGraw blamed you for his incarceration and that he vowed to seek revenge against you. So there's a motive, at least on Zeke's part."

Anne paused to take a sip of her wine. "They said Zeke didn't have many visitors. His mother and sister came occasionally, but he had one regular visitor, his older brother, Zebulon. They said Zebulon came like clockwork."

"Zebulon. That's his name," Doug said.

"I called a private investigator that I've used before and set up an appointment with him for tomorrow morning. I'd like to ask him to check out Zebulon's whereabouts and put a tail on him, if you're agreeable."

Doug nodded. "Sure, if they can find him. But I'm willing to bet that they can't."

"Well, I hope you're wrong. But I should know more in a day or two."

"What about Zeke? Why was he still in prison? His sentence on the drug conviction should have run out years ago."

Anne nodded. "He was involved in a prison brawl where an inmate was killed. Zeke was convicted of murdering the inmate and was sentenced to life in prison."

"How did he die?"

"He hung himself in his cell."

Doug winced. "Any idea why?"

"Apparently he was gang-raped the week before he hung himself."

Doug rose and walked over to the fireplace and stood staring into the flames. "God, Anne, when is this going to end? How many lives have been destroyed because I did a lousy job handling my first case fourteen years ago?"

Anne stood up and walked over to him. "Doug, you can't blame yourself for this."

Doug scoffed. "Why not? Who should I blame?" He shook his head. "I never should have tried that case. I had a good plea bargain and I should have made Zeke take it. But I didn't. And as a result, he took his own life, and now his brother has murdered three women in retaliation against me."

Anne stood there silently.

"Damn it, I just don't see a way out of this." Doug paced in front of the fireplace. "What can I do? I can't predict where he'll strike next."

"Come on, Doug, don't be so hard on yourself."

"Why not? I'm the key to all of this. McGraw's doing this to get back at me. Yet I'm powerless to stop him." Doug stopped pacing and stared into the fire. "Even if I stayed holed up here, I have no doubt that McGraw would still find a victim. He'd still create an opportunity to frame me. He'd probably go after Nellie." Doug looked at Anne. "Or you," he said quietly.

"Doug, please stop doing this." Anne put her hand on his arm and urged him towards the couch. "Come and sit down."

He reluctantly sat down on the couch and took a sip of his scotch. Anne sat quietly watching him.

"What happened to you today?" she asked.

He didn't answer for a moment. "They kicked me out of the firm," he finally said, not meeting her eyes. "Locked my furniture up in storage and washed their hands of me."

"I'm sorry, Doug. I know how tough that must be for you." She put her hand on his shoulder. "You can fight it, you know, when this is all over."

He looked over at her. "Sure, I could sue the firm, but for me it's a lose-lose scenario. Even if the court ruled in my favor, I would never want to practice law there again."

Anne nodded and withdrew her hand. "You're right, it's a no-win situation. But you're a top-notch lawyer, Doug. One of the best tax men around, from what I hear. You'll land on your feet."

Doug managed a smile. "Thanks."

"It's hard to stomach though, isn't it?"

Doug leaned his head back on the couch and closed his eyes. "Yeah. It sure is."

After a moment, he sat up and looked at his watch. "Dinner should be about ready. Let's go and see what Samantha's been up to."

Samantha was helping Nellie set the table in the kitchen. "Perfect timing," Nellie said, when she saw them. "We're just about finished setting the table and dinner's ready to be served. I hope you don't mind eating at the table in here instead of the dining room. Samantha and I thought that it would be a little cozier in here."

"Good choice," Doug said, picking Samantha up and putting her on his shoulders. "While you get the food on the table, I'm going to give this young lady a pony ride."

He started off down the hallway at a trot, while Samantha giggled with glee. "Canter, pony, canter," Anne heard her shout.

"Doug's very good with children. I'm surprised," Anne said, smiling at Nellie.

"Yes, honey, he sure is. Doug loves children and they love him too." Nellie said, stooping to open the oven door. "Why does that surprise you, Anne?"

Anne shrugged. "I don't know. I guess because Doug doesn't really seem much like a family man. I wouldn't think that he would have much experience with kids."

Nellie stopped serving and wiped her hands on her apron. "Anne, family has always been very important to Doug, and is probably even more so because he lost his parents so suddenly." She shook her head. "Everyone thinks Doug's such a playboy and that he'll never get married. Well, I know that man better than just about anyone, and I'll tell you why he's never settled down. It's because he's just waiting for the right woman. He may not even know that himself, but I know it."

Anne picked up a plate, irritated with herself for being so interested in Nellie's assessment of Doug as a family man. "Come on," she said. "Let me help you get dinner on the table."

They finished putting the food on the table just as Doug and Samantha came back into the kitchen.

"Oh, yummy. This looks so good," Samantha said. "I love mashed potatoes." She climbed up on a chair and pulled the chair next to her over closer. "Come on, Doug, sit next to me."

"I would be delighted to," Doug said, scooting Samantha's chair in and holding out the chair on his other side for Anne.

"Can I say the prayer?" Samantha asked. Then, without waiting for an answer she reached out and held Doug's hand. "All hold hands," she said, matter-of-factly.

Samantha bowed her head and squeezed her eyes tightly closed. "Dear God, thank you for this good food and please take good care of my mommy and daddy and give them a hug and kiss for me. Amen. And thank you for my new friend Doug and please take good care of him too. Amen."

Doug picked up the platter of fried chicken and served some to Samantha, and Anne saw the tender expression that crossed his face as he looked at the little girl.

"Come on, now," Nellie said, "eat up everyone. There's enough here to feed an army." She passed the mashed potatoes to Anne. "I hope you don't mind my country cooking. This used to be Doug's favorite dinner when he was a little boy. Fried chicken, mashed potatoes and gravy, corn muffins, fried apples, and green beans. He won't eat it much anymore, though. Keeps insisting that it isn't healthy, that a meal like this has too much fat." Nellie was directing her comments to Anne, talking about Doug as if he weren't there. "Well, everyone needs some fat in their diet. It's not healthy to cut out fat entirely, that's what I keep telling him, but he doesn't listen. I guess that he thinks I'm just old-fashioned, but if you ask me, good wholesome food is still good wholesome food. That hasn't changed any over the years."

Anne smiled. Nellie was a gem. She looked at Doug, who seemed to have tuned Nellie out. "Doug?"

He looked over at her.

"I was impressed with the two guys you have out at your front gate. They parted the sea of reporters and had us through the gate in no time. Very smooth. Where did you come up with them?"

"Manse Security. I've used them before from time to time. They're top notch. Dealing with the media is a cakewalk for them. They're trained for much heavier duties. Still, I thought it couldn't hurt. They sure make coming and going a whole lot easier."

"No kidding." Anne looked at her watch. "Say, speaking of coming and going, I don't like to eat and run, but it's almost seven and it's a school night, so Samantha and I had better finish up and head on home."

"No-o-o-o. I helped Nellie make a cherry pie and she promised me I could have some of it for dessert with vanilla ice cream, and you can't make her break her promise to me." Samantha's bottom lip stuck out in a pout and tears welled up in her big brown eyes.

Doug laughed, looking at Anne. "That's pretty hard to argue with."

"I think I'm outnumbered," Anne said, smiling. "I guess we can stay for a piece of pie." She turned to Nellie. "This was a delicious meal, Nellie. Thank you so much."

"You're welcome, Anne. I hope you and Samantha will come back again soon."

Anne rose and began picking up the plates. "Let me clear off the table while you and Samantha serve the pie."

Doug pushed back his chair. "I have a phone call I have to make. Just save my piece. I'll eat it later."

Nellie shooed him away with her dishtowel. "Oh, come on now, Doug. You know you won't eat any pie. You're just making excuses."

Doug grinned. "Then give my piece to Samantha," he said, tickling Samantha on his way out of the room.

C H A P T E R

55

Doug used the phone in his study to place a call to Patrick Talbot, the head of Manse Security. Anne's mention of the security guards had given him an idea.

"Patrick, Doug Cummings. Sorry to bother you at home."

"No bother, Doug, that's why you have this number. What's up?" Patrick asked.

"First of all, your guys are great. They're working out perfectly. Now I have some more serious work for you to do." Doug told Patrick about Zebulon McGraw and what he suspected him of. "I want you to find him."

"You know that's not our main expertise, Doug. Our people are trained to protect. They're not investigators *per se*. But we'll do our best. We'll get started on it first thing tomorrow."

"Fine. And there's one more thing. I want you to protect a woman by the name of Anne Sullivan, only she can't know that you're guarding her."

"Do you mind if I ask why she can't know, Doug?"

"Because I don't want to give her the opportunity to refuse your services, Patrick. I think she's in danger, but she doesn't know it and I don't want to frighten her. At least not yet. And even if she were aware of it, I don't think she would ever agree to let you provide protection for her."

There was a brief silence. "You think she's slated to be victim number four?"

"Maybe."

"Okay, Doug," Patrick said. "Tell me where to find her."

They worked out the arrangements and Doug was heading back to the kitchen when he met Anne and Samantha in the hallway.

"Hey, are you finished with that pie and ice cream already?" he asked Samantha.

She nodded. "Yes. But I couldn't eat it all, so Nellie letted me save some for the next time I come over."

"Great. I hope that will be soon." Doug turned to Anne. "Thanks for coming over."

Anne smiled. "Thank you for inviting us. Dinner was delicious. I'll call you tomorrow. I'm going to meet with that investigator first thing in the morning. I'll let you know if he has any insight to offer."

Nellie appeared with Anne's coat and Doug helped her on with it. "You girls stay warm now," he said, opening the door. "It's pretty wet and nasty out there tonight."

"Let me see if it started snowing yet," Samantha screamed, as she ran out the door. Her feet hit the icy pavement and shot out from under her, sending her sliding in a heap towards the driveway.

"Samantha, are you okay?" Doug asked, hurrying over to the little girl. "Watch it, Anne, stay inside," he called over his shoulder. "It's solid ice out here."

Samantha lay there whimpering, and Doug picked her up and cautiously made his way back to the house. Once inside, he handed her to Anne.

Anne hugged her and looked her over. "That was kind of scary, wasn't it? Your feet slid right out from under you. But you're fine now."

"I don't feel fine," Samantha sobbed. "It hurt a lot."

"I know it did, sweetie," Anne said. "We'll hold hands when we go back out there, so neither one of us will fall down on the way to the car, okay?"

Doug shook his head. "You'll never make it home in your Jag, Anne. I doubt you could even make it up my driveway. It's a sheet of ice."

"What do you suggest I do?" Anne asked.

"I could drive you home in the Range Rover, but four wheel drive isn't much help in ice like this." Doug shook his head. "I can't believe it froze up so quickly. I should have checked earlier." There was a brief silence. He could hear the ice rain pelting the slate roof.

"I don't want to go back out there. I'm scared," Samantha said, still sniffling.

"I agree with Samantha," Nellie said. "I don't think any of you should be venturing outside tonight. You have plenty of guest rooms, Doug. Why not just have Anne and Samantha stay here tonight? I'm sure the roads will be better by morning."

"Yeah." Samantha jumped out of Anne's arms. "That would be so much fun. We could have a sleep-over."

"Oh, I don't know," Anne said. "I don't want to put you out."

"It's no trouble at all," Doug replied. "Nellie's right. It would be foolish to attempt these back roads tonight. We have plenty of room for you to stay here."

"I guess you're right," Anne said.

"Where do we get to sleep?" Samantha asked. "Can I pick the room?"

"Sure you can, princess," Doug replied, holding his hand out to her. "Come on, I'll give you the grand tour."

He climbed the stairs with Samantha and gave her a choice of the three upstairs guest rooms.

"Where are you going to sleep?" Samantha asked.

"My room's right over there," Doug replied, pointing towards his bedroom door.

"Then I want to sleep in this room, right next to you. Besides, I really like this room because it has a rocking horse in it."

"That used to be my rocking horse when I was a little boy. You can ride it if you want to," Doug said.

"Was this your room when you were little?" Samantha asked.

"Yes, it was. And my parents slept in the room where I sleep now."

Samantha looked at Doug curiously. "Where are your parents now?"

"They're in Heaven," he said quietly.

"Do you miss them?" she asked.

Doug nodded.

Samantha reached up and hugged him. "I know. I miss my parents too. They're alive in Heaven though, and someday I'll get to be with them again. You'll get to be with your parents too."

The sound of Nellie's voice interrupted them. Doug turned to see Nellie and Anne climbing the stairs.

"There are clean linens on the beds, and you should find toothbrushes and any toiletries you might need in the drawers in the bathroom," Nellie said. "I've got some bottled water here for you to drink. Don't drink the tap water. There's nothing wrong with it, but it has a lot of iron in it and it just doesn't taste very good. You know the well water out here, yours is probably the same way. Is this the room you've chosen then, young lady? I love this room."

The three of them followed Nellie into the bedroom.

"Thank you both; your hospitality is wonderful," Anne said.

"Wait a minute," Samantha said, looking in the dresser drawers. "We don't have any pajamas."

Doug laughed. "You're right, Samantha. Let me see what I can come up with."

Doug left the room and returned a few minutes later carrying two of his shirts. He leaned down and held up a T-shirt to Samantha. "It's a little big, but it will make a nice long nightgown for you."

Then he stood up and handed a folded dress shirt to Anne. His fingers lingered briefly as they touched hers. "I hope this is all right."

Anne blushed and drew her hand back. "It's fine, thank you."

"Well, I'll say good night then. I hope you both sleep well." Doug reached down and gave Samantha a hug and kiss. He nodded at Anne. "See you in the morning."

Doug went back downstairs and turned on the security alarm, then checked the locks on all the doors and windows.

Confident that everything was secure, Doug stretched out on the couch in his study, not yet ready for sleep. As he watched the embers from the fire glow in the darkened room and listened to the sleet dance on the window panes, Doug tried to make some sense of the hellish turn his life had taken.

CHAPTER

56

Anne rolled over and looked at the clock on the nightstand. The red digital numbers shone brightly in the dark bedroom. Twelve-fifty-nine. Only eight minutes had passed since she'd last looked at the clock. Why couldn't she fall asleep? She was exhausted. She rolled onto her back, and listened to the even rhythm of Samantha's soft breathing coming from the next bed.

She heard Doug come upstairs just before midnight, but since then the house had been quiet. She assumed that he was asleep by now. Anne sighed and turned onto her side. The storm was still raging outside, and she closed her eyes and tried to concentrate on the irregular rhythm of the icy rain skittering across the windows.

Tap, tap-tap-tap, tap-tap, tap, tap-tap-tap. Anne pulled the covers up over her shoulders and nestled into the soft mattress. Tap-tap-tap-tap, tap-tap, tap. The sleet skipped on endlessly.

She listened for what seemed like an eternity then glanced at the clock again. One-twelve. This wasn't working. She sighed and flipped the covers back. Maybe a cup of hot tea would help.

Anne opened the bedroom door and peered out. Doug had left the hallway light on, but the door to his room was closed. She quietly made her way down the stairs, which were dimly lit by a lamp in the hall below. She paused at the bottom and searched the wall until she found the switch to light the long, dark passageway to the kitchen.

The stone floor in the hallway was cold on her bare feet, and Anne shivered and rubbed her arms briskly as she hurried towards the kitchen. She wished she'd thought to put something else on. Doug's cotton shirt provided little warmth.

A light was burning over the stove, and she found a copper tea kettle on the counter and filled it with water. She turned on the gas burner, and she stood for a moment warming her hands in front of it. Then she searched until she found some herbal tea and a teacup, and stood by the stove, waiting for the water to boil.

The wind had picked up, and she could hear the ice-coated tree branches creak as they were tossed about by a strong gust. Anne folded her arms across her chest and shivered as she listened to the wind howl eerily then gust to a high-pitched whine. She heard scraping sounds as tree branches brushed against the house, and then a loud crack resonated outside the kitchen door.

Anne hurried to the door, found a switch for the outside porch light and peered through the glass door panel. The bare branches of the graceful trees that surrounded Doug's house glistened with ice, and as she watched the wind whip the brittle branches, she saw the lower limb of an oak snap in half and hang from the tree. The pine trees swayed heavily with each blast of air and were so weighted down with ice that the lower branches bent almost to the ground. One pine branch, about eight feet long, had smashed through the porch railing and lay wedged between the stairs and what remained of the banister. That must have been the loud crack she'd heard.

The tea kettle started to whistle, and Anne walked back to the stove and switched off the gas. As she turned towards the table to get her teacup, she had the odd feeling that someone was watching her. She glanced quickly towards the hallway, but no one was there.

Anne carried the teacup back, set it on the stove, and poured the boiling water into it. Steam rose from the cup, warm and comforting, and she watched the honey gold of the tea ooze out of the bag as hot water swirled around it. She dipped the bag once, then again, and left it in the cup to steep for another minute.

The wind roared fiercely outside and she heard another loud crack, this time from the direction of the front of the house. The lights dimmed for an instant, then went back to full power. Oh, God, she hoped they didn't lose power. Sometimes it took days for power to be restored to the rural areas.

Anne removed the tea bag and threw it away, and was halfway down the hall when she realized that she'd left the porch light on. She set the teacup on the hall table and hurried back to the kitchen.

As Anne reached for the switch to turn the porch light off, she glanced outside again. The pine branch that had damaged the porch now lay at the bottom of the steps, along with most of the railing. Broken limbs littered the lawn, and smaller branches tumbled about in the wind. She sighed and turned the porch light off, but in that instant, she caught the sight of a shadowy movement outside and quickly switched the light back on.

Anne gasped and took a step backwards. There was a man on the porch, just outside the door, his hand outstretched as if he were reaching for the handle. He pulled his hand back when the light hit him and stared at her. He was dressed in a canvas hunting jacket and camouflage fatigues, and his camouflage cap bore the words, "Born to Hunt." He was unshaven, and frost clung to his whiskers and to the short hairs that protruded from his nose.

A numbing fear gripped Anne, and she knew in her gut that the man was Zebulon McGraw. She froze, transfixed, waiting for him to make the first move.

The eyes that stared at her were pale green, almost gray, and he squinted slightly, studying her, with an odd emotionless expression. Then the corners of his lips curved upwards, into a slow grin, and he lifted his hand and pointed an outstretched finger at her.

"Pow," he mouthed, and he winked at her as he made a shooting motion with his hand.

Anne flipped the light switch off and turned and ran, as fast as she could, down the hall and up the stairs. She burst through the door into Doug's room and stumbled in the dim light towards his bed.

"Doug," she called, breathlessly, as she reached the bed. She grabbed his arm and shook him. "Doug, wake up. He's here. McGraw is here."

Doug threw the covers back. "What's the matter?" he asked, sitting up and rubbing his hand across his eyes.

"He's here, Doug. Zebulon McGraw is here. I just saw him."

Doug frowned. "Calm down, Anne. Tell me exactly what happened."

Anne took a deep breath. "He's outside. I was down in the kitchen, and I saw him, on the back porch, right outside the kitchen door. I was literally face-to-face with him."

"Goddamn it." Doug rushed to the closet and switched on the light. He reached up and took a shotgun down from the top shelf, then grabbed a box of shotgun shells from a drawer. He quickly cracked the gun and inserted two cartridges into the barrel, then closed the gun and leaned it against the wall.

"How do you know it was McGraw?" he asked, as he pulled navy sweatpants on over his boxers.

Anne hesitated. How *did* she know? "I'm not sure. I just know."

Doug tugged a sweatshirt over his head then picked up the shotgun and shells. "Wait here," he said, as he started out of the room.

"No. I'm coming with you," Anne replied, following him out into the hall.

Doug didn't argue with her, and she followed him silently down the steps. He motioned for her to stop behind him at the entrance to the kitchen, then slid cautiously around the corner, over to the door, and flipped the outside light on.

"Do you see anyone?" Anne asked, after a moment.

Doug glanced at her and shook his head, then peered outside again. "I don't see him, but that doesn't mean he's not still out there."

He watched attentively for a few more moments, then took a golden-brown oilcloth coat off a hook on the wall and stepped into a pair of green rubber barn boots.

"What are you doing?" Anne asked.

He punched a series of numbers on the keypad next to the door. The panel beeped twice then displayed a green light. "I'm going after him."

Anne walked over to the door. "Don't be ridiculous, Doug. You can't go out and hunt McGraw down with your shotgun. Let me call the sheriff."

He didn't look at her as he emptied the box of shotgun shells into his coat pocket and picked up the shotgun. "I want you to lock the door behind me and turn the alarm back on. The code is four-eight-six-eight." He glanced at her. "That's 'hunt' on a telephone keypad, in case you forget."

Doug reached for the door handle and Anne held his arm. "Doug, please. Don't go out there."

He gently removed her hand. "Stop worrying. I'm not going to do anything stupid." Then he opened the door and slipped outside.

Anne let out a sigh of relief as she saw Doug jog slowly across the yard towards the house. It seemed like he'd been gone for an hour, but in reality it probably hadn't been more than ten minutes. As Doug came closer, Anne saw that he was limping slightly and holding his side. She disarmed the alarm and opened the door. He slipped as he reached the first porch step, and clutched the broken railing for support.

"Doug, are you all right?" she asked, stepping out onto the porch.

Doug glanced up at her and she saw streaks of blood on the side of his face.

"I'm fine. Get back inside." He carefully climbed the icy stairs, then grabbed the edge of the open door, and ushered Anne ahead of him back into the house.

"What happened to you? Did you find McGraw?" Anne asked, as she reached out to help him pull off his coat. The shoulders and collar of his coat were coated with ice, as was his hair, and his cheeks were bright red. She could see now that the blood on his face came from a gash on his temple.

Doug shook his head. "I didn't find McGraw, but I did find his tracks. There were definite footprints in the ice that I was able to follow as far as the barn. Then it looks like the son of a bitch took off across the pasture towards the woods."

Doug set his shotgun down and shrugged out of his frozen coat. "Thanks," he said, as Anne took the coat from him. "Damn, it's cold out there." He blew into his hands, then winced as if the movement were painful for him, and put a hand on his side.

"What happened to you?" Anne repeated. "Why are you holding your side?" She moved Doug's hand away and carefully pulled up his sweatshirt. His rib cage was scraped and bloodstained, starting about mid-chest, and Anne traced her fingertips gingerly down to his waist.

"Ah. Take it easy." Doug winced, but didn't make a move to stop her. "A tree limb fell on me and knocked me down the hill behind the barn. I just got a few scratches. I'm fine." He flinched as Anne eased down the waistband of his sweatpants.

Doug had a deep laceration right above his hip bone that was oozing blood. Anne gently inspected the wound. "Doug, this cut looks nasty."

Doug moved her hands away and pulled his sweatshirt down. "I'll take care of it later. First, I want you to tell me exactly what happened when you saw McGraw. What were you doing down here, anyway?"

Anne took a deep breath. "I couldn't sleep, so I came down to make a cup of tea. I was down here for about ten minutes I suppose, and just before I went back upstairs I looked outside and there he was, standing on the back porch. It looked like he was reaching for the door handle."

She shivered and drew her arms against her chest. "I suppose he might have been out there all along, watching me, I don't know. At any rate, we just stood and stared at each other for a moment. And then he pointed his finger at me, like it was a gun, and made a shooting motion. Then he flashed me a hideous grin."

Anne took a deep breath, and shook her head. "I felt like I was frozen. I just stared at him for a second, and then I turned the light off. I don't know why. Just a silly reaction, I guess, so I wouldn't have to look at him any-more." She looked at Doug and shrugged. "That was it. Then I ran upstairs to get you."

"Describe him for me," Doug said. "I only have a vague recollection of what he looked like, and that was fourteen years ago."

Anne closed her eyes for a moment, and pictured McGraw in her mind. "He's tall, probably around six feet, and thin, I think. At least his face is thin. I couldn't see the rest of his body because he was wearing a bulky hunting jacket. He had on a camouflage hat that had 'Born to Hunt' printed on the front of it. He was unshaven, and he has pale green eyes, almost gray."

Doug didn't say anything for a moment. Then he turned the deadbolt on the kitchen door, keyed the alarm code into the panel, and picked up the phone.

"Who are you calling?" Anne asked.

"The guard at my front gate," Doug replied. "I want to get someone down here to keep an eye on the house."

"Do you think McGraw will come back here tonight?" Anne asked.

Doug shrugged. "Who knows? I think it's unlikely. I would think he'd be heading for shelter somewhere. But we're not dealing with a rational individual, and there's no predicting his next move. I want some extra security around here, just in case."

Anne studied Doug while he spoke on the phone with the guard. He stood slightly hunched over, with his hand pressed against his side. The injury on his hip was obviously bothering him. She went to the sink, filled a bowl with warm water, and gathered some dish cloths. When Doug hung up the phone, she motioned towards the kitchen table.

"Sit down and let me clean up those cuts."

Doug shook his head. "I'm fine, Anne. Really. I'll wash up when I get upstairs."

Anne patted the table top, next to the bowl of water. "Please."

Doug still hung back. "Anne, come on, don't make such a big deal over it."

She smiled at him. "There's no need to be embarrassed."

"I'm not," he replied, giving a little half-laugh.

"Great. Then come and sit down."

Doug shook his head, but he walked over and sat down on the edge of the table.

"It'll be easier if you take your sweatshirt off," Anne said.

Doug grimaced as he raised his arms to pull the sweatshirt over his head, and Anne reached out and helped him.

"You really don't need to do this," he said again.

Anne just smiled and pressed a wet cloth to the wound on his temple. As soon as she began to wipe the laceration with the warm, wet cloth, it started to bleed again. Anne washed off the blood and inspected the wound. It was small, about an inch long, and not very deep, but it could probably have used a few stitches. She cleaned it thoroughly and then folded a fresh, dry cloth into a square and held it against the cut.

"Here, hold this," she said to Doug.

He placed his hand over hers, applying pressure to the makeshift bandage, and Anne slid her hand away. She dipped a clean cloth into the bowl of warm water and went to work wiping the streaks of dried blood off the side of Doug's face. His cheek was lean and firm against her touch, and the rough stubble of his whiskers made a soft, scratching sound as she scrubbed. Anne traced a streak of blood down to the solid line of his jaw and cleaned some blood from his sideburn. His hair was wet from the melted ice, and she put the cloth down and gently probed his scalp for any hidden lacerations. When her fingers reached the area just below his temple, Doug closed his eyes and sighed.

"Headache?" Anne asked.

Doug nodded.

"I'm not surprised." She placed one hand on either side of his head and began to rub both his temples lightly.

"That feels good," he mumbled, eyes closed.

As she continued the massage, Doug moved his head slowly to one side and then the other, as if to stretch his neck. Anne slid her hands around to the back of his head and traced the muscles that ran from his neck down to his shoulders.

"God, Doug, you're tight as a drum."

He smiled, eyes still closed. "I don't know why, with my relaxed lifestyle."

Anne kneaded his shoulder muscles, and Doug dropped his head forward, allowing her to work on the taut muscles that ran up the back of his neck. She started at the base of his skull, letting her fingers travel slowly towards his shoulders, making small circles as she worked to loosen the tight network of knots.

The wind howled fiercely outside. Anne glanced at the back door. The porch light was on, and she could see that the storm hadn't let up any. Branches still tumbled willy-nilly across the back yard, and ice pellets skittered along the porch floor. It almost seemed surreal, the chaos outside, the threat of Zebulon McGraw still lurking out there somewhere, and yet inside, in the shelter of the kitchen, with Doug, she felt surprisingly safe, and somehow removed from it all.

Doug moaned softly. "That feels great. Remind me to get injured around you more often."

The sound of Doug's voice brought Anne back to reality and, suddenly, she was all too aware of the fact that Doug was only half-dressed and she, wearing nothing more than his thin cotton shirt and a pair of panties, was giving him a massage. *God, what was she doing?* She abruptly ended the massage and carried the bowl of water to the sink, putting some distance between them.

"I'm going to get some clean water," she said, wondering if her casual tone sounded as forced to him as it did to her. "Do you have a first-aid kit somewhere?"

Doug gave her a puzzled look. "Yeah, there's one in the cabinet in the mud room. I'll go get it." He stood up slowly and walked stiffly towards the small room next to the back door.

Anne took a deep breath and adjusted the faucets until the water reached the proper temperature. He's your client, she chided herself. Nothing more. *Keep it that way.* She filled the bowl with warm water and was waiting for Doug at the table when he emerged with the first-aid kit.

"Thanks," she said, hoping he didn't notice the slight tremble in her hand as she reached out and took the first-aid kit from him.

Doug perched on the edge of the table. "Thank you. For the massage. It really helped."

Anne just nodded, and busied herself inspecting his head wound. The bleeding seemed to have stopped, so she applied some Neosporin to the cut and covered it with a Band-Aid. "There, that should take care of it. Hopefully, it will heal without a scar," she said, turning her attention to the cuts on his side.

Anne cleaned up Doug's side and ribcage, and spread a thin layer of Neosporin over the area. When she had finished, she gingerly rolled down the waistband of Doug's sweatpants and inspected the gash above his hip. Blood had started to harden over the wound, and Anne soaked a cloth in the warm water and pressed it against the area. After a moment she removed the cloth and gently washed around the cut. When she had cleaned it well enough to see inside, she pulled on a pair of surgical gloves and carefully probed the laceration.

"This is a really deep wound, Doug. I hope I can clean it properly." She took a packet of gauze out of the first-aid kit and opened the bottle of hydrogen peroxide. "I'll do the best I can, but you might want to have a doctor look at it tomorrow."

Doug grinned. "I kind of like the doctor I have right now."

Anne ignored him. "Ready? This may sting a little."

Without waiting for Doug's reply, she held a towel below the wound to catch the overflow and poured hydrogen peroxide directly into the cut.

Doug pulled away from her. "Aahhh. Jesus. What happened to your earlier bedside manner?"

Anne smiled and bent down to inspect the cut. "It actually looks pretty good. I'm going to flush it out one more time just to be safe."

Doug grumbled something unintelligible but sat still while she poured the liquid into the wound again.

"That should do it," she said, using some gauze to dry the area. Then she spread a generous gob of Neosporin on a large antiseptic gauze bandage and applied it to the cut.

"Here, hold this in place while I cut some tape," she said, waiting for Doug to put his hand on the bandage.

Anne cut a long strip of tape and carefully secured the top edge of the bandage. Then she cut two smaller strips and taped down each side.

"Okay, you can let go now," she said, cutting one final long strip.

She applied the final strip of tape to the bottom edge of the bandage, and ran her fingers across Doug's lower abdomen to secure the strip in place. Doug drew a sharp intake of breath and pushed her hand away.

"Sorry. Are my fingers cold?" she asked.

He shook his head and smiled wryly. "Not exactly."

Anne blushed and rolled the waistband of Doug's sweatpants back up, then began packing the first-aid supplies back into the case. She could feel Doug's eyes on her, but she didn't look up.

"Come and have a drink with me in the study," he said quietly.

She didn't answer right away, and he cupped his hand under her chin, gently forcing her to make eye contact with him. "Neither one of us will be able to fall asleep if we go to bed now. At least I know I won't. I need to unwind." His fingers trailed away.

"It's late, Doug," Anne said quickly. "Besides, Samantha's upstairs alone. If she wakes . . ."

He held a finger to her lips and silenced her. "Why don't you go and check on Samantha, and I'll start a fire."

Anne tried to summon up the resolve to say no, but he reached out and held her hand, intertwining his fingers with hers.

"Come on," he said, leading her towards the door.

58

Bright sunlight streamed through a crack in Doug's bedroom drapes and he glanced at the clock on his nightstand. It was almost eight o'clock. His eyes felt like sandpaper and he rubbed them, then flopped on his back and ran his fingers through his tousled hair.

It had been after five o'clock when he'd finally gone to bed, but even then he'd had a hell of a time falling asleep, knowing that Anne was in bed in the next room. He smiled at the irony of it. It was proper payback, he supposed, since he'd often been accused of not wanting to spend the night with a woman after having sex with her. Last night, he'd been the one who had regretted having to sleep alone.

Doug gave a low chuckle as he remembered the hard time he'd had parting from Anne the night before. Their first attempt at good night had been down in the study, in the glow of the dying embers of the fire, but they had ended up making love again. When they finally came upstairs, they had lingered in the hallway until just before dawn.

The thought of seeing Anne spurred Doug into motion, and he sat up and threw the covers back, wincing at the tugging he felt from the injury on his side. He rose and walked stiffly to the window, then drew back the drapes and looked outside. The day had dawned clear and mild, and the night's ice was melting into a myriad of streams that ran restlessly down the driveway. No "snow day" today. He'd better hurry if he wanted to catch Anne before she left to take Samantha to school.

Doug quickly showered, re-bandaged his wounds, and dressed. By the time he made it downstairs, Anne and Samantha were already seated at the kitchen table eating breakfast.

"You two are up early," Doug said. He gave Samantha a kiss on the top of her head and locked eyes with Anne across the table. She smiled at him and blushed, then quickly looked away. Doug walked around to where Anne sat, and stood behind her, lightly rubbing her shoulders. She reached up and slipped her hand into his for a moment, but then let go.

"Hey, Doug. Look what Nellie made for us," Samantha said. "Blueberry pancakes. And mine is shaped like a heart."

Doug let his hands trail through Anne's hair, which was down and slightly wet, as he turned his attention to Samantha. "Wow. You must be pretty special, young lady. Nellie never makes a good breakfast like that for me," he said, taking a seat next to Anne.

Nellie didn't respond to Doug's teasing. She just smiled as she placed a plate of fruit and toast in front of him and hummed to herself as she walked away.

"Did you see that all that nasty ice from last night's storm is gone?" Doug asked Samantha.

"Yup," Samantha replied. "I guess we'll have school after all."

"What's happening at school today, anything special?" Doug asked, taking a sip of his orange juice.

The little girl wrinkled her brow. "I don't remember," she finally responded. "But after school, Aunt Anne is going to take me to Huckleberries for lunch and ice cream."

A guilty look crossed Anne's face. "Oh, honey, I'm not going to be able to do that today after all. I have an important meeting that I have to go to. How about if we go to Huckleberries tomorrow?"

"That's not fair. You promised," Samantha cried.

"I know I did, sweetie. But this meeting is really important. I have to do it today."

"Your meetings are always more important than me. You never have time to do anything with me anymore," Samantha folded her arms across her chest and stuck her bottom lip out in a pout.

"Samantha, you know that's not true. Please try to understand," Anne replied.

Doug interrupted them. "Anne, look, I'm sure that your meeting with the investigator can wait another day. Please don't change your plans with Samantha. I'll have Manse Security investigate McGraw."

"Thanks, Doug," Anne said, "but I really don't want to postpone the meeting. Samantha will understand."

Samantha sat silently with her arms crossed, scowling at Anne.

"All right. What if I pick Samantha up from school and take her to lunch?" Doug asked.

"Great idea," Samantha said. "Don't forget the ice cream. Aunt Anne always lets me get ice cream at Huckleberries."

"Right," Doug said, smiling. "What's Huckleberries, anyway?"

"It's a restaurant," Samantha said. "Right near my school. It used to be somewhere else, and then they closed it, but everyone missed it so much they opened it up again."

"Look, Doug, that's very kind of you to offer, but I can't infringe on your day. Samantha's lunch can wait until tomorrow," Anne said.

"Believe me, it is hardly an infringement on my day," Doug said. "It's not like I have anything else on my agenda, Anne. Honestly, I would really welcome the break from what is otherwise looking like a very long day."

Anne looked at the two of them. "Are you sure? Taking a child to lunch at Huckleberries can be quite an experience, especially if you're not used to kids."

"Trust me, I think that with Samantha's help I can probably muddle through," Doug said, smiling at Samantha.

"All right," Anne said, but she still didn't look entirely comfortable with the idea.

Doug leaned over and touched Anne's hand, forcing her to look him in the eye. "I'll take good care of her. I promise."

She blushed. "I know you will. Thank you."

Samantha clapped her hands. "Yippee. We're going to have so-o-o-o much fun."

Anne smiled at her. "I'm sure you will, sweetie. Now finish eating your breakfast. I need to talk with Doug about something."

She turned to Doug. "Do you have a minute?" Her eyes met his, but her expression was guarded.

Doug nodded. "Of course." He stood up and pulled Anne's chair back for her. She walked ahead of him down the hallway and didn't speak until they reached the door to his study. Then she stopped and turned to him.

"Can we go in here?"

"Sure." He gestured for her to go first and closed the door behind them.

Anne walked to the window and stood facing away from him, her arms folded across her chest. Concerned, he went over to her.

"Anne?"

She didn't respond.

He put his hands on her shoulders and gently turned her around. "Talk to me."

She bit her lip and looked down. "I'm not sure what to say."

He grinned. "How about, last night was incredible?"

Anne smiled and Doug lifted her chin until her eyes met his. "Last night *was* incredible," he said, softly.

She nodded, but her smile faded. "We can't do this, Doug."

His hands slid down to her waist and he kissed her forehead. "We already did."

"I know. But we can't continue. Not as long as I'm your lawyer."

Doug shook his head and put his finger to her lips. "Don't."

She frowned and looked away, and he let go of her. "Don't keep pushing me away, Anne," he said quietly.

Anne took a deep breath and made eye contact with him. "I made a mistake last night, Doug. I gave in to my feelings, without any regard for principles or ethics. And it was wrong."

"Anne."

She held up a hand to silence him. "Please hear me out."

Doug sighed and backed away, leaning against the desk. "Fine."

She gave him a tight smile. "Regardless of the feelings I have for you, or we have for each other, what happened between us last night boils down to one thing. I slept with my client. And that's unethical. It's something that I would have sworn that I would never do."

Doug interrupted. "It's just an arbitrary rule, Anne. It doesn't apply to us."

She narrowed her eyes and shook her head. "Why not, Doug? Because you're above the rules?"

"No. It doesn't apply because that rule is meant to protect the client. To prevent lawyers from using their position of power to take advantage of their clients. That's not what's happening here."

She shook her head. "It's also meant to ensure that a lawyer remains as objective as possible. To make sure that her decisions are based on sound legal theory, not emotions. If we're involved in a personal relationship, I'm not sure that I can do that."

Doug studied her for a moment. "What are you suggesting?" he finally asked. "That we put our feelings on hold?"

Anne nodded. "Basically, yes. Maybe I can't control how I feel about you, but I can control what I do about it."

He snorted. "That's ludicrous. That won't make you any more objective."

"Perhaps not. But that's the only way I can do it. Please try to understand."

Doug stared at her. What choice did he have? He could either agree to her terms, or, what? He sighed and nodded grimly. "Fine. I'll play it your way."

"Thank you," Anne said softly. "I'll call you later." Then she left the room.

"To be continued," Doug muttered, sinking into his leather desk chair.

Doug picked up the phone and called Patrick Talbot at Manse Security.

"Doug, hi. My man told me someone was prowling around your property last night."

"That's right, Patrick. It had to have been McGraw. I'd like you to put a man outside my house."

"I've already taken care of it."

"Great. Now what about protecting Anne Sullivan? McGraw saw her here last night, so I'm more concerned than ever about him targeting her. Is everything in place?"

"Yes. I just received word from my man. He said Ms. Sullivan just left your place and he's on her tail."

"Thanks, Patrick."

Doug hung up and wandered the house for a while, looking for something to occupy the morning. He read the *News* and *USA Today* and sorted through his mail, but he couldn't keep his mind off Anne. Out of nowhere, he'd catch a whiff of her perfume. Or imagine her touch. Finally, he couldn't stand it any longer, and decided to go out for a ride.

Billy helped him tack up Chancellor and Doug set off through the back of his property towards the woods. Chancellor hadn't been worked in a couple of days and he was up, spooking and shying, looking for trouble. The horse broke to a canter and Doug tried to bring him back to a trot, but Chancellor refused and cantered in place, tossing his head.

Doug was working up a sweat, fighting with him, so he brought Chancellor to a halt, took his jacket off, and hung it on the fence. "All right, buddy." He patted the thoroughbred on the neck. "Have it your way."

Doug eased up on the reins and Chancellor took off, galloping too fast at first, but then he settled into a nice forward canter, softly snorting his contentment as he flew along. The footing was surprisingly good, in spite of the storm the night before, and Doug let Chancellor hop over a few coops and canter on until they reached the river.

"Whoa, boy," he said as they approached the river's edge, and the horse came back to a walk. Chancellor cautiously made his way down the bank, and they walked slowly through the river, as the normally quiet current rushed past them with the overflow from the ice storm.

Chancellor was calmer now, and Doug gave him a loose rein and let him choose his way through the rocky riverbed. They rounded a bend and Chancellor headed over towards the sandy bank and the trail into the woods, towards home. But as they neared the river's edge, Chancellor stopped, raised his head high, and stared off into the trees.

"Go on," Doug clucked to him, and urged him on with his legs.

Chancellor started up the bank, but then stopped again. His ears pricked forward as he listened. This time, Doug heard it too. The soft snapping of branches as something made its way through the underbrush.

Doug could feel Chancellor's heart beating fast and he patted him and let him stand for a moment, waiting for whatever it was to move on. The rustling stopped and Chancellor lowered his nose, relaxed once again, and climbed up the steep bank out of the water.

Doug let Chancellor stop for a moment to shake off the cold water from the river, and then kicked him onward. They had picked up a trot and were heading up the narrow trail towards the gate into Hunting Hollow, when Doug spotted a man crouched behind a tree. His camouflage jacket almost hid him from view.

Doug halted Chancellor and called out. "Hey, what are you doing here? Step out in the open so I can see you." A twig snapped as the man shifted his weight, but he didn't respond to Doug's command. "You're not allowed back here. This is private property," Doug shouted.

The man remained silent, so Doug turned Chancellor off the trail and headed through the woods towards him. As they approached, the man leapt up and sprinted towards the fence line. The sudden movement startled Chancellor, and the horse reared, spun around, and bolted back towards the trail. Doug got the horse under control and turned back, just in time to see the man hop over the fence into the back pasture of Hunting Hollow.

"You son of a bitch," Doug swore. The fence line was far too overgrown for Doug to attempt to jump it where the man had climbed over, so he galloped Chancellor towards the gate.

The gently rolling pasture at the back of Hunting Hollow was clear but for a few clumps of trees, and Doug raced to the top of the first knoll and stopped. He tried to keep Chancellor still as he looked around, searching for any sign of movement. He could see most of the pasture from that vantage point, but the man was nowhere in sight.

It's McGraw, I know it is, Doug thought. It has to be. Doug's heart thumped wildly against his chest. He wouldn't let Zebulon McGraw get away from him, no matter what happened.

"*McGraw,*" Doug yelled. Dead silence greeted him. "You can't hide forever, McGraw," he called out. "Why don't you come out and face me like a man?" Still nothing. "Give it up, McGraw." Doug's voice echoed across the quiet countryside.

Doug spotted the man the instant he left his cover in the trees and dashed back towards the woods. But this time Doug was prepared. He kicked Chancellor into a gallop and easily overtook him.

Doug circled around him and saw for the first time that the man was carrying a hunting rifle. Doug rode up close and cracked his hunt whip at the gun. The strike hit home and the long thong whipped the man's hand, causing him to drop the weapon. He backed up, holding his hand.

"You're fucking crazy, man," the man screamed. "I didn't do nothing. I was just out here trying to get me a deer. Just let me be. I'll get off your damned property. I didn't do no one no harm." The man sank to the ground, and scampered sideways.

Doug lowered the whip and stared at the man. Anne had described McGraw as being tall and lanky, with whiskers. But this guy was short, almost stocky, and his face was clean-shaven. Damn it. He wasn't Zebulon McGraw. Just some damned deer hunter.

Doug backed Chancellor away from the man and motioned for him to get up. "Sorry. I thought you were someone else. You better watch yourself sneaking through people's property like that. You might get yourself hurt."

The man stood up, still rubbing his hand, and eyed his rifle lying on the ground.

"Go ahead and take it," Doug said, nodding towards the rifle. "Just don't use it around here. This whole property is posted with 'No Trespassing' signs. Next time, make sure you obey them."

The man picked the rifle up and started towards the woods, never taking his eyes off Doug. When he was a safe distance away he stopped and held his gun above his head, waving it in the air. "You're nuts, man. I've got a fucking Remington here, and you're acting like you're Indiana Jones." The man snorted and shook his head, then lowered the gun and took off at a run.

"You're fucking nuts," he yelled back over his shoulder.

CHAPTER

60

Doug's encounter with the deer hunter had made him late, and he raced the Range Rover along Foxcroft Road towards Samantha's school. Good thing he'd had the security guys at his gate to usher him past the media that gathered in front of his farm.

He shook his head as he thought about what had happened that morning with the deer hunter. What a fool he had been to automatically assume the man was McGraw. He shuddered, thinking of the dire consequences that could have had.

As he pulled up in front of the school and parked the Range Rover amid the Suburbans and minivans, he saw several groups of moms and kids already streaming out of the old ivy-covered brick building. Doug parked and hurried inside. He climbed the stairs to the second floor, where he was faced with several classroom doors, all opening into the crowded little hallway. He hesitated, trying to remember which one Anne had said was Samantha's.

Gretchen Moore came over to him, with a cute little red-haired girl in tow. "Why, Doug Cummings, what on earth are you doing here?" She embraced him much too tightly. "I haven't seen you since Sallie Rogers' dinner party."

Doug ignored her question. "Do you know which classroom is Mrs. Kennedy's?" he asked, backing away slightly.

Gretchen looked surprised. "Sure, it's that one over there," she replied, pointing towards a door in the corner.

"Thanks, Gretchen," Doug said, moving off.

The door to the classroom was closed and Doug hesitated, not sure if he should go in.

"They're still having their prayer session," one of the women waiting by the door said. "Better wait out here."

"Thanks." Doug moved away from the door. He leaned against the wall in the opposite corner and stood self-consciously among the group of young women waiting for the class to let out.

He thought he recognized a few faces from the hunt field, but most of the women were strangers to him. As Doug waited, he half-listened to their idle chatter, mostly about tennis and riding. Then he shifted uneasily as the conversation turned to him.

"You had better be more careful about riding out alone now, Marion," a hefty woman dressed in a pink warm-up suit said. "I've always told you that you should have a buddy system anyway, in case you get hurt out there. But now you'd be crazy to hack out alone."

"Why?" a petite blond woman dressed in riding breeches asked. "You mean because it's deer hunting season? Don't worry, I wear my blaze-orange vest. No one's going to mistake me for a deer, no matter how drunk they are." She giggled and looked around.

"I'm not talking about the deer hunters, Marion. I was referring to the murders."

"Oh, that. I thought they caught the guy and he was in jail," the one named Marion responded, frowning.

"They did," another woman said. "But he's out of jail on bond. Don't you read the papers, Marion?"

Marion blushed. "Sure, I read all the horse show results. And sometimes I read the "People" section in the *News*, if I have time."

The woman in the pink warm-up suit spoke again. "Actually, we have one of the mothers here to thank for putting Doug Cummings back out on the streets," she said, shaking her head. "Anne Sullivan's his lawyer. She's the one who got him released."

"Anne Sullivan? Who's she?" Marion asked.

"God, Marion, get with it. She's a tall blond. Pretty. Always all dressed up. You know, looks like a lawyer."

Marion nodded. "Oh, yeah, she's kind of stuck-up. Doesn't really talk to anyone."

"Exactly."

Suddenly the conversation stopped. Someone must have recognized him.

What a mistake, Doug thought. I should have learned by now that going out in public these days is asking for trouble. He breathed a sigh of relief as the classroom door finally opened.

Doug hung back to let the moms in first, but Samantha spotted him from the doorway and screamed excitedly to her teacher, "Mrs. Kennedy, my friend Doug's here. Can I go now?"

Doug walked up to the pair and returned Samantha's enthusiastic hug, then held out his hand to Mrs. Kennedy. "Hi, I'm Doug Cummings. I believe that Anne Sullivan made arrangements with you for me to pick Samantha up from school today."

The teacher smiled warmly at him. "She certainly did, Mr. Cummings, and Samantha has talked of nothing else all morning long. I'm delighted to finally meet the man I've been hearing so much about." She wrung her hands and blushed slightly. "I mean, all the wonderful things I've been hearing about you from Samantha."

Doug nodded and turned to Samantha. "Are you ready, princess?"

"Um-hmm," she said, taking Doug's hand. "My coat's out in the hallway." She reached up to give her teacher a hug. "Bye, Mrs. Kennedy. See you tomorrow."

They walked to Huckleberries and placed their order at the counter, amid jars of jelly beans and rock candy. Then they carried their drinks to a booth.

Doug looked around the small restaurant that was cozily decorated with green and white checkered vinyl tablecloths and stained glass ceiling lamps.

The preschool crowd was everywhere, running free, while their mothers sat together and socialized. The kids giggled and shrieked as they played songs on the jukebox and danced together in the aisle, and no one told them to shush and sit still. No wonder they liked to come there.

"Do you want to go and play with the other kids?" Doug asked Samantha.

"No, that's okay. I'd rather sit with you. I get to see them every day."

"Great. So, what did you do in school today?" Doug asked, trying to start a conversation, well aware of the stares directed at them.

Samantha shrugged. "Stuff."

Doug almost laughed out loud. Serves you right, Cummings. Why did you ever think you could pull this off? He took a deep breath.

"Stuff? What kind of stuff?" he asked Samantha. "Stuff like, what horses like to watch on TV? That kind of stuff?"

Samantha giggled. "No, silly. Stuff like A,B,Cs. And we learned some new songs. And we learned about the Indians and the Pilgrims."

"Really? Tell me what you learned about the Indians and the Pilgrims."

The ice was broken and Doug settled back and listened to Samantha chatter happily away. After she finished telling him about the Pilgrims, Samantha showed Doug two small plastic horses that she brought along in her coat pocket. Samantha made a paddock fence on the table out of sugar packets and played happily with the horses while they waited for their food to arrive.

The chaotic, casual atmosphere was somehow soothing to Doug. Everything about the place was so foreign to him, it helped take his mind off his problems. Even the staff was unique. Doug couldn't help but smile at the waiter who brought their food to the table. The man's whiskered face obviously hadn't been shaved in days, and he was dressed in camouflage pants and a gray T-shirt, with an apron tied around his waist. Doug bet he'd be out in the woods hunting deer the minute his shift ended.

They ate their lunch and then went back up to the counter for Samantha's ice cream. She ordered mint chocolate chip in a cone, which she ate while they walked to The Upper Crust, Middleburg's famous bakery, for a cookie.

Samantha seemed to have fun, and she looked disappointed that Doug had to leave right away when he dropped her off at Anne's house.

"Can't you just come in and play for a little while?" she asked.

Doug shook his head. "Not today, Samantha. Can I take a rain check?"

The little girl furrowed her brow. "What's a rain check?"

Doug laughed. "It means that I hope you invite me again on a day when I can say yes."

"Oh. Okay. Maybe tomorrow." Samantha reached up and hugged him. "Thank you for taking me to lunch, Doug. I had so-o-o much fun. I love you."

Doug returned her hug. "I had a great time too, Sam. Let's do it again soon."

As he straightened up, he saw her smile fade.

"Did I say something wrong?" he asked.

The little girl shook her head. "No. It's okay. It's just that my daddy used to call me Sam. He was the only one. No one else has called me that since he went up to Heaven."

"I'm sorry, Samantha," Doug said, crouching down in front of her and holding her hand. "I didn't know. I don't want to make you sad."

She shook her head and looked at him solemnly. "It's okay, Doug. I like it when you call me Sam. I think my daddy would like it too."

"All right. Sam it is." He gently tousled her hair and straightened up. "You better get inside now. If you catch a cold, your Aunt Anne will never forgive me."

Doug rang the doorbell and heard the sound of approaching footsteps. Ingrid opened the door, a magazine clutched to her chest. Although she greeted Doug with a polite smile, he could see the remnants of tears on her face. She had obviously been crying.

"Hi, Ingrid," Samantha shouted as she ran past the nanny. "I'm going to get my stuff so we can play horse show."

Ingrid smiled after Samantha. "Okay, honey," she said, sniffling.

"Are you all right?" Doug asked.

Ingrid nodded, sighing deeply. "I was sorting through some of Anne's old magazines and started reading this article about what that French au pair did to that poor little boy," she replied, opening the magazine and showing Doug the article. "I just don't understand how someone could ever hurt a child. It makes me want to scoop Samantha up and take her someplace where no one could ever harm her." Ingrid's slight Swedish accent was more pronounced than Doug had noticed before.

Doug nodded. "I know. It's tough. Kids are so trusting; it's hard to comprehend what kind of person could violate that innocence." He reached out and gave Ingrid a light squeeze on the shoulder, wondering if he should stay around for a while. "Are you going to be okay?"

She nodded. "Ya. Thank you. I'll go and give Samantha a big hug. That will make me feel much better."

"There you go." Doug smiled at her. "Tell Samantha good-bye for me and that I'll see her soon," he said, opening the front door. As he stepped outside, he heard Samantha call out to him.

"Doug. Wait."

He turned around and knelt down to her as she raced up to him. She was obviously distraught about something. "What's the matter?" he asked.

"I forgot my horses at Huckleberries." Her bottom lip quivered and she looked ready to cry.

Before Doug could respond, Ingrid picked her up. "It's okay, sweetie. Let's go call Huckleberries right now and have them find your horses for you. Then you can pick them up after school tomorrow. That way maybe you can have lunch there again tomorrow."

"Do you think they'll be okay all night without me?" Samantha asked.

"Oh, ya. I'm sure they'll be just fine," Ingrid replied, giving her a hug. "Come on. Let's go and give them a call."

"Okay," Samantha said.

"So, everything's all right?" Doug asked.

Samantha nodded and reached out to give him a hug. "Bye, Doug. I hope I see you soon."

He smiled at her. "Me too, Sam."

Doug waited until Ingrid locked the door behind him. As he was walking to the Range Rover, he saw Samantha waving good-bye from the front window, and he smiled and waved back.

Then he opened the car door and put his hand in his pocket for his car keys. As he pulled the keys out, something else fell to the ground, and Doug leaned down and picked it up. It was a woman's necklace. A gold chain with a diamond solitaire on the end. How the hell did it get in his pocket?

Christ. He slumped into the driver's seat. It looked like the necklace that Anne had been admiring on Leslie the night of the Hunt Ball.

Zeb waited until Cummings' car was out of sight before he stepped out from behind the bushes. He still wore the apron that he'd stolen from the restaurant, and he grinned as he thought about how easy it had been to pose as Cummings' waiter at lunch.

Zeb fished the kid's two plastic horses from his pocket as he stepped onto the porch and rang the doorbell. He heard footsteps and then saw the nanny's face look out at him through the glass in the front door.

"Ya? May I help you?" She had a funny-sounding voice.

Zeb smiled and held the plastic horses up for her to see. "The kid left these at lunch today. They asked me to drop them off here on my way home."

"Why, I just called Huckleberries and they told me they weren't able to find the horses," the nanny replied.

"Yeah, well, that's because I was already on my way here with them." Zeb held the horses closer to the glass. Come on, bitch. Open the door. "See. Here they are. Wouldn't the kid like to have them back?"

"Ya, of course." The nanny reached down and turned the dead bolt, then opened the door just a crack. "Thank you," she said, sticking her hand out.

Zeb heard footsteps in the hallway behind the nanny and then the kid's face appeared in the doorway.

"You found my horses," the kid squealed, tugging open the door.

"Yeah. You left these at lunch today." Zeb smiled at the kid, but didn't hand over the horses.

The kid smiled back at him. "I remember you. You were our waiter at Huckleberries."

Zeb nodded at her. "That's right, I was. I saw you playing with the horses at lunch, and when I found these at your table I figured you'd be missing them."

"Oh, I did miss them. These are my favorite horses. I have a whole collection. Do you want to see them?"

"Oh, no, sweetie," the nanny said. "You know your Aunt Anne doesn't allow us to have strangers in the house."

"He's not a stranger," the kid replied. "Doug and I met him at lunch today." She reached out and took Zeb's hand. "Come on."

Zeb pushed his way in before the nanny could argue and followed the kid down the hall.

"Well, I guess it will be okay if he only stays a minute," the nanny said.

Zeb grinned. A minute was all he needed.

62

Doug ignored the ringing of the telephone as he closed the front door and turned to hang his jacket up in the closet.

"Oh, Doug, I'm so glad you're finally home," Nellie called out as she hurried down the hallway towards him, wringing her hands on her apron. "It's Anne on the phone. She's been calling frantically for the last hour."

Doug's pulse quickened. Anne must have some news about her meeting with the investigator. He walked into his study and picked up the phone on his desk, sinking into his chair and kicking off his shoes.

"Hi. What's up?"

Her voice was angry. "Where the hell have you been, Doug? I've been looking all over for you."

"I've been out driving around. I turned my cell phone off, because some reporter got my number and wouldn't leave me alone. Why? What's so important?"

"What's so important? Samantha. That's what's so important. Didn't you think I would be worried when I got home and she wasn't here? You were supposed to have her home hours ago. And where's Ingrid?"

Doug glanced quickly at his watch. It was almost five o'clock. "Wait a minute, Anne. Calm down. I did bring her home hours ago. I dropped her off around two-thirty. And Ingrid was there when I dropped Samantha off. The two of them must have gone somewhere." He forced his voice to be calm, but a chill crept up his spine.

Doug's mind raced as he thought about where Samantha and Ingrid might be. Then he remembered Samantha's toy horses and he breathed a sigh of relief. "I'll bet I know where they are, Anne. Samantha left her toy horses at Huckleberries. They probably went to retrieve them."

"That's impossible, Doug," Anne replied. "Ingrid would never take Samantha anywhere without my permission. Even if there were an emergency, she wouldn't leave the house without leaving me a note or getting in touch with me. Besides, they didn't have a car. They couldn't have gone anywhere."

Doug tensed. No car. That ruled out the possibility they'd returned to Huckleberries for the horses. "Are you sure they're not playing somewhere outside?" he asked.

"Do you think I would have called you if I thought they could be playing somewhere outside?" she demanded.

Doug had no response and the phone line lay silent for a moment.

"I'm calling the sheriff," Anne said.

"I think you'd better do that. I'll leave right now. I should be there in fifteen minutes. And, Anne, try to calm down. There's probably some simple explanation as to where Samantha is."

"I'll calm down once we've found Samantha," Anne said, and she hung up the phone.

"Damn it." Doug stood up and slammed his fist on the desk. *Samantha*. It had never entered his mind that McGraw would go after Samantha. He had only asked Manse Security to look after Anne.

A sheriff's deputy was already at Anne's house when Doug arrived. Anne was pacing the hall with a cordless phone in one hand and a sheet of paper in the other.

"I've called all of Samantha's playmates," she said, tapping the phone against the sheet of paper. "Samantha's not at any of their homes. None of them have seen her since she left school today."

Doug glanced at the sheet of paper and saw that it was a directory of the students in Samantha's class. "What about Ingrid? Doesn't she have friends they might have gone somewhere with?" he asked.

Anne shook her head and folded her arms against her chest. "No. Ingrid wouldn't do that. I already told you that, Doug."

The deputy interrupted. "Miss Sullivan, we need to explore all the possibilities. Like I told you before, you need to stop thinking like Samantha has already come to some kind of harm. We get calls like this all the time, and it usually turns out that there is some kind of misunderstanding about where the kid is supposed to be."

Anne glared at him. "That's not the case here, Deputy, and we've already wasted too much precious time making phone calls. We need to get a search party organized, and we need to do it as soon as possible."

The deputy held his hand out to quiet her. "Okay, ma'am. I'm waiting on another deputy to arrive. He'll take charge of that. In the meantime, it'd be a big help if you could provide me with photographs of Samantha and Ingrid. And some kind of personal objects that would carry their scent. Maybe one of Samantha's favorite stuffed animals and an article of Ingrid's clothing. And while you do that, I'd like to ask Mr. Cummings here some questions, since he was the last one to see the girls."

Anne set the phone on the hall table. "Fine. I'll be right back."

The deputy waited until Anne was out of earshot, then looked at Doug and winked. "She's understandably a little emotional right now. I think it'd be best if we keep her occupied."

Doug glared at him and shook his head. "Don't write her off as some hysterical female, Deputy. She has good reason to believe that this is no innocent misunderstanding. There's some background here that you need to know."

"Okay," the deputy said, pulling out his notepad. "Why don't you fill me in? I'd like all the background. But first, let's start with today. Tell me everything that happened, starting with when you picked Samantha up from school today."

Doug replayed the day's events for the deputy and was just finishing up when Anne returned.

"I dropped Samantha off here around two-thirty," Doug said.

"Was the nanny here when you dropped her off?" the deputy asked, looking up from his notes.

"Do you think I would have left her here otherwise?" Doug asked.

The deputy's face turned red and he looked down at his notes. Doug sighed. "I'm sorry. Go ahead and ask your questions. Yes, Ingrid was here."

"Did you go inside the house with the girl?"

"Just briefly. I talked with Ingrid for a few minutes and then I left."

"Do you know if she locked the door when you left?" the deputy asked.

Doug nodded. "Yes. I waited while Ingrid locked it. Were there any signs of forced entry?"

"No. But Miss Sullivan said that the front door was unlocked when she got home."

The deputy looked down at his notes and frowned. "Did the girl or the nanny say anything at all to you that might have indicated what plans they had for the afternoon?"

Doug thought for a moment. He recalled the conversation he'd had with Ingrid. "No," he said slowly. "Not really."

"Are you sure?" Anne demanded. "You looked like you remembered something."

Doug frowned. "I just remembered something that Ingrid said to me. I don't think it means anything."

"Come on, Doug. Tell us," Anne ordered.

Doug repeated the conversation he'd had with Ingrid, including the girl's comment that she felt like taking Samantha away somewhere, to protect her from harm.

Anne stared at him. "Are you saying that you think Ingrid took Samantha?" she asked.

Doug shook his head. "I'm not sure. You know her better than I do, Anne. It just seems such a coincidence that Ingrid would say that, and now they're both gone."

"I don't think she did it," Anne said, shaking her head. "Ingrid loves Samantha. She would never harm her."

"Is that the background that you wanted to tell me about?" the deputy asked.

Doug shook his head. "No. It's something else entirely. It has to do with the person who has been committing the murders around here."

A door opened behind him. Doug turned to see Clyde Dickson walk through the front door.

"Well, look who's here," Dickson said. "We've really got to stop meeting like this."

Neither Doug nor Anne responded. Dickson walked over to the deputy and took the clipboard from him. He glanced over the report.

"So you were the last person to see the little girl and the nanny, huh, Cummings? What a coincidence."

Doug didn't respond and Dickson continued. "Where have you been from the time you say you dropped the kid off," he looked down at the young deputy's notes, "around two-thirty, until the time Ms. Sullivan reported them missing?"

"I went for a drive," Doug said.

"You went for a drive? Come on, Cummings. Surely you can do better than that."

Doug's cheek muscle twitched as he clenched his jaw. He wouldn't give Dickson the satisfaction of responding.

Dickson handed the clipboard back to the other deputy, reached into his shirt pocket, took out a stick of gum, and folded it into his mouth. He stared at Doug and chewed noisily.

The other deputy cleared his throat. "There's something else. I didn't have time to write it in my report yet, but Mr. Cummings was just telling us that the nanny made some mention earlier about running off with the child."

Dickson laughed. "That's convenient, Cummings. Make up a conversation with a missing person that you can use to draw the blame away from you. You never cease to amaze me."

"What will it take to make you start treating this murder investigation seriously, Dickson?" Doug demanded, stepping forward so that he towered over Dickson. "Did it ever enter your mind that you might have prevented the deaths of Babs Tyler and Leslie McCashin if you had concentrated on actually looking for Nancy Williams' killer, instead of just working on building your case against me?"

Dickson just sneered at him, and Doug took a step backward, struggling to control his temper before he did something he would regret.

He took a deep breath. "There's a little girl and her nanny out there somewhere, Dickson, and you better figure out a way to find them. Before it's too late."

"Don't you tell me what to do, Cummings," Dickson said. "You're not conducting this investigation. I am. And your attempt to cast the blame elsewhere and throw me off track isn't going to work."

Doug shook his head. "You're unbelievable." He walked back to Anne and pulled her aside. "My presence here isn't helping things," he said quietly. "I think I should wait outside. Dickson's not going to focus on anything other than me as long as I'm here."

Anne nodded.

"I'll be right out front if you need me." He touched her softly on her back before heading outside.

Doug stood just outside the door, where he could hear what was going on inside.

"Quite a relationship you have with your client, Miss Sullivan," Dickson said. "Wonder what he did to make a pretty lady like you so loyal to him? Even now after your little girl's disappeared."

"Stop right there," Anne said. "You're out of line and you know it. And if you think that I am going to let you sidetrack Samantha's investigation because of your personal animosity towards Doug Cummings, you are sorely mistaken. The way you've conducted this entire investigation has been pathetic, right from the start. You've broken the rules, if not the law, every step of the way. I promise you, Deputy, I'll file charges against you, and I won't give up until I have your badge, unless you launch a real investigation, starting right now, into Samantha's disappearance."

Doug didn't hear a response from Dickson.

Then he heard Anne's voice again, softer this time. "She's just a little child, Dickson. Samantha needs all of our help. Right now. It's her only chance. Please."

Come on, Dickson, Doug thought. How can you resist that?

"All right," Doug heard Dickson say. "I'll get a team started combing the area for her, but mark my words, Miss Sullivan, the trail's going to lead right back to Cummings."

"Thank you," Anne said. "Who'll notify the FBI?"

Doug walked away from the door and sat down on a bench at the end of the porch. He leaned forward and rested his head in his hands. He couldn't get Samantha's face out of his mind. Smiling, as she waved at him from the window. He could almost feel her tiny arms around his neck as she had hugged him good-bye. "I love you," she had said. Why hadn't he said it back?

The front door opened and Anne walked over and sat down next to him. "Dickson is organizing a team to search for Samantha and Ingrid. They should be here soon."

"I'll join them," Doug said.

Anne shook her head. "You can't do that, Doug."

"Why not?"

"I should think that would be obvious. You're their prime suspect."

"That's bullshit, Anne. I don't care what they think. I'm still going to help search for Samantha."

Anne shook her head wearily. "Please don't argue with me. If you go along, you'll only hamper the search. They all be focusing on you, rather than concentrating on looking for Samantha."

Doug didn't argue. He knew she was right.

"Please go home, Doug. There's nothing else you can do here."

"What about you?" He put his arms around her and tried to draw her against his chest, but she stiffened and pulled away.

"Don't," she whispered, shaking her head. "I want to be alone." Tears filled her eyes and she rose from the bench and walked back towards the front door.

Doug stood up. "Anne."

She stopped, but didn't turn her head towards him.

"I'll wait at home. Promise me you'll call, if you need me."

Anne nodded, and then walked into the house, without even glancing in his direction.

63

Doug spent a sleepless night in his study, waiting for the phone to ring. Now it was dawn, and Anne hadn't called. Maybe that was good news. He knew he should try to force down some breakfast, so he went to the kitchen and turned on the coffee maker. As he waited for the coffee to brew, he turned on the *Today Show* and watched Katie Couric laugh as an animal trainer handed her a monkey.

Doug poured a cup of coffee and sat down at the table. Just as he brought the cup to his mouth, the *Today Show* went off the air. "We interrupt this broadcast with a special newscast from your local area," a man's voice announced. The image on the screen switched to the studio of the local NBC affiliate, and a blue banner across the bottom of the screen read, "Middleburg Murders."

"Oh, God, no." Doug slammed down his coffee cup and the hot liquid splashed over his hand. He grabbed the remote control and turned up the volume as the anchorman spoke.

"We have late-breaking news regarding the recent string of hunt-country murders. We take you now to Susan Gregory, who is on the scene out in Middleburg. Susan."

"Thank you, Bob. For those of you who just tuned in, I'm at the Safeway in Middleburg where the fourth victim in a string of recent murders was found just this morning. The body of Ingrid Bjorn was discovered by a grocery store clerk early this morning, in a dumpster in this Safeway parking lot. Ms. Bjorn was reported missing late yesterday, along with young four-year-old Samantha Remington. Samantha has not yet been located."

A wave of nausea gripped Doug. He reached for the phone, but then hes-

itated, the receiver in midair. Who could he call? Not Anne. Not yet. He needed to know more first. Doug slowly replaced the handset and turned his attention back to the newscast.

A yellow and white rescue squad unit was visible in the Safeway parking
lot behind the reporter. The vehicle's siren was silent, but its red and white
lights flashed ominously in the drab morning light.

"Tell us, Susan," the Washington anchor was saying, "is there any news
at this point as to the whereabouts of the little girl?"

The reporter shook her head. "No, Bob, there isn't. And although the
authorities have not yet confirmed it, there is a widespread presumption here
that this killing is the work of the serial killer who has been on the loose in
the Middleburg area. There's mounting fear among the locals that this
community may need to brace itself for the worst as far as little Samantha is
concerned."

The picture on the screen showed a group of men with search dogs in a
wooded area. "As you can see from this footage we shot earlier this morning,
Bob, a widespread search for Samantha is being conducted in the wooded
area surrounding her home. Authorities tell us that the search party was
organized within hours of the time Samantha went missing yesterday and
continued throughout the night last night. But so far, they've uncovered no
clues in her disappearance. Back to you, Bob."

The solemn face of the anchor filled the screen. "That's the very latest on
the tragic early morning events out in historic Middleburg, Virginia. We will
of course be bringing you the breaking news on this situation as it develops
throughout the day. And now, back to the *Today Show* in New York."

Doug turned the volume down and fought the despair that surged through
him. He had been holding out a faint hope that Samantha and Ingrid would turn
up unharmed. That maybe Ingrid really had taken Samantha away somewhere.
But now, there was no doubt in his mind that McGraw had Samantha. Doug's
hand trembled slightly as he picked up the phone and dialed Anne's number.

"Hello," a female's voice said breathlessly after the second ring.

"Anne?"

The voice was stiff. "No, I'm sorry, Ms. Sullivan's not available right
now."

"This is Doug Cummings. Who is this?"

"Hi, Mr. Cummings. It's Cyndi. From Anne's office." Her tone grew
friendlier.

"Where's Anne? Is she all right?"

"She's not taking any calls right now, Mr. Cummings," Cyndi replied.

"That's not what I asked you, Cyndi. I asked you if she's all right."

"She's doing as well as can be expected under the circumstances." Cyndi's voice was guarded. Doug figured that Anne was probably in the room.

"Has she received any news at all about Samantha? Any leads?"

"No, Mr. Cummings. We've heard nothing."

"What about Ingrid? Have you received any details about her death?"

"Yes. It looks as if Ingrid was strangled to death. She didn't suffer the violent beating like the other women. I guess we can take some small comfort in that."

Doug closed his eyes and sighed. "Is there anything I can do to help, Cyndi? Does Anne need anything? Should I come over?"

There was silence for a moment, then Doug could hear whispering in the background. Cyndi came back on the line. "No, Mr. Cummings. Please don't come over here. Anne just wants to be left alone right now. Besides, the media is camped out in front of Anne's house. You definitely should not come over."

"All right, Cyndi," Doug said, feeling rebuffed. "I get the message. Will you promise to call me if you hear any news about Samantha, or if Anne needs anything?" Cyndi assured him that she would and he had her write down the private phone number in his study. He was no longer answering the main telephone line.

Doug was about to hang up when Cyndi stopped him. He heard whispering again at the other end.

"Mr. Cummings, Anne wanted me to tell you that an FBI Agent is going to be contacting you. His name is Chester Rawls. Anne said that I should tell you to please cooperate with him. She says he's a good guy. Not like Deputy Dickson."

"Of course I'll cooperate with him. I'll help the search for Samantha in whatever way I can."

"Thank you. I'll tell her," Cyndi said, hanging up.

Doug sat and stared at the silent telephone. He couldn't just sit around while the deputies and the FBI searched for Samantha. He had to do something to help.

He walked to the window and stared out at the distant hazy Blue Ridge

Mountains, trying to come up with a plan. Doug's mind raced as his eyes swept across the familiar rolling landscape. McGraw must have a hiding place of some sort out there. And it couldn't be very far away. That was the only way McGraw could have followed him as closely as he had.

Doug pounded his fist on the counter. Damn it, he knew the area as well as anyone. He wouldn't just sit at home and do nothing. Yes, he had promised Anne he'd stay out of the way of the search party, but he hadn't promised her he wouldn't search on his own. Doug rushed upstairs to change into his riding clothes.

Just as Doug came downstairs and was heading out the door to go to the barn, the phone in his study rang. He hurried back to answer it.

"Mr. Cummings, it's Brian at the front gate. There's a man here by the name of Chester Rawls. He's FBI. I checked his credentials. Do you want me to let him in?"

Shit. Doug glanced at his watch. "Sure, Brian, send him on down to the house."

Doug studied the tall black man who stood at his front door. Chester Rawls fit the mold of an FBI Agent. Dark glasses, gray suit, white shirt, thin tie, sensible black shoes. Doug led him into the study and sat down behind his desk, motioning for Rawls to take a chair opposite him.

"I know you're here to question me," Doug said, "but first, tell me if they've found any leads in Samantha's disappearance."

"No, Mr. Cummings," the FBI Agent replied. "We haven't found any leads."

Doug smiled wryly at him. "Would you tell me if you had?"

Rawls met his gaze and just smiled back at him. The ground rules had been established.

"Okay, Rawls. Go ahead," Doug said, leaning back in his chair.

Rawls flipped open a small spiral notepad and took a pen out of his coat pocket. "Tell me everything that happened when you picked Samantha up at school and took her to lunch. I want to know who you and she talked to, who sat at the table next to you, who your waiter was, everything you can remember."

Doug picked up a pen off the desk and fiddled with it, trying to decide exactly what to say. Finally, he put the pen down and sat forward. "Look, Rawls, I'll be happy to answer all of those questions if you really want me to. But, quite frankly, that would be a total waste of our time. There wasn't anyone at school or at lunch that day that abducted Samantha and Ingrid. This is the work of a man by the name of Zebulon McGraw. A sick, dangerous man, who apparently will stop at nothing to get at me. He's killed before and he'll kill again. It's up to us to find him before Samantha becomes his next victim. Let's just dispense with all this bullshit about 'who did it,' and let me tell you everything that I can about McGraw."

Chester Rawls didn't respond right away. The agent studied Doug carefully for a moment, as if sizing him up, then finally nodded. "Okay, Cummings. Miss Sullivan mentioned McGraw to me. Tell me what you know."

Doug sighed in relief. He told Rawls all that he could about Zebulon McGraw and his apparent pattern of behavior. As they walked to the door, thirty minutes later, Chester Rawls turned to Doug and motioned towards his riding clothes. "You sure picked an unusual time to go out for a ride, Cummings. What with everything that's happened and all. I don't suppose you'd do anything stupid like go out looking for McGraw by yourself, now would you?"

Doug didn't answer and Rawls went on. "Because if I thought that you'd do something dumb like that, I'd be obligated to prevent you from doing so."

Doug opened the door. "Don't give it another thought, Rawls. I'm just going out for a ride."

"Right," Rawls replied. "Do you mind telling me where you're headed?"

"I'll be heading east, across Foxcroft Road, into the Nine Mile Woods."

"The Nine Mile Woods?" Rawls repeated slowly. "Sounds like a good place to get lost."

CHAPTER

64

Clyde could barely contain his anger as he listened to Sheriff Boling babble on from across the desk. Blah, blah, blah. None of it meant anything. The sheriff was just trying to justify his own lack of courage to go after Cummings.

"So you see, Clyde, I think it's quite possible that we have a copycat killer on our hands here. Not that I'm about to release that to the media, mind you. That would really panic this community. But this most recent slaying, the nanny, I'm not convinced it was done by the same guy. The killer of the first three victims—and by the way I am convinced that they were all committed by the same man—was getting progressively more violent in the beatings of those women. And this lady, she wasn't beaten at all. It just doesn't fit the profile."

Clyde didn't bother to respond. He wouldn't waste the energy.

The sheriff continued. "Clyde, you know that I've not been persuaded that Doug Cummings is responsible for the first three murders. I know that you are convinced of his guilt. As is Timothy Shaw. But I'm not. And since I have my doubts that the nanny was even killed by the same guy, I surely won't authorize going after an arrest warrant for Doug Cummings in the nanny's death. Not until I have proper proof. I want you to back off of Cummings. Right now, our priority is to find the missing girl."

Clyde scowled and shook his head back and forth. "You forgot to mention the fact that Cummings was the last one to see the nanny and the kid alive, Sheriff. Isn't that scenario getting a little old by now?"

The sheriff didn't respond and Clyde rose from his chair. "Sorry for taking up your time, Sheriff. I'd better get back to work."

Clyde walked into the outer office, but didn't stop at his desk. He kept right on going, kicking his waste can as he went by. He wasn't about to sit around doing any damned paperwork.

Clyde drove the short distance to Timothy Shaw's office and stopped at the receptionist's desk. "Is Shaw here?"

"I'm sorry, but Mr. Shaw is in a meeting."

"Well, this is important. Tell him that Clyde Dickson is here and I need to talk to him."

The receptionist reluctantly picked up the phone on her desk and punched two numbers. "Mr. Shaw, there's a Clyde Dickson here to see you. He's says it's important." She listened for a moment and nodded her head. "Yes, sir. I'll tell him." She hung up the phone and waved her hand towards a row of seats. "Mr. Shaw said you are welcome to wait if you want to, but he doesn't know how long he'll be tied up in his meeting."

Annoyed, Clyde took a seat and picked up a *Sports Illustrated* magazine. When he had finished leafing through it, Shaw still hadn't come out. Clyde threw the magazine on the table and ignored the stern look the receptionist gave him. He looked at his watch. Shaw had already kept him waiting for over half an hour. A young woman dressed in a suit walked out of Shaw's office, and Clyde stood up and grabbed her arm as she walked by.

"Look, I've got places I need to be. I've got a date with the media in a little while. Tell your boss that I need to see him now."

"Excuse me?" the young woman said, raising an eyebrow.

"Do I need to spell it out for you? I need to see Shaw. Go and tell him."

"I'm not in charge of Mr. Shaw's schedule," the woman said, turning to go.

"You're his secretary, aren't you?"

"No, I'm not. I'm an attorney who works with Mr. Shaw. And you . . ."

Before she could finish her sentence, the door to Timothy Shaw's office opened and Shaw walked out.

"What are you doing here, Dickson?" he asked.

"I came to find out when you're going to charge Cummings with the nanny's murder. I want to be the one to arrest him," Clyde replied.

Timothy Shaw led Clyde by the arm into his office and shut the door behind them.

"Listen, Dickson, I'm not going to let you go off half-cocked again this time, like you did after Leslie McCashin's murder. No one's going to arrest

Cummings until we have solid evidence, iron clad, linking him to the nanny's murder."

"Aw, come on, Shaw. What are you going to do? Wait until he does it again? Wait until he kills the kid, if he hasn't already?" Clyde asked.

Timothy Shaw just glared at him, his hands on his hips.

"You could at least have his bail revoked," Clyde said.

"On what grounds, Dickson?" Shaw demanded. "Should I tell Judge Hitchin that you have a feeling that Cummings did this one too, and ask him to lock Cummings up until we can find the evidence to prove it? We don't even have the fiber test results from the lab on the McCashin murder yet."

Clyde didn't respond. Shaw pointed his finger at him. "This is my case, Dickson, and I will not let you screw it up. I want Cummings every bit as much as you do, but I'm not going to get caught with my pants down in front of Judge Hitchin again. My people are conducting the investigation now. By the book. You back off Cummings and stay out of our way. Do I make myself clear?"

Clyde shook his head in disbelief. Jesus Christ. Everyone was afraid of Cummings. Because of his money.

"Yeah," Clyde said, opening Shaw's office door. "You're clear all right."

As Clyde stormed out of the building, he consoled himself with the fact that he had an interview with the media that afternoon. Just because Shaw didn't have the guts to try Cummings in court didn't mean that Cummings couldn't be tried in the media.

CHAPTER

65

It was late afternoon by the time Doug returned home. He hated to quit for the day, but he knew that the light would be fading soon and his horse was tired. He'd covered a great deal of ground without finding any signs of McGraw or Samantha. But at least he'd eliminated that area from his search. He'd head out in another direction first thing the next morning.

After checking with Nellie and learning that Anne hadn't called, Doug turned on the television, searching for any developments regarding Samantha. There were none, but the media was milking the story for all it was worth. There were interviews with Samantha's teachers and the parents of her playmates, and heart-wrenching scenes of Ingrid's friends weeping over the nanny's tragic death. There were stories about Doug's connection to Anne and Samantha and to the other recent murder victims. And about his arrest for the murder of Leslie McCashin. There were scenes of the search party combing the woods for Samantha.

Doug sat on the couch in front of the fire and picked at the dinner that Nellie had fixed him. He was channel surfing when he hit a *Premier News* show and Samantha's face filled the screen. The rich voice of reporter Martin Stone was recounting the events leading up to her disappearance. The image faded back to the reporter standing in front of the weathered stone facade of the Red Fox Inn in Middleburg. "While this quaint little town struggles to come together in an effort to locate little Samantha Remington, the residents here are strongly divided in their beliefs as to whether local socialite Doug Cummings could be responsible for Samantha's disappearance and for the string of recent hunt-country murders."

A photo essay of Doug appeared, blending a dichotomy of romantic hunt-country images with those of a fast-paced, high-powered Washington lifestyle. The pictures flashed from Doug on horseback, smiling at a young woman riding beside him, to Doug dressed in his scarlet, dancing with a scantily clad woman at a hunt ball. Then to the sharply contrasting images of Doug testifying before Congress, and attending a black-tie event at the Kennedy Center.

Stone's voice-over summarized the tragic turn of events that Doug's life had taken. "Until recently, multi-millionaire Doug Cummings was regarded as one of the most sought-after bachelors in Washington and was on virtually everyone's list as one of the top tax lawyers in the country. Today, Doug Cummings is preparing to stand trial for murder and has been ousted from his prestigious Washington law firm. Who is the real Doug Cummings? And was he the kind of man to commit murder? Tonight, you're going to hear several differing opinions on that subject. First, we'll go to Clyde Dickson, the sheriff's deputy in charge of the investigation into the Middleburg murders.

"Deputy Dickson, as you know, Doug Cummings has already been charged with the murder of Leslie McCashin, and earlier today Sheriff Boling released a statement saying that Cummings is, quote, 'a person of interest' in the ongoing investigation of the other Middleburg murders. Can you shed any light on what Sheriff Boling meant by that?"

Dickson's flushed face filled the screen. "Sheriff Boling's just trying to be politically correct, that's all. Let me put it this way. We believe the Middleburg murders were all committed by the same person. We've conducted a thorough investigation and we have narrowed it down to one suspect. *One.* Doug Cummings. He's already been charged with the rape and murder of Leslie McCashin, and it's just a matter of time before he's charged with the other murders as well. *Person of interest.* He's that all right."

Martin Stone was back in front of the camera. "Well, you've heard the unequivocal opinion of local law enforcement, now here's what some of the local residents had to say about Cummings."

The picture flashed to a hunt meet and Richard Evan Clarke on his horse. "Doug Cummings is a good man. He's my friend. I have full faith in him. I need not say more." Richard nodded politely at the camera before turning his horse and walking off.

The camera shifted to Wendy Brooks, who paused as she was tightening the girth on her saddle, and stared thoughtfully into the camera. "Doug's a playboy. Everyone knows that," she said, shrugging her shoulders. "He's been juggling women all over this county for as long as I can remember. I think that this time he just got in over his head."

"Thanks, Wendy," Doug muttered. What little appetite he'd had for Nellie's dinner was gone now. He placed his knife and fork on the plate and settled back against the deep cushions of the couch.

The scene moved to Middleburg, and Jack Byron, a local accountant, was interviewed as he was entering Middleburg Merchant's Bank. "Mr. Byron, you and Doug Cummings both serve on the board of this bank. What do you think of the allegations against Mr. Cummings?" Martin Stone asked, holding the microphone towards Byron.

Jack Byron started to walk past the reporter then stopped and looked at the camera. "You want to know what I think? I think that it's neither your business nor mine to speculate about the charges against Doug Cummings. That's what we have courts for." He looked disdainfully at Martin Stone and walked through the double doors that led to the bank lobby. But before the doors closed behind him, he turned around and stopped one door with his foot. "For the record, though, since you asked, I'd say there's not a chance in hell that Doug Cummings is guilty."

Gretchen Moore was on the screen next, standing in front of Samantha's school, dressed in a harvest gold L.L. Bean barn coat, freshly pressed jeans and driving moccasins. Her auburn hair was sleeked back in a bun and clipped with a plaid bow.

"I saw Doug Cummings right here the day Samantha disappeared. He had come to pick up Samantha from school, and I recall thinking at the time that he was acting very odd." She paused. "Do I think he did it? I hope not. But I guess time will tell."

Gretchen went inside and the reporter did a stand-up in front of the school, with mothers and children passing behind him. "You've heard varying opinions as to Doug Cummings' guilt or innocence from several of his peers. Now you're going to hear from a man who's worked for Cummings for almost twelve years."

Doug watched as the image faded to John coming out of the Southern States feed store, a bag of grain in his arms. John looked nervous as he responded to the reporter. "I never talked to no camera before, and I don't know why you want to hear from someone like me anyway, but if it will help Mr. Cummings, I sure don't mind talking to you." John shifted the heavy bag of grain and then continued, looking directly at the camera. "Mr. Cummings is one of the best folk I ever knew around these parts. He gave me a chance when no one else would and now he's doing the same for my boy Billy. Ain't no better man I ever knew than Mr. Cummings. I tell my children every day, you stay honest and try your hardest, and maybe some day you can make something out of your life, like Mr. Cummings did." John shook his head. "Mr. Cummings ain't no murderer. No, sir. I'd stake my life on that."

"As you can see, there's no lack of opinion out here on the subject of Doug Cummings' guilt or innocence," Martin Stone said, back in front of the camera again. "What's almost ironic," he said to Rick Bradford at the anchor desk in New York, "is that Middleburg is best known as a safe haven for the rich and famous, and yet now it is one of their own that many out here believe is guilty of this horrendous string of murders."

"That's quite some story, Martin," Rick Bradford said. "And there certainly doesn't seem to be a shortage of conflicting opinions about Doug Cummings. Martin, I also heard that Cummings had assaulted our camera crew. Can you shed any light on that report?"

"Yes, Rick, Cummings went after our camera crew last week. He apparently roughed the cameraman up pretty good, confiscated his camera, and then stole their van. From the accounts I've heard, Cummings was pretty violent and the incident was apparently unprovoked. The crew was reportedly parked outside Cummings' estate on the public road, evidently not trespassing on his property or invading his privacy in any way."

"That's quite something. Have you been able to reach either Cummings or Anne Sullivan for comment about any of this?"

"Anne Sullivan was understandably too distraught to speak with us on camera, but she did issue a statement through her office saying that she, quote, 'had full belief in Doug Cummings' innocence in the crime for which he had been charged' and that she was, quote, 'confident that a jury would acquit him when he had his day in court.'"

"No comment from Ms. Sullivan about any suspected involvement on Cummings part in little Samantha's disappearance?"

"No, Rick," Stone said, shaking his head. "And no comment from Doug Cummings. In fact, we were unable to contact him at all. He's holed up at his Middleburg estate with armed security guards at the gate, and he hasn't been answering his telephone."

"Thank you, Martin," Rick Bradford said, gathering his notes and turning full face to the camera. His brow furrowed under his thick mane of graying hair and his deep voice was somber. "Of course, the network will be keeping you informed on this story as the events unfold and, in the meantime, I hope you'll all join me tonight in saying a prayer for the safe return of little Samantha Remington. That's it for tonight's edition of *Spotlight America*. See you tomorrow evening. Good night."

Doug clicked the television off and tossed the remote control on the coffee table.

CHAPTER
66

Anne sent Cyndi home for the night and wearily climbed the stairs. She was grateful to finally be alone. A strong storm was raging outside and a deep rumble of thunder shook the house, causing the crystal chandelier at the top of the stairs to make a faint tinkling sound as she walked under it. The lights dimmed briefly, then came back on.

Great, Anne thought, as she entered her bedroom. All I need right now is to have the power go out.

Although she knew she wouldn't be able to sleep, Anne started to undress for bed anyway. She had to stick to her routine. That was all that kept her going.

Anne had just stripped to her bra and panties when the lights flickered off again, this time for good. She groped her way over to the bed and reached for the flashlight that she kept on her nightstand, but it wasn't there.

Damn. Samantha must have been playing with it again.

A flash of lightening illuminated the room long enough for Anne to spot the quilt she kept folded on the foot of her bed. She grabbed for it and wrapped it around herself. She gingerly made her way over to the front window and looked out. The power outage must be a big one. The countryside was dark as far as she could see.

The wind was wickedly whipping the trees around her house, and another flash of lightening revealed the maze of branches that littered her lawn. Anne whirled around as she heard the sickening crash of breaking glass from somewhere downstairs. She assumed a branch must have broken a window, but she listened intently for any other sounds coming from within the house. A long, deep rumble of thunder rolled over the landscape and slowly faded away.

It was quiet for a moment, but then Anne heard what sounded like the creaking of a door. It's probably just the wind, she told herself, but she clutched the quilt more tightly to her. Another crack of thunder echoed outside the window, and as it diminished Anne heard more creaking noises, closer this time. Her pulse quickened as a rush of adrenaline surged through her, and she forced herself to take a deep breath. She turned and looked towards the doorway to her room, but it was shrouded in darkness. Had she closed the door? She couldn't remember. Since Samantha had disappeared, she had started locking her bedroom door at night. But had she done so tonight? She was almost certain that she had not.

A loud creak sounded close by, in the vicinity of the hallway, and Anne's mouth went dry. She hadn't imagined it. Someone was in her house.

She started towards the door just as a stroke of lightening brightened the room, but stopped short as she saw the dark figure of a man standing in her bedroom doorway. There was nowhere for her to go, no means of escape, and she stepped back against the wall and slid down to the floor, trying to make herself as inconspicuous as possible. She stared into the darkness, but could see nothing. It was McGraw. It had to be.

The floor boards creaked again, closer now, and she could sense his presence, so intensely that she felt she would touch him if she reached out her hand. Her heart thudded rapidly in her chest and she held her breath. Another floor board creaked. Right in front of her. So close that she could hear his breathing. Then she sensed a movement, and a shower of water droplets splattered her face.

"Miss Sullivan?" a man's voice called from somewhere in the house. "Are you all right?"

Anne gasped in surprise and heard the man in front of her curse. Footsteps pounded heavily across the floor as he ran from her room. Anne stayed where she was and listened to the slow tread on the stairs as the other man approached. He carried a flashlight and Anne watched as the beam from it shone up the stairs and into the hallway.

"Miss Sullivan?" he called out again.

Anne didn't know who he was, but she was certain that he had saved her from the man who had just left.

"I'm in here." Her voice sounded strange to her, as if it were coming from inside a tunnel.

The beam from the flashlight quickly appeared in her doorway and scanned the room, stopping when she was in its spotlight. Anne put her hand up to shield her eyes from the light, and the man lowered it and hurried over to her. "Are you all right?" he asked, crouching down in front of her and aiming the flashlight towards the floor so that it cast a dim light over both of them.

Anne nodded. The man was dressed in jeans, a bomber jacket, and a navy-blue cap with FBI embroidered on the front. She had never seen him before.

"Who are you?" she asked, then jumped as rapid footsteps sounded from the hallway and descended down the stairs.

"Stay here," the FBI man ordered as he rushed out of the room.

Anne heard the front door open and then it was quiet. After what seemed like a long while, she heard the front door close again and footsteps on the stairs. The FBI man called out to her, "I was too late. He got away."

Anne stood up and was waiting for him when he entered her room.

"Who are you? And what are you doing here?"

"My name's Edward Dorsett, ma'am, and I work for Manse Security." He handed Anne a second flashlight.

"Thanks," Anne said, turning the flashlight on and studying him for a moment. "What's with the hat?"

"Oh, that. I used to work for the FBI, a while back. I do private security for Manse now."

"Why are you here? I didn't hire you," she said, frowning.

"No, ma'am, you didn't," the man replied. "Mr. Cummings engaged me to look after you."

"Doug?"

"Yes, ma'am, that's right," the man replied. "Doug Cummings."

Tears filled Anne's eyes. She'd turned down Doug's offers for help and shunned his phone calls, but he was still looking after her.

She reached out and shook the security guard's hand. "Mr. Dorsett, thank you for being here. For what you did for me tonight. Do you think he'll come back?"

"I'm not making any bets on that one, Miss Sullivan," he replied. "I'll be prepared either way. You just keep your bedroom door locked and I'll be right outside here in the hallway, watching over things."

Anne nodded. "Thank you. Good night."

She locked the door firmly behind the security guard and curled up on the bed, still clutching the illuminated flashlight.

67

Doug spent the night on the couch in his study, not wanting to be far from the phone, and when it finally rang around seven-thirty the next morning, he lunged to answer it.

"Good morning, Mr. Cummings, it's Cyndi, from Anne Sullivan's office."

His heart skipped a beat. "What's happened?"

"Oh, nothing regarding Samantha," Cyndi replied. "I'm calling to let you know that Anne has arranged for another lawyer to represent you today when you appear for the DNA testing."

"What?" Doug couldn't believe it. Taking a DNA test was the last thing on his mind right then. "In light of all that's gone on, don't you think we could postpone the DNA tests?"

"No, Mr. Cummings. Anne does not want to do that. She doesn't want to give Mr. Shaw any grounds to petition the court to revoke your bail," Cyndi replied.

Doug grunted gruffly in response, and Cyndi continued with her instructions.

"You have an appointment at nine o'clock this morning with Tom Sanders at his office in Leesburg. He's with Harrison, Thomas and Albright at one-twenty-one King Street. He'll go over the specifics with you and then take you over to the lab for the testing. Anne had me brief Mr. Sanders on your case, so he should be all set. If he has any further questions, he can ask you when you get together in his office. Anne asked me to assure you that you'll be in very good hands."

"How's Anne holding up?" Doug asked.

"She's coping," Cyndi replied.

"Tell her I'd like to talk to her."

Cyndi hesitated for a moment and Doug heard a rustling, as if she were covering the mouthpiece with her hand. "Uh, Mr. Cummings, Anne's not where I can talk to her right now. But I'll pass on your message."

Why the hell wouldn't Anne even talk with him? He slammed his palm against the top of his desk. "Damn it. All right, tell Anne I'll do the DNA testing," he said.

Cyndi sighed softly. "Yes, Mr. Cummings. I'll tell her. Thank you."

Doug glanced at his watch. He'd better hop in the shower if he was going to make Sanders' office by nine.

Doug was tempted to show up in jeans with the two-day-old growth of beard on his face, but in the end he got out his razor and donned a turtleneck sweater, tweed jacket, and wool pants.

As Doug drove through Middleburg on the way to Sanders' office, he couldn't help but notice the neon flyers taped on the *Hunt Country* news boxes. "Special Section—The Middleburg Murders." He slowed down as he passed the news box in front of The Coach Stop, and caught a glimpse of the newspaper's front page headline. "Authorities Warn Locals, Lock Your Doors." Sharon had come through. Doug sped up and headed towards Leesburg.

He parked on the street in front of Sanders' law firm and found Tom Sanders waiting for him in the lobby. Sanders led the way back to his office and motioned for Doug to take a seat.

"So, Sanders, tell me what to expect today," Doug said, easing into a chair across from Sanders' tidy desk.

"Well, Mr. Cummings, your part is really quite simple," Sanders said, a southern drawl softening his otherwise nasal tone. "We'll go to the lab and you'll give them the samples. I'll be there to make sure that the samples aren't corrupted and that the tests are conducted properly. There's really quite some room for error in DNA testing if the proper procedures are not followed." Sanders' eyes darted around his desktop while he talked. "I'm very experienced in DNA testing. I have a medical degree as well as a law degree, and I've published several articles on the subject. That's why Miss Sullivan called me."

Great. An academic. "Look, Tom, I wasn't questioning your qualifications," Doug said. "I simply want to know what I'll be expected to do this morning."

"Why, just provide the samples, that's all," Sanders replied.

"Come on, Sanders. Do I have to spell it out? What kind of samples do they need?"

"Oh, sorry. I should have explained." Crimson spots appeared on Sanders' pale cheeks. "They don't need a, uh, semen sample. Hair, blood and saliva. That's all. They can establish DNA from any one of those."

Doug let out a sigh of relief. "Fine. Let's be on our way." He stood up and headed for the door.

The testing didn't take long and Doug was back home by noon. Nellie said the private line hadn't rung, but he called Anne's house anyway and got Cyndi. She told him there was still no news about Samantha, and he caught himself before asking if Anne was available. He didn't need to be rejected twice in one day. He quickly changed into his riding clothes and hurried down to the barn.

Doug's search that afternoon was as disappointing as the day before, and by the time he returned home, it began to rain again. He closed the front door and went upstairs, without bothering to check in first with Nellie. After changing into jeans and a sweat shirt, he went back down to the study.

Nellie must have heard him come in because she'd started a blazing fire, and Doug settled down in the arm chair next to it. He closed his eyes and sighed, leaning his head back against the cool, soft leather of the chair. He'd never give up his search, as long as Samantha was still out there. But did he really have a chance in hell of finding her?

Doug sat there until long after dusk, then finally got up to turn some lights on. He sat down at his desk and was toying with the cord on the telephone, debating whether or not to call Anne, when he heard the front doorbell ring. He got up and walked to the door, wondering who could have gotten past the security guards at the gate.

It was Anne. The light outside the front door cast shadows on her pale, drawn face, and Doug was shocked by the way she looked. The last two days had taken their toll on her. She wore a baseball cap and outback coat to protect her from the evening's chilly drizzle, and as she stood there, raindrops rolled off the brim of her cap.

"Come in," Doug said, stepping back. "Here, let me take your coat," he said, reaching out to help her.

"No, it's okay. I'll only be staying a minute," Anne said, but then let Doug take her coat and cap anyway.

She stood with her arms folded protectively across her chest, shivering slightly. "I just wanted to tell you about a phone call I received this afternoon from Sharon Duncan. She's that reporter for *Hunt Country*."

Doug interrupted her. "Anne, you're freezing. Let's go in the study and sit by the fire."

"No, Doug, I'm fine. Please let me finish. I think you'll want to hear this."

He nodded.

"Anyway," Anne continued, "Sharon called me to say that if you are a suspect in Samantha and Ingrid's disappearance, or Ingrid's murder, she could provide you with an alibi."

Doug's pulse raced. An alibi? How was that possible? He'd been alone after he'd dropped Samantha off that afternoon.

Doug kept quiet, and Anne continued. "It seems that Sharon's editor at *Hunt Country* was upset that she hadn't produced a major story about you or any of the murders, so he ordered her to follow you, figuring she'd be in the right place when a story broke. On that day, when Samantha and Ingrid disappeared, Sharon followed you from the time that you left your farm to pick Samantha up at school until you finally went home again early that evening. She's willing to sign an affidavit that she saw you drop Samantha off at my house around two-thirty that afternoon and that you were never near Samantha or my house after that time." Anne made an attempt at a smile. "I already called Clyde Dickson and told him. I'm sure you can imagine how he took the news."

Doug slowly let out a sigh of relief. "Did Sharon see anything that might help us find Samantha?"

Anne shook her head. "No, she was concentrating on following you."

Anne turned towards the bench where Doug had put her coat. "So, that's it. I figured I'd deliver the good news in person."

"Anne, wait. Don't leave yet." She stopped and glanced back towards him. "Don't take this wrong," he said, "but you really look terrible. When was the last time you ate something?"

Her eyes filled with tears and she looked away. "I can't," she whispered, shaking her head. "I've tried, but I just can't."

"I know, but you have to. It won't do Samantha any good if you end up in the hospital. How about letting Nellie make something for you? Even if it's just some soup."

Anne shook her head as she reached up and wiped her tears away.

Doug put a hand on her shoulder. "Please?"

She stared at him for a moment, and then nodded slowly. "All right. Maybe some soup."

He smiled. "Good. Go and warm up in the study. I'll find Nellie."

Anne was sitting on the raised stone hearth in front of the fire when Doug returned. Her arms hugged her knees tightly against her chest.

He handed her a cup of hot tea and sat down next to her. "Do you need to call and let anyone know you're here? In case there's any news?"

Anne shook her head. "No. I sent Cyndi home. Everyone has my beeper number. I've told them just to use that. I'm not answering the phone anymore. Too many calls from the media."

Doug nodded and they lapsed into silence for a moment. He cleared his throat. "I've tried to keep up to date on things through Cyndi. From what she tells me, it doesn't sound like they've had any real breakthroughs in the investigation."

"No. None at all."

"I had a visit from Chester Rawls yesterday. He seems to be pretty well focused on things. Has he been helpful?"

Anne shrugged. "He hasn't come up with anything. But at least he's not following some personal agenda like Clyde Dickson. Rawls seems to really believe that McGraw's behind this."

"Where has he been searching, do you know?" Doug asked.

"Anywhere they think McGraw might have a hideout. They've checked everywhere from the motels in Leesburg to the woods around my house. Rawls thinks that it's more likely that McGraw is in some remote place, maybe in an abandoned tenant house or barn. But their search for those kinds of places has been slow."

"What about the investigator that you hired to check out McGraw. Has he found any trace of him?" Doug asked

Anne shook her head. "No. He's been staking out McGraw's house, but so far he's seen no sign of him."

Nellie arrived with two mugs of soup and warm bread, which she set on the coffee table in front of the couch. "Oh, honey, my heart has been breaking for you and little Samantha," she said to Anne. "I pray every day when Doug goes out on his search that he'll come home with her."

"Thank you, Nellie. Please keep praying." Anne turned to Doug, her eyebrows raised.

Nellie nodded and left the two of them alone. As soon as the door closed behind her, Anne asked, "Your search? What did Nellie mean by that?"

"Anne, look, I know that you asked me not to join the search for Samantha, but I just couldn't sit around doing nothing. Besides, I'm intimately familiar with this area. I hunt around here twice a week. It would have been foolish for me not to be part of the search. And don't worry, I didn't interfere with Dickson or Chester Rawls' FBI team or the search around your house. I was on horseback, combing the woods in this area. I stayed out of everyone's way."

Anne shook her head. "You might be right, but you shouldn't have done it without telling me."

Doug sighed. "Anne, you and I both know that if I'd told you, you would have tried to talk me out of it."

She didn't argue with him, and Doug stood up and leaned his hand against the mantle, staring into the fire. After a few moments of silence, he turned to Anne. "Let's get something straight here. Samantha's out there somewhere, and I'm going to help find her. Like it or not, no one's going to stop me. That's just the way it is."

To Doug's surprise, Anne nodded at him. "Thank you," she said.

Doug held his hand out to help her up, and motioned towards the couch. "Come on. Let's try some of Nellie's soup before it gets cold."

They drank their soup in silence for a while, and then Doug set his mug down and turned towards her. "You've avoided me since Samantha disappeared, Anne. Why'd you finally come over here today?"

She shrugged. "I wanted to tell you about Sharon Duncan."

Doug narrowed his eyes. "Are you sure? Or were you avoiding me because you weren't entirely sure that I was innocent until Sharon called you?"

"No," Anne said, shaking her head. "Absolutely not. I never thought you would harm Samantha."

He reached out and brushed a strand of hair out of her face. "Then why wouldn't you talk to me on the phone?"

Anne sighed and leaned her head back against the couch. "I don't know. I just needed to deal with my grief alone."

Doug ran the back of his hand lightly down her cheek. Once again, he was aware of just how exhausted she looked. "Have you been able to get any rest at all?"

She shook her head in response.

He ran his fingertips over the space between her eyebrows, smoothing out tiny stress lines. "I've been concerned about you being alone. I worried that McGraw might come after you."

She nodded. "I figured that."

He smoothed her hair back and stroked her temple. "Why do you say that?"

"I met your friend from Manse Security last night. He told me that you had hired him to look after me."

Doug frowned. "How did you meet him?"

"Someone broke into my house when we lost power during the storm. I have no proof that it was McGraw, but my gut tells me it was. Your guy came to the rescue."

Doug sat forward. "Holy Christ, Anne. Why didn't someone call me?"

"There was no reason to. Your guy scared him off. That's all there was to it." Anne smiled at him, but there was a quiver in her voice.

Doug reached out and pulled her towards him, and she rested her head on his shoulder. "I promise you, I'm going to get the son of a bitch," he whispered.

CHAPTER

69

Zeb waited in the lawyer bitch's bedroom for her, but it was already after midnight, and his gut told him she wasn't coming home tonight. She'd be spending the night at Cummings' house.

He shook his head in distaste. What a slut. He was beginning to hate her almost as much as he hated Cummings.

It still pissed him off that he'd been interrupted the night before by the fucking FBI man. His plan had been flawless. Even the weather had cooperated. But then Cummings had to go and screw it up by hiring a bodyguard to protect his precious lawyer.

Zeb shrugged off his anger. It made no difference. It had just delayed things a bit. He would still kill the lawyer bitch, just as he'd planned. It was only a matter of time.

Zeb waited for her until three o'clock and then decided to call it quits for the night. He'd go after her tomorrow. And in the meantime, he'd leave her the present he'd brought for her. It gave him a rush, just to think about it. He'd stolen the idea from the barn girl's killer after he watched him drive Cummings nuts with souvenirs from his victims. He had a souvenir for Cummings too. He was just waiting for the right time to deliver it.

Zeb placed the kid's shoe in the middle of the downstairs hallway, and as he slipped out the front door he decided to leave it hanging open. Just to give the lawyer bitch a little thrill when she came home.

70

Doug awoke to the graying light of dawn, with Anne still asleep in his arms. He shifted slightly to ease his stiffness, and lay there quietly for a while, enjoying the comforting feeling of Anne next to him. He eventually slipped out from beneath Anne and placed a pillow under her head. He was sitting in the chair across from her when she awoke an hour later.

"Oh, my God, I fell asleep." She struggled to sit up. "What time is it?"

"Stop worrying. It's okay. It's still early." Doug smiled at her. "How do you feel?"

"I'm not sure," Anne said, reaching up and smoothing her hair back away from her face. "Better I guess."

"How about letting Nellie make you some breakfast?"

Anne made a face and shook her head.

"Please?"

She sighed. "Oh, all right."

"Come on. Let's go see if we can rouse Nellie." Doug held out his hand and helped Anne up off the couch.

They found Nellie already at the stove, and Doug left Anne with Nellie while he went to shower and dress. When he returned, Anne was talking with Nellie and picking at a plate of pancakes.

Anne looked up at him in surprise. "Are you going out already?" she asked, indicating his boots and breeches.

"Um-hmm," Doug responded, grabbing a banana. He pulled out a chair next to Anne and sat down.

"I want to come with you," Anne said.

That was the last thing Doug had expected. He shook his head. "That's not a good idea, Anne. There's going to be some pretty rough riding."

Her eyes flashed angrily at him. "Oh, I see, it's no place for a woman, is that it? This is a guy thing, where you go out and catch the villain single-handed?"

"That's not what I said," Doug replied, keeping his voice even. "I just don't think you're up to it."

"Well, it's kind of you to be concerned, but I'll be fine. I'm coming with you," she said.

Doug sighed. There was no question that Anne would hold him back. On the other hand, he knew that she needed to feel like she was doing something to help find Samantha.

He nodded at her. "Okay."

Anne gave him a small smile. "I'll run home and get changed. It won't take long." She placed her napkin on the table and pushed back her chair.

Doug stood up. "I'll drive you."

"You don't have to do that."

"Yes, I do. I'm not letting you go home alone into a house that has been standing empty all night."

She opened her mouth, as if to argue, but then closed it again. "Thank you."

Doug held out his hand. "Come on. I'm ready if you are."

He decided to take the Porsche, and he popped the sunroof and let the fresh air swirl around them. As they passed through his front gate, Doug motioned to the guard assigned to Anne that he didn't need to follow them.

The drive passed mostly in silence, and they had just turned off the main road and headed down the driveway towards Anne's house when she grabbed Doug's arm.

"Doug, look!"

"What's the matter?" Doug asked.

"My front door's open," Anne said, pointing urgently towards the front of the house.

"Reach under your seat. There's a gun. The clip's in there," he said, motioning towards the glove box.

Anne handed the gun to Doug when he pulled the car up in front of her house. "You shouldn't have that, you know," she said. "It's a violation of your bail."

"Thanks for the warning, Counselor," he said as he jammed the clip in.

"You'd better wait here. Lock the door."

"No. I'm coming with you."

He didn't have time to argue. "Okay, but stay behind me."

Doug stopped short as soon as he walked through the front door. A small white canvas sneaker lay in the middle of the foyer, its laces limp and untied. It was crusted on one side with what looked like dried blood.

Anne gasped and covered her mouth with her hand. "Oh, my God."

Doug held her by the arm. "Is it Samantha's?"

She nodded.

"Okay. Don't touch it. Call nine-one-one."

Doug searched the rooms downstairs, even though he was pretty sure that McGraw would no longer be there. When he returned to the foyer, he found Anne leaning against the wall. Her color was as bland as the sneaker.

"Did you call nine-one-one?" he asked.

Anne nodded.

"Good." Doug tucked the gun in his coat pocket and leaned down to inspect the shoe. "I know this looks bad, Anne, but I bet it's not Samantha's blood."

"Why do you say that?" Anne asked.

Doug stood up. "If McGraw had harmed Samantha, I don't think he would hide it. That's not his style. He likes to show off. And this doesn't fit with his scheme to frame me. I think he's just playing cat and mouse with me. With us. Like with Nancy's hunt whip and Babs' picture. And a few days ago, I found a diamond necklace in my jacket pocket. I'm quite certain it belonged to Leslie."

"You didn't tell me about that. When did that happen?"

"The day Samantha disappeared. I went riding that morning and left my jacket on the pasture fence. Then I wore it to take Samantha to lunch and when I put my hand in my pocket, I found the necklace."

"But why would McGraw do that?" she asked.

Doug shook his head. "Because he's sick. I think he leaves these 'souvenirs' to drive me nuts. It's quite clever, actually. He knows I can't turn them over to the police, because no one would believe my story about how I got the things. It would only incriminate me more."

They heard approaching sirens, and Doug walked over to the open front door. Two sheriff's cars raced up the drive. Thankfully, Dickson's was not among them.

Doug hung back and let Anne do most of the talking, and he waited impatiently on the front porch while the deputies conducted a search and collected evidence. Their efforts were meaningless as far as he was concerned. None of it would help them find McGraw.

The only thing he was interested in was an analysis of the blood on the sneaker. One of the deputies promised that he would take it directly to the lab and call as soon as he had the results.

After the deputies left, Anne went upstairs to shower and change, and Doug insisted on waiting in the hallway outside her bedroom. He couldn't shake the eerie feeling that McGraw was still close by.

As they settled into the Porsche, Doug handed the gun back to Anne. "Could you put it back under your seat please?"

Doug was halfway up the drive when Anne cursed and began tugging at her door handle. "Stop the car," she ordered.

"What the hell?" He slammed on the brakes and managed to stop the car just as Anne struggled out of her door.

Doug jumped out and ran around to Anne. She stood next to the car with her right hand held out awkwardly in front of her. Doug saw that her palm was covered with blood.

"My God," he said, examining her hand. "What happened?"

"It's Samantha's other shoe," Anne said, pointing towards the floor in front of the passenger seat. Doug followed her gaze to the small sneaker that lay there. It looked like the mate to the one they'd just seen back at Anne's house, except that the blood on this one was still wet.

"That son of a bitch," Doug swore. He pulled a handkerchief out of his coat pocket and wiped off Anne's hand. "Is there any chance that Samantha's shoe could have been there when we were in the car earlier?"

Anne shook her head. "Absolutely not. I would have found it when I got the gun out."

Doug picked up the sneaker with his handkerchief and placed it in the trunk. "That means McGraw was there the whole damned time we were in your house, Anne. He's probably still sitting in the woods laughing at us right now."

Anne scanned the tree line. "So, what do we do now?"

Doug steered her towards the passenger door. "We go find him."

71

The barn was quiet when they arrived, and Doug found a note on the tack room door from Billy, saying that he had taken Doug's broodmare, Miss Molly, to the vet in Charlottesville and would be gone until early evening. Doug smiled as he read it. The grammar in the note wasn't perfect, but it was quite a contrast to when Billy wouldn't even attempt to read or write. Nellie had already brought Billy a long way.

The horses were in their stalls, munching hay, and Doug left Anne in the barn while he went inside the tack room. As he reached into the cupboard for clean saddle pads, a magazine lying on the counter caught his eye. Doug set the saddle pads down, picked up the magazine, and flipped through it. There it was. The au pair article.

Doug sensed a movement behind him. He turned to see Anne smiling quizzically at him. "Catching up on your reading?"

He shook his head. "This is the magazine Ingrid was reading when I brought Samantha home." He showed her the article.

"Where did you find it?" Anne asked.

Doug gestured towards the counter. "Right here. Lying out in the open where I'd be sure to find it."

"How long do you think it's been there?"

Doug put the magazine back on the counter. "It definitely was not here yesterday afternoon when I returned from my ride. That means it was either put here last night or this morning."

"But he was at my house then too. How does he manage to get around like that, without being spotted?" Anne asked.

Doug shook his head. "I'm not sure. He must have transportation of some sort. But my hunch is that he mostly travels on foot, through the woods."

"He certainly can't do that with Samantha in tow," Anne replied.

"Exactly. Which confirms my suspicion that he's holding her captive somewhere close by." He handed the saddle pads to Anne and reached for the bridles. "Come on. Let's get going."

Doug carried the tack to Huntley's stall and slid the door open. The big gelding immediately walked over and nudged him, looking for a treat. He patted Huntley on the neck and reached into his coat pocket for a sugar cube.

"This is Huntley," he said to Anne, as he put the horse's halter on. "His size can be a little intimidating, but he's a gentle giant. You'll be fine on him." Doug took Huntley's sheet off and grabbed a brush from the grooming box.

"Here, let me do that," Anne said, reaching for the brush. "You go get your horse ready. I can tack him up by myself."

Doug nodded and carried his tack to Chancellor's stall at the far end of the barn. He quickly tacked-up Chancellor, led him outside, and retrieved his gun from the Porsche. Just as he stowed it in the leather sandwich case that was attached to his saddle, Anne led Huntley out of the barn.

"Everything okay?" he asked.

Anne smiled. "Huntley's a perfect gentleman. I'm sure we'll get along just fine."

Doug checked Huntley's girth, pulled the stirrups down, and gave Anne a leg up. Then he walked Chancellor a few yards away, and swung himself up into the saddle.

"Ready?" he asked. She nodded, and Doug set off at a trot, moving briskly down the grassy area between the horse paddocks and across the large empty pasture at the rear of Hunting Hollow. He stopped to open the gate that led into the Bellevue Woods and then picked up a trot again. The trail through the woods was not wide enough for the two of them to ride abreast, so Doug took the lead on Chancellor and Huntley dropped back and followed behind.

The leaves were all off the trees now and thick on the ground, allowing the wintry sun to filter randomly through the barren branches. Pockets of sunshine danced gracefully on the trail as the limbs overhead swayed in the breeze, and Chancellor snorted and spooked playfully at a patch of sunlight. Doug breathed deeply and his sigh mixed with the horses' soft breathing and the crunching and snapping sound their hooves made on the footing beneath them. Doug let Chancellor break into a canter as the trail climbed uphill, then pulled up at the top of the rise, where the path gave way to a small clearing in front of a stone wall.

Anne was a little short of breath and Doug raised an eyebrow at her. "Are you all right?"

"I'm fine," she said, gasping slightly as she spoke. She paused and took a deep breath. "I guess I'm just a little out of shape."

"Sorry. I'll take it easier." Doug looked around. The stone wall was a big one. It had a slight drop on the other side, making the landing a little tricky. He figured Anne would have a problem jumping it. "There's a gate farther down the fence line. Let's go through down there," he said, walking towards the gate.

"Where are we?" Anne asked. "Is this still your property?"

Doug nodded. "This fence is my property line. We're about to cross over into the back of the Symington's farm, Foxfield. They have about a thousand acres with a couple of old tenant houses and barns on the property. There are several service roads leading back here, as well as the way we came through the woods. It's perfect hiding ground. Easy access and plenty of shelter."

The first building Doug took them to was an old dilapidated barn. It wasn't much of a structure anymore. The red wooden sides were faded and cracked, and many of the boards were broken or missing. The barn's gray roof sagged and the hayloft door hung tentatively by one remaining rusty hinge. Still, it afforded plenty of shelter as a hideout. They approached it quietly across the pasture, and then Doug left Anne under cover in a clump of trees while he slowly circled the building.

"I don't see any sign of life around here," he said as he trotted Chancellor back to her. "Let's go inside."

They rode up to the barn, then dismounted and led the horses inside. The musty odor of the interior was potent but not unpleasant, a mixture of old hay and animal smells. The milking stalls that lined one side were still relatively intact, and the remainder of the barn was empty but for a wheelbarrow, minus the wheel, which leaned against a center post, and an old plow that rested in one corner.

Doug headed towards a ladder, which led to the hayloft suspended over the lower third of the barn, and Anne silently followed his lead. As they passed by one of the milking stalls a pigeon flew out, narrowly missing their heads, and Anne shrieked as she and Chancellor both jumped to the side.

Anne clasped a hand to her chest. "Sorry. I guess Chancellor and I are both a little spooked today."

Doug smiled but didn't say anything, and as they reached the hayloft ladder, he handed Chancellor's reins to her. "Let me take a look up above." He grabbed the ladder in both hands and gave it a good shake, before putting his full weight on it.

The thick cobwebs Doug brushed from between the rungs as he climbed gave him a good indication that he wouldn't find any signs of recent activity above. As Doug stepped off the ladder, a mouse scurried away across the loose hay scattered on the floor. Doug walked the loft, but there was no indication of human habitation.

"There's nothing here," Doug called to Anne, as he started back down the ladder.

"So, what's next?" Anne asked as they led the horses outside.

"We'll head over that rise." Doug pointed towards the tree line at the top of the hill to their east. "There's a machine shed over there and a vacant tenant house."

The machine shed proved to be a disappointment, and they moved on towards the tenant house. It was well secluded, down in a valley. A perfect hiding place. As they approached, Anne grabbed his arm and silently mouthed, "Shhh."

"Look, see the car?" she said quietly, pointing towards the tail end of a white car protruding from a screen of trees behind the house.

Doug followed her gaze and nodded. They rode slowly and studied the layout. The house had two stories. There was a door in front and, from what they could see as they headed towards the back of the building, at least one other entrance at the rear. What appeared to be shades or white sheets hung in the windows, all drawn closed, except for one small upstairs window.

"This could be it," Doug said, pulling Chancellor up and dismounting. He took his cell phone out of his pocket and handed it to Anne. "If I'm not back out in ten minutes, call nine-one-one."

"What would you like me to tell them? I'm out in some pasture; I don't know where exactly."

"Tell them you're at Foxfield Farm, at the tenant house down in the valley. They'll know where that is."

"Really?" she asked.

"Yes. The rescue squad is intimately familiar with all of these farms. They have to be to attend to the people who get hurt in riding accidents. Trust me, if there is a way to get there by vehicle, they know where it is. Even if it's in the middle of a pasture."

Anne frowned. "Doug, wait. Let's talk this through. What if you go barging in there and it turns out that a tenant is living there?"

"No one lives here. I know this place. I ride through here all the time," Doug replied.

"Well, maybe someone just moved in."

"I know that the Symington's stopped renting this house out a couple of years ago because the farm road that leads here gets washed away every time Goose Creek get high, and they got sick of paying to repair it. Besides, why would a legitimate tenant hide their car in the bushes?"

Anne shrugged. "I don't know. They probably wouldn't. I just don't want you to do something that you might regret later."

"Come on, Anne. So what if I barge in there and surprise some innocent person? Who cares? What if I don't go in and McGraw is in there with Samantha? What then?"

"I wasn't suggesting we leave. Couldn't we just watch for a while and see if anyone comes out?" Anne asked.

"No. I'm going in now." Doug held Huntley so Anne could get off.

Anne dismounted and Doug handed Chancellor's reins to her. Then he opened the sandwich case, took out his gun and put it in his coat pocket.

Anne's eyes widened. "My God, Doug."

Doug smiled grimly at her and nodded. "I know. 'It's a violation of my bail.' I'll only use it if I need it." He turned away and started towards the house, but hadn't gone more than a few yards when Anne stopped him.

"Doug."

He braced himself for an argument and turned around.

"Please be careful."

Doug nodded and continued towards the house. He circled the house from a distance and approached the back door from the far side of the structure.

Doug couldn't see anything through the tightly drawn shades covering the window next to the entrance, so he put his ear to the door and listened. He might have heard a voice; he wasn't sure, but it was definitely far off, not coming from close to the door. He reached out and tried the door knob. It turned easily in his hand. Doug took a deep breath and pushed it gently, cringing at the slow creak it made as it swung inward.

The door opened into a kitchen, void of any furniture, obviously unused for quite some time. A brownish greasy square on the yellowed linoleum flooring was telltale evidence of the stove that used to stand there, and the door on an old Frigidaire hung open, showing off its empty mildewed interior.

Doug walked cautiously across the small room and paused at the door. A narrow hall formed an "L" that led to a staircase straight ahead and left to another room. He paused and listened. No more evidence of the voice he thought he had heard.

Doug crept along the hall to the other room and looked inside. It too was empty. Peeling wallpaper and threadbare beige carpeting gave the room a desolate feel, and a damp musty smell from years of mold and mildew permeated the stale air. Doug stood gazing at its emptiness. Had he jumped to conclusions? Then a loud thump sounded overhead, followed by a series of softer knocks and a rustling sound, like something being dragged back and forth across the floor.

Doug raced quietly to the stairs and ascended them carefully. He could see three doors at the top of the stairs. The one straight ahead was a bathroom and the one to the right opened into a small bare room. The door to the left was closed.

Doug's heart raced as he approached the closed door, and he paused briefly outside and listened. He heard another series of thumps and a stifled moan.

Doug withdrew his gun from his pocket, opened the door, and stepped into the room. Sunlight streamed in through the bare window and cast a shadow on two figures lying on the floor in the middle of the room.

Doug quietly crossed over towards them, but as he got closer he saw what they were doing and he stopped. It was a teenaged boy and girl. Naked. Having sex.

The girl saw Doug first. "*Travis.*" She pounded her partner on the back. "Someone's here."

"Huh?" The boy turned around and saw Doug. "Oh, my God," the boy said, grabbing the girl and trying to cover her with the blanket that lay beneath them. "Don't hurt us, man. Please."

Both of their eyes were fixed on the gun in Doug's hand and he lowered his arm. "Relax. I'm not going to hurt you, but you have some explaining to do. I'll wait downstairs for you to get dressed."

Doug went outside and motioned for Anne to come down, then sat on the front steps and leaned back against the side of the house. He breathed deeply, trying to slow his surging adrenaline. Just as Anne arrived, the kids came out.

The girl's flushed face was almost the same shade as her fiery hair and she was sniffling. "Sir, you're not going to tell on us, are you? My parents would kill me." The boy held her protectively, but looked scared to death himself.

Doug stared sternly at them, and shook his head. "No, I'm not. But you better have learned a damned good lesson from this."

"We have, sir," the boy said and some of the color started to return to his cheeks.

"All right, then. Go on home." The kids raced away, hand in hand, and the white car sped down the drive moments later.

"What was that all about?" Anne asked. She handed Doug his cell phone and then sat down next to him, still holding both horses' reins.

Doug explained what had happened.

"Why were you so stern with them?" Anne asked.

He shook his head. "I don't know. I guess I overreacted. When I went in and heard them upstairs, I was so sure that I had found McGraw's hideout. I thought I'd found Samantha."

Anne put her hand on his arm and studied him solemnly for a moment. "Do you really think we have a chance of finding Samantha?"

He covered her hand with his. "Yes, we do. There's a place out there somewhere, just like this, that McGraw is using as his hideout. There has to be. It's just a matter of time until we find it."

He stood up, took Chancellor's reins from Anne, and secured his gun back in the sandwich case. "Come on. I'd like to check out an old mill house that's not far from here."

Anne nodded, and Doug held Huntley for her and gave her a leg up. She groaned a little as she sat down in the saddle. Doug glanced at her.

"We should go back now if you don't feel up to it," he said. "Going to the mill will probably add another forty-five minutes to the ride home."

"No, I'm fine. My muscles will loosen up as soon as we get going again." Anne gestured towards the hillside. "After you."

They trotted across the pasture, heading back towards the Bellevue Woods. The terrain was straightforward and they made good time. When they reached the gate into the woods, Doug stopped and swung down off of Chancellor to open it.

"Damn," he swore, fussing with a padlock on the chain that held the gate closed.

"What's the matter?" Anne asked.

"Someone's put a padlock on this gate. Probably Melvin, the Symington's farm manager. Melvin gets furious any time a rider carelessly leaves one of their gates open, and he padlocks it shut for a week or two to teach everyone a lesson. The problem is, there's no easy way around this one." The coop next to the gate was a good four feet high. Far beyond Anne's ability.

"What are our options?"

Doug thought it over. "I can try to take the gate off the hinges, but it's pretty rusty. I don't know if I can get it off. Or, we turn around and go back."

Anne shook her head. "No. We've come this far, I don't want to turn back. If you take the jump, how long would the ride to the mill be from here?"

"Five, ten minutes max. But this jump is very trappy. I don't want you to risk it."

"I wasn't suggesting that I go along. I'll wait here. You go. If you think that the mill could be his hideout, I want you to check it out," Anne said.

"Are you sure you'll be all right here alone?" Doug asked.

Anne nodded. "Unless you think Huntley will have a problem when you ride off."

"No, he should be fine. Why don't you just walk him a little ways down the fence line so he's not standing right here when I jump."

Doug waited while Anne walked Huntley away, then cantered Chancellor up to the coop and hopped over into the woods.

Doug hadn't been to the old mill in years. He used to play there often as a child, pretending that the ruins were an old fort where he and his friends would hide and fight off the enemy.

As he approached the clearing he slowed to a walk and listened. He could hear the rush of the water in Goose Creek behind the mill. He decided to risk tying Chancellor to a tree while he went inside, hoping to God that the thoroughbred wouldn't spook at something and break the bridle and take off.

All that remained of the mill house was a stone shell with some remnants of the old mill wheel and mill stone. Most of the roof was missing, and as Doug went inside, he realized that it didn't offer much shelter as a hiding place. Still, as he stood there, he had an overwhelming feeling of someone else's presence.

Doug inspected the mill house, and the hard heels on his riding boots made his footsteps sound unnaturally loud in the eerie silence that surrounded the mill. He walked the interior of the mill house, but it was empty, and definitely uninhabited. Doug found some footprints outside, but figured the odds were they belonged to a deer hunter.

Doug walked back over to Chancellor and untied him, but he was unable to shake the eerie sensation that he wasn't alone. He mounted and gathered his reins to ride off, then stopped and headed back to the mill house one more time. He stood and looked in through the open doorway, and Chancellor whinnied and danced uneasily, as if he sensed something too. Was he missing something? Finally, he shook his head and turned away. There simply wasn't any place there to hide.

Zeb clamped his hand firmly over the kid's mouth. They could hear footsteps overhead and the kid was squirming, trying to get loose.

"Shhh. I told you to be quiet," Zeb hissed at her, tightening his hold. "You don't know who's up there. It's probably a bad guy. You be a good girl now and be quiet and I'll give you a surprise."

The footsteps receded and the kid stopped struggling and slumped weakly against him. "I want to go home," she whimpered.

Zeb let go of her. Damn. That had been too close. He knew he shouldn't have waited so long to kill the kid. He should have killed her the first day, like he'd done with the nanny. But he loved watching how crazy it made Cummings, not knowing whether the kid was dead or alive. Out there on his horse all day long, searching for the kid.

Zeb dug through the pile of fast food wrappers on the floor and came up with a candy bar. "Hey, kid, you want a Milky Way bar?"

The kid almost grabbed the candy bar from him. Zeb watched her rip the wrapper off and stuff the candy bar in her mouth. Damned kid was always hungry. And it wasn't easy finding food around there. The closest McDonald's was half an hour away in Leesburg, and he had to drive almost twenty minutes to get to the nearest 7-Eleven.

Zeb heard movement above him again and he grabbed the kid. It wasn't footsteps he heard this time. What was it? He cocked an ear and listened.

Thump. Thump. Thump. Thump. Then silence.

Zeb tightened his grip on the kid's mouth, but she wasn't struggling. It seemed like she was listening too.

Thump. Thump, thump, thump.

Then he heard a horse whinny. And a man's voice.

"It's okay, Chancellor. Calm down, buddy."

Holy shit. It was Cummings up there.

Thump, thump. Thump. Thump. Thump. Thump. The hoof beats faded away and it was quiet again.

The kid stared wide-eyed at him and he took his hand off her mouth, but didn't let go of her.

"That wasn't a bad man up there. That was Doug. I recognized his voice," she said tearfully. "You said when he found us, I could go home."

Zeb scowled. God, he was getting tired of her. "Yeah, well, he didn't find us yet. 'Cause he didn't see us. You have to wait until he sees us."

The kid shook her head. "I don't want to wait any longer. I want—to—go—home—now," she wailed.

The kid was sobbing and Zeb shoved her down on a pile of blankets in the corner. "There. You take a nap now. I'm going to go out and get us something to eat. If you take a long nap while I'm gone you can have another candy bar when I get back."

The kid grabbed at him. "Please don't take the light with you when you leave. I'm afraid all alone here in the dark."

Zeb shook her hand off his arm. "That's your punishment for being bad and not wanting to play the game anymore. Now just shut your eyes and you won't know how dark it is."

Zeb turned the camping light off and crawled to the door at the end of the tunnel. He could still hear the kid whimpering, but she was quieter now. He figured she'd cry herself into a good long sleep.

Zeb carefully secured the tunnel door from the outside and then sat down on the creek bank, planning his next move. The question was, who to kill first? The kid or the lawyer bitch?

Doug decided to hack back a different way, down the service road that led to the old mill. He had gone a couple of hundred yards when he spotted an old Ford truck parked at the edge of the road in the underbrush. Its red paint was dulled orange with age and rust, and it didn't have any license plates. Someone had spray painted "Farm Use" in white paint on the tailgate.

Doug frowned. It didn't feel right. It was an odd place to abandon a truck. He got down off Chancellor to inspect the vehicle more closely. Doug opened the glove box and found a small spiral notebook with a chewed up pencil stuck through the twisted silver binding, some bailing twine, and one crumpled work glove. Other than that, he didn't see any sign of personal belongings. The bed of the truck contained a shovel and an old corn broom.

He led Chancellor around to the front of the truck and opened the hood. The engine was thick with years of old oil and grime and Doug reached out and touched it. Some of the oil was fresh. It hadn't been long since it had been driven.

Doug walked around to the back again. There were deep tracks in the mud where the truck had been driven off the road, and they looked like they had been made recently. He stared farther down the road and saw a series of tire tracks. It looked like someone was driving the truck in and out of there on a regular basis. But why?

Doug checked inside again to make sure there weren't any keys in the ignition, then climbed back up on Chancellor. He didn't know what significance, if any, the truck had, but he would sure send the Manse security guys to check it out when he got back to the farm.

He decided he had already left Anne alone for too long, and headed straight up through the woods towards where he had left her. When he got to the coop, Doug called out a warning to Anne so that Huntley wouldn't be spooked when Chancellor jumped over. "Anne, I'm back. Heads up over the wall."

Chancellor cantered the jump easily. Doug pulled him to a stop on the other side and looked around for Anne. He had expected her to be waiting where he had left her, but she was nowhere in sight.

"Anne?" His deep voice sounded unnaturally loud in the stillness of the pasture. There was no response. He called louder. "Anne?" But the only response was his voice reverberating back to him.

Doug scanned the pasture, shielding the sunlight from his eyes with his hand. At first he saw nothing, but a movement in the trees at the crest of the hill caught his eye. He squinted, trying to see better, and then groaned. It was Huntley, grazing quietly with all his tack on. But Anne was nowhere in sight.

Doug kicked Chancellor into a gallop and sped up the hill, and his heart raced into a sickening thud. It was déjà vu of the day he'd found Nancy.

Huntley lifted his head and looked at Doug and Chancellor as they approached, chewing contentedly on the wad of grass in his mouth.

"Good boy," Doug said quietly to Huntley as he rode up next to him and grabbed his dangling reins. They were broken in the middle, right next to the buckle. As he knotted them back together, Doug's eyes searched the wooded area, but still saw no sign of Anne.

With Huntley in tow, Doug made his way carefully through the patch of trees. He moved quietly but quickly, his senses alert to any movement or sound. The terrain grew rocky and rose steeply in front of them, and Doug held Huntley's reins more tightly, leaning slightly forward in the saddle to take his weight off Chancellor's back.

They had almost reached the pasture on the other side of the thicket, when something tumbled noisily down through the bushes about fifty feet away. Doug hurried in that direction, and arrived in time to hear some scrambling and a muffled voice mumble, "Shit."

"Anne?"

"Doug, thank God you're back. I lost Huntley," Anne's voice reached him through the undergrowth, before she stepped out into view. Her breeches were streaked with mud down the back of one thigh and a rip over her knee revealed a nasty cut. She was carrying her hard hat in one hand and her other hand grabbed out at trees and branches for support as she navigated the steep, rocky earth.

"What happened?" Doug asked, as he hopped down off Chancellor and tied both horses to a branch. He hurried over to Anne and held out his hand, helping her climb over a boulder and down onto the path.

"Some deer ran out of the trees right in front of Huntley and he spooked. I wasn't expecting it and I fell off. At first he came back over to me, but then, just as I had my foot in the stirrup and was about to get back on, another deer ran out and he whirled around and I ended up on my back. That time he took off into these trees, and so I followed him in here trying to catch him. I obviously had a worse time of it than he did." She looked at where the horse was tied. "Is he okay?"

"He's fine. What were you doing up here in the first place? I thought you were going to wait for me down by the woods."

"Huntley was getting antsy just standing around, so I decided to let him trot around a little," Anne replied, reaching down to brush some of the dirt off of her breeches.

"Way up here?"

Anne shrugged in response.

"Did you stop to think that I might be worried about you if I got back and you were gone?" Doug asked.

"Quite honestly, no, I didn't. Falling off wasn't part of my plan. I thought I'd be back before you returned," Anne replied.

"Great," Doug groaned. "Falling off wasn't part of your plan. What about running into McGraw? Did you ever stop to think about that?"

Anne sighed. "Doug, I didn't run into McGraw and I didn't plan for this to happen. It was an accident. There's no reason to get upset about it. Besides, what's the difference whether I waited for you down by the woods or up here? If McGraw were after me, he'd get me either place."

Doug exhaled. "The difference is, I expected you to be down there. And I was scared to death when you were gone."

Anne studied him for a moment. "I guess it's obvious you didn't find anything at the mill."

Doug shook his head. He knelt down and carefully peeled the torn beige material away from the wound on Anne's knee. She had a deep gash, split diagonally across her kneecap. Doug touched it, but eased up when she winced. "I don't think you did any major damage, but it needs to be cleaned out good and you could probably use some stitches."

Doug stood up. "Look, Anne, I'm sorry about the way I reacted. I just don't want anything to happen to you."

She gave him a faint smile. "I know. Thank you."

He put his arms around her and drew her close. "I'm sorry I haven't found Samantha," he whispered.

Anne nodded against his chest and put her arms around his waist. He sighed and closed his eyes, breathing in the faint, fruity smell of her shampoo.

After a moment, Doug reluctantly pulled away. "We better go," he said, casting a wary eye at the sky. "We're supposed to have a cold front move through here today and they're predicting some nasty weather again. From the looks of those clouds, there's a pretty good storm brewing."

"That's it? That's the end of our search?" Anne asked.

"Only for today," Doug said.

Doug untied Huntley and led him over to Anne. He saw that blood was still oozing from the gash in her knee. "Are you going to be okay to ride back?"

"Do I have a choice?"

He shook his head. "Not really."

"Then I'll be okay."

Doug kept the pace to a brisk walk, knowing that trotting would be painful on Anne's knee. They had just reached the pasture with the Symington's tenant house when a bitter wind started to blow. Doug frowned, looking back at the darkening horizon.

"Are we going to make it in time?" Anne asked.

"It'll be close."

Sleet started to pelt them and Doug looked at the ominous sky. "Come on. We better hurry or we're going to be dumped on."

They had reached the gate into the woods and they hurried through it. At least the trees gave them some shelter from the freezing precipitation.

Anne was starting to shiver. "Let's trot, Doug. My knee's okay."

They trotted the remainder of the way through the woods, slowing only long enough for Doug to open the gate into his back pasture. The precipitation was all rain now. Chilly and soaking. They didn't talk much and as they reached the last stretch towards the barn Doug turned to Anne. Her lips were bluish and her skin was pale.

"Are you all right?" he asked.

Anne nodded stiffly. "I'm just cold, that's all."

They reached the barn and Doug jumped off Chancellor. He held Huntley's reins, helping Anne as she slid off.

"You go into the tack room," Doug said. "There are some wool coolers in there to wrap up in. I'll put the horses away and be right there."

"I'll take care of Huntley," Anne insisted through chattering teeth.

"Don't be ridiculous, Anne. You're freezing."

Anne nodded as she took Huntley's reins from Doug and led him into his stall. "I know. And so are you, Doug. Just let me get Huntley's tack off and throw a cooler on him. You take care of Chancellor and then we can both go inside and warm up."

Doug shook his head. He knew there was no sense in arguing with her, so he hurried down the aisle with Chancellor, grabbing a rub rag from the rack in the darkened wash stall as he passed by.

Anne's frozen fingers tugged on the billet straps of the saddle, trying to release the girth, and she almost had it when Huntley shied at something and jumped away.

"Huntley, hold still," she said, as she moved towards him. The horse backed up and snorted, and then someone grabbed her from behind.

He clamped one hand over her mouth, locked his other arm around her neck, and pulled her head back. Anne gasped. *McGraw.*

He stood much taller than she, and it felt as if he could snap her neck with the slightest of efforts. He hauled her silently from Huntley's stall into the empty wash stall across the aisle. Anne fought the impulse to struggle. She knew there was no sense in it. McGraw had her overpowered. It was better to save her strength.

She could hear the echo of Doug's boots as he came up the aisle towards them. The footsteps stopped at the tack room and a door opened, then closed, and the footsteps continued towards them once more.

"Anne?" Doug called out as he walked past them, towards Huntley's stall.

Anne felt breath, hot and rapid on her ear, and McGraw shoved her forward, thrusting them both into the aisle as Doug stepped back out of Huntley's stall.

"Stop right there, Doug, or I'll break her beautiful neck."

Doug stopped in his tracks. "Langley? Jesus Christ. What's going on here?"

Langley? Anne stared at Doug. Who was Langley? It was McGraw who had hold of her, wasn't it? She attempted to see the face of the man who held her, but she couldn't move her head.

The man Doug had called Langley laughed. "It's not your turn for questions, Doug."

Doug took a step towards them, and Langley tightened his arm around Anne's neck. "Back off, Doug," he said.

Doug held his hands up in submission. "Okay, Langley. Don't hurt her. Whatever is going on here, it's between you and me. Just ease off. I'm not going to do anything."

"Get in that stall over there." Langley took his hand off of Anne's mouth and gestured towards Miss Molly's empty stall. "Now."

Doug walked slowly towards the stall, still keeping his hands raised. "Just take it easy. I'll do whatever you say."

Langley followed behind Doug, still keeping his iron hold around Anne's neck. "Get over along that wall." He wrenched Anne's neck roughly as he gestured towards the wall adjoining the next stall.

Then Langley held his hand out to Doug. "Give me your cell phone."

Doug reached into his pocket for the phone and Langley grabbed it out of his hand.

"Now put your hands behind your back and through the bars."

Doug gave a brief hesitation and Langley jerked his arm upward, lifting Anne off her feet.

"Okay," Doug said quickly, putting his hands behind his back.

"Good. Now you stay just like that, and I won't hurt her. You move a muscle, and I snap her neck. Understand?"

Doug nodded and Langley drew Anne back out of the stall. He dropped Doug's cell phone onto the brick barn aisle and stomped it with the heel of his riding boot. Then he pulled Anne towards a stall with a nameplate that read, "Junior."

"Open the door," he ordered, letting up slightly on her neck. Anne slid the door back and Junior immediately walked over to them. "And keep that colt away from here."

Anne shooed at Junior to back off and Langley reached with his other arm to grab the lead rope off of the hook on the stall door. "Tie this around his wrists." He pointed at Doug's arms sticking through the stall grill.

Anne's fingers were so stiff from the cold that she could barely get them to work, and she fumbled weakly with the thick cotton rope.

"Do it!" Langley ordered, and kicked out at Junior as the young horse approached them again.

"I'm trying," Anne said, finally managing to loop a knot.

Langley ripped the end of the rope out of Anne's hands and drew the knot closed, then braced his foot against the wall and tugged with the full force of his weight to tighten it. He wrapped it around a few more times and tugged at it again, finally seeming satisfied when blood formed on Doug's wrist where the rope cut into it.

Langley pushed Anne ahead of him out of Junior's stall and closed the stall door. Then he shoved her back into Miss Molly's stall, slid the door closed, and reached down to pick up something off the stall floor beneath the water buckets.

Anne was free in the stall now and she looked at Langley's face. She recognized him. He had been seated with Leslie at the hunt ball. He was the man who had called Anne, "Doug's flavor of the week." Anne looked questioningly at Doug. What was going on?

Doug raised his shoulders and shook his head slightly. He obviously didn't know either.

Doug turned his attention to Langley. "Langley, she's shaking. Why not let her go in the tack room and get a blanket? She's going to freeze to death standing around in those wet clothes."

Langley just laughed. "No need to worry, Doug. Her death won't come from freezing. I'll make sure of that."

Langley stood in front of Doug and waved the object that he had picked up. It looked like part of a tree branch, with a rope looped through one end.

"Look familiar?" Langley asked.

Doug frowned. "It's my twitch."

"It'll make a nice little package when they find this, don't you think, Doug? Look. This is Babs' blood right here." Langley pointed to a spot on the twitch. "And this is Leslie's. See?" He held the twitch in front of Doug's face and smiled. "You can even see a little bit of Leslie's fabulous black hair."

Anne struggled to make sense of what he was saying. Was it possible that McGraw wasn't the killer after all? That this guy was? Had *he* kidnapped Samantha?

Langley lowered the twitch, backed away, and walked over towards Anne. "Her hair will look nice on here too, don't you think, Doug?" He reached out and held a strand of Anne's hair, and let it slide slowly between his fingers.

"Let her go, Langley," Doug said. "You've got me. Just let her go."

Langley spun around and smiled at Doug. "I'm not going to kill you, Doug. I'm looking forward to watching you waste away in prison. I'm disappointed you haven't figured that out by now."

"You've already done enough, Langley. They're going to lock me up with all the evidence you've already given them. When they have that twitch, they'll throw away the key. You don't need her."

Langley snorted. "You think I'm going to just let her walk away from here? Sorry, Doug, but that's not part of the plan. She has to go." He turned back to Anne and gripped her by the hair, pulling her face close to his. His breath was sour and Anne turned her head to the side. Then Langley released her, laughing, and reached out and ripped her shirt open with one rough yank. "Ah. Very nice. You sure know how to pick them, Doug."

Doug kicked out with both legs and sent Langley sprawling to the stall floor. Langley cursed as he scrambled up and lunged at Doug. He grabbed Doug's right arm and gave it one quick downward thrust, hitting Doug's forearm on the stall grill. Anne heard bones snap and saw that Doug's arm stuck out at an odd angle where it was tied behind him.

Doug gritted his teeth. "Tell me why you did it, Langley. Did you kill all of them just to frame me?"

Langley walked over and looked out the stall window and then turned back and smiled at Doug. "I didn't start out to frame you, Doug. Not when I killed Nancy." His lips drew back in a snarl. He clutched the twitch in front of him, twirling it as he spoke. "I just happened to come across Nancy in the woods that day. As fate would have it, I was out searching for some stray hounds, and Nancy was looking for you."

Langley narrowed his eyes at Doug and began to pace the stall. "I tried to talk with Nancy, just talk with her, but she kept riding away from me. She was in such a hurry to catch up with you."

Langley's voice rose in anger. "I grabbed her arm to stop her, so we could talk, but then Sunday spooked and Nancy fell off. She wasn't injured, but she lost her helmet and the fool horse galloped away. I got down off my horse to help her, but she told me to leave her alone. And then she turned her back on me and started to walk off after her horse. She wouldn't give me the time of day. It really pissed me off, so I picked up a branch, and I swung it at her."

He smiled fleetingly. "I didn't mean to kill her. I just wanted to stop her, so we could talk. But I got carried away and I hit her harder than I meant to. Then, of course, I had to strangle her, so she wouldn't tell anyone what I'd done."

He grinned at Doug. "Of course, I was delighted to learn that they suspected you of killing Nancy. But it wasn't then that I came up with the plan to frame you. No. It was after I killed that bitch Babs that it dawned on me how easy it would be to set you up for both murders. And that notion was simply too tempting to resist."

Langley waved Doug's twitch in the air. "You see, it was this that gave me the inspiration."

Doug frowned at him. "Where did you find my twitch?"

Langley smiled. "It was pure luck. Dr. Mitchell was at my barn one afternoon and received a call on her cell phone from Babs, looking for your twitch. It seemed that Dr. Mitchell had been using your twitch at your barn and had inadvertently put it in her truck. Babs was frantic to get the damned thing back right away. Said you were pissed off at her. But Dr. Mitchell was headed over to the Mare Center to stitch up a weanling who'd put his leg through a fence, and she didn't have time to run by your place. I like Deb Mitchell, so I offered to take the twitch to your place for her."

Langley's lip curled up, like he had a bad taste in his mouth. "When I got to your place, Babs was her usual bitchy self. Not in the least bit grateful that I had gone to the trouble to return the damned thing to her. She didn't even say thank you. Just bitched at me for taking so long."

Langley raised the twitch in the air, holding it like a baseball bat. His knuckles were white where he gripped it with his fists. "And then Babs made her fatal mistake. She ordered me to leave so she could lock up the barn and go home. *She* told *me* to leave. I still had the twitch in my hands so I slammed it right into her skull. *Splat.*"

He swung the twitch violently. "But that didn't shut the bitch up. She still taunted me. She threatened to tell you what I'd done to her, Doug. So I hit her again. And again. Until she finally shut up."

Langley lowered the twitch and looked at Doug. "When I realized that I had killed her, with your twitch, that's when I came up with the idea to blame it on you." He sneered. "It was so simple. They were already suspicious of you. Especially Deputy Dickhead. I gambled that the medical examiner wasn't sophisticated enough to tell the difference between the injuries caused by this twitch and the branch I used on Nancy."

He ran his hand down the twitch. "Nancy's blood isn't on this, but I figured that deputy wanted you badly enough that somehow he'd find a way to explain away the absence of Nancy's blood." He laughed. "And, of course, I made sure you had no alibi for Babs' murder. That was a nice touch I came up with, using the rag with the deer scent so Huntley wouldn't load and you had to miss the hunt meet. Don't you agree? And all those nice mementos I left from all your victims. Did you appreciate those, Doug?"

Doug didn't reply and Langley walked over to Anne. His eyes roamed her body hungrily for a long moment, and then he reached out and stroked her breast lightly with the side of the twitch. "I'm going to take my time with you," he whispered, his face only inches away from hers.

"Langley," Doug called, diverting his attention from Anne. "Why'd you kill Leslie?"

Langley looked at Doug and shrugged. "Everything was taking too long. They should have arrested you after they found Babs. But they didn't. So I decided to help it along. I figured they needed some more evidence. That's when I came up with the button idea."

He paused and smiled. "That was truly brilliant. I didn't know who the lucky lady would be, but I was sure that someone would throw herself at you at the hunt ball that evening, and she'd become victim number three. I just had no idea it would be Leslie."

Langley frowned, a faraway look on his face. "Beautiful Leslie. Too bad she was such a slut. She came on to me all evening at the hunt ball. She thought I looked *'so-o-o handsome in my scarlet.'* And she went on about *'how fascinating it must be to be an honorary whip for the Hunt.'*"

Langley imitated Leslie's voice in a high-pitched tone and waved his hands about coyly. "She said I must be *'such a good rider to ride out in the woods all alone like that.'*"

Then Langley lowered his hands and his voice returned to normal. "Leslie stuck her tits in my face when we talked, and she rubbed her crotch against me when we danced, but then, at the first opportunity, she ran outside in search of you, Doug. Just like Nancy."

Langley threw back his head and laughed. "Poor little slut, Leslie. She was so disappointed that she didn't find you. But don't worry, I satisfied her needs before I killed her."

Anne gasped and Langley turned on her. "What?"

"She was still alive when you raped her?"

Langley scoffed. "What did you think, I fucked a corpse? No, my dear. That's not how I get my kicks. She was very much alive and able to enjoy every minute of it." He reached out and flicked his fingers inside Anne's bra. "As you will be, my dear."

"What about Ingrid?" Doug interrupted.

"The nanny?" Langley waved his hand nonchalantly. "Funny thing, that twist of events. I didn't kill the nanny. That was someone else's handiwork. But it doesn't matter. They'll still pin it on you."

Doug scowled in disbelief and glanced at Anne, but kept talking to Langley. "What about Samantha? Where is she?"

Langley smiled. "You're dreaming if you think I'd tell you, Doug." He shook his head. "You pathetic ass. Conducting your heroic searches every day. I couldn't risk having you actually find the girl. No. That would ruin everything. That's why I decided to put an end to this today." He threw his head back and his laughter echoed through the barn. "Deputy Dickhead will cream in his jeans when he finds the beaten corpse of your beautiful lawyer."

Doug's eyes met Anne's and he inclined his head towards the door, motioning for her to make a run for it. But Langley's eyes caught Doug's nod, and he wheeled around and sent the twitch cracking into Doug's temple. Doug's body slumped towards the floor, held up only by his arms, tied behind him through the stall grill.

Doug was roused by a terrible pain shooting through his right arm. Something was pulling on it, and he could hear a faint popping as his broken bones grated together. His mind was fuzzy and he closed his eyes again, trying to stop the roaring noise inside his head. Then he remembered what had happened and he struggled to his feet. Everything seemed to sway for a moment and he leaned against the stall wall for support. He couldn't let himself pass out again. He took a deep breath and waited for his balance to settle, then looked around the barn. Anne and Langley were gone.

The unbearable agony in his arm began again and Doug looked over his shoulder. It was Junior, tugging at his arm. The young horse was chewing on the knot in the rope that held Doug captive.

"Good boy," Doug muttered through clenched teeth. He moved his hands, shaking the rope, trying to encourage the young horse. Junior kept tugging on the knot and after what seemed like an eternity, Doug felt the rope begin to loosen. *Come on, come on. You've almost got it.*

As the rope loosened, Junior became more animated, flipping his head with every tug. Black dots flashed before Doug's eyes and he nearly passed out from the pain. He took several slow, deep breaths, and the dizziness passed. Finally, the rope eased enough for Doug to wiggle his good arm out, then turn around and slip the rope off of his broken arm. Junior pulled the lead rope away and tossed it up in the air.

Doug stood still for a few moments and cradled his broken arm with his other one. When he felt steady enough to move, he hooked his right hand through his belt, immobilizing his broken arm the best he could, and crept quietly out of the stall. The barn appeared to be empty.

He moved cautiously towards the tack room. His gun was still in the sandwich case attached to his saddle. But just as his hand reached for the doorknob, he heard Langley's voice coming from within.

"Stop whining." Doug heard a slap. "I'm not going to kill you yet. I want Doug to watch."

Doug quickly looked around the barn. He had to find something to use as a weapon. His broken arm undoubtedly gave Langley the advantage. Doug's eyes searched the barn aisle and he spotted a steel pitchfork at the far end. He was about to head towards it when he saw the doorknob turn and heard Langley's voice. "I'm going to go see if Doug's finished with his nap."

Doug flattened himself against the wall to the side of the door. The element of surprise was his only weapon now. When Langley stepped out, Doug jumped him instantly and locked his left arm around Langley's neck. He threw his full weight against Langley and tried to slam him into the aisle wall, but Langley overpowered him. Langley twisted out of Doug's grasp and grabbed him in a headlock from behind.

"You son of a bitch, I'm going to kill you," Langley hissed in his ear. "I'm going to kill you and keep Anne for myself."

Langley shoved Doug towards Miss Molly's stall, and Doug lunged to one side, trying to dislodge Langley. Langley stumbled briefly, but quickly regained his balance.

"Nice try, asshole," Langley said, jerking hard on Doug's neck, lifting him off the ground.

Anne's voice stopped him. "Stop right there, Langley."

Langley wheeled them around and Doug saw Anne walk out of the tack room towards them, a pistol leveled in their direction.

Langley laughed. "You're not going to shoot me. You can't get at me without hitting Doug."

"Let him go, Langley," Anne ordered, not more than ten feet away.

"You know there's not a chance in hell of that happening," Langley replied.

The distraction had caused Langley to loosen his grip, but Doug still couldn't get free of his hold. Doug watched Anne carefully. She must have taken his gun out of the sandwich case. But would she actually use it? He wasn't sure, but at least she was buying them some time.

"Move out of the way, Doug," Anne said, motioning slightly with the gun.

Doug stared at her. Was she totally out of it? It was obvious that he couldn't get out of the way.

Anne aimed the gun at Langley's lower half and locked eyes with Doug. "I said, move out of the way, Doug."

Doug shook his head "no," but she nodded in return and her eyes begged him to obey her.

Doug's eyes held Anne's for a moment, then he gave a quick nod, inclined his head to the left, and silently mouthed "one, two, three." On three, he summoned all his strength and twisted his lower torso to the left, an instant before the shot rang out.

"You goddamned bitch," Langley screamed. He dropped his hold on Doug and grasped his right thigh with both hands. Bright red blood spread quickly through the beige material of his riding breeches.

"Where's Samantha?" Anne demanded.

Langley straightened up and sneered at her. "'Where's Samantha? Where's Samantha?' I'm so sick of hearing about poor little Samantha. You'll never see her again, you bitch."

Anne's outstretched hands trembled slightly as she raised the gun towards Langley's chest. "Tell me where she is."

Langley laughed at her. "You really want to know where Samantha is? I'll tell you where she is. She's waiting for you in hell."

Langley leapt forward at Anne, and she fired again, this time hitting him square in his chest. A look of disbelief flickered across his face and he stopped and staggered backwards. "You fucking bitch," he gasped.

Anne pulled the trigger again and Langley sank to his knees in the aisle. He coughed once and frothy blood spewed from his mouth. His hands fumbled briefly at his chest, where a large red stain spread across his shirt, and he opened his mouth as if he were trying to speak. But he only managed to make a gurgling sound as he toppled over onto his side. Then he was still.

Anne walked forward slowly, until she stood above him, and emptied the rest of the clip into his motionless body.

76

Doug took the gun out of Anne's hand and dropped it on the ground next to where Langley lay. He put his good arm around her and tried to draw her away from Langley, but she resisted. Tears began to trail down her cheeks as she stared at Langley's body.

"He killed Samantha," she whispered. "She's really gone."

Doug swallowed hard and cleared his throat, unable to speak.

Slowly, Anne averted her eyes from Langley and looked at Doug. "We weren't even looking for the right guy, Doug. McGraw must have just been stalking you. He didn't take Samantha. Or commit the murders. Langley did."

She stood with her arms clenched to her chest and was shaking so hard that her teeth chattered. Doug put his arm around her again and walked her towards the tack room.

"Come on. Let's go inside."

Anne followed silently, but stopped at the threshold and reached for the door jam.

"What's the matter?" Doug asked.

She swayed and lifted a shaky hand to her forehead. "I'm just a little dizzy."

"I'm not surprised," Doug replied. "You're freezing." He tightened his hold on her and drew her into the room as he kicked the door shut with his foot. "You need to come inside and warm up."

He lowered her onto the leather couch. "You okay while I get some blankets?"

She nodded, but her face was alarmingly pale.

Doug hurried to the closet and as he lifted a stack of wool coolers off the shelf he heard Anne call out his name. He turned and saw her start to stand, then pitch forward onto the coffee table. Her head knocked over the large bronze horse that stood in the center of the table, and she collapsed and tumbled to the floor.

He dropped the blankets and hurried over to where she lay, on her back, in the narrow space between the couch and the coffee table. Doug quickly shoved the coffee table aside and knelt down next to her. She was motionless, with her eyes closed and her head turned to the side.

"Anne, are you all right?" he asked, not really expecting a response.

Anne didn't react and Doug gently moved her head so that she faced forward. The side of her face was streaked with blood, but he saw no visible wound. He smoothed back her hair and found a gash above her ear, about three inches long, which was bleeding profusely.

Doug rose and grabbed the wool coolers, covered Anne, and then pulled the vet kit out of the cupboard. It was cumbersome, working with just one hand, and he had to fumble through the box for a moment before he found a package of sterile gauze pads. He ripped the box open and wet several pads with cold water. Then he grabbed the cordless phone off the cradle on the counter and returned to Anne.

Anne was still unconscious, and he knelt next to her and pressed the gauze pads firmly against her head wound. Her lips had taken on a bluish tint and Doug feared that she was going into shock. She was breathing, but it seemed shallow and weak.

"Anne?"

No reaction. Doug dropped the surgical pads long enough to pick up the phone and press nine-one-one. He placed the phone between his ear and shoulder and then applied pressure to her wound again.

The phone seemed to ring forever, but finally he heard a woman's voice.

"Hello, nine-one-one. Please state your emergency."

Doug drew a deep breath. "This is Doug Cummings. I'm calling from Hunting Hollow Farm. On Millville Road. I need an ambulance."

"What is your emergency, sir?"

"She's unconscious. She has a head wound and I think she might be in shock or hypothermic."

"What are the nature of her injuries?"

"I'm not sure. She's freezing. She passed out. And when she fell, she hit her head."

"Okay, sir. I'm going to dispatch the ambulance. Do you have anything you can use to keep her warm?"

"Yes. I've covered her with some blankets."

"All right. That's good. Now please give me your exact location. Are you inside the house at Hunting Hollow?"

"No. I'm in the barn. Tell them to follow the drive past the house to the barn. I'm in the tack room. And please, tell them to hurry."

He dropped the phone and shifted so that he could lean against the couch. His fingers held the makeshift bandage in place, and he ran his thumb lightly across Anne's forehead and down her cheek. She was still unresponsive and stone cold to his touch.

Damn it. If Anne had merely fainted, she should have come around by now. Was she in shock? Or suffering from hypothermia? Or was her head injury serious enough to render her unconscious? Maybe it was all of the above.

"Hang in there, Anne. It's going to be all right," he murmured. He continued to stroke her face and talk quietly to her and then, finally, he heard the far-off wail of an approaching siren.

Doug heard car doors close and then voices in the barn. He called out. "We're in the tack room."

The tack room door swung open, and Carol Simpson entered with a security guard. Doug recognized him as one of the guards who had been stationed at his gate. A frightened-looking teenage boy peered curiously over Carol's shoulder.

"Radio for the sheriff," Carol said to the guard, handing him her two-way radio, as she crossed the room and knelt down in front of Anne.

"Who is she and what happened to her?" Carol asked, as she pulled her stethoscope out of her pocket and reached for Anne's wrist beneath the wool cooler.

"Anne Sullivan. And I'm not exactly sure what happened, Carol. She just passed out. She's been in those wet clothes and exposed to freezing temperatures for a couple of hours now. When she collapsed, she hit her head. That's how she got this gash," Doug said, pulling the gauze pads away so Carol could see the wound.

"Cooper, go get me some blankets out of the ambulance," Carol called over her shoulder towards the boy.

"Yes, ma'am," the boy replied.

Carol stared at Doug grimly as she took Anne's pulse, then looked away and shoved the stethoscope back into her pocket.

"Is she going to be okay?" he asked.

Carol glanced at him. "You'd better hope that she is."

"What do you mean by that?" Doug snapped. "Of course I hope that she is."

"I mean that Langley Masterson is lying dead in your barn aisle, Doug, and this woman is unconscious with a head wound. That's not a very good scenario, given how the other ladies were murdered. Assuming that you have a plausible explanation for what happened here, I'd say you'd better hope that this lady can back you up."

"Carol," Doug began, but she held her hand.

"Don't tell me about it, Doug. The sheriff's on his way. You do your explaining to him."

Doug bit back a response. There was no use arguing with her.

As she unfolded one of the blankets the kid had brought and tucked it tightly around Anne, Carol glanced at him. "You know, you don't look in very good shape yourself, Doug."

She fished a small flashlight out of her medical bag. "Look at me," she ordered, aiming the light towards his eyes.

Carol shined the light first in one eye, then the other. "Looks like you have a pretty good concussion," she said, putting the flashlight back in the bag.

"Why do you have your hand hooked through your belt like that?" she said, nodding towards his arm.

"Don't worry about me. I'm fine," Doug replied. "Just take care of Anne."

"Cooper, come over here and look after Mr. Cummings," Carol said, turning her attention back to Anne.

The kid approached him, followed by the security guard.

"Is there anything I can do to help, Mr. Cummings?" the guard asked.

Doug tried to think clearly. "Is anyone stationed at the gate?"

"Yes, sir. One man," the guard replied. "He's fending off a whole flock of reporters."

"Then I think it's best if you go back up to the gate. Direct the authorities down here to the barn when they arrive, and help keep the media out."

The guard nodded. "Yes, sir."

"Mr. Cummings, are you able to move over here?" the kid asked, pointing towards a chair along the wall.

Doug ignored him and looked at Anne. Carol had wrapped her in more blankets and her color looked a little better, but her eyes were still closed. "How is she?" he asked Carol.

"I'm warming her up," Carol replied. "Now go on and let Cooper have a look at you."

Doug slowly rose and sat down in the chair. There wasn't anything he could do to help Anne. She was in good hands.

"Can you loosen your hand from your belt, sir, so I can check out your arm?" Cooper asked.

"It's broken," Doug replied. "It feels better if I keep it immobilized like this."

The kid cleared his throat. "Yes, sir, I imagine it does. But we have an inflatable cast I might can put on it. Let me take a look see."

Doug sighed and painstakingly removed his hand from his makeshift sling.

"Now this might hurt a bit, Mr. Cummings, but I need to roll your sleeve up so I can see your arm. I'll try to be as gentle as possible."

Cooper shifted Doug's arm so that it lay across his lap, and Doug gritted his teeth as pain shot through him. He leaned his head back against the wall and closed his eyes.

God, he hoped that Anne would be all right. But what about Samantha? Had Langley really killed her? Something about the way Langley had said Samantha was dead didn't ring true. It had seemed more like he'd said it just to taunt Anne.

The chilling realization hit him that if Samantha were still alive, if Langley had been holding her captive somewhere, the secret of her location had died with him. If she were still out there, locked up somewhere, she'd starve or freeze to death. He had to find her. But how? What had he overlooked?

Doug opened his eyes and put his hand on Cooper's arm. "Cooper, hold on for a minute. I need to ask you something. Did you grow up around here?"

The boy nodded. "Yes, sir, all my life. I live right across the woods from here, over on St. Louis Road."

"If you wanted to hide somewhere around here, where you had easy access in and out, but no one was likely to come across you, where would you go?"

The boy frowned at him.

"I know it's a strange question," Doug said. "But it's important. I really need your help. Just say the first place that comes to mind."

Cooper thought for a moment. "Well, the tunnel under the old mill by Goose Creek, I guess. That's where I'd go if I didn't want anyone to find me."

Doug remembered the farm truck he had seen near the old mill house and how he'd had that eerie feeling that someone else was there. His pulse quickened. "Tell me about the tunnel."

"It's just an underground tunnel that runs from the spring house, down by the creek, to the mill wheel. My friends and I discovered it a few years back. The entrance by the spring house had been closed up with stones, but we pried them away and found the door that led to the tunnel. It was a big deal with the Historical Society. We even got our names in the paper. It was pretty awesome, actually. They've boarded it up now though, just so no kids get hurt in there or anything."

Doug's heart jumped wildly. "How big is it? Could a person fit through it?"

"Oh, sure. As long as you crouched over," the boy replied.

Doug heard a voice crackle over Carol's radio, announcing that the sheriff's car was five minutes away. He had to get out of there.

He sat forward in the chair. "Cooper, you're doing a great job, but I've had just about as much pain as I can handle with this broken arm. Could you go get that cast you mentioned earlier?"

"Sure, Mr. Cummings. It's in the ambulance. I'll be right back."

Doug waited until Cooper was gone, then tucked his hand back into his belt. After making sure Carol wasn't looking, he eased quietly out the side tack room door.

Doug took the Range Rover and drove out of the farm the back way, across the dirt service road. The jostling from the ruts in the road sent waves of pain racing through his head, and he struggled to keep the car straight, as nausea threatened to overcome him. Doug slowed the car and opened the window, letting the icy fresh air blast his face. He breathed in deeply and gradually felt the nausea subside.

When he reached the smoother pavement of Foxcroft Road, he picked up speed again. The road that led to the old mill was off of Millville Road. Doug slowed and made the turn, then painfully negotiated the road's twists and turns as he headed for the mill.

The late afternoon sun was dimming and Doug knew that he only had an hour or so of daylight left. He pressed the accelerator harder.

As he made his way along the dirt road through the woods, Doug noticed that the truck he'd seen earlier was gone. He pulled up as close as he could to the mill house and shut off the engine, then climbed out of the car and opened the tailgate, searching in the back for a flashlight. He found jumper cables, a tow rope and some road flares, but no flashlight. He did find a bomber jacket though, and he slipped his left arm through the sleeve and snapped up the front, leaving his broken arm immobilized inside.

Doug didn't bother going back into the mill house, but headed straight down to the spring house by the creek, where the boy had said the tunnel entrance was located. The embankment was steep and he was out of balance with just one free arm, but he managed to stay on his feet. The going was easier once he reached the path that ran along the creek's bank. Doug moved more quickly, and had a surprisingly easy time finding the door to the tunnel.

He saw a well-worn path of footprints leading up to the entrance.

The door was kept closed by a single board, slung across at about chest height. It was lodged firmly between the stones that surrounded the opening and then fastened in place with a bundle of shiny new fencing wire. The door opened out, and it was clear from the way the barrier was fashioned that it was meant to keep someone from coming out of the tunnel, rather than to deter anyone from going in.

He quickly loosened the wire from the board. Come on, Sam, please be inside, he prayed. The board slid out easily, and Doug reached down and turned the door handle.

"Samantha?" he called out as he pulled open the door. "It's Doug, Sam. Are you in there?" There was no response and he opened the door wide and peered in.

The tunnel was narrow and dark and the dim light that spilled in through the doorway did little to illuminate the dingy space. Doug stepped inside and stood for a moment. He waited for his eyes to adjust to the darkness. The air in the tunnel was stagnant, and the pungent odor of urine mixed with a moldy dankness and musty rodent smells.

The ceiling was too low for Doug to stand up straight, and he bent down and carefully crept along through the darkness. At the far end, beneath what he assumed was the mill wheel, the tunnel ended at a small square room, which was almost in total darkness. Doug knelt down and felt his way around the floor. The room was obviously empty. Along the wall behind him, he felt a paper wrapper of some kind, and then as he moved over further, he found a pile of empty containers and next to that a heap of blankets. His hand brushed against a small hard object, and as he picked it up he felt the legs, the tail, and then the head. It was a small plastic horse. He grasped the horse in his hand and swallowed hard. This was it. This must have been the place where Langley had been hiding Samantha. But he was too late. Samantha was gone.

"Damn it." He shoved the pile of rubbish away and slumped back against the wall. *"Goddamn it."*

Doug's voice echoed eerily back to him and a hollow feeling of despair flowed through him. He closed his eyes against the sting of tears, and gently fingered Samantha's plastic horse. He could still picture Samantha playing with her horses when they'd had lunch at Huckleberries. Cantering the plastic horses around the table top and jumping them over the sugar packets.

Happily humming as she . . .

"I'm sorry."

Doug jumped at the sound of a quiet voice coming from somewhere in the darkness.

"I'm sorry I ate the last candy bar. Please don't be mad at me."

"Sam?" Doug groped his way in the direction of her voice. "Oh, my God, Samantha. You're still here."

He groped the pile of blankets and then felt her small face. He picked her up with his good arm and scooped her onto his lap. "It's Doug, Sam," he whispered as he held her tightly, gently rocking her back and forth. "You're safe now."

78

Doug carried Samantha out of the tunnel, but his strength was dwindling and he had to stop and rest before making the trek back to the Range Rover. He sat on a rock outcropping and held Samantha on his lap. Daylight was fading fast, but Doug could still see well enough to check Samantha over. She was dirty and disheveled, and her small face was thin and pale, but she didn't appear to have suffered any serious physical harm.

He smoothed her hair out of her face. "Are you okay, Sam?"

Samantha nodded but tears welled up in her eyes. "It was scary in that dark place. And I didn't like the man who took me there."

Doug took her hand in his. "Who was the man, Sam? Did he tell you his name?"

She shook her head. "He wouldn't tell me his name. He said it was a secret. But you know him. He was our waiter."

Doug frowned. "Our waiter? What do you mean?"

"He was our waiter. At Huckleberries. When we ate lunch there."

Doug caught his breath. "Are you sure?"

Samantha nodded. "Yes. He brought my horses back to me." She buried her head against his chest. "I'm hungry. Can we go home now?"

Doug held Samantha as he tried to make sense of what she'd told him. Was it possible? Was it possible that neither Langley nor McGraw had taken Samantha? That it was a total stranger? A waiter from Huckleberries?

He stood up and picked Samantha up with his left arm. His priority right now was to reunite Samantha with Anne. After that, he'd concentrate on finding out who had abducted her. "Hold on tight, Sam. We're going home."

Samantha wrapped her arms around his neck and rested her cheek against his shoulder.

Doug carried Samantha slowly up the embankment. He was unsteady on his feet, and he didn't want to risk stumbling and falling with her. When he reached level ground the going was much easier and he picked up the pace. They made it to the Range Rover just as the graying daylight disappeared into dusk.

He tried to get Samantha to buckle up in the back seat, but she refused to let go of him, so he climbed into the driver's seat with her on his lap.

"Turn the heater on. I'm freezing," Samantha said, huddling closer and shivering against him.

"You bet, young lady. Heat is coming right up." Doug reached awkwardly around the steering wheel and turned the key with his left hand, expecting the engine to turn over instantly. But the engine just let out a hum. He released the key for a moment and then tried again. Same response. Just a faint hum.

Doug tried the radio. It worked. And the headlights. They worked. So it wasn't the battery. Maybe the engine was just cold.

Doug waited a moment and then tried one more time. But the engine still didn't turn over.

Damn. He banged the steering wheel with his fist. This was all he needed. The car wouldn't start, and he didn't have a cell phone to call for help.

Samantha raised her head from his chest. "What's the matter? Why don't you start the car?"

Doug sighed. "Something's wrong with it, Sam. Let me take a look under the hood."

Doug opened the door and started to get out, but Samantha clung to him. "Don't leave me here alone in the dark. I want to come with you."

Doug took a deep breath. He felt like he was about to collapse. "Please, Samantha. Stay here. I'll be right in front of the car where you can see me. Look, I have the headlights on."

Samantha's bottom lip quivered and she began to cry, but she let go of him. Doug patted her on the arm. "It's okay, Sam. I'm not going to leave you. I just can't carry you and fix the car at the same time. Okay?"

Samantha nodded and wiped her tears away.

Doug forced a smile. "Okay. I'll be right back."

Doug stepped out of the Range Rover and released the hood latch, then walked around to the front of the vehicle and opened the hood. The light was dim and he leaned down close to get a better look at the engine.

"Hey, Cummings. You looking for this?"

Doug jumped and whirled around. A tall, thin man wearing camouflage clothing stood in the beam of the headlights, holding a metal cap with wires extending from it.

The man took a step forward and dangled the cap in front of him, flashing him a chilling smile. "I don't think you're going to be driving anywhere tonight."

Doug's heart thumped wildly in his chest. The man's West Virginia drawl was vividly familiar. He recognized it from the cell phone call the night of the hunt ball. It was McGraw. Fear gripped his stomach. He leaned against the front bumper for support.

Doug ignored the voice in his head that screamed at him to grab Samantha and run. He'd be lucky if he made it twenty yards. He forced himself to breathe evenly. His only hope was to stall for time until he could come up with a plan. He stepped forward.

"I'm glad you finally decided to come out and face me, Zebulon."

McGraw scowled at him and drew his arm back and pitched the cap into the woods. "Cut the crap, Cummings. You ain't glad to see me. I'm your worst fucking nightmare."

Doug held his hand up. "Look, I know you blame me for what happened to your brother. But nothing you do to me can bring Zeke back. It will only make things worse. You'll end up in prison yourself."

"Shut up, Cummings."

"Come on, Zebulon. Let's talk this through."

"I said shut up."

"Okay. Okay. I'll shut up. You talk, Zebulon. Tell me what . . ."

McGraw whipped his arm up and aimed a rifle at Doug's chest. "I said, shut the fuck up."

Doug stopped. "Okay," he nodded.

McGraw laughed. "There, now. You ain't as dumb as I thought you was. Now go and get the kid out of the car."

Doug didn't move. "Leave her out of this, Zebulon. Let's keep this between you and me."

McGraw leapt forward and thrust the gun barrel into Doug's chest, forcing him to step backwards until he was pressed against the car. "Let me make it real clear to you, Cummings. Get the kid out of the car or I'll blow your guts all over the engine."

Doug studied McGraw. The man was angry. And obviously full of hatred. But not out of control. His eyes were cold and determined. Doug didn't doubt for an instant that McGraw would happily pull the trigger, if provoked. He nodded. "Okay, Zebulon. I'll go get her."

McGraw backed up. "Go on, then. Go and get her," he said, waving his rifle towards Samantha.

Doug walked around slowly to the open driver's door and found Samantha huddled in the driver's seat with her knees drawn up to her chest and her arms wrapped around her legs. She was rocking back and forth. "That's him. The bad man. He's out there. I heard him. I don't want him to take me back to the dark place," she whispered tearfully.

Doug put his hand on her shoulder. "Is he the waiter, Sam?"

She nodded.

"Okay, Sam. I won't let him hurt you. I'm going to take care of you. You just have to do exactly as I say. All right?" Doug held his arm out and Samantha nestled against him and locked her arms around his neck.

"There you go. Good girl. Now just hold on tight and do what I say. Everything's going to be all right."

He carried Samantha back towards the front of the car, deliberately stopping just short of the beam from the headlights, so that McGraw was looking into the light, but he was not.

"Okay, Zebulon. Tell me what you want from me."

McGraw stared coldly back at him. "What I *want* from you? What I want is for Zeke to still be alive. But you can't give me that, can you, Cummings?"

Doug shook his head. "No, Zebulon. We both know I can't do that."

McGraw nodded. "Right. We both know you can't do that. So, what can you offer me?"

"All I can offer you is an apology. I'm truly sorry about what happened to Zeke in prison. I don't know what else I could have done for him, but . . ."

McGraw raised the rifle towards him. "Be-e-e-e-p. Wrong answer. Try again."

Doug didn't respond. Something off in the distance caught his eye. Behind McGraw. A pair of headlights. No. Two, three pairs of headlights. Moving slowly towards them through the woods. Hope surged through him. He looked back at McGraw. "You tell me. What do you want from me, Zebulon?" he asked, struggling to keep his voice calm.

"Come on. Smart lawyer like you. Think about it. You took my brother's life away, so what I want from you is . . .?"

"Retribution."

"Eh?"

"Revenge."

McGraw laughed. "Bingo. And how will I get that?"

Doug stole a quick glance at the headlights. They were closer now. Soon McGraw would be able to hear the vehicles. Keep him talking. Distract him. That's all he could do. "Revenge won't help anything, Zebulon. What good do you think it will do to . . ."

"Shut up, Cummings. I'm the one asking the questions here. How will I get my revenge?"

Doug shrugged his shoulders. "I don't know. You tell me."

"Come on, Cummings. You're just afraid to say it. You know what I want. What I'm going to take. Now say it." McGraw waved the rifle at him. "I'm going to take your life. As payment for Zeke's. Say it."

"Zebulon."

"Say it."

Doug shifted Samantha in his arm and held her tighter. The first set of headlights was almost to the clearing. "You want my life as payment for Zeke's."

"No. I don't *want* your life. I am going to *take* your life. As payment for Zeke's. Say it."

The beam from the first set of headlights broke into the clearing. All McGraw had to do was turn his head slightly and he'd see them. Doug took a slight step backwards. Poised for flight.

"Look, Zebulon, I know you're angry. But think it through. Taking my life won't bring Zeke back. You'll just be sending yourself to prison. Why not stop before it's too late?"

McGraw snorted. "You're a fucking idiot, Cummings. You know I'm going to kill you, but you're still trying to use your smart lawyer talk to distract me. Well, guess what, asshole? It ain't working. Your time for talking is over." Zeb aimed his rifle at Doug's feet. "I think I'll start at the bottom and work my way up. Any last words?"

Doug knew he'd never outrun McGraw, but he wouldn't just stand there and be gunned down. He tightened his grip on Samantha and started to turn away, when she lifted her head from his shoulder and pointed a finger at the three sets of headlights that bore down on them. "Who's that?" she asked.

McGraw turned to look behind him, and in the same instant Doug took off in the opposite direction towards the mill house. "Hold on tight, Sam," he whispered. He ran through the dark, heading for the shelter of the mill house, surprised at how quickly he was able to move. Adrenaline had taken over.

He heard McGraw swear behind him. "Fucking A." And then McGraw's footsteps pounded after him.

A hollow voice from a bullhorn broke through the night. "Stop where you are. This is the FBI. Drop your weapon. We have you surrounded. I repeat, stop and drop your weapon."

Doug stumbled on a root and Samantha cried out, but he regained his balance and ran on. He could see the gray stone walls of the mill house in front of him. He was almost there. Just a few more yards. But McGraw was right behind them, closing the gap.

Doug heard a shot ring out from McGraw's gun the instant he felt it tear through his leg. And then he seemed to fall in slow motion. With no free hand to break his fall, he took the impact on his right shoulder, and shielded Samantha with his body. In one quick motion, he released his grip on her and pushed her forward.

"Crawl, Samantha," he whispered. "Stay close to the ground and crawl to the building ahead. I'm right behind you."

Samantha didn't move and he shoved her forward. "Go, go, go. Crawl. Now."

Samantha still didn't crawl forward, and just when he was ready to grab her and cover her with his body, he felt her start to move.

"Good girl. That's my girl. I'm right behind you."

Ping, ping, ping. Three warning shots whizzed through the trees above them and the voice boomed over the bullhorn again. "Stop and drop your weapon at once or we will open fire."

"Fuck," McGraw swore, and the sound of his footsteps veered off to the right. Doug listened to the snapping of branches as McGraw tore through the woods.

McGraw was gone. At least for now. Doug inched his way forward, using his left arm and right leg. He knew the bullet had shattered his femur and he felt blood pumping from the bullet wound in his thigh. The rest of his body was growing numb, and he feared he would soon lose consciousness. He had to get to Samantha.

Inch by inch, Doug moved forward until finally his hand scraped the cold, stone surface of the mill house wall. He rested his head on his arm for a moment and then summoned the strength to pull himself up onto the stone floor inside the building.

"Samantha?" he whispered.

He felt her small hand on his arm. "I'm right here."

He closed his eyes in relief. "Good girl, Samantha. You are such a brave girl. Come on. Let's move into the corner over there."

Doug slowly dragged himself to the corner, then leaned against the wall and pulled Samantha close to him. She was shivering uncontrollably and he unzipped the front of his jacket and pulled it around her.

He wasn't sure how long he sat there, hugging Samantha and fighting unconsciousness, when he heard the sound of approaching footsteps. Slowly, cautiously, someone was making their way around the outside of the mill house. He shook Samantha to get her attention and put his finger to his lips.

"Shhh," he mouthed.

Samantha nodded at him and put her hand over her mouth.

The footsteps were on the other side of the building. So soft and quiet that he could barely hear them. Doug cocked his head and listened. The footsteps moved around the far end of the building and slowly made their way along the side. He could hear them distinctly as they grew closer. Down the side of the building and around the corner. Towards the door. Approaching the area where he and Samantha sat.

Doug pulled the jacket tighter around Samantha and cradled her head against his chest with his hand. There was nothing he could do now. Except wait. And pray.

He saw a dark figure enter the doorway and stop. Was it McGraw? It was a tall man. That's all he could make out in the dark. And as the man turned towards him, Doug saw that he was holding a gun in his outstretched hand. Not a rifle. A handgun.

The man turned slowly as he looked around, and then his gaze seemed to stop where Doug and Samantha lay. He stepped towards them and Doug held his breath. He still couldn't see if it was McGraw. He blinked against the darkness, trying to see. He didn't think the man was wearing camouflage clothing, but he just couldn't see for sure. The man stopped next to them and crouched down.

"Cummings?"

Doug let out his breath and relief flooded through him. It wasn't McGraw.

"Yeah. It's me."

"It's Chester Rawls, Cummings. Are you okay?"

Doug nodded. Then he held the front of Chester Rawls' jacket and pulled him closer. "It's McGraw, Rawls," he whispered. "He's still out there. You have to find him."

"Okay, Cummings. We're on top of that. I've got agents combing the woods. Right now, my priority is to get you out of here safely. Are you okay? Can you make it back to the car?"

Doug shook his head and let go of Rawls' jacket. "I can't walk. McGraw shot me in the leg. Just get Samantha out of here. You can send someone back for me."

"No-o-o-o," Samantha wailed, clinging to him. "I don't want to go without you."

"Shhh. It's okay, Sam. I'll be right behind you. Just like before. Now go with Mr. Rawls. He's a friend of mine and he's going to make sure you get home safely. You do whatever he says, okay?"

Chester Rawls ignored Doug and took a walkie-talkie out of his pocket. "I need backup and the ambulance. I'm in the mill house. I've got Cummings and the girl."

"Yes, sir. We're on our way," a voice squawked back at him.

Chester Rawls put the walkie-talkie away. "Don't you worry, young lady. We're not going to leave anybody behind here." Rawls held his hand out. "I'm Chester, and you must be Samantha."

Samantha nodded.

"I've been looking all over for you, Samantha," Rawls said.

Samantha wrapped her arms around Doug's neck. "You don't need to look for me anymore. Doug founded me. He rescued me from the dark place."

"Yes, Samantha. I can see that he did. You're lucky to have a friend like Doug."

"Um-hmm. And you rescued us now, so I'm lucky to have a friend like you too."

Rawls patted her on the arm. "Thank you, Samantha. I'm honored to be your friend."

Doug tugged on the front of Chester Rawls' jacket again. "Rawls."

"Yes, Cummings?"

"How'd you find us?"

"A young kid from the rescue squad. He told me that you'd been asking him about hiding places. Told us how to get here. Told me you were in pretty bad shape too. That's why I brought the ambulance."

"Where did you talk to him? Were you at my barn?" Doug asked.

"Yes."

"Did you see Anne?"

Rawls nodded. "Yes. She gave me the headlines about what happened."

Doug breathed a sigh of relief. "So she was conscious. How is she?"

"She's going to be just fine. But she's worried about you. She asked me to find you and bring you home safely."

The darkness of the mill house was suddenly flooded with light and Doug shielded his eyes with his arm. He heard several car doors slam and then a sea of faces seemed to surround him.

Chester Rawls stood up. "Okay, we need a stretcher over here. We've got a gunshot wound to the leg. Agent Perkins, take Samantha into the ambulance and stay there with her. Campbell, Stoke, Watkins. Cover us. We've got an armed fugitive out there."

Doug squeezed Samantha's hand as the agent came to lead her away. "It's okay, Sam. Go on. It's nice and warm in the ambulance. I'll be right there."

Then he closed his eyes.

Chester Rawls' voice was down at his level again. "Hey, Cummings, don't fade out on me here."

Doug opened his eyes.

Rawls smiled at him. "Hang in there, Cummings. I may need your help again."

Doug held his hand up. "Find McGraw, Rawls. Promise me you won't give up until you find him."

Rawls reached out and took Doug's hand. "You have my word on it."

Chester Rawls backed away as they moved him onto the stretcher, and as he was being loaded into the ambulance, Doug saw Rawls and another agent take off into the woods.

The rear doors of the ambulance slammed closed and Doug looked around for Samantha. She was lying on a bench across the aisle, wrapped in a wad of blankets, with her head resting on the FBI agent's lap.

He reached across the aisle and squeezed her hand. "Are you warming up?"

She nodded, her eyes half closed.

"Good. Why don't you take a little nap? I'll wake you up when we get there."

The EMT put a hand on his arm. "I'm sorry, sir, but I need to get an IV started."

Doug squeezed Samantha's hand once more, then released it, and held his arm out to the rescue worker. Another EMT moved his leg, and Doug closed his eyes against the pain.

He drifted off and was awakened some time later by someone tapping him on the shoulder. He opened his eyes and saw the female FBI agent leaning over him.

"I'm sorry to wake you, Mr. Cummings, but Agent Rawls said you'd want me to." She pointed to the cell phone she held in her hand. "Agent Rawls just called me, sir. They got him. They apprehended McGraw."

Six Months Later

The parking area in front of Samantha's school was full, so Doug turned the corner and parked the Range Rover in the lot behind the building. He limped slightly as he hurried up the gravel drive. Time. That's what Dr. Gannon kept saying. Just give the leg time to heal properly and the limp should disappear.

As he rounded the corner, Doug saw Anne standing on the school porch with her back towards him, looking out at the street, tapping her fingers against a white, wooden column.

He walked up behind her and slipped his arms around her waist. Anne jumped and spun around, but she broke into a smile when she saw it was him.

"I'm sorry I'm late," he murmured, brushing her hair back and kissing her on the forehead.

"It's okay, I already saved seats for us." She gently touched his cheek. "You look tired. Did you get any sleep last night?"

"No, I worked until it was time to shower and change to drive out here. But the long night was worth it. We have the Tycoon Technologies due diligence about wrapped up. Mark is putting the finishing touches on it this morning." He ran his fingertips lightly across her stomach. "What about you? How did you sleep?"

"I missed you, but I slept fine."

"What about Samantha? Any nightmares?" Doug asked.

Anne shook her head. "No, and she stayed in her own bed all night."

"That's three nights in a row."

Anne nodded and crossed her fingers. "I know. I think it's a good sign."

The sound of a chime drifted out the open front door of the school. "I think that's the signal the graduation ceremony is about to begin," Anne said. "We better take our seats."

Anne had saved seats for them in the front row of folding metal chairs that were set up in the large meeting room of the school. After they were seated, Doug glanced around the room and saw Timothy Shaw watching them. Doug nodded at Shaw, and they exchanged smiles.

Shaw had turned out not to be such a bad guy after all. He'd dropped the murder charge and publicly apologized to Doug, and, despite strong opposition from Langley's family, had declared Anne's shooting of Langley to be self-defense.

Shaw was working relentlessly on Zebulon McGraw's prosecution. McGraw's trial for Ingrid's murder was set to start in two weeks, and after that, Shaw would try McGraw for Samantha's kidnapping, and for attempted murder and assault with a deadly weapon against Doug. Shaw was asking for the maximum sentence on each charge and was determined to see McGraw spend the rest of his life behind bars.

The music started and groups of preschoolers marched in. Doug lifted the video camera that Anne had brought and started to film. The children sang songs and each graduating child came forward to receive his or her diploma from the headmaster. Samantha was next, and Doug reached down and held Anne's hand as he looked through the viewfinder.

"Our next graduate is Miss Samantha Remington," the headmaster announced.

Doug leaned over towards Anne and whispered, "Soon to be Samantha Cummings." Anne squeezed his hand as Samantha took the diploma and curtsied to the audience.

A flash went off, and Doug looked over to see Sharon Duncan lower her camera and write down something on her notepad. Doug had given Sharon an exclusive on the story of the murders, and she had also written a series of articles on Clyde Dickson, exposing his mishandling of the murder investigation. Dickson had been fired by the sheriff and was working as a private security guard, patrolling the food court at a factory outlet mall in West Virginia. Sharon had sold her articles to several of the major national publications, and a few of them had offered her a job, but she had chosen to stay at home and continued to cover the local community for *Hunt Country*. Sharon made eye contact with Doug and they both smiled. Then Doug turned his attention back to the ceremony.

Following the graduation, there was a reception with punch and cookies, and Doug was standing by the door, watching the kids run around, when he felt a hand on his shoulder.

"Doug, that was a wonderful ceremony," Richard Evan Clarke said. "Thank you for inviting us. Samantha looks great. How is she doing?"

"Very well, all things considered. She continues to receive counseling, but I think she's going to be fine."

"That's great, Doug. And how about you? How's business at the law firm?" Richard asked.

"Starting a new firm definitely presents a challenge, but so far it's going quite well. I have a good group of young lawyers working with me and we're building a solid client base."

Richard chuckled. "You're a master of understatement, Doug. I'll bet that with all the legal work Tycoon Technologies generates you don't need any other clients."

Doug just smiled.

"What about your bride? How's the mother-to-be feeling?" Richard asked.

"Anne had a rough bout with morning sickness early on, but she seems beyond that now and she's feeling much better." Doug pointed her out across the room and smiled. "Look at her. She's never looked more beautiful."

As if sensing that they were talking about her, Anne looked over at them, and blushed when she caught them staring at her.

Richard smiled. "I couldn't agree more. You're a lucky man, Doug Cummings."

Doug nodded and his smile faded. "Yes, I am. Sometimes everything seems so perfect that I'm afraid it can't last."

Richard clasped him on the back. "Don't talk like that. You've more than paid your dues with the hell you've been through. Go and enjoy your family. I'll see you at the Hunt board meeting next week."

Doug said good-bye and walked over to Anne and Samantha.

"Does anybody here still have an appetite for lunch?" he asked, picking Samantha up and giving her a hug.

"I do, I do," Samantha screamed.

Doug smiled at her and put his arm around Anne. "Let's go, then. I'm sure Nellie has fixed quite a spread at home."

They said good-bye to Samantha's teacher and the headmaster and went out the front door of the school.

A woman wearing a red bandana was kneeling on the brick sidewalk that led to the street, weeding a flower bed. Doug stopped with Samantha in his arms and let Anne go first as they eased by her. Doug was annoyed that the woman had chosen such a busy time to weed along the narrow walkway, and he wondered fleetingly whether the school had hired a gardener. Thomas, the maintenance man for the school, normally took care of the grounds by himself.

The woman stopped her weeding and looked up at them as they passed, smiling at Anne and nodding at Doug.

"Nice day, ain't it?" she asked.

Doug hesitated for a moment. He thought he might know the woman, but not as a gardener. He stared at the woman's face, but he couldn't place her. Maybe without the bandana . . . Doug shook his head. It was probably because she was out of context. If he saw her in a different setting, he might recognize her.

Doug stepped around her. "Yes, it's a gorgeous day," he replied, smiling, and moved on to catch up with Anne, who was waiting for him by the street.

The woman's smile faded as she stared at Doug's retreating back. Her eyes narrowed, and she reached up and fingered the heart-shaped locket she wore around her neck. Inside were pictures of her brothers, Zeke and Zebulon.

G L O S S A R Y

Blood - The foxhunting practice of wiping blood from the dead fox on the face of a rider who witnesses their first kill.

Butt bar - A restraining device at the rear of a trailer stall, to prevent a horse from backing out of the trailer.

Check - An interruption of the chase during a foxhunt.

Coop - A wood panel jump, fashioned after a chicken coop.

Couple - Two hounds, used for convenience in counting.

Covert - An area of woods or brush where a fox might be found. Pronounced "cover."

Field - The group of people foxhunting, excluding the master and the staff.

Fixture - The time and place where the hunt meets.

Foxhunt - A hunt with hounds, followed by riders on horseback, after a fox.

Full cry - The sound of a pack of hounds in hot pursuit.

Gone to ground - The fox has taken shelter.

Gone away - The fox has left the covert and the hunt is on.

Hack - A leisurely ride, usually cross-country.

Hand - The way a horse is measured, from the ground to the highest point of the horse's withers. One hand equals four inches.

Hilltoppers - A group of foxhunters who generally go at a slower pace than the rest of the field and usually do not jump. Also referred to as the "second field."

Hounds - Foxhounds. They are never called "dogs."

Huntsman - The person who controls the hounds.

Hunt breakfast - A meal served after the hunt. Usually hosted by the property owner where the hunt meet was held.

Kill - When the hounds destroy the fox during a foxhunt.

Line - The trail of scent from the fox.

Master - MFH (Master of Foxhounds) - The person in command of the hunt.

Meet - The assembling of a foxhunt at a certain place.

Melton - A wool hunting coat.

Run - A period during which the hounds are actively chasing after the fox.

Scarlet - A red coat worn by certain select members of the hunt. Also referred to as a "pink" coat, after the British tailor, Mr. Pinque, who designed it.

Scent - The smell of the fox.

Stirrup-cup - A drink served to mounted riders before the hunt.

Stock tie - A plain white tie worn around the neck, tied in a square knot and fastened with a plain gold safety pin.

Tallyho - A hunting cry when the fox is sighted.

Twitch - A device used to twist a horse's upper lip, in order to attract the horse's attention so it will stand still.

View - To see the fox.

Whipper-in - A person who helps the huntsman control the hounds. Also called a "whip."